Hit Me
with a
Rainbow

To Phil,
With warm
wishes for
all good Things,

James Kirkwood

BY JAMES KIRKWOOD

Novels

There Must Be a Pony!
Good Times/Bad Times
P.S. Your Cat Is Dead!
Some Kind of Hero
Hit Me with a Rainbow

Nonfiction

American Grotesque

Plays

There Must Be a Pony!
U.T.B.U. (Unhealthy To Be Unpleasant)
P.S. Your Cat Is Dead!

Musicals

A Chorus Line (*coauthor*)

JAMES KIRKWOOD

Hit Me with a Rainbow

A Novel

DELACORTE PRESS / NEW YORK

Published by
Delacorte Press
1 Dag Hammarskjold Plaza
New York, N.Y. 10017

Manufactured in the United States of America

First printing

Designed by Giorgetta Bell McRee

LIBRARY OF CONGRESS CATALOGING IN PUBLICATION DATA

Kirkwood, James.
Hit me with a rainbow.

I. Title.
PZ4.K593Hi   1980   [PS3561.I72]   813′.5′4   79-19469

ISBN: 0-440-03397-7

For Peggy Hillmer
with love

Hit Me
with a
Rainbow

CHAPTER 1

Kelly inhaled deeply; this enabled him to speak in a rush of false energy on the expulsion of breath: "You are perverse, you're a traitor, you are! I ought to cut you off—" laughter fed by despair broke up his speech for a second "—without a cent!" He sighed, coughed: "You're not even worth speaking to anymore, I'm not going to talk to you anymore. That's a promise—you're a total dud!"

"Kelly, are you all right?" Her voice was tinged with disappointment, confusion and concern.

"Yep," he called out over the cassette of Mozart's Greatest Hits.

"Who are you talking to?" Rhetorical, unless someone had managed to climb in the bathroom window twenty-three floors up.

"Monologue to a Dick," Kelly muttered to himself, shaking the last few drops off the traitor, then putting it back in his pants and flushing the toilet. Another sigh as he rinsed off his hands and muttered: "I was just speaking to my—member." A little laugh at the oddness of that word. "Not a member in good standing," he said as an afterthought, then: "Christ, I made a pun."

Stepping out of the bathroom into her bedroom, he would as soon have stepped into an open elevator shaft. The amenities had to be got through. There she was, stretched out on her bed in her slip—slips were the most attractive article of clothing possible to him . . . their clingability!—looking more heavenly than anyone who had to perform the basic bodily functions had a right to, now reaching over and stopping the cassette.

"Were you talking to me?" she asked.

"No."

"I didn't think so." She fingered the bedspread. "Kelly, did I—was it anything—"

He cut her off. "No. Just me. Not you. Ma-me!" His occasional stutter could be counted on for perfect timing.

"Oh . . ." Jody was not only beautiful, she was bright, too. Taking her cue from his tone and abbreviated speech, she decided not to pursue the whys or wherefores. "You're so attractive, you know I think you're attractive."

He would catch the tossed bones like a gentleman.

"You are," she went on, sitting up on the bed. "That's all there is to it." She caught the look in his eyes and threw decorum to the winds. "You're so fucking vulnerable." (Although when she spoke such a word it rolled off her tongue like: "Coffee with sugar, please.") "You know who I told a girl friend you reminded me of? Montgomery Clift. You have that same . . . appeal."

The rash of books had brought about a Montgomery Clift retrospective and he got this a lot lately.

"So—" She spoke hesitantly now. "Shall we talk?"

His Aunt Peg used to say: "If you're leaving—leave. If you're going to stay, get away from the door, take off your coat, sit down and have another drink." He would follow her advice. "If you don't mind," he said, "I think I'll leave."

"Will I see you again?" She sat up straighter.

"No, I don't think so." He tossed a few bones of his own.

"You're beautiful and sweet and bright," he said without looking at her.

"Would you like to spend the night and just . . . cuddle?" She laughed, blushed. "—Such a ditsy word, but it's not to be knocked." Then: "Would you?"

"Ya-yes, but—no, not really. Please—I'm leaving now."

"Kelly . . . ?"

But he was already out of her bedroom, crossing the living room, snatching up his coat on his way to the door.

Waiting for the elevator, he glanced back down the hall, hoping to Christ he wouldn't see her front door open, wouldn't have to eke through another farewell sentence or two.

Kelly sat in a bar getting drunk. Because that's what young, about-to-be-twenty-seven-years-old, attractive—so they say—guys do when they can't get it to work. Can't get it up. When Peter Pecker will not dance to the Piper's tune.

One of those neighborhood bars where everyone knows each other well enough for in-house requests to the bartender.

"Hey, Nick—put on the news, it's ten after eleven!" a redheaded man called out.

"Yeah," said a fortyish, plump, tarty type two barstools removed from Kelly, "that'll cheer us up!" Turning to the redhead, she said: "You see the *early* news?"

"Yeah."

"So—what do you think happened since seven? The world come to an end?"

"I like the news."

"Hmn," she muttered down into her glass, "I like peanut butter but I don't spread it around."

Kelly chuckled at her irrelevancy. She sensed it more than heard him, swiveled on her stool. "You ever had chicken baked with peanut butter?"

"Na-no," Kelly said.

"You haven't lived. You come to Betty's, I'll make you

chicken baked in peanut butter—so good it could hurt you!" Jabbing her head forward, she squinted at Kelly, did a take, ducked back again. "Christ, you come to Betty's, we'll skip the peanut butter and get right to dessert—you! When'd you fall in—huh? Hey, look, everybody," she announced to the assembled, "we got a winner here!"

Kelly almost spit up his drink: winner, shit, lady, are you wrong.

"Betty," said the bartender, winking at Kelly, "lay off the customers."

"Nick," she countered with supreme wit, "go fuck yourself!"

"I tried—" he said as Betty joined in and they both finished: "—*but I threw my back out!*"

General laughter from Nick, Betty and a few others. Then a quick gasp from Betty at the recently turned-on news. "God, look at Maggie Banner—is that gorgeous? You know, when I look at her, I understand dykes. I really do. I'd bump titties with her any day."

"Hey, Betty—" Now a real warning from Nick.

"I already told you—go fuck yourself." After six vodka stingers, Betty was beyond turning back. The tongue was out for the night. "And she's gotta be pushing fifty, she's gotta. Oh, she's still with that opera singer—he's a hump, too. Turn it up, Nick!"

Kelly glanced at the screen to see a shot of Maggie Banner and Raffaello Tucci walking down the corridor of a terminal at Kennedy Airport as a voice-over reported: ". . . back in the States for the first time in almost a year with her world touring companion, Raffaello Tucci, former bad boy of the Met." Then a quick cut to a close-up of Maggie Banner, who was asked: "How does it feel to be back in the United States?"

An easy yet dazzling smile and the husky-voiced reply: "It's always good to come home. I mean, home is where the home is." She became immediately serious: "One thing people in this country sometimes forget—everything works. Things work here. Other countries all have their strong suits but in the United States things work. You can actually make a phone call without chancing a nervous breakdown."

"Will you be coming out of retirement?"

"I don't know, we'll see."

"What have you got to say to all your fans—any message for the people who've been waiting for two years for a Maggie Banner picture?"

"Yes," she said without a moment's hesitation, "vote! I've just come from South America. Vote—try to elect a president for once with brains and charisma. Out of—what?—over two hundred million people, there's got to be someone can do the job right. Just vote and think." A quick wink into the camera. "Excuse the soap box, but I troop it with me."

"Atta girl," Betty called out.

Raffaello Tucci took her arm and started to guide her away. "One last question—what did you miss most of all about America?"

Maggie Banner pulled in, swinging her head in a small circle as if it were impossible to summon up a specific answer. Then, raising a hand to her chin, she said in a level, considered voice: "Oh, that's such a difficult question. So many things. But I suppose I'd have to say—" She bit her lip in thought: "—the toilet paper."

The bar applauded as the newsman broke up and they switched to coverage of a fire in the Bronx.

"Oh, God, I love her!" Betty said.

And Kelly loved her, too. But everyone loved Maggie Banner. To Kelly she was a combination of Anne Bancroft and Carole Lombard—he'd seen her on the Late Show—and perhaps a touch of Ava Gardner—a dash of her basic lostness—with a sprinkling of Jill Clayburgh. No, she was herself—unique.

And he was Montgomery Clift. And, he thought, just about as dead.

So he ordered another double, turning his thoughts to a promotion he was up for. He didn't much like his job, but he still wanted the promotion; he wanted to win *something*.

"You like blizzards? I like blizzards—everyone's so

friendly!" This from Betty, glancing out the window at the incredible whiteness that covered New York.

"Yes," he said, realizing he would have to put in time with Betty and he might as well be done with it.

He would have too, if a beefy Italian had not stuck his head in the front door and shouted: "Hey, Betty—c'mon, we're going over to Gino's place. Come on, right now. He's throwin' a bash!"

"Tony—my gumba!" Betty shouted. "I'm practically there." She grabbed her purse and turned to Kelly. "Come on, cute-ass, we're gonna party. It's only three blocks."

"No, thanks, I have to work early."

"Oh, c'mon!"

"No, I really—"

"Nobody's gonna have to work tomorrow, everything'll be closed. Whaddaya do?"

Without a moment's hesitation Kelly replied: "Undertaker."

"What—*you?*" He grinned and nodded enthusiastically. "Jesus!" Betty shouted farewells to a few of the regulars and was gone.

Kelly knew certain people were turned off by that reply. There were also certain people turned on by it. At a party of sophisticated folk he never gave that reply. He'd have a hit on his hands—he'd never get off the hook without a detailed account. He gave them "Computer Programmer" or "Marketing Research." That was a yawner for the in crowd. But Undertaker did just fine with people like Betty. Your average lower-middle New Yorker didn't want to get into deadies.

The truth—"I'm in publishing"—sounded too much like movie dialogue and he never used it with strangers.

With Betty gone, he was left alone with his problem. THE problem. The malfunctioning, nonfunctioning persistent problem. As his best friend, Lenny, had once said, "Well, Jesus, Kelly—look, you're bright, you're young, you're talented, you're attractive—so what if you can't create the world. (Lenny's euphemism for "doing it.") Is that all there is in life?" After a second he answered himself: "No, but it's

high up on the list, right before hot fudge sundaes actually."
Then: "Oh, Jesus—Kelly!"

The problem imposes a massive list of do's and don't's and
carries a long list of "have tried."

You do keep an apartment that is meticulous in its order,
design and essential tidiness. Because you have too much
time, it, your cave, becomes a never-ending project. So well
organized it's boring. You do well at your job because—you'd
fucking well better do well at something if you can't do well
at fucking. You have hobbies up the kazoo. My God, are you
an authority: photography, the stock market, theater, opera,
cinema, chess, sketching; you speak French well, Italian
passably and you're even thinking of taking Greek. You keep
your sense of humor finely honed; you live off it, because if
you don't have humor, you don't have a chance. Anyhow.
Period. Paragraph.

You work out at the gym three times a week because you
want to keep your body as fit and young-looking as possible
because every day/week/month is time lost and you want to
stay the way you were in case the goddamn thing ever gets
working. Should it ever "get the spirit" you don't want it attached to an old man's withering loins. You look into a mirror coated with sarcasm; your image bounces back on rays
of irony. Your secret smirks at you at odd moments. You are
in on your problem, you understand the reason but you cannot find a solution. And what is the sense of knowing the
cause if you cannot correct the effects. That is the sticky-
bitch of it. You know why just as well as you know your
twenty-seventh birthday is about to hit you on the head, but
you cannot do diddle-dee-squat about it.

There are avalanches of "don't's" that grow as time passes.
You don't look too longingly, or lovingly, at a pretty girl if she
is in position to notice, because you cannot follow through
with the promise that sort of gaze carries. You don't believe
in God much anymore because what he/she/it/them have
done to you is so perverse that if you did believe, you'd go
around shitting in St. Patrick's Cathedral and blowing up
synagogues. Except—there are always exceptions—you do,

every-once-in-a-great-while-take-it-all-back, get down on your knees and pray to Christ to set you right. You don't— oh, you don't do a lot of things. Besides the things you can't, that is.

The "have trieds" list belongs to *The Guinness Book of World Records*. There was, naturally, in the beginning, psychoanalysis, psychotherapy, group therapy and assorted other therapies. There was yoga, yogurt, TM, est, mind control, hypnosis, self-hypnosis, tap dancing, erecto-cremes, splints and various other marital aids, potions to apply, liquids to imbibe, pills, massages, hallucinogens, pot, coke, Quaaludes, mirrors, black lights, glo-lights, poppers, herbs, diets, acupuncture, every kind of music from the Love Death and Pavane to a Dead Princess, to Judy, Ethel, Barry, Neil, Abba, the Beatles, Bee Gees, to *Swan Lake* and the film score to *Ryan's Daughter*. Then there were the serious attempts: contemplation, long discussions with a few close friends (very few), isolation, complete celibacy (no fancy handwork), meditation. And reading—everything from Freud and Jung to *Your Ass-hole Is Your Own Best Friend*. There had been whites, blacks, mulattoes, Spanish, German, Swedish, redheads, blondes, brunettes of every age, size, shape, disposition and description.

And, yes, he'd tried men. A man. Why not? Although he had a hunch that was a bummer because if you keep looking at the female gender and their accoutrements—legs, breasts, behinds, waists, hair, eyes—and you never do that with men, you have a clue you're not exactly going to suffer premature ejaculation if you try it with one. That's not to say he never looked at men's parts. He didn't have penis envy; he had a fine (looking) one of his own. He had "operational envy." He could not help wondering if he could tell which ones worked and which didn't. But he went to the Y to exercise and swim and fellows were always asking him if he'd like a drink or a cup of coffee. So he let the one who was by all probable-popular standards and tastes the sexiest—best build, best personality, best hair, eyes, best everything—pick him up. *Nada*. Oh, yes, a great body massage and he ended up getting Gary's life story, which was interesting. But—not really a serious twinge. Just a lot of envy looking at the athletic porno-Polaroid collection which proved Gary eclectic in both preference and performance.

And he'd tried threesomes. Twice. With Pauline and Dorinda and Jeanette and Kit. And even a foursome—with Lenny and two girls from Jackson Heights.

And he'd tried . . .

The worst part, of course, was—he was exceptionally horny. Feeling. In his mind. To himself. By himself. Oh, yes, it did work when he was alone. Masturbating. But that was so one-sided, so unsatisfying. All it did was relieve tension and permit sleep. Not a good clean sleep. A messy, fretful one. And it worked, occasionally, during the preamble to "creating the world." But it would not work in the honeypot. Oh, no. It would approach the Gates of Heaven, it would even make a tentative entrance. But once inside, certain death awaited. Suffocation by fornication.

Of course, the most perverse part—his blockage was taking place during the sexual revolution. When creating the world was no big deal, when people were actually deriving mutual benefits such as: immense enjoyment, wish fulfillment, relaxation and, most importantly, love. The girl/woman no longer thought the boy/man owed her the rest of his life/labor/soul for this reciprocal satisfaction. When women could own up to their own attractions; not only own up, but do something about their desires without getting their heads shaved and wearing scarlet letters. Let alone trimming their psyches.

What a time! To be dead in.

And the bottom line was not simply to fuck or not to fuck. Not at all. It was the capacity to love completely. It was the ability to please the object of his affection in the fullest, deepest sense. It was the lack of being the complete animal, the sense of not being able to fulfill by far the healthiest reason describing our presence on earth—to love. That was what could bring him to tears, both shed and unshed.

Now that he had reviewed his problem, something he did

automatically, to the point of tedium, in the hopes that, as in the case of misplacing a watch or a ring, you can worry up an answer to the mystery—he surprised himself completely by slipping, unknowingly, into the next phase, without having realized it. The next phase being the ultimate solution.

CHAPTER 2

He was amazed. He had paid his bar bill, gone out into the snow-filled night, and was approaching the East River more by instinct than plan. He didn't recall leaving, didn't even feel the cold. He had been doing this lately. After his yearly lung checkup at the Strang Clinic on East Thirty-fourth Street, he'd suddenly found himself going up in the elevator at the Empire State Building. Soon he was standing on the observation platform with assorted double-knits, their ice cream–coned children and Instamatics. He had found himself strolling across the Williamsburg Bridge one night after dinner in Little Italy.

Naturally the outright thought had occurred to him many times: pull the plug, call it quits, leave the building, buy the farm. But the notion seemed to have taken on a life of its own. He'd even bought a mail-order .38 revolver, with the idea in mind that now, living in New York City, one ought to have some means of protection in one's own home. Still, why did he often take it out and fondle it? Why did he buy a trashy paperback chronicling the last days of Freddie Prinz? Why had he collected all those books by and about people

who were clinically dead, then came back with such tanta-
lizing accounts of that gauzy in-between world no traveler is
supposed to return from. In the back of his mind there was a
sneaky hunch—this just might be the way. His investiga-
tions into the nether world were becoming more frequent,
more persistently subconscious than conscious.

The snow. The snow kept falling, soft and thick again over
the former frozen masses of it, as Kelly lurched across the
deserted East River Drive and then stood looking down at
the blackness of the water, polka-dotted with large Ivory
Flakes one moment, black again, more polka-dots but none
lasting, except for occasional sinister floes of ice bobbing by.
He stood wondering what it would be like. More and more,
drowning appealed to him. Such a clean way to go. No
razors and slit wrists and blood spurting all over. No brains à
la Hemingway. No fighting your way to the surface, choking
on your own mucus from an overdose, only to be found and
pumped out. Water was swift and clean. Did your whole life
really pass in front of you in a second? "Christ, I hope not!"
he said out loud. He'd lived through it enough. No more
reruns, please.

The East River was seductive, much more so than the
Hudson, which he'd checked out last Sunday late afternoon.
The Hudson was too calm, too broad, too . . . dull looking is
what it was. The East River was vibrant, its currents easily
seen; swirling with life, it should be able to absorb life into
it. Wondered how long it would be until he was found, who
would find him and—it was how treated when found that
gave him pause. Treated like . . . what? A frozen piece of
waterlogged meat? Would they reach out and catch him
with a hook? What did it matter—he'd be dead. Nevertheless. There's always a nevertheless, isn't there? Or would he
lie trapped beneath a dark, rotting pier until winter's end?
Not a pretty sight for some teen-age Hispanos taking their
first spring dip in the river.

A torrent, a whirling torrent of icy wind swept up off the
water and hit him in the face, reminding him for the first
time of the cold. "Jesus—freezing!" It was freezing. "It's too

cold!" He laughed at the lame excuse: "Well, Your Honor, see, I couldn't quite get myself to commit suicide because— well, it was just too *cold*!"

So he turned, inching back across the pedestrian way, back toward his apartment on Sixty-third off Second. Skidding down the ice bank onto the drive itself, he slipped, fell easily, landing on his knees, palms down in the snow in front of him. Lifting his hands, he brushed the snow off and realized he was in a kneeling position. After a lone car had muffled by on the far lane, ice chains sounding an even tattoo, he remained where he was. Looking up into the falling snow, he said: "Oh, c'mon—just one fucking miracle— please!" He laughed. "Okay, I'll rephrase that—just one miracle . . . please!"

He'd gone right from work to his ill-advised date with Jody, so once back in his orderly apartment he opened the folds of *New York* magazine, which he'd taken from his mailbox. Four birthday cards and the phone bill. Glancing at the clock, he saw it was after three. Quickly he undressed, put on a T-shirt and got into bed. Sitting up, he opened the birthday cards, a funny one from Roger and Norma in San Francisco, a funny-dirty card from Lenny in Chicago, then he opened the envelope without a return address. Inside was a blank file card; on it was scotch-taped the definition of pat·ri·cide. It had been cut from a dictionary.

Sighing, he was neither angry nor upset, merely curious as he checked the envelope to find, as he thought, it was from New Jersey. Some demented person with nothing else to do had been throwing these little darts at him for a year now. It could have been any one of a number of people. Crumpling the letter and envelope up and throwing them on the floor, he wondered how whoever it was had tracked him down.

The fourth envelope was the most important. He had saved it until last, although he knew it would contain no personal message. He opened the envelope tentatively, gently sliding the card out and unfolding it. A simple birthday card with a "thinking of you" message and only the signature: "Love, Bethel."

He pressed the card between the palms of his hands and closed his eyes, conjuring up her image. For an instant she floated before him, the wide eyes, the generous mouth, the shining hair and flawless skin. The frame froze for an instant before her features contorted, her eyes reflecting the terror he had witnessed the last time he had seen her.

Shaking his head, he got up, walked to the bathroom, took two aspirins to counter the drinks he'd had and hurried back to bed. The first part of his slumber was the heavy, drugged sleep of one who'd drunk too much. That out of the way, he slipped into a version of his basic recurrent nightmare, a nightmare that plagued his sleep three or four times a year and one he'd done happily without for several months:

Morning, and he was leaving for work. Stepping out into the hallway, he realized he was without his overcoat. He searched the apartment frantically, looking under things, behind furniture, in the bathroom and kitchen. Panic struck when he glanced at the clock and saw it was almost ten. He must hurry or he'd be late for work; with the chance of a promotion coming up he didn't need that. He rushed out into the hall and only then did it occur to him: he hadn't looked in the closet. Running back, he flung the closet door open.

His father, clad only in his clerical collar and a worn athletic supporter, gaunt and thin and propped up in death, faced him. The eyes wide open, glazed, milky-opaque. The gray-outlined rib cage seemed about to burst through the dead-white flesh of his chest. As Kelly stood hypnotized by this specter, his father's corpse tipped forward, falling in slow motion toward him. Kelly tried to scream but his vocal cords refused to sound.

He ran from his apartment, alternately stumbling and falling down the stairs and out into the street where the air was so freezing he could feel the sweat congeal over his body, gripping him in a clammy mold of fear.

Cut. He was in front of his office building. Running into

the lobby, he pressed the elevator button. The door slid open to reveal his father propped up against the rear wall of the elevator, gaunt and rigid in death as before.

"Oh, God, no!" Kelly swung up from the waist in bed. He could hear the last echoing sounds of his words bounce off the walls. He had ended the nightmare himself. After so many years, he was getting good at aborting them. There had even been a subliminal sense during it that it was, in fact, a nightmare. Nevertheless. He'd paid his dues, though; his breath came in short jabs; as in his dream, he was damp with perspiration.

Reaching for the Kleenex from his bedside table, he mopped his face. He almost laughed, but not quite. Falling into that particular nightmare after the missive from New Jersey and the card from Bethel was too classic. If he'd had to tell an analyst, it would be boring in its predictability. Analysts! They'd certainly not helped him. He thought of the majority of them as charlatans. What was it Lenny said? "I can't imagine two psychiatrists being introduced to each other at a cocktail party and not breaking into hysterical laughter at their mutual fraud!"

He'd had his midslumber exercise and soon fell back to sleep.

CHAPTER 3

The following day at work was strange. The blizzard rearranged the working lives of so many New Yorkers, juggled the schedules of so many businesses, that something halfway between a holiday atmosphere and emergency-alert existed. Kelly himself, struggling with a hangover and little sleep, was edgy, punchy, constantly pulling himself together. Along with another employee, Stanley Giles, he was candidate for a promotion to head up a new Paperback Original department at Parade Paperbacks, a company which mainly reprinted hardcover titles, how-to books and other nonfiction works but had resisted paperback originals and was only now starting up that department long after the other houses. Small but prestigious, they hoped.

Kelly had long been concerned about the promotion, but other problems had taken precedence and he'd kept this one under the counter. Now that the promotion was to be announced the following day, his anxiety suddenly burst into full bloom. This was brought to his special attention by everyone all day long saying, "Good luck tomorrow, Kelly!"

They were undoubtedly saying, "Good luck, tomorrow!" to Stanley Giles, too.

Sometime during the afternoon Kelly made a pact with himself. Or the devil. Or his guardian angel. He told himself if he got the promotion it was a sign that his entire life would alter. Changes would be made, giant steps taken. He would be rocket-boosted onto another level. He acknowledged the childlike naïveté of belief in such a sign. But he often played these games: if I get to Fifth Avenue and Forty-ninth Street before the next crosstown bus comes by, Consolidated Metal will go up three more points, I'll sell and make two thousand dollars. If the lady in the purple coat sits on my side of the bus . . . or whatever. The old step-on-a-crack game.

By late afternoon his hangover and lack of sleep were catching up with him. His work for the day was finished and this allowed time for his brain to play Ping-Pong, until his nerve ends played hell, blinking and twitching, flashing hot and cold. If they held a majority conference and came out with anything approaching a majority decision, they could undoubtedly tip him out of his swivel chair onto the floor. He wanted to go home, but he didn't want to chance being marked "missing" in the event a phone call or summons came from the boss, Big Daddy, Hanley Meister.

Standing up, he walked to the window of his small office and glanced at his watch. He looked forward to five o'clock, when he could leave. Tomorrow would take care of itself; what would be would be.

He stood staring out his window. The snow had stopped again. It was that time of winter twilight, all chilly grays, when the emptiness of the evening ahead yawned open in front of him. It was the acknowledgment of the emptiness that knotted his intestines and froze his bowels.

Soon he slipped into his part-time hobby: looking down from his office window, he wondered if a dive out from the building—feet springing with a mighty thrust from the ledge, more than a mere jump—might enable him to clear the sidewalk and land in the snow-covered street. Not that the snow, from the eleventh floor, would exactly cushion his fall, but at least he could avoid ringing the gong on some luckless pedestrian. He could also pick a time when the street was empty of cars; the prospect of denting someone's hardtop didn't appeal to him either. If he chanced down upon a Volkswagen, for instance—absolute chaos.

He knew how to swim but nothing fancy. Wished he knew how to execute a swan dive; that would be a graceful way to go. He wondered if anyone in those last desperate moments had ever had the sheer cool class to swan dive from the Golden Gate Bridge or the Empire State Building. Talk about dives—that would be a dive!

Footsteps approached the door. "Kelly?" The voice belonged to Stanley Giles, his competitor. Kelly remained standing stock-still. A grin spread across his face. If he ever *were* to jump, it would be worth waiting until Stanley was leaving the building. Not a direct hit, only a good close miss. Nothing ever shook Stanley Giles up, but that would give him a start. On second thought—no! After Stanley recovered from the initial shock—and had his suit cleaned—he'd turn the experience into a riveting anecdote. He'd be dining out on it for years.

"Kelly?" Soon he heard Giles's cocksure footsteps clack on down the hall.

Needing an independent activity for the last twenty or so minutes he must put in, Kelly walked back to his desk and took the *New York Post* from his drawer, glad to have avoided a conversation with Giles and one of those "let's go next door and have a may-the-best-man-win drink" affairs, which Giles would undoubtedly have suggested.

He opened the paper to a feature article about the Copacabana, which had reopened, not as a disco, but as the old Copa, restored as it used to be, a full-fledged nightclub. The new owner, a rich real estate developer from Houston, declared Studio 54, New York, New York, the other discos and in spots were fine, but a city like New York should also have a place for people who want to sit down for a change, be waited upon, served good food and see the best entertainers in the world. Lena Horne was the opening attraction. She was an all-time favorite of Kelly's; in a burst of optimism, he decided to splurge and see her.

He looked up the ad for the Copa on the entertainment page, phoned and made a reservation for the following night, his birthday. Lenny thought he might be able to fly in from Chicago for a long weekend and they'd take in the dinner show. Immediately it occurred to Kelly that if he got the promotion, there'd be a double reason to celebrate. Just as quickly he censored himself for projecting ahead to the possibility: perhaps he was putting a jinx on the promotion by anticipating any festivity honoring it. He was about to call the Copa and cancel the reservation—they could always just show up, what with the blizzard he was certain they'd get a table—when another knock at the door to his office interrupted his frazzled on-again-off-again thoughts.

The game was on: if he could get out of the building without talking to anyone outside of the usual "good-nights," he would get the promotion. Quickly he slipped out of his chair, stepping to the side of the large closet-cupboard unit, placing himself between it and the corner of the adjoining wall.

"Kelly?" It was Grace Emory.

He caught a quick flash of himself hiding behind a piece of furniture in his office. Hiding! If the door were opened just a crack, yes. If it were opened all the way, he'd be only half-hidden. That was even more absurd.

"Kelly?"

He felt like a kid; a grin widened his mouth. Despite the ridiculousness of his position, he remained where he was, shoulders hunched up, crammed between the closet and the wall, thinking: a few more seconds and she'll leave.

But the door opened and, of course, there he was staring at *where it had been.* Grace Emory, sighting the half of him immediately, inhaled a little catch-breath of surprise. Still grinning, Kelly felt his cheeks pump up to a blush.

Recovering from the cramped-up sight of him, Grace said, "Hi, I didn't know we were *playing.*"

"I was just tha-thinking," he said, feeling the moisture eke out along his sides below his armpits.

"There?" she asked. "All scrunched up like that?"

"Yes." He shrugged with attempted casualness, as if he always did his thinking jammed back there between the closet and the wall.

She indicated his desk. "Ever tried one of the drawers? If it's cozy you want—" They both laughed as Kelly stepped away from the closet. "Anyhow, *whatever* you're into now, I just wanted to wish you—happy birthday." In response to his questioning look, she added: "Tomorrow, isn't it?"

"How did you know?"

She sighed. "I cooked dinner for you last year."

"Oh, yes," he said, the memory of the whole of his tentative courtship of her obscuring any individual incident.

"Anyhow, birthday, promotion, blizzard and all, I thought maybe we could have a drink on your way home from the office. I have to be at French class at six thirty so I won't take up your whole evening."

"Well, I—"

"Unless you're busy, of course."

"No, I'm not busy," he said.

She smiled at him. "So—a drink?"

"Ah—sure."

"I'm not twisting your arm?"

"No," he said. "No," he repeated. "Not at all. I—"

"One more word and I'll *know* I am."

"I'd like it," he said simply.

"Good."

He watched his last serious failure leave the room. Not the best prospect to be faced with a specific failure on the eve of his birthday. Not healthy. He still liked her, liked the tininess of her, her pulled-togetherness, her sass and candor. If there had been anyone in the last few years he could have opened up to, outside of Lenny and Roger and Norma, it should have been Grace.

But he had had a disastrous experience with Pamela, a girl he was certain would understand. He had told Pamela the entire saga the Friday evening of a skiing weekend in the Catskills. She had listened attentively; afterward she looked at him for a long moment, then actually broke into laughter, saying: "Why Kelly, you're something, telling me all that just to get me into *bed!* You're terrible, just *terrible!* I'll go to bed with you, but you don't have to make up bizarre stories like *that!* My God!" When he finally convinced her he was not making up a story, her face turned to clay and she uttered one final, "My God!"

Thinking to let the matter simmer down overnight as long as they had separate bedrooms anyhow, he attempted to give her a good-night kiss; the way she recoiled, someone could have been dangling a rattlesnake in her face. The next morning she was gone before breakfast, leaving him a short note: "Dear Kelly, I have to get back to the city. I simply don't understand you. I'm sorry. I'm also confused. Let's take a breather."

He did exactly that. He never called Pamela again and she never called him.

He should have taken another chance with Grace. But he'd been so sure of Pamela. Still, he should have spilled it all out to Grace, he knew that now. Too late—she was engaged, on to other matters.

"Good Christ!" he said, standing up abruptly. "If I could only get rid of it."

He heard the echo of his own voice, winced at the sounds reverberating off the walls. He was talking to himself more and more lately. Dangerous sign this.

CHAPTER 4

They fought the snow-choked streets and sidewalks for five blocks before stepping into a small bar-restaurant on Fifty-sixth between Fifth and Sixth avenues. The walk at rush hour, slipping, dodging and bumping into others slipping and dodging, had been hazardous enough to feed them with small talk. And even a few laughs.

Now, sitting in a corner near the fireplace, Kelly found the soft lighting and comparative quiet a letdown. Their first drink was passed in alternate drifts of silence or clumsy attempts at appropriate conversation while picking at over-salted peanuts. To his chagrin Kelly eventually heard himself asking Grace if she'd seen a certain French film.

Boring, I am boring!

The question caught her in the middle of a sip. "We must have more to talk about than that," she said, putting her glass down. "How do you feel about tomorrow?"

He wanted to say unstrung, but he bluffed through: "I think I have a good chance."

"Good for you!" she said. "You and Stanley have been with the company about the same time, haven't you?"

"I've got six months more. Not because of that, though. I think I'd be more selective. I don't care much for the work I'm doing now, but to be in charge of choosing paperback originals, even if the department is starting up small—I'd like it."

"And Meister?"

"I think he likes my work." Kelly shrugged. "He also likes the—the outgoing, rah-rah type, and Stanley's a—"

"Stanley's a kiss-ass," Grace snapped.

Kelly laughed and lit the cigarette she held out. "Thanks," she said. "I hope you get it if you really want it." She blew a thick puff of smoke out and away from their table. "So— what have you been up to?"

"How do you mean?" he asked.

"I mean," she said with a trace of impatience, "what have you been doing with yourself?"

"Oh . . ."

"All right," she said, aware of his hedging, "how's the stock market?"

"Fine, I've had a good six months." He told Grace of several stocks he'd picked that had done exceptionally well. She asked how his photography was coming along and he spoke of some new equipment he'd bought for his darkroom. She asked if he'd taken any fascinating pictures lately and he told her of some good shots he'd taken in Brooklyn where the freighters dock.

"Don't you enjoy taking pictures of people?" she asked. "I find people more interesting than things, don't you?"

"Yes," he said.

She gave him a moment to elaborate, then she exhaled, "Uh-huh—well!" at his short reply. Along about this time she began tapping her fingers on the top of the table. He ordered another drink and they sat in silence until it arrived. She took a sip from her glass and looked him in the eye; she spoke simply and directly. "Who all do you see nowadays, Kelly?"

"No one in particular," he shrugged.

"Oh, fascinating," she said. "How are they?"

Aware of his inadequacy, he grinned at her. "I mean—"

"Are you happy?" she asked.

He thought for a moment and lied. "Relatively."

"Great!" she snapped.

In spite of their past relationship, they had not been lovers and since the night they'd tacitly agreed to give up trying, they hadn't seen one another socially. Yet she was treating him with all the impatience and a bit of the digging sarcasm of a one-time lover. And he liked it.

He took a large gulp of his drink, straining for a sentence that would be personal, that perhaps would voice his regrets or even say he missed her. Before he could assemble the words, she felt the hopelessness of their conversation and acknowledged it by setting her glass down sharply. "I really don't think I'd better finish. The temptation to stay into the wee hours with all this talk is too great as it is." She glanced at her watch. "Besides, I'm bad enough at French without being drunk. I'm only taking it because Freddie and I are passing through France this summer. I hate the rudeness of the Parisians and this time I want to be able to give it back to them."

He paid the check quickly and they left. Out on the side-walk he asked if he could drop her in a cab.

"No, I like to walk in the snow. It's only Sixty-fourth between Madison and Fifth."

"I'll walk you there."

"Promise not to talk my ear off?"

"I'll try not to." He grinned at her.

When they got to Fifth Avenue, she said, "Seen any good plays lately?"

"No," he replied, smiling.

"Thank God," she sighed.

Outside in the air he felt light-headed. He wanted to enjoy this sensation, but he felt burdened. The gaggle of unspoken words inside his head bound him up and refused to allow the liquor freedom. Although Grace was no more than five foot three to his five eleven, she paced their walk, her stride becoming somewhat militant by the time they reached Fifth

Avenue and Fifty-eighth Street. Light snow had begun to fall as she led the way uptown; the streets and sidewalks were already banked high with crusts of white. Soon they ducked their way past an island of ten or twelve people waiting in vain for cabs under the canopy of the Pierre Hotel.

By the time they approached Sixty-first Street, Grace was walking so fast he was surprised she hadn't slipped and fallen. At the corner, about to squeeze through a narrow gorge cut in the snowbank, she suddenly turned to him. He stopped, thinking she was about to say something.

Her brow was gathered up in wrinkles and her mouth did seem to be assembling words, but a small, sharp shake of her head canceled this out. Her right arm shot out in front of her; she slammed the flat of her hand into Kelly's stomach and sent him sprawling backward into the snow. He cried out—almost cawed, the sound of a downed bird—and sat there too stunned to speak.

Several people standing under the canopy fifteen or so yards away laughed and pointed at them. Grace stood defiantly where she was.

After a moment Kelly said, "What was that for?"

"I felt like it."

"You did?"

"Yes, I did. That's what you need, a good push. You ought to give *yourself* a good push!"

Kelly extended an arm for leverage; Grace ignored his outstretched hand. "You can get up yourself. You're not a cripple." She added in a mumble: "Even if you treat yourself like one."

"What?" he asked.

"I said," she shouted at him, *"Peruvian Tin just went up two points."*

Kelly picked himself up and brushed the snow from the back of his overcoat. Then, facing her, he said, "I'm glad we got together this evening."

"Charming, I'm sure," Grace replied. She stood there looking at him. He was concentrating on her eyes, which seemed about to spurt tears, when she cocked her head, muttered something incoherent, and sent him sprawling back into the snow again.

This caused a heightened commotion from the group under the canopy as Kelly cried out in anger, "What's the matter with you, anyway?"

"Nothing!" she said, willing back tears. "Nothing's the matter with *you,* either, except you make me mad."

Kelly sprang to his feet. "You're not exactly endearing yourself to me, either."

"Hey, little miss," a plump lady in a mink coat called out, "you're some bully!"

A hoot of laughter echoed from the woman and her friends. Grace snorted in their direction and quickly stepped out into Fifth Avenue toward the Central Park side of the street.

"What did I do?" Kelly asked, following her.

She wheeled on him in the middle of Fifth Avenue. "Nothing! You didn't do *anything.* You never do anything! That's it!"

Her words struck him as true as they did forceful, and he shouted back at her: "So—what's it to you!"

"Great!" she cried out. "He *shouted*! He raised his voice. There *is* someone living inside there." A cab honked at them. "Oh, shut up!" she yelled at the driver. She hopped over some rough spots in the street and scrambled up onto the sidewalk.

Their treatment of one another during their courtship— both of them inching along over evenings made of egg- shells—came winging back at Kelly with retroactive vio- lence. "Why didn't you ever talk to me like this when—"

Again she wheeled on him. "Because I had such a crush on you I was afraid to open my mouth for fear of scaring you off. So we both pussyfooted around until we were all pussy- footed out. We never even had a fight! We didn't even— Oh!" she exclaimed, brushing away a strand of hair that had fallen down across her forehead. "What are we talking about it now for?"

"You started it," he offered.

"Somebody has to start something with you," she snapped, adrenaline high once again, dredging up more exasperation from the past. "You'd never talk about—never *tell* me anything about yourself. It was like three months of being out on a blind date."

A gust of cold wind swept across from Central Park and slapped him; the vodka inside him kicked out at it and he added a savage mental boot of his own. "I had a—I ra-really loved you!"

"Then why in Christ's name didn't you ever make a pass at me! Why didn't we go to bed?"

"Because—*because*! Oh, shit, I can't go into it now."

She reached out and took his hand. "Oh, Kelly, I made up that something—I don't know, something happened once." He looked up at her again. "Yes, I mean to you," she said. "And I'll bet it was a pip!"

"It was a pip all right!" He was immediately surprised at the strength of his reading.

"Ah-hah! See, I knew, I—but you'd never—" She squeezed his hand. "Some nights when we'd have a couple of drinks or a smoke, you'd get that delicate one inch off the ground and I'd see something bubbling up in you, right back there behind your eyes and I'd think: tonight he might just explode in a whole shower of words. But it never happened, the pressure escaped, the high wore off, and it never happened."

"I know. I was—I had such a feeling for you, I was ja-just taking it easy."

"And vice-vice. I was taking it easy, not wanting to come on strong, wanting to let you take the initiative. We were both so easy, we just fizzled out. Huh?" He only shook his head. "I'm sorry I pushed you," she said. "Freddie and I had a fight and I was taking it out on you." She glanced at her watch. "I'll be late. Good-night, Kelly. And happy birthday. Some night maybe you and I'll have dinner, if you'd like, and we'll really talk. *I'd* like it."

"So would I," he replied.

"Good. I'll keep all my crossables crossed for tomorrow."

He said good-night; she was about to release his hand,
which she'd been holding all this time, when she suddenly
flung it down by his side and took a quick step back from
him. "You see," she said, as if she were continuing a sentence, "if I were you, I'd give up a job with a publishing
company, especially one like ours, even if I were senior edi-
tor."

"I have to live."

"You told me once you'd worked eight thousand dollars in
the market up to seventeen; you said now you'd had some
more good times, so you must have more."

"For a rainy day," he said.

Grace held a hand out, palm up. "It's *snowing* now!" She
snorted. "What did *that* mean? I'm a little fashnoofkaed myself." Putting her hands on her hips, she said, "You know
what I think? You ought to go on your travels."

"Where?"

"Anywhere! Knock around, kick up some dust, see the
world, get some dirt on you, get out of whatever rut you're
in, for God's sake, before it's too late!"

"I never knew you to—" He broke off, shaking his head.

"To what?" she asked.

"—get so worked up."

"Yes, I get worked up, because I see you all set to turn
into a dried-up bachelor and it's ridiculous and I worry about
you. There!"

"I worry too," Kelly said.

"Then for God's sake *do* something! Do something different for a change. Surprise yourself!"

"Like what?"

"Like—how the hell do I know! Just do it!" In an instant
she was convulsed in laughter, taking Kelly right along with
her. "My God," she shrieked, "look at us—I mean *me,* pushing you down in the snow *twice* and shouting—and—it's so
late for all that. Oh—oh, Lord, people are *funny,* aren't we?"

"Yes," he laughed.

"Oh, my God!" She turned from him, making her way
through the thick snow with the determination of a terrier.

He could still hear her laughing, chattering and clucking to herself about the human condition half a block away.

How he'd missed his chance with her a year ago! In spades he had; he was certain of it now. He could kick himself all the way to Staten Island. Instead, promotion, birthday, blizzard, THE PROBLEM, and all—he got rip-roaring drunk.

CHAPTER 5

He had not staggered home until almost three o'clock, having hit Studio 54, a new disco called Erasmus High, a singles bar and Babette's Watering Hole, where he'd been absorbed into a group of merrymakers led by a thin, attractive, exposed nerve end, Muffy, obviously rich from the way her group deferred to her. She supplied them all with the strongest pot Kelly had ever inhaled. From time to time her friends would call her "Little Dick." "Hey, Little Dick," they would say, "can I have another hit?" Finally Kelly had the temerity to ask her why she was called "Little Dick." Looking him squarely in the eye, she said: "Because my mother is called Big Dick!"

At various times during the evening he announced: "I'm going to quit my job, go on my travels, see the world, get some dirt on me!" He no more meant this than he'd have thought of signing up for a course in hang-gliding. It was a hedge against the promotion. But it sounded good, this parroting of Grace's advice, although he had no idea how to implement it, had he actually taken it seriously.

Kelly finally pulled a disappearing act. Little Dick had

begun zeroing in on him in a heavily stoned yet frenetic state. If he did not need anything, he did not need another close encounter of the worst kind. He barely managed to get home in time to pass out.

Awakening was not fun. The bright glare of cold daylight violated his bedroom, which was freezing. He staggered to the bathroom, swallowed two aspirin, cursing himself for not taking them when he went to bed. He felt the radiator, pure ice. Without checking to see if the oil supply was low, the superintendent had let the furnace run out. There would probably be no hot water either. The tap proved him right. He looked at his watch—8:40. He'd forgotten to set the alarm.

Shaking his head, he quickly went to the kitchen and placed a large pan of water on the stove for shaving. He poured a glass of orange juice and gulped it down. His thirst was tremendous; he drank a second glass and felt dizzy. He placed another smaller pot on the stove with water for instant coffee and reached for his usual box of cereal, but his stomach sent a strong negative response at the prospect of food and he withdrew his hand.

Returning to the bathroom, he took an Alka-Seltzer and gazed at the shower with longing. He'd have given anything for a warm shower. It wasn't until he lathered himself and stood in front of the bathroom mirror that he was seized by an attack of nerves regarding the promotion. Lifting the razor to his face, he made a few unsteady passes at his cheek. Was he shaving or dueling with himself? His hand, jerking this way and that, refused to respond to his commands. He nicked himself several times and winced as he applied a styptic pencil to the smarting cuts.

Taking a first sip of coffee, he thought he might be sick to his stomach. He went back to the bathroom and brushed his teeth again. It was nine fifteen when he was ready to leave. Already fifteen minutes late, he would be half an hour late by the time he reached the office.

The hallway was even colder than his apartment, and he tugged up the collar of his coat. When he stepped out onto the snow-covered sidewalk, the glare of the sun together with a brisk, chilling wind and the grinding roar of a garbage truck stopped him completely.

He ducked back into the vestibule of his building, hesitating only a moment before unlocking the inside door and hurrying back up the four flights of stairs. Entering his apartment, he went directly to the bathroom cabinet where he retrieved a small plastic prescription container labeled Valium. He snapped the cap off only to find a small drift of yellow powder at the bottom.

It was not his day, even though it had barely begun. Glancing in the mirror, he noticed a smear of pink on his shirt collar from the cut on his neck. He raised his hand and with a trembling finger blotted the nick. He met his eyes in the mirror and said, "You're a mess." Laughing nervously, he thought back to the night before and, most of all, to Grace. He didn't feel like going on his travels; he felt like going back to bed. What the hell had he been doing out until three A.M. the night before an important day? Did he have a secret self-destruct button?

He had never in his life taken a drink in the morning. But his mind was made up, he needed the hair of the dog, needed anything he could take to help get him through. In the kitchen he opened a can of tomato juice. Pouring it into a glass, he dotted it with salt and pepper, hurried into the living room and splashed a tot of vodka in the tomato juice. After stirring it with a bottle opener, he raised the glass and took a sip.

The tomato juice was cold to his palate. He could barely perceive the alcohol content, so he poured in another splash of vodka. He stirred it with his finger and drank again. There was no doubt this time; above the cold of the juice a heavy overlayer of warmth was suspended oillike. He tracked the warmth as it flowed down from a tang in the back of his throat to his stomach. Smacking his lips together, he walked to the window and pulled open the drapes. At that moment, a scattered cloud front slid under the sun, dulling its glare. He took another drink and checked his wristwatch: 9:28. The time merely registered as time, not some ticking demon to be raced. He downed a healthy swig from his glass and smiled. The butterflies were no longer beating their wings quite so furiously against the walls of his stomach. If he left now, he could walk to the office and be there in ample time for the meeting. In over three years he had rarely been late to work. Finishing his drink, he realized he was no longer aware of the cold, nor did the announcement at ten loom over him like some trembling avalanche.

But he was still thirsty; he hurried into the kitchen and emptied the can of tomato juice into his glass. Walking back into the living room, he poured a slug of vodka into it and in three successive gulps finished it off. Now he felt a kick. He set the glass down, hiccuped and laughed.

The world was softer when he stepped out of the building onto the sidewalk for the second time. The wind was still brisk but as he turned, walking toward Fifth Avenue, it was at his back, helping him glide along over the packed snow. The snowstorm had turned New York into a small town. Pedestrians nodded and occasionally spoke to one another as they picked their way along over heavy drifts or inched gingerly over the icy spots. Even the drivers of cars reacted with a paternal vigilance, starting up slowly at intersections and braking with equal care.

One block from his building an enormous black woman, great puffs of frosted breath coming from her mouth, lumbered up the steps from the subway holding a small girl by the hand. She slipped on the sidewalk and sat down easily on her backside. Clapping her hands together, the little girl giggled: "Oh, Tessie, you're funny!" "I'll funny you," the woman said, then laughed so hard she was unable to get up. A young boy from the newsstand joined Kelly and they hauled her to her feet as she warned them, "Watch your backs, babies, I weigh a full ton." She laughed again and thanked them.

Turning into the lobby of his building, Kelly thought what a pleasant, tilted walk to work it had been. In the elevator he was unable to suppress a grin. He always felt the urge to laugh in elevators, but usually he was able to control himself.

His high spirits were tainted when he entered the front office of Parade Paperbacks, however. The perpetually harassed switchboard operator–receptionist, who was attempting to deal with the phones, a delivery boy and an impatient man with an artist's portfolio; the chatter of secretaries; the noise of the typing; all this activity, while most familiar, seemed jarringly out of place to Kelly this morning. It was a day to be outside, not cooped up in an office. Parade Paperbacks wasn't paying attention to the storm.

He remembered the first day he had attended summer school. He'd been seized by an intense attack of claustrophobia. The office was overheated, too, just as the schoolroom had been humid and stuffy. He removed his overcoat as he walked past the desks in the large front office, almost expecting one of the secretaries to chide him for being late, to say he was wanted in the principal's office. Bumping against the last desk, he received a distracted look from Miss Herman, an unattractive, dark-complexioned girl with goldfish eyes and a fine line of fur edging her upper lip. He stifled an impulse to suggest a shave and realized he was not only a bit high, he was drunk.

As soon as he entered his office he raised the window a good two feet; the cold air rushed in and he blotted the dampness on his forehead with his hand. There was a scribbled note on his desk from Grace Emory, saying Mr. Meister had asked to see him around nine fifteen and ending with, "Good luck this morning." He was pondering how to interpret this bit of news when Grace appeared in the doorway.

"Oh," he said, "I just got your note. I wonder what for?" In contradiction to the way in which alcohol usually affected his speech, his words came out with unusual lightness; he wondered if she noticed anything; if she did, she gave no sign.

"I don't know. I just heard his secretary mention it and thought I'd let you know."

"Thanks, I just got in."

"So I see," she said, smiling and indicating his coat, which he held folded over his arm. She glanced down at the floor, then back up at him. "Kelly, I'm sorry about last night. I don't know what—"

"I liked it," he grinned at her.

"What?" she asked, as if she hadn't heard him correctly.

"I liked it," he repeated.

She cocked her head. "You look exceptionally well today."

"I do?" he asked with surprise.

"Yes, you've got good color."

"Well," he replied, "a drink for breakfast always gives me a bit of a flush."

"Sure," she said, "me, too." She crossed her fingers. "Good luck, see you later." She walked away down the hall.

Grinning, he spoke to the print of a whaling ship upon his wall. "Tell the truth and nobody believes you."

The clock on his desk read 9:57. Hanley Meister was a punctual man. If the meeting was scheduled for ten, it was meant to begin at ten. Kelly left his office and proceeded down the hall to the meeting room. He was still gliding, even without the wind at his back. He made no stop, indulged in no last-minute preparation, as he usually did, before entering the room; he simply opened the door and walked in.

Mr. Weiss was engaged in conversation with Mrs. Vance. Mr. Loganthal and Mr. Deems looked over some printed matter and Miss Mosley was pawing through her handbag. They glanced up and variously nodded or spoke a word or two of greeting. Kelly said, "Good-morning," and sat down next to Mr. Loganthal and across from Miss Mosley, who returned to the contents of her purse with squirrellike attention.

Her two front teeth were bared. Kelly decided it must require a goodly effort to draw her lips together over them.

He studied her closely. As much as she reminded him of a squirrel, there was also something of the bird about her. The top of her head was flat, her hair curling down in featherlike wisps over her rather high forehead like some comic female canary. Yes, she was a cross between a squirrel and a canary. He giggled as Miss Mosley snapped her purse shut and looked up at him.

"You're in a happy mood, Kelly," she chirped, wagging a finger at him. "Must know something."

Mr. Mahoney and Mr. Bissinger entered the room, followed shortly by Stanley Giles, looking sleek and overfed and smelling of lemon cologne. He sat to Kelly's left. Good-mornings had barely been exchanged when the small door at the end of the room opened and Hanley Meister entered, followed by his secretary, Mrs. Emhardt, who took her place next to him and prepared to take notes.

The principal's office, Kelly thought. How dry it is. He glanced around the table. How dry they all are. Except for Miss Mosley and Stanley Giles, who quivered with ambition and told endless jokes and anecdotes in an attempt to cover up the insane drive behind his shifty eyes, they were interchangeable gray blobs. Miss Mosley and Stanley Giles were not gray, but neither did they inspire in Kelly a desire to fraternize beyond the office level of workaday relations. As for the rest of them, the color was gray and the room was stuffy and—the Big Gray Daddy himself had finished shuffling through his papers and was speaking.

"I know you'll be glad to hear that *Watch That First Step* has sold over seven hundred thousand. We expect to go over a million by May."

There were nods around the table and muttered indications of approval. Hanley Meister went on to speak about several new books they were dickering for, and Kelly glanced around the table at the intense gray faces hanging on to every word, expressing their enthusiasm in tight little smiles that snapped shut the minute Hanley Meister acknowledged them.

Kelly suddenly leaned back away from the table. He didn't

really feel part of the meeting. He was certainly observing it, monitoring it, but from a distance—rather like watching it down the long end of a telescope. He squinted his eyes, blurring his focus and increasing the illusion. Close as he actually was to the people around the table, he felt that if he reached out he would not be able to touch any one of them.

Again the parallel between school and Parade Paperbacks struck Kelly. If an industrious schoolboy projected himself into his concept of a business firm, he might well end up with a prototype of Parade Paperbacks and its system of meetings, interoffice memos, progress reports, bowling team, rewards and office contests. There was even a pool for guessing the "sleeper" of the year.

Today it all seemed ridiculously stuffy and G.I. to Kelly.

The principal finished reciting a few other figures and cleared his throat. He looked at Kelly and beamed a kindly, fatherly smile at him. "I wanted to see you earlier, Kelly. Perhaps we can have tea after the meeting." Hanley Meister was a confirmed Anglophile.

Kelly nodded.

"Before we get on to other matters, Stanley Giles is going to head up our Paperback Original Department and I'm certain that—"

CHAPTER 6

Kelly was not sure exactly what made him stand; it was probably not the shock of the announcement as much as Stanley Giles's hand coming to rest upon his shoulder in sympathetic understanding. Also, and he could have made this up, it seemed the hand arrived at its destination just a mite early. Anyhow, there he was standing.

"Kelly . . . ?" It was Mr. Meister's voice.

"Yes!" he replied, uttering the word as if it were the definitive answer *and* end to a long discussion. Kelly was congratulating himself upon the force with which he had imbued that one simple word, when an unexpected hiccup ruined the effect. He started to raise his hand to his mouth and was about to say, "Excuse me," when he realized that would undoubtedly weaken his case. As it was, the hiccup did provide a certain staccato punctuation to his "Yes!" and he decided to leave it that way.

Turning to make his exit, he noticed little furrows above the bridge of Miss Mosley's nose; she had also gone to the considerable bother of shielding her teeth. Out of the corner of his eye he was also aware of Mr. Bissinger and Mr. Mahoney sliding back their chairs and standing up as Mr. Meister repeated, "Kelly?"

He shut the door behind him and heard the principal call his name out once more, in a firm tone this time. He walked quickly down the hall and, nearing his office, heard the door to the conference room open and the buzz of conversation trickle down the hall after him. He also heard a pair of footsteps leave the carpet of the meeting room and strike out on the bare hallway. If anyone was chasing him, he hoped it would be Stanley Giles, but a quick glance over his shoulder disappointed him; it was Mr. Mahoney. Realizing if he took the time to enter his office and retrieve his overcoat he would be trapped, he continued straight ahead toward the outer offices and the reception room.

"Kelly . . . Kelly!" There was a whine to Mr. Mahoney's voice which only made Kelly quicken his pace. "Kelly—wait up!"

He broke into a trot as he entered the large front office. Five secretaries were at their desks and they all turned to look at him. One of them, Miss Grossbard, stood up. "What?" she asked.

Without thinking, Kelly threw his arms up in the air and shouted: "Mice!"

This brought all of the secretaries to their feet; Miss Herman screamed and jumped up on her chair. He clicked through the door to the reception room, now empty, and ran across to the heavy wooden doors leading to the outside hall. He was aware that the footsteps behind him had broken into a trot, too.

"We're having an interoffice chase," he said.

"Did you say something?" the combination switchboard operator–receptionist asked from behind her window.

"Genitalia!" Kelly said, opening the door and turning left for the bank of elevators. He spotted a red coat disappearing into the end car. "Wait!" he called out. Skidding across the marble floor, he jumped into the elevator and slammed his fist against the "door close" button.

In the time it took for the doors to shut, he heard Mr. Mahoney skidding across the marble floor after him. "Kelly, what the devil is the—" He caught only an elongated glimpse of Mr. Mahoney's flushed face as the doors came together and the elevator began its descent.

He burst into a nervous giggle and leaned against the railing of the car, alternately laughing and gasping with relief. He became aware of the only other passenger, a chubby, oval-faced young lady wearing a red cloth coat. She had backed into the far corner of the elevator and stood clutching her purse to her stomach with two dimpled fists. Definitely prepared for assault, she stared bug-eyed at the floor indicator above the doors. Kelly laughed harder at the sight of her terror. She bolted out of the car the second the doors opened, not caring that it was only the third floor. Two men entered the car and glanced with faint amusement at Kelly, still panting to control himself.

A taxi, one of the few abroad in such weather, dropped off four businessmen at the curb as Kelly walked out onto the sidewalk. Ducking into it, he stifled an impulse to shout, "Bellevue and step on it!"—and gave the driver his address.

Suddenly the hilarity dropped out of his adventure and he was left sitting in a puddle of noncomprehension. What in Christ's name had happened? A tiny pain shot across his forehead and for a moment he experienced a throwback to the early morning's hangover. He was drained; although he'd only been up a little more than two hours, the vodka and his behavior at Parade Paperbacks had wiped him out.

He conjectured the scene that must have followed his abrupt departure and was enlightened by the knowledge that, to all intents and purposes, he had quit. He reproached himself for not coming out and saying it. As if to rectify this, he said: "I quit."

"What?" the cabbie asked.

Everyone was asking him "What?" today.

"Nothing," he mumbled.

Kelly had a question for himself: he asked himself what he was going to do, but what he had already done was more than enough to cope with. He felt swamped; again it was as if he were looking down the wrong end of a telescope, only this time he was observing himself sitting numbly in the back seat of the cab.

When he was let off at his address he climbed the stairs, his fatigue increasing with each step he took. Cold as his apartment was, it was still a haven. He was standing in the center of the room in quiet amazement to find himself home so soon when the phone rang. It startled him and he jumped a step to the side. Out of annoyance he rushed to it, snatched the receiver up, said, "I quit!" and slammed it down.

There, he thought, that makes it official. He took his jacket off and the phone rang again. It rang all the while he was undressing and stopped only as he crawled into bed. He had just settled snugly under the covers when it rang again. In a final burst of energy he bolted out of bed and picked the phone up, jiggling the small metal button until he had broken the connection. When he heard the dial tone, he got the operator and had her put him through to Western Union. He addressed the telegram to Hanley Meister and the message was brief:

> I quit.
> (Signed)
> Kelly McDermott

He had no sooner hung up when the phone began ringing again; he carried it into the dressing room, wrapped it in a heavy sweater and placed the bundle, now whirring faintly, in a drawer.

Falling into bed, he pulled the covers over him and was asleep within minutes.

He was vaguely aware of his doorbell ringing two different times, but there was a short in it so the ringing was more of a muffled static buzz and not all that intrusive. He merely turned on his stomach and, dragging a pillow over his head, was lost in sleep again.

He toyed with awakening for what seemed ages. It was finally the heat in his apartment that caused him to stagger out of bed and open a window. The three radiators were going full blast now and he turned the center one off.

Thick snow fell again; it was dark outside the windows but only a slate-gray color, not entirely black. Looking at his clock, he saw it was ten minutes after five. "Took care of *that* day!" he muttered. He was ravenously hungry; walking to the kitchen, he noticed two yellow envelopes sticking under his front door. The first telegram read:

> Have tried phoning all day, first at
> office. Grace says you walked. Con-
> gratulations. Airports closed again,
> can't make it anyhow. Boss had
> heart attack, all sitting shiva or
> whatever. Give 'em hell. Phone me.
> Congratulations twice. Come visit.
>
> Lenny

Kelly puffed up, proud once again of his defection. The second telegram said:

> Take the long weekend. Please see
> me Monday morning. Know we can
> work out something.
>
> Hanley Meister

"I've already *taken* the long weekend," Kelly said. The last sentence of the telegram needled him. It was too placating, patronizing even.

When he opened the cupboard, a jar of peanut butter caught his eye. He made himself a thick sandwich of peanut butter and grape jelly and devoured it. He made another and washed it down with a glass of milk.

Returning to the living room, he was filled with emotions as mixed as any he'd ever experienced. He walked to the dressing room, opened the drawer, and lifting out the bundle containing the phone, he could feel the sensation in his fingers and hear the muffled ring of it. He quickly unfolded the sweater and answered it. It was Lenny from Chicago. Within minutes Kelly blurted out an account of his last few shaky days and his leave-taking at Parade Paperbacks.

When he finished, all he could hear was Lenny's laughter. "Oh, Kelly—Jesus Christ, you did it, you did it! I wish I was there, I'd give you a big hug, the Croix de Guts, and a bottle of champagne! You were never that happy there; you were happy to be working, that's all."

"But what do I do now?"

"Who cares, who gives a hot sitz bath? Relax awhile, Grace was right, hit the road, bum around. Write a book; you were always talking about it. Why don't you write the story of—" Lenny's voice dropped to a hush. "Christ, write about what happened in your *family*. You're nuts if you don't. Whatever you do, don't sit around and mope. Go out tonight and celebrate! You made a change. How many people are able to make changes in their boring-assed lives? Huh? We don't get to make changes after they put us in our boxes, you know. That's it."

They talked for fifteen minutes and by the time Kelly said good-bye, Lenny had so filled him with adrenaline he was into a natural high. He'd no sooner put the phone down when it rang again.

"Kelly?" It was a woman's voice. "Kelly?"

"Yes."

"Oh." There was a sigh. "It's Grace."

"Oh—hello, Grace!"

"I've tried phoning you several times. Is everything—I mean are you all right?" There was a touch of wonder in her tone, indicating perhaps he wasn't quite the known quantity she had presumed.

He replied in a cheery voice: "Yes, I'm fine."

"Your friend, Lenny, called from Chicago—"

"Yes, I just talked to him."

"Oh, good. Ah—I have your coat. I brought it home. I thought you might need it over the weekend." She sounded warm and concerned.

"Thanks."

There was a pause. "You certainly turned the place upside down. The whole rest of the day was . . . I don't know . . . weird. Kelly?"

"Yes."

"Good for you!"

That was two counties heard from. He suddenly wanted to see her; he also remembered the reservation he'd made. "Listen, Grace, are you busy tonight?"

She hesitated before answering. "I don't think so. Why?"

"I've got a reservation for the dinner show at the Copa to see Lena Horne."

"You have?"

The surprise in her voice annoyed him and he gave no further explanation, only inviting her to join him.

Her reply was tentative. "Kelly, I'd love to. I think I can . . ."

"Could you let me know for sure?"

Again she hesitated before speaking. "You see, Freddie and I had a terrible row on Tuesday. We'd planned dinner and a movie tonight, but we haven't seen one another or spoken since he slammed out of here. So I guess I can."

He explained to her that the show began at nine, that if they wanted to eat first they should be there by eight.

"I'd rather eat after. And Kelly—" She broke off.

"Yes?"

"If Freddie comes by or—"

"Just call and let me know."

"I hate to leave it that way . . ."

"I'll understand. I'll pick you up about eight fifteen."

"I'd better plan to meet you there, Kelly. Just in case."

"All right. See you about a quarter to nine. I'll wait upstairs."

"I'm looking forward," she said, and hung up.

He took a bath, as joyful as it was warm. If there was ever a night he needed company—and now he had it! He could sift through the unanswerables with Grace. He sat up in the tub with a splash. Tonight he might even tell her—his secret, is what he thought of it as. He sloshed from side to side and made a firm promise to tell her everything.

The hour from seven to eight was interminable. At eight, fully dressed, he fixed himself a vodka martini and watched a television special on South Africa. He started to make a second drink, then stopped, digging around instead in his special stash drawer in the night table until he came up with half a joint he'd been keeping. He smoked it, hoping this might allow him the freedom of opening up with Grace. The possibility that she might actually be breaking up with Freddie rattled around in the back of his mind. He didn't wish it exactly. Nevertheless. This might just turn out to be a very special night.

At eight thirty, feeling pleasantly light-headed, he prepared to leave the apartment, all the while praying the phone wouldn't ring. He sighed with relief as he quickly locked his front door and walked down the stairs.

An unbelievable amount of snow had fallen again since he'd been in his apartment. The streets were adrift; sidewalks that had been cleared during the morning were blanketed once more, and the strips of pavement that had been neglected for the past twenty-four hours were either impassable or had been cut through by narrow gorges barely wide enough for one person to slip through.

A gust of wind swatted him as he came to the corner of Park and Sixty-first. The smoke and drink were working together now and he felt a sense of adventure merely being out. He looked south on Park Avenue and saw the lights of the apartment buildings and shops, empty now, shining the softest pastel through the thick snowflakes. For as far as he could see, only five or six cars were under power. The rest stood humpbacked in snow by the curbs, like so many frozen buffalo. Sound was muffled. New York looked incredibly beautiful and snug; he thought of all the cozy activities taking place under shelter, wondered how many people right now in the city were engaged in "creating the world." Fire one, fire two . . .

The going was slow and by the time he made his way up the steps to the Copa on Sixtieth between Madison and Fifth, it was almost a quarter to nine. He gave his name and was greeted ebulliently by the head maître d'; it was definitely an off night. "Ah, yes, Mr. McDermott—for two," he beamed, as if the entire establishment were waiting only for Kelly's arrival.

"I'm being met here," Kelly said, giving his coat and rubbers to the hatcheck girl.

"Would you care to wait at your table?"

"I'll just wait up here."

"Yes, or you can sit in the bar if you prefer."

The maître d' left him to attend to a party of four. Kelly stepped into the lounge where he sat down and ordered a vodka gibson on the rocks. Turning on the stool, he faced the foyer so he could see Grace when she arrived. Excitement and anticipation caused him to gulp the drink down and he ordered a second. He had just about finished it, eyes glued to the entranceway, when he heard a fanfare followed by a muffled introduction. Glancing at his watch, he saw it was ten after nine. The maître d' ducked his head into the lounge. "Miss Horne is going on now. Would you like to wait at your table? I'll bring the young lady down as soon as she arrives."

Kelly paid for his drinks and followed the man to the head of the stairs, where he felt obliged to use the handrailing. He'd consumed a total of two peanut butter and jelly sandwiches, a glass of milk, one vodka martini, two vodka gibsons and had a smoke since awakening and he was feeling the freight. He grinned—*the last of the swingers*. At the bottom of the stairs the maître d' turned him over to another maître d', saying, "Mr. McDermott, table for two."

There was a burst of applause from the darkened room as Lena Horne made her entrance from the upper level down the opposite stairway to the left of the room. The maître d' guided Kelly to a table on the balcony level of the club directly overlooking the dance floor. Though it was not on the main floor, the vantage point for seeing the show was excellent. The tables on the main floor were three-quarters occupied, while those on the second level were barely half-filled.

Below him Lena Horne stood in the spotlight, snugly poured into a gold lamé gown, singing her opening song, a specially written upbeat number. She looked as cool as ever; her skin glowed not with heat but with a coolness, Kelly decided. No teeth were ever whiter as she flashed her tight oblong smile and her mouth tugged over in a wicked twist that cinched a double entendre. She was well into her third song when the maître d' tapped Kelly on the shoulder and whispered, "Telephone." Kelly followed him to a phone in an alcove behind the staircase.

"Kelly?" It was Grace.

"Yes."

"I'm at the corner store," she whispered. "I made an excuse. Kelly, I'm so sorry, I really am. I was just getting dressed when Freddie came by with flowers and the whole works, including apology. I planned on coming anyhow, but he lost a very important case in court today. He's in a dreadful mood, he's got a bad cold and I—"

"That's all right," Kelly said, faking it.

"I know, but—"

"Listen, I understand."

"You're not alone, are you?"

He remembered he hadn't given any details, only that he'd reserved a table. "No," he lied, "friends from Cleveland."

"Oh, good. Still, I wish I could be with you. How're you feeling? About today, I mean?"

"Okay."

"Let's get together tomorrow. We'll have a talk and you can get your coat. In the afternoon—is that good for you?"

"Sure."

She apologized again, he told her to forget it and they hung up.

He was bitterly disappointed. When he sat back down at his table a waiter took his order for another drink, which he didn't really want. The evening had turned sour and he felt a dismal sense of isolation creeping over him. He did his best to shake this feeling off; though it took all his concentration, he forced himself to give his attention to Lena Horne, and by the time she'd impeccably delivered some twenty songs spanning almost fifty minutes, he was hypnotized to a surprising degree by her artistry. She was forced to beg off.

The lights came up; the regular band was replaced by a smaller combo that played a strange but interesting combination of Latin-disco music. A few couples drifted onto the floor while others called for the check, having seen the main attraction. Kelly had nursed his last drink through the entire show and was now feeling severe hunger pangs. He ordered linguini with white clam sauce, a large salad and garlic bread.

Experiencing a major slump because of Grace's no-show, he also fully realized it was his birthday and—how grimy, to be spending it alone in the Copa-fucking-cabana! A wave of anger swept over him, which was better than self-pity, although, in all honesty, there was no one to aim the anger at but himself.

A stir of excitement at the foot of the stairway, to the right of Kelly's table and behind him, caught his attention. He turned to see the assistant maître d' back away from his reservation stand, humble-fashion, clearing a path, as the head maître d' glided down off the last step onto the maroon carpet and turned back toward the stairs, flourishing one arm out before him, his body executing a formal half-bow.

He extended his arm, a long, thin hand took his, and Maggie Banner stepped down off the stairs. She nodded and smiled at the maître d' as Raffaello Tucci appeared and took her by the arm. She turned to her escort and, although her smile broadened, it seemed to tighten somewhat. They moved forward a few short steps while the rest of their party cleared the stairs.

Two men, one middle-aged, square-built, thick-necked,

black brush-cut hair; the other, older, graying, a sensitive look upon his handsome face, followed them directly. The older man, Raffaello Tucci's former coach and manager, was impeccably dressed in a dark gray suit; the younger of the two wore an expensive black mohair number which fit too snugly, a white-on-white shirt in company with a white-on-white tie. He reeked of the midsixties.

The last two of the party caught Kelly's attention: a woman, at least six feet tall, large-boned, ungainly and fierce of face, carrying a fur coat over her arm and wearing a small-print dress of purple, blue and yellow, a dress that showed off the corseted her beneath. Her body wrestled the clothes; she simply did not seem at home dressed up. She reminded Kelly of a prison matron—she should be wearing a uniform of sorts, not a dress-up dress. She was followed closely by a blue-jacketed, turtlenecked younger man with long, curly auburn hair and large brown liquid eyes that belied the street-tough look of his otherwise rugged face and muscular build.

When the party had assembled in a loose cluster, the maître d' nodded once again, whereupon they followed him across the upper section of the club toward the stairs leading down to the dance floor and the ringside tables. Only two tables separated Kelly from the aisle they traveled. Nudges and brief sounds of recognition spread from table to table as, even in this short amount of time, the entire upper level of the club became aware of Maggie Banner's presence.

She took small steps, smile intact, looking neither to the left nor to the right, acknowledging the attention she drew only by her erect carriage, the upward tilt of her head; and by smiling at no one in particular, she smiled for everyone. Then, for a moment, as she reached out and placed her right hand on the railing at the top of the stairs, she paused, glancing to her left, and the beam of her glance landed upon Kelly. She was still smiling.

Kelly averted his eyes for a split second, looking back up again to see what he expected, that she was moving on. Then, one foot poised in the air for descent, she suddenly, in the manner of a quick doubletake, stopped and turned back to him. Her smile hit him once more; he was again about to look down, would have, in fact, if at that moment his attention had not been caught by the complete change in her expression.

CHAPTER 7

Her smile did not alter slowly or flicker and fade. It vanished. Her eyes, bright, shining and alive, ceased broadcasting their nondirectional effervescence and assumed an opaqueness as they regarded him. A tiny frown, two wrinkles between the brows only, appeared—as if she had suddenly remembered something of vital importance.

"Ooops, sorry. Maggie, did I—"

"No! No, dear . . ."

The tall woman, engaged in conversation with the young man, had stepped on her heel. The moment was gone. Maggie Banner, full of reassurance, gave her complete attention to the woman, glanced down briefly at her foot and proceeded down the stairs.

Of the rest of the party, only the young man, mouth slightly pursed, looked at Kelly, a brief glance, somehow tipped with the humor of a shared secret.

A sense of heady intoxication, far and away beyond any stimulants indulged in, swept over him. He could not believe she'd really focused on him. Perhaps the cumulative effects of the last few days were providing him with delusions. He looked behind him to see if he could possibly have misinterpreted her gaze; perhaps it was aimed at someone else. The two couples seated there appeared oblivious as they dove into their food.

Heightened sounds of recognition came from the floor below and he looked down over the balustrade to see the party of six being seated at a ringside table to the right of the dance floor, almost in a direct line with his table. He thought it odd they were given a table with a profile view of the entertainment instead of one squarely facing the bandstand.

Maggie Banner was seated with her back to Kelly, Raffaello Tucci to her left, the young man to her right. The prison matron, flanked by the other two men, sat facing the second level and Kelly. Of the seven couples dancing, each managed, in turn, to maneuver close to their table, where a waiter stood taking orders.

Kelly's waiter circled him slowly, eyes glued to his empty glass, until he felt obliged to order another drink. When he looked back down, Raffaello Tucci was helping Maggie Banner out of her fur coat and leading her out onto the dance floor. She wore a brown wool dress with long sleeves; a wide burnt-orange belt circled her waist. The brown of the dress set off her tousled, smoky-blond hair. She was thinner than he'd remembered and also taller. Tucci held her closely, keeping his right hand, fingers outspread, firmly pressed against the small of her back, which was toward Kelly.

He could see Tucci's face clearly as it caught a beam of light aimed at the bandstand. Kelly thought his face more striking, the features better defined, than photographs of him showed. His black, thick but neat eyebrows almost met, but not quite, over the bridge of his prominent aquiline nose, hooding his dark brown eyes (one of them glass), giving him an intense look as if he were forever concentrating on something or someone—almost the look of a hypnotist.

Though Kelly was an opera buff, he had never seen Tucci. The one-time tough-boy tenor of the Met had lost his voice eight years ago, before Kelly's opera-going days. He did have Tucci on several albums, and though the quality of the voice was erratic and tended to soar out of control, sharping now and then, there was a raw, belting joy about it that was exciting to hear.

Through myriad magazine and newspaper articles, many of the unorthodox circumstances of Raffaello Tucci's life and career were known to Kelly: born in the Stuyvesant section of Brooklyn of a large Italian family, began singing as a boy at block parties, sent to Italy to study voice by a flush uncle high up in the Cosa Nostra, finally returning to the United States for his debut at the age of twenty-seven at the Metropolitan, where he spent six tumultuous seasons scrapping with management, cosingers and at times the audience. He was even known to walk offstage during the first act of *Don Giovanni* and flatten a talkative stagehand.

But he packed them in. The Italian population of New York worshiped him and even those who criticized him, for both conduct and tone, flocked to see his performances, never knowing what controversial incident of prank or temperament they might miss. Most of all, though his charm was sometimes boyish, fresh and frisky, when he settled down to serious business there was a solid layer of sex appeal underneath. He was catnip to the ladies.

Raffaello Tucci was an opera freak and the freakishness of his personal life paralleled his career. After many publicized romances he surprised everyone by courting and marrying the pretty but plain daughter of a wardrobe mistress at the Met.

From time to time he had suffered from nodes on his vocal cords. Two years after his marriage, while laying on a high C in the aria *Di Quella Pira* during a performance of *Il Trovatore*, he burst a blood vessel and hemorrhaged. Raffaello Tucci's singing days were cruelly and abruptly ended. Some called it a tragedy; others claimed he had it coming, saying he never took care of, let alone improved, the natural gift he was born with.

The Italian Big Boys looked after their own. He was swept up, embraced and made their legitimate front for a casino in Las Vegas and a hotel in Miami. He was also made a millionaire and allowed to multiply that original sum by being "let in" on various good investments: oil, real estate, stock and other ventures not so legitimate.

It was said that the sheer drama of the loss of his voice seemed to sustain him for a year or so. Only when that nightmare evening at the Metropolitan was stale news did his embitterment, deep and unrelenting, settle in.

From then on, with a certain regularity, his name would pop up in the papers: a waiter slapped around, an airplane steward roughed up. His name was bandied about in a Senate investigation of the Mafia but he was not called to testify; he was not considered active in the organization; he was only "their boy."

Then a car accident outside of Tucson. He was drunk. He lost his wife, who was pregnant, and, for added punishment, his right eye. After this latest misfortune, though he was no longer singing, he was dubbed "the tough luck tenor of the Met."

Now and then a picture based on his life story was rumored, but by this time his public image was none too lovable; also, his career had been a relatively short one so that even now, though only in his midforties, teen-agers might know the name in context with his brawls, with only a vague knowledge that he had been an opera star who, when he appeared in the opening bill of the Met season one year, caused a society columnist to warn the women of the 400: "Girls, wear the paste ones tonight, it's you against the Cosa Nostra."

Down on the floor the couple moved together without speaking. Raffaello was swamped and spilling over with love of Maggie Banner. His emotions wracked him, made his stomach a banjo of constricted muscles, and caused a tremor in his fingertips.

Time was when she would beat him to the draw, or at least equal him, with protestations of her affection. Lately, however, she displayed a disquieting calm and he found himself racing ahead, rattling off his feelings like a schoolboy, pounding them at her as if he could make up in quantity, at least, words for the two of them and fill the void left by her silence.

He knew the foundations were shaky, but the moment he acknowledged the trembling, he switched on a kinescope crammed with rhapsodic memories of the good times together, focused mainly upon *her* happiness as reflected from him. With such a storehouse of mementos to fondle, how could there be any permanent damage?

It was true they had experienced their troubles lately. And they were mainly his fault, he knew that. He would change, ease off, stop pressing her. Also, she was exhausted, and no wonder, from their world travels. Now she was back home where she wanted to be; she would relax. All he had to do was use his head, play it cool, and their relationship would mend and be as it was in the beginning.

He accepted his do-it-yourself snow job, adding a qualifying phrase: *try not to love her so terribly much!* Even as he counseled himself, he gave her a little involuntary squeeze and mumbled aloud: "But I do."

"What?" she asked softly, drawing her head away from him.

"Nothing," he said. "Nothing."

"Oh," she replied, resting her head back up against his shoulder.

Everything was a sign to Raffaello. Every gesture, look, sentence. Now, even a simple "Oh." A month ago she wouldn't have let him off the hook, she would have teased whatever it was out of him. But now she let it drop with a simple, unprotesting "Oh."

His snow job had melted; he was suddenly miserable.

And Maggie Banner, though experiencing her own discomfort over the anguish she was soon to inflict upon Raffaello, was obsessed by the young man she had seen sitting alone on the upper level.

So like the first one! Not the face as much as the quality. Or perhaps there is a resemblance? She closed her eyes, trying to assemble a picture of her first lover, but twenty-some

years was a long haul and the fingers of her memory could
only graze the aura of him, mainly the feel of youth, the sen-
sitivity, cleanliness and unspoiled . . . not innocence exactly, but the undamaged *expectancy* of youth. However,
time blurred the features.

Raffaello eased the pressure of his fingers upon her back.
She could feel his fingers tremble slightly; she knew she
was the cause and it made her sad again. He, too, was aware
of the trembling and, in order to quell it, he held her tightly
once more.

She sighed at the rude imbalance, the inevitable tilting of
the scales, that brings each love affair bumping to the
ground, and he asked if she was feeling well.

"Yes, Raf, I told you—"

"I love you," he whispered in her ear. "I've got you—like a
virus. Where's a cure for a virus like you? Each day it gets
worse. You think I like it? If penicillin worked, I'd take an
overdose!" She chuckled. He pressed her closer to him, waiting for her to speak. When she didn't, he suffered a mild attack of temper: "Jesus, Maggie—"

She read it and immediately said, "I love you, too, Raf."
And although she had already finalized plans for leaving
him, she could still say she loved many things about him:
she loved his magnetism; she loved their physical relationship, the wild, complete freedom of it; she loved his unexpected and quite sophisticated bursts of humor, loved his
playing tough guy tongue in cheek. And more than she
loved his strength and manliness, she loved his childish
pride and stubbornness, his fears and superstitions and the
traces of lostness behind the mask of polished assurance.

There were parts of him she loathed, too: his occasional
bursts of cruelty and his absolute selfishness. Most of all, it
was simply not possible, in her predicament, to exist one
more day within the suffocating grasp of his love for her.

Kelly watched them, wishing he could see her face. Then
slowly, as they danced, Raffaello Tucci turned her until she
was facing away from the bandstand, her chin resting on his

shoulder. Her eyes roamed upward to the balcony and found the object of her curiosity.

Excited and confused, Kelly once more glanced down, running an index finger around the edge of a plate in a slow circle. This independent activity finished, he could not refrain from stealing another look. Without lifting his head, he slowly raised his eyes. *Her* eyes seemed still to be directed toward him, but they were half-closed, heavy-lidded, and he could not be sure.

As if to answer the uncertainty he felt, she lifted her head slightly, opened her eyes and smiled. It was a far different smile than before, lasting only a moment, not a full smile, only noticeable by a widening of the mouth at each corner, a slight parting of the lips, which pressed her cheeks upward, accenting her already angular cheekbones, followed by a small tug to the right of her mouth, and then it relaxed. But the message it imparted, a subtle, personal "Yes, you" transferred itself to her eyes and remained.

Without his permission, Kelly's head lifted itself up, his neck stretched forward for a split second in complete reflex to this communication, and the smile he felt within rushed to show itself but was struck down by an attack of nerves and ended in a sudden, convulsive twitch. He felt a blush and lowered his head, almost knocking his chin on the drink the waiter was placing in front of him. Kelly mumbled an incoherent "Thank you" and a second waiter arrived with his food.

The band stopped playing to a smattering of applause and couples drifted off the floor to their respective tables. As Raffaello Tucci and Maggie Banner approached their table, the members of their party stood, including the large woman. She leaned forward, said something to the couple, and there was a brief exchange of conversation. Maggie Banner touched her arm, and the woman left, accompanied by the young man, who escorted her up the stairs, across the balcony level, and up the second flight of stairs.

Instead of sitting back down in her own seat, Maggie Banner took the chair which had been occupied by the other woman. Now facing in the general direction of Kelly, she lit a cigarette, glanced up, located him and smiled. Raffaello Tucci caught this and turned in his chair, scanning the balcony level for the object of her attention.

Kelly did not wait to see if the man had spotted him. He quickly picked up a fork and aimed at the linguini, too quickly, in fact, for his knuckles struck the base of his glass and his vodka gibson spilled into the basket of garlic bread. Two waiters appeared from nowhere and, in a flurry of activity, whisked the bread away, mopped up the excess liquid from the tablecloth and took his order for another drink. When they finally left, he was too embarrassed to look back down and riveted his attention to the food in front of him. By this time he was in such a state, eating was purely a diversionary tactic, nothing more. The linguini could have been hay; it had no taste, it was merely bulk to be shoveled into his mouth.

He did not glance back down again until the regular band began to play for dancing. When he did, he allowed his eyes to move slowly to the side and—yes, she was staring at him. A quick nervous grin flashed across his face and in return she lifted her glass in a smiling toast to him. Raffaello Tucci wheeled in his chair and caught sight of the target.

Again Kelly looked down. A drink arrived to replace the spilled one and he inhaled a large gulp without taking his eyes from the small cocktail onions wedged between the ice cubes. He sputtered, coughed and wiped his mouth with his napkin. Feeling another cough coming on, he took a sip to quell it. The antidote worked and he finished off the drink in three successive gulps. The liquor burned his throat and his stomach flushed hot.

Resuming his eating task, he had taken three or four bites when someone tapped his shoulder. He looked up to see the husky man in the tight mohair suit standing over him. Kelly immediately recognized the black crew-cut hair for a toupee.

"Mr. Tucci would like you to dance." When Kelly sat there utterly speechless, the man spoke again, his voice laced with sarcasm. "Ah, not with him—with Miss *Banner.*"

CHAPTER 8

"Me?" Kelly asked.

"Isn't that what I just said?" The man smiled superciliously.

Kelly looked down to the table below him. Maggie Banner and Raffaello Tucci appeared to be having an argument, although the music was too loud for Kelly to hear any words between them. Leaning in across the table, she spoke with animation. Tucci made a grab for her wrist but she jerked her hand away and, as Kelly stared down, wondering what to do, she glanced in his direction, saw him, and suddenly stood up. He expected her to walk away from the table, but she simply stood, shoulders back, head up. Her expression had changed and she was smiling up at him.

"Did you hear me?" the Toupee asked.

"Yes."

"Well . . . ?"

"Wa-well, I—"

"Wa-what?" The man had mimicked him.

"Listen, I—"

"The lady's waiting—Mr. Tucci's waiting," he added.

"Listen . . ." Kelly had no idea of what to say. "Would you tell her that—"

"*You* tell her." The Toupee grinned. "Come along." He grasped Kelly's arm.

"But—"

"C'mon, baby-boy!" He lifted Kelly up out of his chair with a strong grip, so strong the muscle in Kelly's arm ached. As he tried to pull away, the man released him, shoving Kelly ahead of him. *"Good* boy!"

The attention of the room was on whatever scene was being enacted as the band stopped playing for a moment and the place was suddenly bursting with silence. The drinks he'd consumed while sitting down dizzied him now that he was standing up under full sail. He was not aware of the stairs under his feet. There was only a slight fear of being pushed from behind.

Then he was on the main floor and the band trickled into a lazy tune, vaguely familiar to Kelly from years ago. His feet directed him toward the table, but his eyes refused to focus and the blood pumped furiously up into his head.

Soon he stood in front of her. He blinked his eyes to clear his vision and there was her face, glowing in close-up. The sight of her at such close distance was overpowering, as if he'd gone to a Magna Vision film and only been able to get a single in the front row.

Staring at her, he was aware, in his peripheral vision, of Raffaello Tucci sitting to his right and he knew the man was focused on him. Kelly thought if he continued to look at Maggie Banner head on he would black out.

He glanced to the left; the rest of the room could easily have been a mural. Painted people sat motionless at their tables; the few couples who had been dancing had backed away from the floor and stood stiffly at the sides; waiters and busboys leaned together in pairs; even the music came from a marionette band. Kelly especially noticed the eyes of the clarinet player, bulging out and cocked to the left, glued to where the action was.

Raffaello Tucci coughed and Kelly looked back at Maggie

Banner. He was about to say, "I'm sorry," until he realized he'd done nothing to be sorry for—except follow instructions. Still, he swallowed, opened his mouth as if to say something, although he wasn't quite sure what. Perhaps simply give his name.

"Dance!" Raffaello Tucci commanded in a loud voice.

"Oh, Raf!" Maggie Banner said in a low growl, "don't be such an ass-hole."

Kelly almost laughed. Instead, looking down at his feet, which seemed strangely disembodied from the rest of him, he decided to confess: "I'm really not—"

"Dance!" Tucci repeated, reaching out a hand and shoving Maggie Banner roughly in the back.

In a dual effort to catch her as she slammed into him and to maintain his own balance, Kelly found his right arm around her. They stood there close together; her perfume seeped into his nostrils, almost stinging them. "I'm not exactly Baryshnikov," he said.

She grinned. "Might as well dance," she shrugged, "or he'll start throwing things—like you and me!" Putting an arm around his shoulder, she said, "Here we go—easy," and led them off onto the floor away from the table. They stubbed toes immediately and the bark of Raffaello Tucci's laughter grated his ears. "Don't look down," she cautioned. "There we go." They moved off again and after a few steps without a mishap, she added a reassuring, "There . . ."

"Ummn," he mumbled.

"So?" She said briskly, as if to open up conversation.

He took a deep breath. "I'm glad it's a slow one. What is it? I remember—"

" 'Dreams Ago,' from an old picture of mine. I sang it . . . sounded like a pregnant foghorn. Still, I'm glad they're playing it instead of a disco number. At least it calls for contact dancing."

"Ummn," he repeated. Her face was up against his shoulder. He could feel her breath graze his neck right above the collar of his shirt. Her thick hair touched his chin. He made an effort to go into a box stop, but she squeezed him tightly.

"Small steps, hold me closer," she said. "That's right, feel me close, I'll go with you."

"You feel good," Kelly said, surprising himself.

A little laugh as she answered: "We'll show the old bastard, won't we?"

They moved together, not speaking for a while, having hit a stride of sorts. They were the only couple dancing; Kelly became aware of the blur of faces watching them from the ringside tables. The sight made him dizzy. He went off-balance, tipping slightly forward and to the left, but she caught him.

"All right?" she asked.

He mumbled yes, then after a few moments asked: "Can we talk? I think I'm better when we talk."

"All right—shoot."

He chuckled. "I can't . . . think of anything to sa-say. Will you?"

"Talk?"

"Yes."

She cleared her throat slightly. "For openers, I really think—" Brief pause. "I love you."

"What?" He stopped dancing abruptly.

"Keep on," she said, supplying the initiative to get them moving again, then adding: "Oh, I don't mean *marriage* or anything like that." A sigh, followed by a simple throwaway: "Just love . . ."

"I saw every movie you ever made," he said.

"I haven't seen any of yours."

Kelly laughed. "I never made any."

"I said, I love you."

"Tha-that's what I thought you said." He shook his head, muttering: "Jesus . . ."

"—had nothing to do with it. I've lived an entire love affair since I saw you. Sorry you weren't with me." When he didn't reply, she added: "Capsule version—of course."

He could not believe these words; he could not believe the entire situation; he didn't answer; he had no answer.

"It was—" She pressed her lips against his ear. "—lovely."

"I quit my job," he said out of nowhere.

"Good for you," she laughed. "I quit mine, too." Drawing her head back, she glanced around the room. "I'd rather be on a beach," she said. "You make me want to be on a beach. Would you mind?"

"No." He agreed with her. "Yes, that would be nice." Projecting to a beach, he caught a mental picture of himself facing Maggie Banner head on in the bright sunlight. The picture was too clear, too strong, definitely too much for him; it needed blurring and he added, "Could I still be a little drunk?"

"If you wanted to. Would you want to?"

"Ya-yes."

"Why?"

"Because if I weren't, I'd sta-stammer." He shrugged. "See?"

She stopped dancing, pulled away and looked him in the face. "Do you?" she asked. He nodded. "Really? I always have an overwhelming impulse to hug anyone with—" she hesitated "—with a speech thing. Like so." She was about to give him a squeeze when Raffaello Tucci banged his fist down upon the table and bellowed, "Dance—slut!"

A woman two tables away emitted a tiny, choked-off cry of fright. "Christ, he can be cute," Maggie said, turning gracefully, facing Tucci with a smile and bowing her head. Turning back to Kelly, she said, "We'd best resume; the Master awaits." She put her arm around him and once again they moved off together. "But I think you're joshing me, you don't really stammer at all."

"Not when I'm drunk, not much at all anymore. Only when I'm . . . only sometimes."

As they danced past a table of eight people, a man called out: "Atta boy, atta girl, Maggie!"

Maggie drew her face close to Kelly's ear and whispered out of the side of her mouth: "Cool it, cool it—let's have no audible demonstrations." Abruptly pulling away from him, she asked: "You're not alone, are you?"

"Yes." Then he added: "It's my birthday."

"Oh, well, that explains it." She laughed, then hugged him: "Happy birthday." Her left hand suddenly clutched at his shoulder. "I don't know your name."

"Kelly. Ka-Kelly McDermott."

She cocked her head, looked at him, then said: "Kelly Mc-Dermott. Great name, but . . . you don't look like a Kelly McDermott."

"I'm not," he replied in all honesty, without knowing why.

"What?" She laughed the husky laugh he'd heard so often. "I don't believe a word you've said. I suppose it's only fair to tell you—I haven't believed a word you've spoken in all the time I've known you."

They both laughed; again her laughter struck his ear and this familiar trademark reminded him of the spectacular fact that he was dancing with Maggie Banner. He held her tighter, as a person having a delicious daydream is apt to squeeze his eyes shut in order not to lose the thread of it. *I'm dancing with Maggie Banner!*

So thinking, he experienced a moment of light-headedness, executing a few frisky dance variations which she followed as if they had rehearsed. This brought them near the bandstand. "It's ending," she said as the band increased in volume, leading into the final strains. "Our dance is ending. Let's have some kind of a finale here!"

And surely, in heightened rhythm with the band, he managed to twirl her and, full of exhilaration, he exhaled a whispered: "I love you!" He felt a response in her body as they held each other closely in one full final turn, ending in an improvised backbend with the last bar of music.

There was silence for a moment while they looked at each other. Someone from the balcony level began to clap, a table facing the bandstand took up the cue, the table next to it joined in, and steadily the sound of applause increased to a healthy roar. After winking at Kelly, Maggie Banner tilted back her head and he could hear a low throaty laugh beneath the din. "We're a hit," she said.

She then turned to face Raffaello Tucci and, raising her long, thin right hand in a most delicate, ladylike fashion, the gesture no larger than the fluttering of a bird's wing, she thumbed her nose at him. This earned a howl of approval and a further wave of applause followed.

At a ringside table to the right of the bandstand, a short, fat, overdressed lady in her fifties jumped to her feet, holding a pair of bejeweled wrists out in front of her, smacking a pair of pudgy hands together militantly. She stopped long enough to reach over and haul her husband up next to her. The other couple at their table rose, followed by a young man and woman behind them. The gesture caught on, and soon most of the room was at attention.

Maggie Banner took Kelly's hand and led him in a bow to the right, one to the center, and one to the left.

The occupants of one table remained seated. Raffaello Tucci glared down at the tablecloth, the fingers of his right hand turning over a thin gold lighter. The others—Tucci's former manager, the Toupee, and the young man who had escorted the Prison Matron up the stairs and returned alone—appeared to be frozen in time and space.

After the applause had peaked, the band launched into a disco tune and people took their seats. Kelly led Maggie Banner toward her table. The young man started to rise as they approached.

"Sit!" Raffaello Tucci snapped.

As Kelly slid her chair back, Tucci got to his feet. "Now stand." The young man flinched and stood, followed by the other two. The older man reached out a hand and placed it on Tucci's arm. He began to speak but Tucci silenced him with a look and pulled away, turning to Maggie: "A highly overpraised performance."

She regarded him coolly. "Raf, don't be modest. The applause wasn't *for* us, it was directed *against* you."

Kelly realized the room was completely silent again. The band had ceased making music, the dance floor was empty, all eyes were directed at them. Even breathing seemed to be suspended in anticipation of their confrontation.

Kelly was in the midst of wondering what to do next, how to break this frieze, when Maggie Banner sighed, drew her shoulders back, stood up straight and smiled at him. "Thank you for a lovely dance."

She extended her hand to Kelly and he reached to take it. "I enjoyed—" but he got no further.

Raffaello Tucci, with an uncanny instinct for winning a point, quickly and viciously stamped his foot down. The sound cracked back from the wooden dance floor like a shot. In surprise and total reflex, Kelly jumped back from the outstretched hand. It was done. Again Tucci's laugh of delight assaulted his ears. The fat woman across the room jumped to her feet again and shook her fist at him. "Bully!" she shouted.

But it was done and her gesture only magnified the moment more.

The second he retreated, face instantly crimson, Kelly turned inward upon himself with a loathing that vitiated any possible attempt at recovery and left the way only for further retreat. Without looking anywhere save the floor, he turned, walked to the stairs and proceeded up them as the band trickled back into the tune they had been playing.

CHAPTER 9

Kelly sat at his table, head downcast, mind burning: if only he'd stood his ground, taken her hand, held it for a moment and said something, *anything;* if only Raffaello Tucci had *struck* him; if only he hadn't bolted like a frightened rabbit.

He was aware of the four people at the table to his left staring at him. A finger touched his arm, and he looked over to see a man with thinning hair wink at him. "Better than getting her autograph, huh?" Baring lifeless coral gums and a chalky set of uppers, the man laughed at his remark as if it were true wit.

His wife put a hand on her husband's shoulder and leaned over in front of him. "Oh, it must have been a thrill. I mean it was a thrill for us just to see her, but to *dance* with her!"

The other woman gasped, "Here they come now! She's so thin. Isn't it a shame the way they keep themselves so thin?"

The first woman called, "Maggie, oh, Maggie—you're wonderful!"

Still smarting with embarrassment, Kelly was unable to look up; he could only sit glaring down at the glazed remains of the linguini and clam sauce. When he sensed the party had ascended the second flight of stairs, he signaled the waiter for his check. He wanted desperately to get out into the fresh air without further contact with anyone. While the waiter prepared his bill, a brunette girl in her teens, lifeless teased hair wrapped around her head like so much spun sugar, came up the stairs from the main floor of the club and trotted to his table. She clutched a menu and a pen. "Pardon me," she grinned at him, "but you're an actor, aren't you?"

"No."

The grin disappeared and she cocked her head in disbelief. "You're not an actor?"

"No."

"But I thought—are you sure you're not an actor?" There was an unattractive whine to her voice.

"Yes, I'm sure," he said.

"Oh." She started to leave, then turned back. "But you *danced* with her! I thought you were an actor she knew." He shook his head. "Oh," she repeated and left.

When the waiter brought the check he could not resist quipping: "No charge for the dance."

Kelly paid it, overtipping as usual; if the waiter had poured scalding coffee down his front, he would have overtipped. Walking up the stairs, he felt dull twinges behind his forehead, the advance guard of a headache. Why not, he thought, after today? There was a world of sorting out to be done after this day. He presented a plastic chip for his coat and was helped into it by a tough, baby-faced girl whose cheeks shone with a pink coating of greasy makeup. He picked out a quarter, added another fifty cents in change and dropped the coins into her palm.

"Thanks." She plopped them into a tin box behind her.

Kelly was full of appreciation for this terse exchange and headed for the door. Pushing it open, he was momentarily blinded by a flash and heard a man shout, "One more, Mr. Tucci."

When his eyes refocused, he saw Raffaello Tucci and Maggie Banner standing on the steps down in front of him.

The three other members of their party formed a group on the sidewalk to their right. In front of a *Daily News* car parked at the curb, a photographer stood removing a black plate from his camera and slamming another one inside.

For a moment Kelly considered turning and reentering the club, but this impulse to retreat disgusted him. He decided to walk down the steps and pass to their left.

"Hey, fella!" the photographer shouted, "would you clear the background?"

As Kelly took a step down, Tucci, wearing dark glasses now, turned and, grinning, said, "There he is; here's your boy, Maggie!" He waited until Kelly was one step away and repeated the stomping gesture.

Maggie Banner snapped, "Raffaello!"

Once again Kelly was taken by surprise. He flinched but only for a second, continuing down the stairs as Tucci laughed and reached out to pat his shoulder. "You're okay, a little skittish maybe, but—"

"Stop it!" Kelly said. The words came out between clenched teeth.

"Aw . . ." Tucci cooed, his hand coming to rest on Kelly's shoulder.

"Raf, that's enough!" Maggie Banner said.

Kelly caught the flush of embarrassment for him on her face and that was the trigger that made him act. In an instant, bursting with cumulative rage from every insult and rudeness he had ever endured, he jerked his right elbow up to rid himself of Tucci's hand.

There is rumored to be a knockout button, a spot no larger than a quarter, situated on the lower right side of the jaw, and Kelly's elbow, unintentionally but magically, connected with it.

For a moment Tucci remained standing stock-still, his head tilted up and to the right, his dark glasses cocked down on the top of his nose at an absurd angle.

"Je-*sus!*" the photographer said. And a flash caught them poised like living statues.

Then Raffaello Tucci's body slowly swiveled sideways,

tipping forward at the same time, and toppled off the step with the dead weight of a felled tree. His head cracked against the snow-cleared pavement under the canopy and his glasses fell off. His eyes were open and glazed.

Only then did Kelly lower his elbow. He was aware of Maggie Banner, eyes wide with disbelief. Tucci's former manager, the Toupee, and the young man, mouths open, stood where they were. No one moved.

"Jesus," the photographer muttered, snapping a second picture. "Jesus!" he repeated and another flash exploded, aimed at Kelly and Maggie Banner this time. When would someone move, Kelly wondered, feeling himself frozen to the step. Only the photographer seemed capable of action. Oddly enough, the first move was not directed at Kelly, but toward the man with the camera, who now knelt aiming for a close-up of Tucci's expressionless face.

"No pictures," the Toupee growled, stepping forward as the flash went off. The photographer jumped back, bumping up against the car and jarring the driver who sat behind the wheel. When the Toupee kept moving in his direction, he sprang away from the fender and ran around to the street side of the car. This reaction seemed to satisfy the Toupee, who stopped, turned around and stepped off toward Kelly.

He didn't reckon with Maggie Banner. "Leave him alone," she warned.

"Why—you punk!" he said, ignoring her and still moving toward Kelly.

"Morty, leave him alone!" she repeated.

When he continued his approach, she swung her sizable purse back by the straps and brought it slamming forward broadside into the Toupee's face, knocking him backward.

She turned to Kelly. "Run!" she shouted as the Toupee's hands went to his face and he whined, "My eye—Christ, my eye!" "Run!" she repeated. "Kelly, run!"

The tires of the *Daily News* car screamed, spinning in the snow, finally attaining traction and sending the car lurching forward. Still Kelly had not moved. Maggie Banner looked down at Tucci and, as if she'd just walked through a door and seen him stretched out like that for the first time, she jerked her head back and a hand went up to her cheek. Suddenly rocking back and forth in laughter, she faced Kelly again, reaching out and giving him a shove. "Kelly, run! Get the hell out of here!"

Yes, and high time, he thought, taking off down the remaining steps and turning left.

"Oh, God!" he heard her gasp. "They'll *find* him. Stosh," she shouted, "get him! Go after him and bring him—" She stopped abruptly. "You know," she continued, "get him!"

He turned quickly to see the young man, Stosh, start off after him, urged on by Maggie Banner. The Toupee held a handkerchief up to his eye and the older man knelt by the inert form of Raffaello Tucci.

After a few yards the going on the sidewalk became impossible. In places the snow was up to his knees. Kelly waded through a high drift and cut over into the street, glancing over his shoulder at the same time to see that the young man now identified as Stosh had taken to the street, too. When Stosh saw him looking back, he waved his arms and called out, "Wait, guy! Wait for me!"

A snap of cold air struck him in the face, bracing him; the bizarre proceedings of the evening further exhilarated him. I've had an event, he thought. *Event! I've had a major occurrence!* He laughed and ran on down the street.

"Hey, dumb-ass, wait for me!"

But Kelly kept on running. The wind was strong, the night was cold, the events were, indeed, wild.

"Okay—but I'll catch you!" There was an adolescent singsong tease to the reading.

Kelly looked back again to see Stosh setting a solid stride for himself. He heard the muffled roar of a machine as he neared Fifth Avenue and when he reached the corner he saw the huge yellow snowplow crawling south in the middle of the street. Sprinting to clear in front before the machine could throw up banks of snow on either side, he made it by several feet, leaving the plow between himself and his pursuer. Angling southwest toward the square in front of the

Plaza Hotel, he could hear Stosh shouting at him but was unable to make out the words over the whir and scrape of the machine.

By the time he reached Fifty-ninth Street, the initial burst of adrenaline triggered by his knockout of Tucci and escape from the scene of the accident began to wane. He felt the effects of booze and pot in his legs, which became more landlocked every few steps. His breath came in irregular gasps. Kelly stopped, turning around to see Stosh slide down a triangular crust of white the plow had left in its wake. Stosh had lost only a few yards. A lone cab crawled east along Fifty-ninth Street, its light on; Kelly waved, lunging toward it before realizing that, despite the light, it was occupied. This cost time and distance and he lost more time briefly wondering exactly where he was headed. He should be going east toward his apartment but Stosh ran a few yards to that side of him already and he'd have lost more ground.

"Eey—wait up for me—wait, we'll just talk!"

Stosh was gaining. Kelly turned, running at an angle toward the Plaza where a bundled-up doorman waited in vain for a cab for two couples who stood huddled together at the top of the steps.

"Hey—Kel-lee!" How odd to hear his name called with such urgency by a stranger.

It occurred to Kelly to dash into the hotel, then out a side entrance, but as he approached the large metal canopy Stosh called out: "What's the matter—don't you wanna fuck a movie star?"

The look on the doorman's face, together with a frozen, nasal "What'd he say?" from one of the women at the top of the steps made Kelly change course and run past the hotel toward Fifty-eighth Street.

Stosh's moronic laugh floated on the wind after him. Kelly slowed to make the icy corner turn going west, finding it difficult to pick up speed because the sidewalk had been cleared by such a narrow path it was hard not to rattle against the sides. Approaching a wider clearance near the side entrance of the hotel, he barely avoided stepping on a pair of legs sticking out into his path. A well-dressed if somewhat disheveled man lay propped up against a snowbank. He looked up as Kelly sidestepped him: "So I'm a Jew, so what? I'm a happy Jew and you know why? My wife's tumor is nonmalignant." The man was very drunk. Kelly did not slacken his pace as the man called out: "Three cheers for my wife's nonmalignant tumor. I could hug it."

When Kelly had run another fifteen yards, he heard a cry of surprise from Stosh. "Hey, dumb-ass—you kicked your covers off; you'll freeze your kishkas!" The voice was tough New Yorkese; the words were tinged with something else.

Kelly grinned as he came to a narrow breakthrough leading out to the single cleared lane in the middle of Fifty-eighth Street. He turned, performed some tricky footwork maneuvering it, leaped a crusted bank of snow, slipped, almost regained his balance and went skidding down on his side. "Shit!"

"Easy come, easy go!" Stosh called out, defying the laws of gravity and attempting to hurdle the high, frozen banks after Kelly. He barely made it into the street, then he, too, fell. "Kee-rist!"

Scrambling to get to his feet, Kelly turned to see Stosh no more than ten yards behind him, getting up fast and shouting: "What—what are you—some kind of running nut!"

Kelly cried out, "Get away, get away!" as he regained his balance and took off on the slippery roadbed.

This broke up Stosh, who echoed, "Get away, get away— what is *that* mean? Get away!"

Kelly slipped again, fell sideways against the snowbank, but managed to keep to his feet, although he was forced to stop for a few seconds. By the time he was able to gain traction he could feel the presence of Stosh directly behind him.

"Gonna getcha!"

Kelly laughed out of pure nerves and the childishness of the chase, which should have been taking place in a schoolyard, not on the streets of Manhattan. Just when he vowed to make a superhuman effort to charge ahead he heard a heavy rush of breath behind him as Stosh lunged forward, throwing his body at Kelly in a full tackle.

Both went slamming down, Stosh's arms around Kelly's waist. Kelly grunted; Stosh expelled "Gotcha!" on the breath that was knocked out of him. As Kelly scissor-kicked his legs, trying to wriggle out from under him, Stosh tightened his grip and panted: "Ah-ah, that's it, that's enough! Jesus, what is it with you?"

Kelly was about to say, "Get away!" once more but refrained, not wanting to be ridiculed again. Instead, he simply lay there completely out of fuel. He felt the weight of Stosh and the hardness of his body as he climbed on top of him, securing his hold, but he could do nothing about it.

"Hey, what was you runnin' for? I'm on your side, I'm helpin' you!" He felt Stosh's breath against his ear. "Huh? Answer me!"

"I don't know," Kelly gasped. "Someone chases you—you run." Suddenly the utter ridiculousness of the situation occurred to him. Not for a second had he thought why he was running, he simply ran. Now that he did think of it, there was no reason to distrust Maggie Banner's motives in ordering Stosh after him. He repeated, "I don't know."

Within seconds he was laughing, roaring with laughter. And soon Stosh was laughing with him and just as hard, so hard Kelly was eventually able to turn on his side, rolling Stosh off him. Stosh quickly scrambled on top, with Kelly on his back, pinning him down by the arms and facing him.

"Okay, okay!" Kelly gasped, "you got me, let me up!" But he was still laughing.

When they were laughed out, Stosh looked down at Kelly and demanded: "Okay—who won?"

"Who won?" Kelly echoed, confused.

"Yeah, now—*who won?*"

"Oh, that, I mean—*this*. You did."

"Good. Just remember—it's not running the race or playing the game that counts—it's *winning!*" Stosh shook him by the shoulders. "Right?"

"Right," Kelly said. He could only laugh more at the absurdity of Stosh's dialogue with the two of them lying in the middle of Fifty-eighth Street in the remains of a blizzard. Not sure if he was being put on or not, he was certain of one thing only: he was in the presence of a certified character, a young man who could have been a dock worker, by his looks, or a miner, a farmer, but not . . . whatever he was.

Stosh looked him in the eye and asked: "Do you dig being pinned down on your back in the snow in the freezing cold?"

"Of course not." .

"Then let's get the fuck up!" After Stosh removed himself from Kelly, he extended a hand and helped him to his feet. They brushed themselves off, then each other, and walked up the middle of the street toward Sixth Avenue.

"Maybe we can get a cab around Fifty-seventh Street," Stosh said.

The chase had taken the last bit of energy out of Kelly. "I think maybe I just better go home."

Stosh stopped in his tracks. "Home? You gotta be wiggy. Don't you know who that was you decked?"

"Raffaello Tucci."

"Nobody decks Raffaello Tucci and gets away with it." He cocked his head. "Come to think of it, nobody's ever decked him. I don't know why, but they didn't." He rubbed his chin, then opened his mouth wide: "Jesus, what if you killed him!"

Kelly rocked back on his heels. "Killed him?"

"Yeah, it's possible. Not by hitting him—"

"I didn't hit him, my elbow—"

"My ass!" Stosh exclaimed.

"But it was an accident—I didn't mean to."

"Guy, so is life. So what, you didn't *mean* to? Hitler didn't mean to lose the war. Did you by any chance hear his head connect with the sidewalk? F sharp, it was a symphony. And from the look on his face he wasn't about to do no encores."

Another moronic-sounding laugh issued from him, an Elmer-from-the-country hee-haw. Wide open, his mouth showed need of serious repair. Two teeth in the upper left were missing, a front tooth was chipped and the rest showed their fillings easily, a bit of gold, a bit of silver. The gums that anchored them required attention, too. His teeth were a contradiction; otherwise he was well put together, clean, well groomed. Immediately aware of Kelly's dental inspection, Stosh closed his mouth, cutting off his laugh and following it with a cough. "I mean—he could die from whatever people die when they get cracked on the head in the right place. 'Course if that happens, forget it—we'll all head for the Frigate Islands. But if you only knocked him out, then you're gonna get paid back for it."

"But I didn't mean it," Kelly said. "He must know that. I . . . wa-wouldn't hit him."

Stosh giggled: "You wouldn't, but you *did!* Even worse, somebody got it on film!" He threw back his head and laughed again. "Oh—oh, Christ, if they print those in the papers there'll be a fuckin' gang war! Oh—oh—" Once again he shielded his teeth, drawing his lips together in a pursed position that argued with the strength of his face.

"How do you mean?"

"Don't you know whose *boy* he is?" Stosh asked incredulously.

"I read in the papers, about Las Vegas and—"

"Yeah, well, the *Mafia* to put it bluntlike. Ey, we're in luck—lookit!" Three people got out of a cab at the corner of Sixth Avenue. Stosh jammed two fingers in his mouth; the resulting whistle was so shrill Kelly stepped back a foot. "C'mon—" Stosh began to jog, but Kelly still had second thoughts. When he didn't immediately follow, Stosh ducked back, grabbed his arm with a firm grip and pulled him along. "Don't give me trouble, will yah?" The cab cruised down to meet them, edging as far to the side of the narrow cleared lane as possible to allow them room to get in, but when Stosh grabbed the door, it was locked. The driver, weasel-faced under his dirty brown cap, rolled down his window partway: "Where you goin'?"

"Southern Hotel, Forty-second between Broadway and Eighth."

"That'll be ten bucks."

Stosh looked at Kelly: "Fuckin' bandit!"

"What was that?" the cabbie growled.

Stosh nose-to-nosed it with the man, enunciating clearly: "Fuck-in' ban-dit!" Pulling back, he said: "You got that, didja hear that?" He spit it out once more. "Fuckin' bandit!"

"Yeah, yeah . . . okay, I heard it. We got a blizzard, it's ten bucks!"

In a frenzy, Stosh dug under his overcoat into his pants pocket and hauled out a wad of bills. "Here, here . . . twenty bucks, *twenty* bucks—"

"I only—"

"No," Stosh screamed, shoving the bills at him, "take the twenty, you greedy mother-fucker. There . . . there!" He grabbed the man by his coat collar, pulling until his face was halfway out the window. "But one thing—open the door, open it quick, and keep your fuckin' mouth shut. I don't wanna hear one fuckin' word outta you or I'll fuckin' pulverize you!"

"Yeah . . . yeah . . . okay!" There was a click; Stosh opened the door, guided Kelly in before him, then got in himself. Before they settled in their seats, the cabbie turned around and said: "Look I didn't mean—"

Stosh jerked his body forward and shouted with ear-shattering force: "I said not a fuckin' word outta you; you got your fuckin' money, now keep your greedy boring fuckin' mouth shut! You are a piece of shit, but you got twenty bucks for being a quiet un-fucking-bothersome piece of shit, now me and my friend—for that twenty fuckin' bucks— wanna ride in fuckin' peace and quiet!" Stosh turned to Kelly and spoke in a flat, understated voice: "I gotta do something about my fuckin' temper."

Stosh coughed from the energy expended shouting, then, changing characters, he spoke one more sentence in a down-South accent: "Me and mah fren means ta git our twenty dollars' worth if'n we has to shit in here!"

The driver, his face a wipe-out of total befuddlement, gently slid the window shut, giving his head a little involuntary shake as Stosh whispered to Kelly: "I love to blow their fuckin' minds. Especially ass-holes. Have you noticed that the proportion of certified ass-holes in the world is on the rise?" A short burst of laughter. "Now . . . what was we talkin' about?" Stosh caught the expression on Kelly's face. "What's the matter?"

"I—you—you're funny."

"Wait'll you catch the whole act." Stosh made a fist and pounded it against his knee. "Okay, goddamn it, let's get down to business. Okay . . . oh, yeah—see, I'm not saying Raffaello himself would give you a face job—I wouldn't invite you to the same *party*—but mainly it's the friends of Raffaello Tucci you gotta watch out for. They don't like to see him light his own cigarette, let alone get *eighty-sixed.*"

"Yes, but—"

"Yeah, but nuttin'. Christ, you knocked him *out!* What do you think they're gonna do, send you flowers? Mags knows that; that's why she says to go get you."

Kelly thought he'd found a hole: "But he wouldn't even know who I was, my name or anything."

"Ohhh?" Stosh said wisely. "You mean if they print that picture of you nobody's gonna come up with your name? Another thing, let me ask you a coupla questions, just a couple. Okay?" Kelly nodded. "You have a reservation at the Copa?"

"Yes."

"You make your reservations in the name of Burt Reynolds?"

"No."

"You in the phone book?" Kelly nodded again. "Guy, you just passed the test but you flunked the course." He glanced forward to see the cabbie sneaking a look in the rearview mirror. Stosh smacked his hands together fiercely, at the same time shouting in a Louis Armstrong voice: "Abadabada

no lookee, no nookee—Southern Hotel only, chop, chop!"
The cabbie flinched, averting his eyes to the roadway ahead.

Kelly had wondered about their destination. "The Southern Hotel?"

"Yeah, all part of a plan, she'll tell you, don't worry. Oh, I
been meaning to ask you—you *wanted* to see Mag again,
didn't you?"

"Yes, of course."

Stosh shook his head: "Then I don't know what the fuck
you was runnin' for."

In the silence that followed, Kelly wondered if he really
did want to see her again. True, he'd prayed for a miracle,
but there are miracles and miracles. This miracle might be
too much for him to handle.

CHAPTER 10

They were left off at the Southern Hotel in the middle of the overripe block on Forty-second Street between Broadway and Eighth Avenue without a word from the cabbie and only a pursed-mouth final sentence from Stosh: "You've either been a real pussycat—or a turd. Offhand, I'd say—turd wins!"

He led the way into the building and down a long, depressing marble corridor into the garish lobby—three shades of green, from apple to pea to forest, and so many mirrors it was impossible to tell where the true boundaries of the room ended.

Stosh eyed a wilted group of travelers slumped down in two sofas to their left, luggage stacked high in front of them. They looked shipwrecked and badly in need of a leader. "The servants are bushed," Stosh said. "You stay here, I'll knock up the butler."

Walking the length of the lobby to the desk, he picked up a key from the clerk and, signaling Kelly to wait, went to the house phones in the corner. The possibility of this being a trap struck Kelly. What if Stosh had pursued and rescued him only to lead him to a convention of some "friends of Raffaello Tucci" upstairs? As quickly as the notion occurred to him, he dispelled it by acknowledging a newly formed and inexplicable trust in Stosh.

When Stosh hung up the phone he motioned for Kelly to join him at the elevators. "Maggie's on her way." He placed a hand on his chest. "Oh, I feel better now." Stepping into the elevator, he said, "Seven, please." As they rode up, he repeated, "I feel better now. I was worried she wouldn't get away. We had all this planned different for later on tonight."

"All what?" Kelly asked.

"I better leave her tell you."

Getting out of the elevator, Stosh led the way down the hall to an alcove at the end of it. A sudden spurt of retarded laughter burst from him; when Kelly looked at him Stosh quickly put a hand up to shield his teeth. "Would you believe, this is the honeymoon suite! The honeymoon suite at the Southern Hotel—would you believe anyone had their honeymoon here?" More laughter. "Probably a Polack couple—like me." His laughter cut off and he turned to Kelly in all seriousness. "You know any Polish jokes, keep 'em to yourself. Only people can kid about Polacks are Polacks—okay?"

"Okay," Kelly said, suppressing a grin, thinking back to childhood days when kids said: "I don't care what you say about me, but don't call my mother that!"

"Oh, one other thing . . ." Stosh said, ducking his head back away from Kelly and looking at him with a mock-wise expression plastered across his face.

"Yes?" Kelly replied.

"You like to fool around?"

"Fool around?"

"Yeah, you know, neck and fool around? If you ever do—let me know."

Astounded, Kelly could only sputter, "I—ah . . ."

Stosh slapped him on the shoulder. "No sweat. But you never know; in case you ever do—just let me know. Your place or mine or a cruddy motel of your choice!" He caught the look on Kelly's face and broke up. "Hee—ought to see your face! Hee . . . no sweat!" He shook his head then quickly snapped his fingers. "You like lobster salad?"

"Yes."

"You know the difference between lobster salad and a blow job?"

"No," Kelly said.

Tapping an imaginary cigar and beaming a Groucho leer, Stosh said, "Wanna have lunch?"

Again he broke himself up. "Hee . . . I gotcha!" Stosh lifted his hand to knock, but the door opened before he could touch it. The enormous woman Kelly had dubbed the Prison Matron stood in the doorway, now dressed in a flowered housecoat, a fierce grin upon her face.

"Flora!" Stosh shouted. He was immediately smothered in her arms. "We made it," he gasped.

"Yes," she said, squeezing him. "Oh, Stosh, I was so frightened." She pulled him into the room, beckoning Kelly in after them.

He was amazed at her voice; it was high and thin and entirely girlish.

"This is Kelly," Stosh said, extricating himself from the folds of her.

"Yes, Maggie told me." She smiled, looking at him for a long moment, and said, "Hello, Kelly."

With these two words Kelly felt himself fully embraced. "How do you do," he said.

She turned to Stosh. "He's lovely." Kelly looked down in embarrassment. "You are," she said, reaching out and taking his hand. "Come, sit down." Helping him out of his coat and leading him to an easy chair, she added, "Maggie should be here any moment." When she had placed Kelly in the chair, she swung around to face Stosh. "Now—tell me what happened? I mean what *happened?*"

"First of all, what about checking out of the Waldorf?" Stosh asked.

A giggle, rather like a quick run up the high end of a xylophone and as incongruous as her speaking voice, escaped her. "Worked like a charm; I changed cabs three times, bags and all. Three *times*." She clasped her hands together. "He'll never trace us."

"Good girl," Stosh said.

"Now tell me about you," she said. Before he could begin, there was a knock at the door. "Oh," Flora cried, "Maggie!" Kelly smiled as the huge woman skipped to the door, opened it and caught Maggie Banner up in her arms, swinging her around into the room. "Oh, Maggie, I was so frightened!"

Maggie's eyes found Kelly and Stosh as Flora was setting her down. "You're here—thank God!"

"Just this minute," Stosh said.

"Thank God," she repeated breathlessly, untying a large silk scarf from her hair and snatching off a pair of hornrimmed glasses.

"Your coat," Flora said. "Where's your coat?"

"I ditched it," she replied, going to Kelly and taking his hands in hers. "Left it in the subway john." Flora gasped; in reply Maggie said, "Oh, that's right, I probably should have donated it to the Little Sisters of Perpetual Agony—but, honey, there was no time!"

"Your coat, your beautiful coat!" Flora wailed.

Maggie released Kelly's hands. "I don't want to be trapped, Flora, certainly not by waltzing in here with a sable coat."

"But, Maggie—"

Her face tightened, her fingers ran through her hair, her voice was caustic. "I doubt if I'll be needing a fur coat again. Wouldn't you say, Flora?"

Stosh flinched as though he'd been struck and Flora raised a large paw to her chin. "Don't say that."

"Then don't go *on* about things that don't matter."

Nobody spoke; there was such import to the quiet that Kelly was sure he must have missed something. He looked from one to the other; their faces were equally grim.

Stosh finally broke the silence by exhaling a large breath and saying, "Hey, Mags, we made it, we're all here!"

"Yes, we are." She smiled, and the moment was gone. "We're here." She took in the room briefly and just as briefly made it her domain. Winking at Kelly, she said: "Love what you've done to the place."

"What about the lobby?" Stosh asked. "Did anyone—"

"The desk clerk hardly looked up," Maggie replied. "And the elevator operator had his nose in a newspaper. Just the same, I had him take me to the ninth floor, then I walked down. Did you tell Kelly?"

"Not the whole works," Stosh said.

Facing Kelly, she laughed and clapped her hands together. "Would you believe—forty-eight years old and running away?" She shook her head in distaste. "Christ, it's awful being a rotten *movie star;* you can't lie to anyone about your age—every time you pick up a paper you see it there in print. However, as long as we're on it, you don't have a 'thing' about age, do you?"

Kelly grinned and shook his head.

"Good. And as long as we're on it—if you didn't know, wouldn't you say I was no more than . . . forty-*seven*?" Kelly laughed now.

Stosh spoke up: "Anyone in their right mind would say you was no more than thirty-eight and a goddamn good thirty-eight at that."

"Thirty-*eight!*" Maggie shouted in pretended outrage.

"Thirty-six."

"Okay," Maggie said, "I don't want to see any *more* heads broken around here. Enough of the age. Anyhow, Kelly, I'm leaving Raffaello, running away. It was all planned, but who'd have thought—the complications!" She turned back to Stosh. "Now—tell me what happened?"

Stosh launched into his pursuit of Kelly with enthusiasm, adding a few theatrical embellishments of his own. When he finished, Maggie said, "Oh, Kelly, shame! What did you think, didn't you know we were only trying to—" She broke off. "No, of course not, how could you?" She turned to Stosh. "I was terrified he'd get away from you. Before Raf even came fully to, Morty went into action, had them get Kelly's name from the reservation list. My God, I thought, what if he's in the phone book and," she swung around to face Kelly, "you *are!*"

"See, what'd I tell you?" Stosh took a step toward Kelly, giving him a brisk punch on the arm.

Walking to Kelly and taking him by the hand, Maggie said, "I'm so glad Stosh caught up with you, so glad." She squeezed his fingers and her voice dropped to whiskey-contralto: "You ever been kidnapped?"

"No . . ."

"Watch out!"

Being in a hotel room—the honeymoon suite of the Southern Hotel at that—was even more overpowering than sharing her with the crowd at the Copacabana. Kelly was speechless.

"What about you?" Stosh asked. "How'd you get away?"

Maggie released Kelly's hand and stepped back away from him. "Simple. The Copa found a doctor in the house, on the chance Raf had got a concussion—he didn't, simply got knocked out. When Raf came to, just about the time Morty set out to find you all, they took him into the manager's office to give him a further examination. I said I'd wait out in the lounge. Not bloody likely. I took off, walked to Madison Avenue up to my buns in snow. No cabs, and I couldn't see myself standing there waiting for one until morning —Little Eva with the entire Mafia snapping at me once Raf found out I'd disappeared—so I walked downtown until I came to a subway station. That's when I phoned Flora, I was so worried about the two of you." She laughed huskily. "But here we are. We're not a triumvirate anymore. We're —what's four? A quadrumvirate?" A hand flew up to her face. "Can you imagine if they print those pictures of Raf out cold? Kelly, you'll be a national hero!"

"National target, too," Stosh added, "with his puss all over the place."

"Of course," Maggie said in a lowered voice. "We'll have to be careful, really careful. And clever!"

Kelly was overcome by the feeling he'd wandered into a

theater in the middle of the feature. If she were leaving Raffaello Tucci, why not just leave him, why the hide-and-seek,
the Southern Hotel, and these two strangely likable but bizarre companions? He also realized he was suffering from
fatigue provided by the day's other events, which were a
mixture of reality, unreality and pure fantasy. Perhaps it
would be better to come back and see the picture from the
beginning. What he needed was sleep and time to figure out
which way his world was spinning.

He rubbed a hand across his forehead and stood up. "I
suppose—ah, I mean, I ra-really ought to be getting along
home. Then tomorrow—"

"What!" Maggie Banner exclaimed.

"You nuts?" Stosh asked. "He'll already have your apartment staked out."

"No, it's impossible, you can't!" Maggie said firmly.

"Oh, no!" Flora cried.

The reaction was so violent he sat back down. Maggie
went to him. "You must promise not to go near your apartment! Not to go *near* it, not for a while!" She gasped: "You
don't have a girl friend or a boyfriend or a cat or a dog in it,
do you?"

"No," Kelly said.

"Thank God!"

Kelly went on to venture: "If he wasn't really hurt,
though?"

"Oh, baby, baby! You're not dealing with a—" she looked
to Stosh for support "—with the boy next door. It's not a
matter of hurt or not hurt. His ego, where that's concerned
he's a child, an insane child! And the timing couldn't be
worse. If I were still with him, maybe I could reason—" She
broke off. "No, I couldn't. He's beyond reason. Don't you
see, I've left him. When he finds out—"

"But," Kelly said, "he must know I didn't have anything to
do with—"

Without warning she was in a temper. "No!" she shouted.
"No, I can't explain it any further. Not now, not after today.
You'll have to take my word for it. You're a fool even to think

of going home. A fool!" She stood in the center of the room and slapped her hands on her hips. "I want a drink!" It was issued like the Declaration of Independence.

"Maggie . . ." Flora's voice was pleading.

"I need a *drink!* Is there anything or do we have to order it? You said you'd have the place stocked." She caught Flora and Stosh exchanging looks. "What's *that* about?"

"Yes," Flora said, "there's some brandy. Stosh, in the closet in the bedroom."

"And fix one for Kelly," Maggie said.

Kelly shook his head. "No thanks, I've had enough."

"Fix one for Kelly," she repeated. "Here, I'll help you." She followed Stosh into the bedroom and slammed the door.

Flora and Kelly were left staring at one another. He smiled for no reason at all. She sat down on the sofa, folded her large hands in her lap and cleared her throat. Kelly noticed her eyes: how small and round and shy they were, all out of keeping with the rest of her face.

Flora cleared her throat again. "Be gentle with her," she said. "She's had a—"

The door opened and Maggie stuck her head into the room. "You keep your fucking mouth shut!" she snapped.

Flora blushed. "I didn't—"

"Make sure you don't!" She wagged a finger at her and slammed the door again. Immediately it opened and Maggie poked her head out, addressing Kelly: "Incidentally, whenever you hear me use that foul four-letter word I just used— which isn't often and only slips out when I'm driven to it— please think of it as spelled p-h-u-q-u-i-n-g. That way it takes the fucking sting out of it!" She pulled the door shut briskly again.

Be gentle with her! Of all the qualities to *be* with her, that seemed to be the least called for. She bristled with strength at a moment's notice. And, yet, the next second, while the slamming of the door still reverberated in the room, Kelly thought: yes, be gentle with her.

Maggie's voice reached him from the next room. "Stosh, I said—" she shouted, then checked herself, modulating her tone, and he could hear no more. Stosh opened the bedroom door and walked quickly across the room to what Kelly imagined was another bedroom; after a while he returned to the first bedroom, shutting the door after him.

"It's been a day," Flora sighed. She couldn't have expressed Kelly's thoughts more had she been curled up inside his brain. He was feeling lost, a displaced person. More to make conversation than anything else, Flora glanced around the room. "This suite's not as bad as one would imagine, considering the hotel. Maggie's bedroom," she continued, indicating the room Stosh had entered, "is quite pleasant. And ours," she pointed to the opposite door, "is nice, too." She cleared her throat. "Well, at least they're clean."

"Oh," Kelly said, unable to fight back a yawn.

"You're tired, aren't you?"

"Yes, I am; I've had a lot to drink, too."

She stood and walked behind his chair. He could sense her bending over him. "You just sit here." He leaned forward automatically, but she placed a hand on his chest and drew him back. "You sit right here and we'll see what we can do." She began massaging his forehead with the fingers of both hands. Her touch was firm; her huge fingers worked knowingly in a circular pattern back and forth across his forehead. She gave the impression of having touched him before, of knowing him well. It was the touch of a friend, sure, not in the least shy of contact with him, the way her eyes were shy.

"Umn . . ." he murmured.

"We'll take care of our Kelly," she said.

The door opened. "That's a good girl, Flora," Maggie said. She had slipped a soft, powder-blue dressing gown over her dress and carried a tumbler half-filled with brandy.

"I made ours with water," Stosh said, offering Kelly a glass. "Maggie takes it neat."

Kelly held his hand up. "No thanks."

"Drink it," Maggie said without looking at him as she settled herself on the sofa.

Stosh urged him, in a glance, to take the glass. Kelly held it, watching the bubbles spiral up from the bottom and break the surface with minuscule poppings. He looked up; Maggie's enormous eyes were focused upon him and the corners of her generous mouth turned down in a pout. "I really don't need another—"

"I said drink it." She did not raise her voice; in fact the words came out flat and close together, but they added up to a command if ever he'd heard one. Flora's fingers stopped their probing. The corners of Maggie's mouth straightened out and in an instant she was smiling. "It's been quite a night, it's only right to tie it up with a bow. Besides," she added, "didn't you say it was your birthday?"

"Yes."

"Happy birthday, Kelly." Flora smiled.

"So, you see, we must drink," Maggie said, toasting him with her glass. Flora walked over to sit in the chair next to Stosh and, conducted by Maggie, they sang a speeded up chorus of "Happy Birthday," after which they laughed and Stosh and Maggie sipped their drinks.

Somehow, Kelly was reminded of the Mad Tea Party. He said thank you and raised his glass.

"And—to our adventure," Maggie added. "If we can't have adventures—what's the point?"

"To our adventure," Stosh and Flora said together as Maggie tipped her glass, indicating for Kelly to drink.

"Did you know Stosh is practicing to be a stand-up comic? He's going to be the first nationally famous Polish comic. Tell me, Stosh, to what do you owe your fabulous success as a comic?"

"Would you repeat the question?" Stosh asked.

"Tell me, Stosh, to what do you—"

"Timing!" Stosh shouted.

They laughed, then sat in silence for a few seconds until Maggie spoke again: "Stosh doesn't like Polish jokes, though. But he'll tell almost any *other* ethnic story. Ah—give us an Italian one."

Stosh cleared his throat. "What's the difference between an elephant and an Italian housewife?"

"I don't know," Maggie said. "What is the difference between an elephant and an Italian housewife?"

"Oh—about five pounds, a moustache and a black dress!"

Flora clucked disapprovingly and Maggie smiled at Kelly: "Isn't that tasteful?"

I'm in over my head, Kelly thought; I'm out of my league. The brandy and soda tasted bitter; it snapped in his throat as it went down. He smiled. *Out of my league! I don't have a league. And what's more—I don't have a job and I can't even go home! What do I think of that?*

"You smiled," Maggie said. "You should smile a lot. It kicks off your whole face. To your face," she said, raising her glass, "your very sweet face." Kelly joined her in a drink. "And to your eyes—dear eyes!" Another drink: "And that one dimple over there," she added, pointing to his cheek and sipping again.

The absurdity of anyone as incredibly beautiful as Maggie Banner drinking to *him,* to *his* face, *his* dimples, stunned him completely. As he was thinking how ass-backwards this all was, she said: "You're not drinking."

Kelly took another large gulp and a wave of dizziness swept over him. Feeling he might possibly be ill, he quickly stood up. "I really should be going." The three opposite him froze. "Oh, I won't go home. Don't worry," he lied, "I—I have friends I can sta-stay with."

Oddly enough he didn't mind stuttering in front of Maggie Banner; he knew it didn't matter to her; it was the other two he didn't want to embarrass. Is that what it did to people—embarrass them? Well, yes, they were embarrassed for *you.* Didn't want them to be embarrassed for *him!*

"We'd rather you stayed with us," Maggie said. "Wouldn't we?"

Stosh nodded: "You gotta."

"Yes, stay with us, Kelly." He loved the way Flora said his name. It was an embrace.

"Well, I . . ." The dizziness had left and it was safe to sit down.

"At least have your nightcap, then we'll talk about it." Maggie glanced sideways at Stosh. "I know what it is. You're suddenly finding it a bit strange to be with us; it all happened a little too . . . precipitously—there's an apt word. And you'd sort of like to just go home and think about it awhile—right?"

Kelly grinned; that's exactly how he was feeling.

"Come on, nod once if I'm on the right track."

Kelly laughed. "Oh, I can ta-talk."

Maggie winked at' him: "Ga-good for you."

Flora chided her: "Maggie!"

Waving a hand at her, Maggie said: "Oh, Kelly understands me, don't you, Kelly?"

"Yes."

"What he doesn't understand—is Raf and the fact that he is, at times, temporarily insane and I'd bet Elizabeth Taylor's ring this is one of those times. And we don't want you in any danger—that's why we're keeping you here with us. Isn't that right?" Stosh and Flora agreed and Maggie added: "Let's drink to that?"

After they had all drunk again, including Kelly, they sat in silence. Stosh lit a cigarette, Maggie coughed and Flora unfolded her hands, then folded them again, letting them rest in her lap.

It occurred to Kelly that the three of them sitting there opposite him comprised a team. Yes, they're a team, he thought. They're watching me, this is some kind of game. But what do they—

His head bobbed down. The liquid in his glass no longer effervesced; it lay there, settled. He jerked his head up. "Yes . . . ?"

"What . . . ?" The voice was Maggie's.

"Oh . . ." He put a hand to his forehead. "I—I thought you asked me something."

"No," she said, "but I will." She ran a finger around the

edge of her glass, making a little squeaking sound. She looked up and smiled, this time, it seemed to Kelly, shyly. "Do you believe in God?"

"Yes—most of the time." Nodding his head, he quickly added, "Not my father's God."

"Which God is that?"

"Not a vengeful God." He wondered how *that* slipped out?

Maggie jumped up from the sofa. "Oh, no, *not* a vengeful God." She turned to Flora. "Did you hear that?" She raised her glass. "To a mellow God, with a twinkle in his eye, and a heart about the size of . . . Brazil."

"Brazil!" Stosh said, sounding a daffy-duck laugh.

"All right, Rhode Island," Maggie said, taking a sip of her brandy.

Kelly's arm felt leaden as he raised his glass and drank; it was a relief to bring his hand down to rest upon the arm of the chair. Glancing up, he was aware of the blue-on-cream wallpaper moving in spirals behind the opposing team. He shut his eyes tightly for a second; when he opened them, the patterns on the wallpaper danced out at him. He jerked his head back and blinked his eyes, focusing on Maggie Banner's hair, her lovely smoky head of hair. Streaks of silver and beige and chestnut and copper all tousled thickly together. She smiled at him. He wanted to reach out and touch her hair, but what right had he? Looking at all three of them sitting there and feeling the draining away of his energy, he suddenly wanted, in the worst way, to entertain them. Or perhaps it was the other way around; he simply wanted *not* to bore them. Yes, that was it. He leaned forward, wanting to say something. They leaned forward to receive whatever it might be.

"Ah . . ."

"Yes?" Maggie said.

Out it popped: "I killed my father."

Maggie's face lit up immediately. "You did? Oh, now I want to hear all about *that!*"

"You mean—" Stosh drew a cutthroat finger across his neck "—like, for real?"

Kelly nodded. "Um-hmn . . ." He jerked his head to the side, quickly checking Flora out. Her fierce grin was in place as she said: "Why, Kelly . . ." It was not said in censorship, but in total and, it seemed, happy surprise. He was relieved and glad he'd said it. He felt he wouldn't be saying much more and perhaps it was his background in publishing that let him end with a page-turner.

He wanted to say more, but his lips were numb. He put the back of his free hand up to them. Yes, they were numb and thick and dry. He attempted to raise his glass to wet them, but his right hand refused to obey him. It remained locked, clawlike, around the glass, resting dumbly on the arm of the chair. He looked crossly at his clenched fingers. "Hey . . ." he said, reprimanding his hand.

"Is everything all right?" Maggie asked. "Kelly . . . ?"

Speech was beyond him now. No, he thought, everything is *not* all right, but how would you know? You're not me. He was aware of his glass leaving his hand, but he didn't hear it fall. He cocked his head, waiting for a crash, but there was none. The soundlessness struck him funny, but laughter was beyond him, too. He caught movement opposite him. Stosh leaned forward to get up from the sofa, but Maggie stretched out an arm in front of his chest, pressing him back.

They're feasting on me, the three of them, sitting there feasting on me. What expressions did they wear? He peered upward out from under cast-iron lids. They were a blur now. I'm passing out, he thought, that's what I'm—and for one brief second the truth flashed over his head.

"Drink!" he gasped. "—You!" He would have pointed, but the last bit of energy was snuffed out of him and he slumped unconscious in his chair, his head tilted onto his left shoulder.

During his enforced sleep he did not dream or awaken fully but rather he experienced two sensations. A piercing cry, full of terror, penetrated his padded sound barrier. There were words, but he couldn't distinguish them and there weren't many. He experienced no danger, himself, but felt a desire to reach out, to locate the source of panic and quiet it. The other sensation was of a weight upon his chest, at first pressing against him firmly, later merely a weight, warm and soft. He tried to reach up, to touch it, to discover it, but this effort alone drained him, sending him under once more.

CHAPTER 11

Word of an incident involving celebrities spreads quickly, especially if the incident should be one of misfortune. By 2:00 A.M. in Raffaello's suite at the Waldorf-Astoria a gathering of his friends were taking their leave, having conducted a minor wake over his "accident" and the disappearance of Maggie Banner. Their parting shots to Raffaello were full of forced, good-natured ribaldry:

"Listen, Raf, she was too thin anyhow. You want someone—zaftig."

"A stud like you—you probably wore her down. She's off resting; she'll be back for more of that good stuff, don't you worry."

One of the last to go, a maritime union official, Ralph Bianco, put his arm around Raffaello. "Raf, if you want me to find her, give me the word. All I'd need would be her bank, her manager's name, lawyer, something like that to start with."

"No, no," Raffaello said.

"You sure?"

"Yes, she'll—we had a tiff, she's just pulling a—" Raffaello patted his arm; he wanted the man to leave. He'd suffered a certain humiliation in front of these men but the most mortifying item on the list—he felt like crying.

"You give me a call if I can help," Bianco said. Clasping Raffaello's hand warmly, he added, "Pecker up!" and left.

Raffaello closed the door and turned to face the man he could most level with, Victor Barbour. "They mean well." Raf shrugged.

"Sure." The older man smiled. "They love you." Raffaello walked toward the bar. Without thinking, his former coach and manager blurted out: "Raf, don't—"

Raffaello turned abruptly: "Don't what?"

"I thought you were . . ." Victor trailed off, realizing his error.

"Not in over two years, you know that. I was going to fix you one."

"No thank you, Raf."

Raf sat next to him on the sofa. The two men were silent for a while. Victor was careful not to initiate a topic, to let Raffaello have his head. He had observed his deadly calm behavior the last few hours and he knew this to be the most dangerous sign of all. Someone had once said that Raffaello Tucci had at least twelve escape valves and half of them were open at any given time. Now, seeing them closed off, Victor knew, in time, there could be nothing less than a major explosion and he would as soon not be a party to the triggering of it.

After a long while Raf shook his head. "I don't understand," he muttered. "I don't understand." Victor opened his mouth to utter some little placating phrase, but Raf spoke firmly, a tinge of warning in his voice that he would not accept the usual clichés: "She's my life, Victor, She's my *life*!" Raf turned to face him and again he said: "I don't understand. You see, what we had was so—only with Carol did I have this special, this—" He chopped the air with a flattened hand. "—Out of this world, *unworldly*—thing! Two magnets and the moment we met—slam! Together, we'd always be together. Locked, that nothing could separate. Oh, death, yes, but neither one of *us*. I don't understand!"

Again Victor took a breath to speak but Raffaello pressed on. "Something you didn't know, not that I wouldn't have told you, but we didn't see each other around that time, me out west and you back here. When Carol died, after, for almost a year, I never . . . with another woman. I couldn't." Victor's hand came to rest on his knee. "Oh, for months I didn't try, but when I did—I just wasn't able. I went to several doctors. They suggested I go to a—you know," he said, tapping his forehead, "a head man." Raffaello chuckled. "Can you see me going to a psychiatrist?"

Victor kept his silence.

"Then I met Maggie and—the very first time! Like I said—two magnets. And like it never was before, not even with—" He broke off in deference to his wife. "You know, never a word spoken, no little rituals, following a blueprint, the way some women can be satisfied only a certain way, a certain time, a little performance you've played over and over. Not with her. Uncanny the way it happens with us, without ever talking it over or planning or signals. You know that's unusual; how many women is it like that with? But that wasn't all by a long shot. I mean—sex. Except, I'll tell you this, since I met Maggie I've never been to bed with another woman—there's no desire. None. And you know me, Victor. My God, the way I used to play around, it's a wonder it didn't fall off years ago."

Out of enthusiasm for Maggie he began to pace. "Oh, God, she's a woman, Victor. She's one in a million; she's got everything, and always a surprise! On our trip, such curiosity, about everything, everyone. Oh, yes, fun and wild and— but then underneath, like a little girl, tender, gentle. And such a heart, such . . . ah, what?—*humanity*. I never met a man or woman with such humanity." Raffaello chuckled. "And a little bit crazy, too. Everybody interesting is a little crazy, huh, Victor? Such a combination she is!"

Victor nodded. "It's only a matter of time. These misunderstandings, they don't last. You know that, Raf."

"I know, I know. Still, there isn't all that much time."

"Ah, there's always time. Same Raf, always impatient, always—"

"Victor, goddamn it—"

The phone rang and Raffaello snatched it up, saying very little, only mumbling "I see" a few times and ending with: "Yes, keep it watched." He hung up and turned back to Victor. "That McDermott fellow, he's not home. Almost three and he's not home yet. You heard Morty—she sent Stosh after him. You don't think they're together?" Before Victor could answer, Raffaello waved the idea away. "No, what could she see in him? That scene in the club, that was to get at me; she knows how jealous I am."

"Of course," Victor agreed, "just because he's not home doesn't mean he's with her." The older man stretched and stifled a yawn.

"Victor, I've kept you up, you run along," Raf said, taking the man by the arm and standing him up.

"We'll get together tomorrow, Raffaello."

"Sure," Raf said, helping him into his coat. "Maybe we'll drop by the opera some night. I hear that new Greek girl is something."

"Irene Panayiotopoulos. Fantastic, the voice soars, such a Tosca."

"We'll go," Raf said, leading him to the door. "I missed you, Victor. God, the times we've had."

His former coach and manager summed them up with a long, deep-throated "Ahh!"

The two men embraced and brushed cheeks; Raf took his hand, squeezing it and holding it tight. "Jesus, Victor, if she's with him, if she's—"

"Ah, Raf, my boy, my boy," Victor said, shaking his head.

"I've bent your ear enough," Raf said, pushing him away gently. "Call you tomorrow," he added and quickly closed the door.

When Raffaello was alone he could feel the pressure of his tears begging for release. In an instant he was trembling with an uncontrollable mixture of anger, frustration, hatred and love. His eye caught sight of a silver-framed photograph of her on the mantel. He walked quickly to it and with a chopping blow of his arm knocked it to the floor. He heard the glass break, but it was a small snap of a sound, not nearly satisfying enough. He lifted his foot and ground his heel down upon it; the resulting crackle and pop almost pleased him, but not entirely.

He looked to the bar; he couldn't drink, he knew that; everybody knew it. But how he wanted one! He hurried to the bedroom and began undressing. Standing barefoot in his tailored French shorts, he lifted his T-shirt carefully over his head, stretching the neck of it with the spread-out fingers of his hand so as not to disturb his meticulously combed hair. He reached to the back of his head, his fingers nimbly exploring to see if his thin spot still remained concealed by careful combing. He was accustomed to Maggie's combing this one spot for him.

Stepping out of his shorts, he stood there in the nude. He reached down and cupped his genitals in his hands, lifting them up and away from his body in a final freeing gesture. As he held himself, he thought: she'll miss this, she'll think twice before giving this up.

Or would she? Was he still the prize package he'd once been, still the dashing lover boy who made heads swivel, eyes track him, and pulses step up to a trot?

He turned to face himself in the mirror. He still had definition; his chest and rib cage narrowed down to a thirty-four-inch waist. He straightened up, tucked in his stomach and turned sideways. Pretty good for forty-seven. Only three years from fifty. He let his stomach out; still pretty good. He touched his right pectoral. The mound of it was no longer rocklike, but it was firm; it responded when he tightened the muscle of it; it hadn't turned to jelly by any means.

He looked at his face; it was still a handsome face. His face had always pleased him; he felt as if he were admiring a totally different person when he looked at it. There were lines here and there, but they were good lines, lines of character.

He put a finger up to the side of his glass eye. It was a perfect match; nobody but an expert would notice it. Many people he met knew he had lost an eye and he could sense, often, their searching out which one—the left or right?

He smiled; his teeth had always been well cared for. He tucked his chin in and poked the roll of flesh that appeared under it with his finger. There, there was age showing. He jutted his jaw out until the roll disappeared. That's more like it. Slowly he retracted his chin until the roll began to gather again. No, can't walk around like you have a broken neck.

He backed away from the mirror for a brief final summation. Pulling himself in and tightening up, he cocked his head and was forced to agree with himself: he could easily pass for forty-seven minus ten and a damn good thirty-seven at that.

In the shower he soaped himself well, lathering his neck, chest, armpits, stomach and genitals. He remembered the first time he and Maggie had showered together: green tiles, a large cake of lemon-yellow soap with a white braided rope attached to it, the top of that luxurious growth of smoky hair at chin level, the tininess of her standing in front of him as he washed her back, carefully arching away from her so as not to prod her with his excitement.

Even now, as he soaped himself, he was responding quickly to the memory of her. He immediately increased the flow of cold water, rinsing himself and cutting his shower short. He toweled himself dry vigorously, strode into the bedroom and got into his pajamas.

Grabbing a pillow, he dropped it to the floor and knelt upon it, leaning his chest up against the bed and placing his hands, clasped together, on top of the covers.

He smashed his fist down into the pillow; *everything* brought a memory of her: the first time she'd surprised him saying his prayers. They'd been together three weeks. He'd always waited to say them until she took her nightly shower, but this night, their first in New York, after the shower had been running a reasonable amount of time, she suddenly opened the door, having forgotten her shower cap. There'd been no warning, no time for him to spring up from his knees.

Greatly touched, she came to him and they sat on the bed holding hands and talking about God and Heaven and Hell and Fear and Childhood and Superstition. It was a full half-hour before they realized the shower was still running. She turned it off, and they went to bed immediately.

He lifted his head from the pillow and knelt there praying silently:

Dear God, I love her too much. Too much! Don't mess up our time together like this. Sure, have a little game. Like Maggie said, you play games, too. Fine, but don't play around too long. Make her call me. A call . . . tomorrow . . . please!

He whispered a hoarse Our Father and a Hail Mary and ended with: "God bless Maggie and keep her strong and well for me and say hello to Carol and Momma."

Raffaello got up off his knees; as he picked up the pillow he'd been kneeling on, his eye caught sight of a faint smudge, no more than a brush, of orange lipstick. He bent his head down, examining it closer, and rubbed his finger over the spot. It was her lipstick; pressing his nose down into the pillow, he could smell the unmistakable scent of her perfume.

In a violent gesture he flung the pillow away from him. It sailed across the room and knocked over a small lamp on the dresser; there was a flash of light and the lamp was dark. "Jesus Christ!" he shouted. "What are you doing to me! I've taken enough from you—you son of a bitch! Jesus!"

He stood there breathing heavily. He looked down at the bed. At six that very evening they'd performed such gymnastics! Did she do it knowing it would be the last time? She must have; she must have been all packed; it must have been planned because Flora excused herself at the club and . . .

He walked quickly to the door leading to the adjoining suite Maggie had occupied and opened it. The smell of her was pungent. Raffaello moved to the mantel where he picked up a piece of crumpled pink Kleenex. He held it for a moment and on his way to the wastebasket he saw a glass with an orange lip-print on the edge; next to it was a copy of the New York *Enquirer* with its headline: LESBIAN FREEZES GIRL FRIEND, EATS LADYFINGERS. Maggie loved the grisly tabloids.

Dropping the Kleenex in the wastebasket, he noticed it was nearly full. He got to his knees and began sorting through the contents: an empty can of hair spray, an old pair of brocade slippers, another gory scandal sheet, several worn emery boards, more wadded-up Kleenex, a nylon stocking.

He stood up abruptly. God, what was he looking for—her discarded Kleenex, her garbage? What did he expect to find—a card with her phone number on it, a clue? Was she playing a game with him? Was this some sort of joke? She and Flora and Stosh were always up to some prank or other.

He shook his head and walked toward the door. Abruptly stopping in his tracks, he stood perfectly still, as if he could sense from the room itself, from the very atmosphere it held, whether this was a joke or not.

No, the room was empty, dead; there was no warmth remaining, no vibrations left behind. He shuddered.

He'd been in bed for no more than fifteen minutes when he knew sleep was hopeless. He changed positions, now on his stomach, now on his back, curled on his side, again on his stomach, and then on his back once more. He could hear his heart thumping and feel the perspiration seeping out of his pores.

Raffaello wrenched himself out of bed and walked directly to the sitting room where he poured a shot of scotch and bolted it down, warm and neat. It burned, and the smell—like vomit to his nostrils—and the taste of it made him shudder convulsively and cough. His first drink in over two years. Vile, rotten stuff, what had he ever seen in it? To find out, he poured another inch or so and swallowed it. Not much of a burn this time. By the third drink the smell was not so bad and the taste was vaguely familiar, a friend from the past.

By the time the quarter-filled bottle was empty, he felt warm and fuzzy and even a little smugly secure.

Watch out for Raffaello when he's drinking, they used to warn. He's a crazy man, the booze is fire water to him. Nonsense, not at all, he could handle it. He sat in the easy chair next to the phone awaiting Maggie's call. She'd call soon. She couldn't stand to sleep alone. She'd have that nightmare of hers and wake up screaming bloody murder and reach for him but he wouldn't be there. Flora and Stosh could comfort her, all right, but afterward she couldn't fall asleep, held so tightly, in their arms.

She'd call soon enough. She might even just arrive, burst through the door unannounced. She did things like that, she was a creature of impulse.

A thought flicked through his brain. Could she, with him waiting by the phone, now, at this very minute, be sleeping soundly in the arms of that young man?

He lurched up from the chair. "No!" he shouted. "No!" he repeated, aiming for the liquor tray.

CHAPTER 12

Kelly fought awakening for hours. At one point he forged open his iron-lidded eyes a squeak only to see bad, large-patterned floral wallpaper that would not be found in a suburb on the wrong side of Detroit anymore and thought: I'm having the wildest crazy-assed *dreams*. Maggie Banner likes *me,* thinks *my* eyes, *my* smile—good-night. With a grin he gladly slipped back into unconsciousness.

A slight headache nagged him to the surface again but he rationalized, somewhat fuzzily, if he ignored it by sinking back under, he could probably sleep it away.

The smell of coffee, toast and bacon pulled him gently out of his sleep next. A small headache still persisted, but what eventually caused him to snap his eyes open was the sudden radar awareness that he was being stared awake.

There at the foot of the bed they stood, Stosh and Flora, both grinning, Flora with all the gusto of an Amazon preparatory to attack, Stosh showing his bad teeth until awareness made him shield them.

No dream this; there they were. The two of them together

were much bigger than life. Immediately he felt a rush of affection for them and smiled back—until he remembered
vaguely the circumstances of his enforced departure from
the Mad Tea Party.

"You—!" was all he got out.

"Now listen—we hadda, we hadda, 'cause supposin' you'd
left. And you was wantin' to go, yes, you was. Well, here!"
Stosh dug into his pocket and took out a Polaroid photo.
"Remember the old neighborhood?" he asked with what to
him was a sophisticated snort.

Kelly rubbed sleep from his eyes, then looked closely at
the picture: a slightly blurred shot of Lafitte's French Hand
Laundry across the street from his apartment. An overcoated
man with hat, scarf and gloves stood to the side of the door,
leaning against the steps of an abutting brownstone.

"Sorry it's not a better picture but I hadda take it from a
movin' taxi. That's Ollie—guess who Ollie works for? I'll tell
you—Morty. And Morty works for Raf. Capiche?"

Flora nodded. "It's true, Kelly."

Stosh cocked his head. "What—you think Ollie's waitin'
for his *laundry*?" He sounded his subnormal laugh, which,
together with the eerie photograph, made Kelly laugh also.

"They got a watch on you; we knew they would. So we
was just savin' your ass—excuse my French."

Kelly winced; his headache increased with awakening.
Flora read his expression immediately, picked up a large
tray, and set it on his lap. "Fuel, that's what you need." She
handed him a large glass of orange juice and a paper cup
filled with pills and capsules of various sizes and colors. "Vi-
tamins—down 'em, every last one."

He obeyed instructions and while he ate breakfast they
cheerily rehashed the evening before. Kelly glanced at the
unmade twin bed next to him. The powder-blue robe
Maggie Banner had worn lay across it. There were also, on
the chair and bureau, articles belonging to a lady. Had he
slept in the same bedroom with Maggie Banner? He guessed
he had. "Where's—" As he paused, deciding whether to call
her "Maggie" or to be more formal, Stosh answered him:

"Out doing errands. She'll be back soon, her secretary's on the way over."

The second he'd finished the last piece of toast and bacon, Stosh took the tray away. Flora said, "Now, roll over and undo your shorts."

"What?" he asked, glancing over to see her holding a hypodermic needle. "No . . ." He clutched the sheets to him.

"Vitamin B-12, that's all," Stosh said.

"Is that what it is?"

"Yes," Flora replied as Stosh added, "Yeah, what else?"

Kelly sighed: "After last night . . ."

"See," Flora said, shooting a sharp glance at Stosh, "he'll never trust us." Turning back to Kelly, she said, "I didn't know anything about it. I didn't. Did I, Stosh?"

"No—only because you'd spill the beans."

"See?" she said, all chipper again. "Roll over, it won't take a second."

"Do you know how?" Kelly asked.

A peal of girlish laughter. "Oh . . . oh," she struggled to get the words out, "that's what I *am*—a nurse! Oh—did you think I just go around jabbing people?"

So the Prison Matron was a nurse. He unsnapped his shorts, at the same time slipping over on his stomach. Flora peeled them back, pressed a damp cotton pad up against his right buttock, jiggled it and said, "Oh, cute. Aren't they cute, Stosh?"

Stosh uttered "Ummmmm . . ." so wisely Kelly felt the blush in his backside as the needle stabbed him, discharged its load and was withdrawn. "All gone," Flora said, "all over." She took the cotton pad and rubbed it vigorously against the offended spot. "Such cute muffins . . ." He felt a playful series of pats on his buttocks.

"Flora!" Stosh clucked.

She giggled. "I'm sorry, I couldn't help myself, but—we love your body."

"We?" Kelly asked, glancing around.

"Yes, all of us. When we put you to bed, we decided. Didn't we, Stosh?"

Another "Mmmmmm . . ." from Stosh, who approached with a large bath towel, saying, "Lift up?" Before Kelly could even inquire, he added: "For your rubdown—gotta get you in shape for Mags, big doin's afoot."

"I really don't need a rubdown."

"I give good ones; you'll feel a hundred percent better," Flora said, tapping the bed. For the first time she spoke with the authority of a nurse: "C'mon, be a good boy, slip off the shorts!"

To lie there in the nude in front of those two was not the most relaxing idea. Maybe not so much on his stomach but—

As if in answer to Kelly's thoughts, Stosh said, "When you turn over, you get a *towel*, don't worry." He made a clucking sound with his tongue. "Fussy one, ain't you?"

Somehow it was more embarrassing to continue protesting their efforts to help him than to remove his shorts. He lifted his midsection up and felt Flora's hands take hold, slipping them down around his ankles and off. In a few seconds he shuddered "Ahh!" as a splash of cold alcohol hit his back.

"I know," Flora said. Her large hands warmed the fluid as she worked it up his back, kneading the flesh between his shoulder blades.

Kelly heard movement in the living room, then a brisk knock at the door. "Who is it?" Stosh asked.

"Miss Vaughn," a clipped, nasal English voice called out.

"Ah—could I have a robe or—"

"If you think *this* one would even notice—forgetsville!" Stosh snorted.

Stosh opened the door and Kelly swiveled his head around, his left cheek resting on the sheet.

"Lo, Stosh," Miss Vaughn chirped, breezing in. "Flora," she nodded, paying no attention whatsoever to Kelly. She wore a belted polo coat and carried a briefcase. She passed his bed as she crossed the room and Kelly turned his head the other way round to follow her. After Stosh had helped her out of her coat, she tugged at her salt-and-pepper tweed suit and sat in the easy chair, slapping the briefcase onto her knees. "I'm Miss Banner's secretary," she said, unsnapping her briefcase without looking up.

She had dull, mouse-brown hair that fell in a thick bang across her forehead and cut straight down either side of her face, obscuring her ears and ending at her jawline. A bowl-cut affair, most unflattering to the female face, Kelly thought. She wore glasses, silver-rimmed, and there was a flesh-colored bandage across the bridge of her nose, extending to the middle of each cheek.

Shuffling through some papers, she said, "Miss Banner asked me to go over some details with you." She glanced up briefly, but Kelly could not see her eyes. She wore double-thick lenses, the same kind of special glasses Muriel Sproul, who'd sat next to him in history in his junior year in high school, wore. They obliterated her eyes as far as the on-looker was concerned; Kelly marveled that she could possibly see out from such a maze of magnified glass. "Oh," she added as an afterthought, "Miss Banner should be back soon."

Kelly glanced at his wrist; his watch had been removed. "Oh, what time is it?"

Miss Vaughn checked her watch: "Ah—one thirty-five."

"God . . ."

Stosh laughed. "Yeah, time flies when you're havin' fun. Michelle Finn is a bitch, huh?"

"What?" Miss Vaughn asked.

"Nothin'," Stosh said. He'd gone to the bureau and was returning with a glass of water and a pill. "Here, take this." When Kelly hesitated, he said, "A pill to pick you up."

"I'm feeling much better," Kelly offered.

"Do as he says," Miss Vaughn advised. "Miss Banner will want you in the best possible condition."

Her voice and manner contained such clipped authority that Kelly, turning his body to the side, popped the pill into his mouth and washed it down. Miss Vaughn took a pad of paper from the briefcase and placed it on her lap as Flora resumed the massage. "If you don't mind answering a few questions?" She glanced up and the light from the reading lamp next to her flashed in reflection from her glasses, reminding Kelly of a blinker signal.

"Sure."

"Age?"

"Twenty-seven."

"Twenty-seven," Stosh said. "You twenty-*seven?*" When Kelly nodded, Stosh shook his head. "You sure fooled Stosh; I thought you was practically Gerber's."

"Gerber's?" Kelly asked.

"Yeah—baby food."

Flora snickered and Miss Vaughn cleared her throat. "Stosh, could we continue? That is, if it won't discommode you?"

"Whoops," Stoosh shrieked. "Get her!" He turned to Flora. "*Discommode!* Ain't that a terlet?" Stosh and Flora giggled like children.

"You'll have to excuse them," Miss Vaughn said indulgently. "They verge on the aboriginal; I don't see how she puts up with them."

"I like them," Kelly said, surprising himself.

"Hooray for Kelly," Stosh shouted.

A snort from Miss Vaughn. "Impossible. And you like them? I suppose that's your problem. Now then—married?"

"No."

"Engaged?"

"No."

"Divorced?"

"No."

She checked off down a list with her pencil, keeping her lips tightly pressed together. Kelly imagined she had tiny soft gray teeth behind them; he wondered if she ever smiled.

"Miss Banner was curious about your job. You told her you'd resigned, I believe?"

"Yes, I did." He gasped as Flora poured more alcohol on his back. She was working down lower, kneading the flesh around the small of his back and waist. He was enjoying the massage now.

"What sort of job?"

"I worked for a paperback book company."

"Approximate yearly salary?"

Kelly hesitated, then said, "Do we have to go into that? I don't see what—"

"Yeah, that's pretty cheeky," Stosh said.

Ignoring Stosh, Miss Vaughn went on. "It would help ascertain certain . . . Of course, if you'd rather not, I'm sure Miss Banner would respect your wish."

Here I am, Kelly thought, lying nude in the Southern Hotel in front of three strangers, quibbling about telling my yearly salary. He smiled. "It doesn't make that much difference. Around sixteen thousand."

"What—a year?" Stosh asked incredulously.

"Yes," Kelly replied.

"In the *publishing* business! Forget it! I did better than that when I was a hooker, counting the stuff I could hock, of course. Even when I went straight for a year—"

Miss Vaughn snapped her fingers, "Stosh, I'm afraid you'll have to leave the room."

"Aw, what'd I—"

"Do as I say!" Miss Vaughn clapped her hands together. "I know, why don't you trot out and fetch the papers." For the first time Kelly detected a trace of enthusiasm in her voice.

"Yeah. Hey, that's what I'll do." Stosh was equally enthusiastic; he ran to the door and was gone.

"I don't understand," Kelly said.

"Don't understand what?"

"About this interview."

"You will," she said briskly. "Miss Banner has a proposition to make, but first she must know whether it's feasible. Parents?"

"Dead—I mean deceased."

"Do you distinguish between the two?" she asked snidely.

He attempted to explain his correction. "Dead sounds so final and deceased sounds like—"

"What—out to lunch?"

"No." He smiled in spite of himself.

She glanced over her list. "Not married, not engaged. And what is it you people say—going steady?"

"No."

She looked up at him curiously. "No?" She appeared to be mildly surprised. "Any sisters or brothers or similar relations that might presumably be concerned with the publicity and your apparent disappearance?"

"An aunt in Cleveland and two good friends in San Francisco and one in Chicago." Kelly thought about Grace. "And a girl at work I used to go with."

"That's not many."

"No," Kelly agreed.

"Still it's lucky, it simplifies things."

"Oh," he replied, not having the vaguest idea what she was talking about.

"Then, too, being without a job simplifies things even more." She adjusted her glasses before continuing. "And that brings us precisely to the point. Miss Banner will pay you ten thousand dollars to be her companion for a period of . . . oh, I'd say probably not more than four or five months." She paused as Kelly felt Flora's hand leave his back. "Perhaps even less, if so—"

"No!" Flora cried out, "don't say that!" She stepped back from Kelly. "You promised you'd—"

"Flora!" Miss Vaughn was on her feet and at Flora's side. "Flora!" There was animal strength in her voice that startled Kelly. He turned his head in time to see her slap Flora across the face. Not a hard slap; it was controlled, pulled in almost before it struck. Flora's hand went up to her cheek; her eyes welled with tears.

Neither of them spoke. Although Kelly could not see Miss Vaughn's eyes, he imagined her to be in a highly emotional state, too. She tugged her jacket down, smoothed out her white, high-necked blouse and touched her hair gingerly with one hand, pressing the bangs down along her forehead. She inhaled a deep breath. "Enough of that." Speaking with renewed strength, she said: "Stop it; no crying!" Miss Vaughn returned to her chair. "Would you care to be excused, or can you pull yourself together?"

"Yes," Flora replied meekly. As the secretary sat down, Kelly once more felt Flora's hands upon him, but her touch was uncertain now, preoccupied.

Miss Vaughn's eyeglasses flashed up at him. "As I said, Miss Banner will pay you ten thousand dollars to be her companion for," she cleared her throat, "the approximate length of time mentioned. You'd have no expenses. You could look upon the money as—"

"I don't understand," Kelly said. "Why?"

"Why not?" she shrugged. "It's her offer to make, your decision to accept or reject it."

"I don't understand—why me?"

She ignored his question. "There are conditions, of course. She's taking a trip. You'd be allowed to phone or write anyone of your well-being before you left New York, but once you reach your destination, should you accompany her, it would be imperative that you contact no one." She quickly added, "Until your period of employment should be terminated."

"I see." He heard himself reply "I see" in a perfectly calm, matter-of-fact voice, as if secretaries of movie stars were constantly bombarding him with offers to fly off with them and this was simply the most recent proposition up for consideration.

Miss Vaughn coughed slightly. "I take it you will consider?"

A ripple of giddiness swept over him. "Yes," he replied, adding, "what other conditions?"

She thought for a moment. "In the event Miss Banner decided to terminate her agreement with you at any time, under no circumstances would you reveal her whereabouts to anyone. That would be of utmost importance."

The nasality of her voice had begun to irritate Kelly, to penetrate his inner ear. At the same time he was feeling quite buoyant. His body tingled from the massage; he could feel the increased circulation in his shoulders, back and legs. How could he feel irritated and well at the same time?

"Oh, one item more. Slightly clinical and I hope you won't take offense." She cleared her throat. "You're not attracted to members of your own sex—or at least you're normally bisexual?"

He would have taken offense had not the term "normally bisexual" amused him. He grinned. "I believe my appetite is normal," he said, triggering two thoughts simultaneously: appetite, yes; fulfillment, no.

Then, in the next instant, he became annoyed at her for reminding him of his inadequacy. "I'd rather wait to discuss the rest of this with Miss Banner," he said.

"You would, would you?" she asked.

"If you don't mind."

"As you wish," Miss Vaughn said, rising and striding to the door. "I'll see if she hasn't come in."

When she'd gone, shutting the door behind her, Kelly turned to Flora. "I hope I didn't offend her."

"Oh, no!" Flora giggled, "Lord, no!" Within seconds she was doubled over in laughter.

Kelly was amazed; he'd said nothing humorous, at least that he could make out. Flora was still clutching herself when the door was flung open.

Kelly turned his head around. There Maggie Banner stood, minus wig, glasses and nose patch, in Miss Vaughn's clothing. "Voilà Maggie!" she cried, arms spread wide.

This sent Flora reeling back against the wall in spasms. Kelly snatched a sheet from the foot of the bed and pulled himself up to a sitting position. "What's—what's—" But that was all he could say.

CHAPTER 13

"You didn't suspect it was me?" Kelly shook his head and her face lit up as she snatched off a wide band that held her own hair close to her head and, in that gesture he remembered from the night before, ran her fingers through the thick strands of it. "Not even an inkling?"

"No."

"I passed muster then."

"Oh, Maggie, you can travel anywhere in that, they'll never recognize you," Flora gasped, still trying to pull herself together. "You were marvelous!"

"Better than the pregnant housewife in San Francisco?"

"Oh, yes." Flora made a face. "I didn't like that one."

Maggie looked at Kelly, still clutching the sheet to him. "Poor Kelly," she said, going to him. "Forgive me for using you as a guinea pig. But I had to give it a test. You must think we're all—well, squirrelly."

"Um-hmn," he nodded. And it was true. Some of the crazy-quilt, tilted goings-on of the evening before he'd attributed, in part, to his drunken condition. But he was sober now and the Mad Tea Party was still in full swing, well attended by Maggie Banner and Company.

Stosh burst in waving the *Daily News.* "Wait'll you see, Kelly—you're big-time!" Noticing Maggie was no longer Miss Vaughn, he said, "You were great, Mags, a real gas!" He handed Kelly the paper; the front page nearly jolted him out of bed. His gasp of surprise earned a giggle from Flora and a glug of laughter from Stosh.

The large black headline read: KAYO FOR RAFFAELLO. The enormous photo under it was sharp and clear: Kelly, feet planted firmly on the steps, arm crooked in the air, face contorted by a grimace, which seemed totally unlike himself; Raffaello Tucci, caught in midfall, body rigid, dark glasses cocked on the end of his nose, eyes glazed; Maggie Banner swathed in her sable coat, eyes glancing to her left and looking no more concerned than if Raffaello Tucci had stubbed his toe, Kelly thought.

"You know what's a gas," Stosh said, leaning over his shoulder. "Your arm looks like you just followed through with a haymaker instead of conking him with your elbow."

"And me, look at me," Maggie added. "I look rather lahdee-dah about it all, if I do say so." She put a hand under Kelly's chin, tilting his face up. "That expression on your face—some tough guy, huh? Some tiger. Did anyone ever call you Tiger?"

He had to laugh. "No—na-never!"

"Well, I just might. I'm a citizen, I pay taxes." Then she held his face in both hands; her enormous green eyes widened as she drew him in with her gaze. "Kelly, come with me! Come with us!"

She spoke with such intensity, he was momentarily thrown. "I—I don't know . . ."

"I know all this seems peculiar, but there are—" She dropped her hands and walked several steps away. "There are reasons, sound reasons." She turned to Stosh. "Baby, order us a batch of Bloody Marys and a chocolate malted, too. I need energy. And Flora, get Arnold Lefkowitz for me.

If he's not there, don't leave this number, tell him we'll call back. I don't want to take chances; Raf'll be after him."

Flora and Stosh left the room. Maggie lit a cigarette; she'd taken only one puff when she said, "Oh, wait a minute, I forgot," and walked into the sitting room.

Left alone, Kelly picked up the newspaper. He stared at himself, matted out, plastered there on the front page, and, hardly able to believe it, brushed his fingertips across the picture, as if he might be able to lift his features off the page and feel the dimensions of them. Withdrawing his hand, he studied the picture. Tiger, Maggie Banner had called him. Not quite a TIGER, perhaps, but he did look determined.

He would have given anything for a glimpse of Grace's expression when she first saw the picture. He thought of Miss Mosley, teeth completely unshielded in virtual shock, and Stanley Giles, beady-eyed with disbelief, and grinned; he thought of Hanley Meister and laughed out loud.

Maggie walked back in. "Kick out of it?"

He nodded. "I'd be a liar if I said no."

"Here," she said, holding out a brown silk robe with black borders and cuffs, "brought you a present. Happy birthday." He only looked at it. "Take it."

"It's very handsome."

"Like man, like robe," she said, handing it to him.

He felt a tingle, a faint stirring, somewhere way down inside the middle of him and up along the insides of his arms, too. She helped him into the robe and then sat down on the bed next to him. "Now—where to begin? Or do you want to ask me questions? Ask me anything." She took the newspaper from him and put it aside. "Go on," she said. "Let's speak frankly. I will, I *do*."

He fingered a belt loop on the robe. "All right. Then why would you pick me?" He glanced up at her.

She smiled, the same smile he remembered from the night before, a slight pull over to the right and a downward tug. "I didn't pick you, I saw you. You came into my line of vision. I saw you and you reminded me of someone . . ."

She waved a hand behind her. ". . . Way back when. Someone lovely and special, I might add. And I wanted you, then,
there, at that moment. Oh, I don't mean quote wanted you
unquote like they say in books right there on the tabletop at
the Copacabana."

She laughed. "I wanted to feel the touch of you, to talk to
you, to—maybe I only wanted to play with you, flirt with
you. Perhaps, knowing I was leaving Raf, I was anticipating
being alone and I was restless, on the prowl." She quickly
took his hand and pressed it between hers. "Oh, that was
then, last night, when I first spied you. When we danced,
something about you touched me. There was a clean . . .
*un*touched something about you." She looked at him
quickly. "Does that annoy you?" And just as quickly she
waved the question away. "No, I said I'd speak frankly.
That's what got to me. The whole thing triggered by chemistry, of course, pure chemistry on my part, I mean felt by me,
which I God only knows indulged myself in." She hesitated,
pressing the fingers of her right hand against her throat
before continuing. "At this stage of the game, I don't take a
full century to fall in love. I'm permissive with myself. Besides I've always had the capacity to fall in love quickly."
She cocked her head. "Perhaps I mean . . . to *project* myself into a love affair. Do you believe in that?"

"Yes." And he meant it. "Yes, I do," he said, "but—"

"But what?"

In a burst of frankness, he added, "I don't seem to be able
to follow through."

"You don't mean that?" He nodded. There was a full measure of concern in her voice. "Oh, I wouldn't want that for
you."

"I don't want it for myself either."

"We'll fix it then," she said. Kelly laughed. "No laughing,
we will. People can fix things for people. That's part of why
we're here." She touched his hand again, adding, ". . . I
keep telling myself." She frowned. "So—" Jumping off the
bed, she strolled away from him a few paces. "To get on with

the next phase of our long, no *ancient* relationship." She smiled. "Outside on the steps, when you connected with Raf, it was concern prompted me to pursue you, to have you pursued, rather." She returned to the bed and tapped the front page of the newspaper with the back of her hand. "And when I say concern I don't say it lightly.

"Raf's got an adoring fan club. They may be grizzly bears but he's got them charmed." She held a hand up. "Oh, despite what you saw, he can be charming—take it from a birdy who knows. Anyhow, these chums, they figure he's lost enough rounds and they're not about to let him lose anything else." She paused for a moment. "That, I suspect, goes for me, too."

"But you're Maggie Banner—"

"God only knows," she added ruefully.

"I should think if you wanted to leave him, you could just—"

"What? Just walk away? You mean why the disguise, this hotel, all of that?" He nodded. "First place," she said, tapping herself under the chin, "the countenance has been overexposed, it draws crowds. If I were unrecognizable, I wouldn't have to bother. I'd simply go where I'm going and that would be that. If I went as my adorable self, my whereabouts would be common knowledge. Raf would be after me, there'd be scenes, pleading, recriminations."

She paused, obviously thinking how to phrase her next thoughts. "I'll put it this way. I have a little time for—oh, some fun, some excitement before I have this rather pressing commitment. I haven't the time, nor the energy to fritter away. It's easier this way, believe me. Besides, if I persisted, if I refused to go back to him, there might be more than just scenes." She looked Kelly straight in the eye. "I'm afraid of him when he flies out of control. I don't trust his actions. You see, one thing I do know—he loves me very much."

"If he loves you," Kelly asked, "why would he hurt you?"

"Oh, Kelly—he's like a child. If a child's toy is taken away from him, he'd just as soon break it as let anyone else play with it."

Kelly's logical mind made him ask: "If you think he might do something, you could go to the police."

"Don't be naïve!" There was an edge of impatience in her voice. "You don't get protection until *after* the fact. Until the President's assassinated, or the baby's kidnapped, or the secretary's raped. Then the widow gets protection, the baby's parents, the secretary's roommate. Anyhow, wouldn't I look silly." She shrugged, strutting across the room and confronting an imaginary man: "Officer, I've just left this man and I'm afraid he'll do me bodily harm." She laughed, but not for long. "That's why I'm concerned for you. If he can't get at me, somebody's going to have to pay. Why should you end up chopped meat because I gave you the nod? That's why I want you to understand you can't go waltzing around town like any other civilian—not for the time being, not until his attention is attracted to a more pressing matter. Even if he did get sidetracked, there'd be one or two adoring chums would love to earn a gold star by tracking you down some fine day or night . . . and your features are just dandy the way they are. They don't need rearranging."

In spite of the danger she lined out, he felt strangely untouchable, also oddly garrulous. Little granules of energy, and he was certain it was the pill Stosh had given him, were percolating through his veins. He shook his head. "But last night was an accident. He must know by now I had no connection with your leaving—"

"You're being logical," she snapped. "He's not a logical man."

"I know, but still—"

She sprang up from the chair and rushed over to him, grasping him by the shoulders. "I'm bored convincing you. I don't have the time. I can't—" her fingers dug into him "—I can't go on about it!" He sat there stunned. "Do you believe what I say?"

He was taken by surprise. "I . . . ."

She shook him with all the tensile strength she possessed. "Answer me!"

"Yes," he said.

"Do you really?" She slapped him across the face.

"Yes!" His hand covered the sting on his cheek; he antici-pated a break in her attack, an apology.

Instead she shook him again. "Will you be careful?"

An attack of nerves seized him and he spoke on the waves of his laughter. "Ya-yes—ha—I—"

She slapped the laughter out of him. "Say yes and mean it."

"Yes!" he yelled. "Stop it!"

"All right!" she said. "All right." She released him, turning away and walking back toward the chair. "I'm—" and now *she* laughed, "I'm bushed anyway." She slumped in the chair, laughing softly; then she coughed. "I'm bushed," she repeated. She was breathing heavily; underneath her blouse, the rise and fall of her breasts was labored; her head tilted down, chin almost touching her chest. "I—" She gasped and her eyes rolled up at Kelly.

He stood up from the bed. "Yes?"

"Get Flora . . ."

He ran to the door and opened it. "Flora . . ." The sitting room was empty. "Flora!"

"Yes?" she called from the other bedroom.

"Come here, it's Maggie." He realized he had never used her first name before and turned around to look back at her.

From under heavy lids she worked him into focus. "No," she sighed, waving him back, "get away, stay away." She turned her head sideways.

He stepped into the sitting room out of her line of vision. Flora hurried in from the other bedroom and rushed past him.

"Something's wrong. She—" But she entered the room and shut the door, paying him no attention.

CHAPTER 14

He stood in the center of the room, wondering what could have come upon her so suddenly and wishing he could be of help. He could hear hurried but controlled sounds from the bedroom: footsteps, low whisperings, drawers opening and closing.

He walked to the middle window and looked down at the south side of Forty-second Street. The outside world was still there, and to Kelly, in spite of the uncertainty and fears he knew he should be experiencing—safety threatened, jobless—still, standing in this strange, impersonal hotel room with his three newly found, bizarre friends nearby, the world seemed less hostile than ever before.

What kind of a pill had Stosh given him, anyhow?

He was feeling energetically optimistic, a feeling not usually included in his repertoire, so much so that he found it difficult to stand still without having an activity to engage in.

He turned and poked his head into the other bedroom. From the looks of the room—trousers and a shirt of Stosh's and an enormous tent of a housecoat that could only belong to Flora—he imagined they had both slept there. He *had* slept in the same room with Maggie Banner.

He remembered what she had said about him: a clean, untouched look. Untouched—that was for sure. As for clean, he didn't feel all that scrubbed. It was a minor gesture, but he could at least tidy up for her. The bathroom door was open at the far end of the room and he moved toward it.

Fifteen minutes later, bathed and shaved, having used the contents of Stosh's leather toilet case, he walked back into the bedroom. The shower had further braced him. He could feel little explosions of joy or hope or something good blipping up inside him. He would make a point of asking Stosh exactly what that pill was.

He noticed the phone and, on an impulse, picked it up. He gave the operator the number for Parade Paperbacks and when he was connected he asked for Grace. She answered in her modulated business voice. "Distribution, Miss Emory speaking."

"Hello, Grace, this is—"

"Kelly?" she asked tentatively, almost tremulously. Then she whooped his name: "Kelly!"

"Yes," he replied, holding the phone away from his ear.

"Oh, Kelly—Kelly, my God!" There was not only excitement in her voice, there was also a distinct measure of awe and admiration. Then abruptly she was all whispered concern. "Kelly, are you all right?"

"Yes, I'm fine."

"Oh, Kelly—I'm speechless," she gasped, but she wasn't at all. "I mean—Kelly, how exciting! You danced with Maggie Banner! And you *hit* him! Kelly, how marvelous! I've tried calling your apartment every half-hour." Then a gasp. "You're not there, are you?"

"No."

Dropping her voice to spy level, she added: "Because it's being watched, you know."

"Yes, but how did you know?"

"There was a newspaper reporter here; he told us."

"A reporter—there?"

"Yes, wanting to know all about you. Kelly, you're a celebrity!"

"How did he find out where I worked?"

"Oh, he'd already interviewed the super of your building. And the owner, too." Grace sighed. "Kelly, the place has been an absolute madhouse!"

"How do you mean?"

"Well, I mean—just nobody's getting any *work* done. The girls in the outside office are—well, they're honking around like a bunch of geese. Mr. Loganthal's had to bawl them out twice. Miss Mosley's so excited I'm afraid she might bite herself. Mr. Meister's practically passing out cigars—talk about reflected glory. And Stanley Giles is a deep forest green with envy." They both laughed and she said, "It's heaven here today. But Kelly, where are you?"

"At the—in a hotel. I don't think she'd want me to say which one."

"She?" Grace asked. She held her breath while she asked the next question. "Not Maggie *Banner*? You mean you're *with her?*"

"Uh-huh."

"You've been with her ever since—all *night?*"

"Yes."

"You spent the *night* with her—*in a hotel?*"

"Yes."

"Oh, my God! How exciting! Why, Kelly McDermott! *Kelly McDermott!* I can't—well, what's happened to you! Now, Kelly, you've got to tell me every moment, from the very beginning. Promise?"

"I promise." He was going over so well with Grace he couldn't help airing the distinct possibility: "It might have to wait awhile," he added. "I might be going off on a trip."

"On a trip—where?" she asked. Then suddenly: "Not with her, with Maggie Banner?"

"Yes," he replied, trying to keep his tone matter-of-fact. "She's asked me and—"

"Oh—go, Kelly! *Go!*"

"Yes, I think I will," he said, still playing the part.

"Where? Where would you be going?" she asked.

"I don't know," he said, suddenly realizing he didn't. "I think she wants to keep it a secret," he added, justifying his lack of knowledge.

Grace's enthusiasm was only whetted by this. "You don't *know!* That's even better. How marvelous! Oh, Kelly—"

A voice Kelly recognized as belonging to Miss Ayers, the switchboard operator, broke in. "Miss Emory, your Chicago call is on the line."

"Oh, God, yes—tell them one minute." After the click-off she said, "Kelly, I've got to take it, there's a whole mix-up with—anyhow, I'm so glad you called. Kelly, I'm so thrilled for you! Will you write me, let me know—well, just everything?!"

"Yes," he said.

"Oh, and Kelly—can I tell them here that you called and that . . . well, you know, that you're with *her?* I'd like to rub it in a little, it would do them good! Can I?"

He laughed. "Sure, tell them anything you want."

She laughed a little wicked, scheming chortle of a laugh, said good-bye, and hung up.

The conversation with Grace was an added boost to his already hypoed adrenaline. He walked into the living room as the far bedroom door opened and Stosh stepped out. "Hi, guy," he said.

"Is she all right?" Kelly asked.

"Sure," Stosh said, crossing to a tray of Bloody Marys.

"Kelly?" It was Maggie from the bedroom. "Come on in."

He found her lying on the far bed, dressed in a quilted robe, looking quite chipper and sipping the last of a chocolate malted Stosh must have brought her while Kelly was showering. Flora busied herself putting things back into her black kit. She neither spoke nor looked at Kelly. Stosh carried the tray in, passing a glass to Maggie and one to Kelly.

"Are you all right?" Kelly asked.

"Of course." She smoothed out a place on the bed next to her and patted it, indicating for Kelly to sit down. When he did, she placed a hand on his knee. "Might as well level with you. I've been plagued this last year or so with anemia. Pernicious anemia. Isn't that nasty sounding?" She repeated it. "Pernicious anemia!" Suddenly she looked at Stosh, who had put the tray down on the dresser and was simply standing there, staring down at the carpet. "Stosh!" she snapped.

He looked up at her briefly. "Yes?"

"Are you just going to stand there like a Polish statue?"

"No." His voice was flat and toneless, not at all like his usual self.

She looked at Kelly. "Anyway, this anemia—" Stopping abruptly, she glanced back at Stosh, who hadn't moved, then to her watch. "It's almost time for you and Flora to think about leaving, might as well get packed. And try Arnold again, will you?"

Stosh muttered, "Okay," and left the room.

"So," Maggie said, smiling at Kelly, "I suppose we all have our crosses to bear and this anemia thing's mine and it's a bore. I give out at a moment's notice and that's all there is to it. So you mustn't mind. Flora slaps me around, gives me a shot, and I'm fine. Huh, Flora?" She gave Flora ample time to respond and when she didn't, said: "Isn't that right, Flora?"

Flora mumbled something and Maggie stood up from the bed. "Honestly, Flora, when the two of you go into your monosyllabic *zombie* periods, you're infuriating."

"I'm sorry," Flora mumbled, closing her leather bag.

Maggie stared at her a long moment and then waved her away. "You better get organized, too."

"Yes, I was just going to," she said, leaving the room as Stosh called in: "Maggie, I got Arnold."

"My lawyer, won't be a minute," Maggie said, picking up the phone. "Hello, Arnold. . . . Yes, dear, I'm leaving this evening. . . . Do you have the cash? . . . Fine, I'll call you later and we'll arrange to meet. . . . Arnold, has Raf called? . . . Yes, I thought he would. You don't think he'd ever—" she glanced at Kelly briefly. . . . "No, I don't either. . . . I loved seeing you yesterday and Janet and—that godchild of mine. He's a gem. . . . Some godmother you picked for the

Viet Cong! You have my permission to shop around for an alternate, a *sane* one!" She cleared her throat again. "I love you, too, and my love to Janet and the Viet Cong. . . . Yes, he's a terror and—so dear! . . . Call you later, 'bye."

She hung up quickly. Kelly could not help notice how poignant her voice had become. Her back was to him; she didn't turn around immediately, but straightened up and took a deep breath. When she did face him, she was smiling but it was forced. "Funniest thing," she laughed huskily, "my lawyer was over in Viet Nam at the end of the war, negotiating for the State Department, when his son was born. It was such a terrible birth—she was in labor for two solid days—that they began calling the baby the Viet Cong and it stuck. Isn't that mad? He is a terror, but he's adorable." She smiled and gave her shoulders a prideful wiggle. "I'm the Viet Cong's godmother."

Kelly somehow connected Flora's and Stosh's mood with whatever was disturbing to Maggie in her conversation with her lawyer.

"The Viet Cong! Don't you love that for a six-year-old boy?"

"Yes." He smiled at her.

She glanced down at the carpet, then back up at Kelly. "Will you kiss me?" she asked in a quiet voice.

He replied, "Yes," and was immediately terrified.

She stood her ground and let him come to her. She held her head tilted up to him, eyes opened, lips relaxed but not parted. His heart thumped several times as if there were an ungodly knocking at his chest. He wondered if she heard it.

He hesitated a moment; aware of his hesitation, Maggie closed her eyes and brought her hands up to rest lightly upon his shoulders. He moved closer until he came within the warm gravity of her face, and the light breath from her lips grazed his mouth and chin. He touched his lips to her and for a while they rested there together.

Fear gripped him that she might suddenly grab him convulsively, cover his mouth with hers, her body constricted, her arms flung around his back, clutching at him, urging him on to the fulfillment of his masculine role.

But she made not a move.

He pressed his lips gently against hers. He parted them slightly and felt hers part in return, but no more than his. His arms slipped around her, and she drew her hands down from his shoulders across his chest and slid them around his sides until they rested upon his back. He opened his mouth wider and his tongue touched her upper lip, then her teeth, as her tongue came forward to touch the tip of his and withdrew between lips held wider apart, allowing him to be the aggressor.

There was a clash in his body, a heady merger, as drink met pill, combining with the provocation of the moment to produce a tiny mushroom cloud within him. His body jerked forward, and his arms firmed their grasp of her body. The warmth of their two mouths increased while they kissed, and some of this heat seemed to swirl in the back of his throat and trickle down inside him, flowing past his stomach, dropping down farther and spinning in circles, zoning in to settle at the center of his groin with increasing heaviness.

In hesitation and uncertainty he trembled slightly, but she murmured a low pleasurable sound which let him know he was giving satisfaction. Such a tiny sign as this not only reassured him but excited him more. He drew their bodies together and quickened the movements of his lips and tongue.

She placed one hand on the back of his neck, squeezing the nape of it gently between her thumb and forefinger. Her gentleness filled him with gratification and gratification translated itself to joy. A delicious arrow shot down his spine, ricocheted back up to his neck and exploded, flooding over across his shoulders and flowing down his sides.

He was attacked by gooseflesh; he felt each hair on his body standing out erect and he could feel, at the same time, another part of him becoming firm up against the silk of his robe.

He arched away from her in retreat, but she lowered her

hands to the small of his back and drew their bodies up close against one another. She whispered something—no more than a word or a phrase—which he did not hear and, being unintelligible, it somehow doubly excited him. She kissed his neck quickly four or five times from his ear to a point under his chin and brought her mouth back to his lips.

His excitement was complete now and the pressure between their two bodies caused him to pulsate. Responding to this, she moved up against him in a slow, circular pattern. He gasped out of total pleasure and moaned, feeling an abandon so many years longed for that it threatened to drown him. For a split second he wanted to tell her, to voice his joy, but they were locked together now.

It happened quickly: suddenly there was no floor beneath his feet—he was levitated by passion—nothing but the delicious, quivering vacuum of their embrace. Then, as if a switch had been flicked, he was being hurtled off into space.

A knock at the door jarred them back to consciousness. They ignored it; however this consciousness brought an awareness to Kelly of a tickling sensation beginning in his toes, the tips of his toes, swirling around his ankles, creeping up in ever-increasing spirals about the calves of his legs, tightening his kneecaps, locking them; and as it swept up the insides of his legs, an awareness that he would explode when it reached his groin struck him and he quickly wrenched himself away from her.

He turned, facing away from her. Still too late, he feared, when he heard a second and louder knock at the door, followed by Flora's voice: "Maggie?"

"Wait," she called out, walking to Kelly, but not touching him. "You didn't . . . ?"

He held up his hand, mentally forcing back the tide, swimming wildly against the oncoming wave.

In a moment, she snatched the wax-paper container from the dresser and dashed the remains of the liquid up against the side of his face. He sputtered, cried out, and turned to her in astonishment, as the flow of his passion quivered, ebbed and was checked. Their eyes met in mutual surprise.

He put a hand to his face, wiping his fingers down the side of his cheek. He looked at them, then back to Maggie.

She shrugged helplessly, tugging the corners of her mouth down and making a sad-clown mouth. "Chocolate malted!" she said. She tossed her head back and her husky laughter filled the room.

Within seconds they were convulsed, rocking back and forth on their heels; then they were together, hanging on to one another, holding each other and swaying wildly. Maggie's face grazed his, lifting off a blotch of malted milk. She pulled back and they laughed even harder when he pointed to her cheek.

"Maggie!" Flora called again.

"Yes—come in," she gasped.

"You all right?" Flora asked, opening the door.

"Yes," Maggie roared, "saved by a chocolate malted."

"What?" Flora asked, but she received only a series of howls in reply, as the two of them struggled for control.

"Oh, Kelly!" Maggie seized him by the shoulders. "Come with us, won't you?"

And he was so filled with joy by the freedom of his response to her, so filled with the pungent sensation of potency he had just experienced that he laughed back at her: "Ya-yes!"

But she was no longer laughing: her eyes widened, she inhaled a little catch-breath. "You will?"

And his reply was sober, too. "Yes, I will."

Maggie cried out and turned to Flora. "Did you hear that, Flora?"

Clasping her hands together, Flora grinned ferociously.

"Oh, Kelly!" Maggie threw her arms around him; she was laughing again.

Kelly joined her, thinking: yes, by God, I'm going and I don't even know where. This made him laugh all the more.

Abruptly she leaned into his ear and whispered: "Did you really kill your father?"

"Yes . . ."

She pulled away from him. "Oh, Christ, how exciting!"

CHAPTER 15

The day started out for Raffaello as badly as the evening had ended. He'd fallen into a drunken sleep with a lighted cigarette in his fingers. The cigarette had fallen down between the cushions and the arm of the chair and he'd awakened in the midst of the smoldering mess coughing and panicked, with a wracking headache and a badly upset stomach.

A hurried call to the desk brought several bellboys and an assistant manager. The chair was taken out and the *Daily News* and the *Times* were brought in. There, covering the front page of the *News,* was the photograph taken the night before. Raffaello was, in quick succession, amazed at the prominence given the incident, then sickened and finally— enraged.

One of the bellboys returned to clean up and spray the room free of smoke, and Raffaello detected a knowing, wicked gleam of the boy's eyes when he caught him staring at the picture. He sent the boy for Alka-Seltzer and went into the bedroom. His head was killing him and the liquor he'd consumed was eating away at his insides.

Most of all—Maggie hadn't called.

One hand to his forehead, he flopped down on the bed and despite his misery, or perhaps because of it, fell asleep immediately. The bellboy's insistent knocking awakened him. He grumbled and called out: "What—yes?"

"Alka-Seltzer," the boy called out.

"Son of a bitch, I was asleep," Raffaello groaned, once more aware of his headache. The boy knocked briskly several times. "Stop it!" Raffaello shouted, staggering to the door. "I was asleep, for Christ's sake!"

The bellboy stood there, a wise look on his freshly scrubbed early-morning face, holding out a small tray. "Sorry, sir, but you ordered it."

Raffaello felt slightly foolish; of course he'd sent for it. He reached toward the tray with an unsteady hand. As he lifted the glass he was seized by a small spasm and some of the water sloshed over the side. It was important that he maintain his poise, and Raffaello glanced up to see if the boy had noticed. There was no doubt from the shining eyes and pursed mouth that he was suppressing a grin.

In one of those gestures for which he was well known, Raffaello quickly flicked the glass of water in the boy's face. That would wash the smirk away! The boy ducked back in surprise but the reason for the gesture was apparent enough; he didn't say anything, only brushed a hand over his mouth and back across his chin.

Raffaello was immediately overcome with shame, such a ridiculous, uncalled-for little gesture; there was even something feminine about it. Recoiling with disgust, he took the tray, walked to the bureau, got a twenty-dollar bill and handed it to the boy without a word. The boy nodded a sober-faced thank-you and backed off.

After he'd taken the Alka-Seltzer, Raffaello lay back down on the bed, but there was to be no more sleep for him. There was penance to do; he had to put in time berating himself for his conduct with the bellboy. He could imagine the expression on Maggie's face had she been witness to it. Don't step on the little guys, she had said when he started after a rude tie salesman in a Madrid department store; save your energy for the big boys, the real villains.

There was also the matter of his drinking to contend with. He had yet to reprimand himself for going off the wagon. After all this time, two years, how could he succumb so easily! Every time he'd had a fight with Maggie he knew she expected him to pick up a glass and drain it—God only knows, in spite of her condition, she couldn't stay off the stuff—but sobriety had become a badge of strength to him. And then, last night, he'd taken to the bottle like a nursing infant.

He was not finished censuring himself, either, for his behavior at the Copacabana. Could this possibly have triggered her leaving—no, no, he'd been over this a dozen times. Flora had excused herself before he'd sent for that McDermott fellow to dance with Maggie. Further proof she hadn't arranged for a rendezvous with the young man and *then* left him. Although his conduct earlier had been reprehensible, he must keep the sequence of events straight in his mind.

Raffaello knew he was in danger of swinging out of control; he could feel the warning signal deep inside him, a little tickle of a dizzying sensation, the same way he could tell if bad weather was on its way by the small ache around his eye. He told himself he must not lose his balance, he must keep himself tightly reined, try to keep mannerly. That was it, he must keep his manners about him. He was going through a crisis but he must maintain his equilibrium. He would show Maggie and the world he was not the temper-happy Peck's bad boy he was often made out to be.

Then the calls began. Phone calls from television and radio reporters, from newspapermen and gossip columnists, from friends in New York and California and Las Vegas who had just got the word.

And one call from a jilted former girl friend who, whenever word of a New York visit by Raffaello reached her, delighted in phoning and blasting him with his own recording of "Di Quella Pira," the aria he was singing when he lost his voice. He hadn't known who it was until two years ago when he'd been in New York. The girl's mother had walked in during the call and Raffaello heard: "Jenny, turn that sound down, whatever—" Jenny had hung up, but too late; he'd heard the name and it all fit: she'd been a poor loser, a vengeful customer if ever there was one.

The next time she called, record player tuned to frantic, he'd waited until the aria ended, then said: "Don't I know you? Aren't you the girl with the one long black wiry hair, rather like a corkscrew, growing out of her left tit?" She slammed the phone down quickly.

But here she was again, just wouldn't give up. Today, the minute he heard the music, he simply sighed: "Oh, Jenny!" and hung up.

To the various newsmen he was civil; he maintained his control. No, he had no comment to make; no, he had no idea where Maggie Banner might be; no, he would prefer to say nothing more. (Oh, but he could tell them a choice bit of news, if he wanted. But—no, it was unthinkable, he could never violate her most sacred confidence.)

Calls from friends were more trying. He could not be so impersonally cool as with reporters and newsmen. Friends required more patience, especially those who were slightly overeager in their solicitude, who were excited, even secretly pleased the minute misfortune's breeze tipped their noses. The Trouble Sniffers, Maggie called them.

But Raffaello kept his pledge of allegiance to good manners and fended them off one by one with a minimum of fuss, a bit of the old boyish charm, and a few face-saving lies.

By noon his headache was gone, although he was still experiencing tremors, vibrations in his stomach and unsteady hands. He was torn by a strange mixture of emotions. In a way there was something satisfying, almost exhilarating, about the attention he was receiving. The phone had hardly stopped all morning. No matter what, Raffaello Tucci was back in the limelight; what happened to him was still front-page news. On the other hand, though he was assured of the curiosity of the press and the concern of his friends, he was becoming bored with their calls and tired of his own voice. He'd been clinging to the hope that Maggie would call; each time the phone rang his stomach jumped and this took a toll on his nerves. He was fast running out of patience.

He hadn't taken a morning drink, badly as he could have used one. He wouldn't take one either; he would not allow that particular gain to be torpedoed by Maggie, no matter what anguish she inflicted upon him.

The phone rang; he almost didn't answer it but something, a sly tease of a hunch, told him that after all the other calls—it just might be her. He let it ring several times, so as not to appear anxious, then lifted the receiver tentatively. "Hello?"

"Hello, Raf?" It was Morty. "Just checking in. McDermott never showed at his apartment, not all night, and Raf . . ."

"Yes?"

"He hasn't shown up at work either." There was a pause, then Morty said: "I don't know . . ." He left the end of the phrase not only dangling but dripping with insinuation.

"So?" Raffaello snapped, trying to remain calm but bristling at the suggestion in the simple words: I don't know. In the end, he couldn't let it alone. "What do you mean—*you don't know?*"

"I mean—beats me where he is."

"Then why didn't you say that!"

"Look, Raf, I only—"

"I don't give a goddamn *what* you don't know. Find out where he is, do you hear me?"

"Sure, but—"

"Find out, then call me. And don't bother me until you do!" Raffaello slammed the phone down hard. He glared at it, sitting there dead and black. He was, in an instant, trembling with rage that Morty's insinuations might have some basis in fact.

It was one thing if she wanted to go off with Stosh and Flora and play a little game of hide-and-seek. Maggie was erratic, a creature of impulse, just as he was. But it was quite another kettle of fish if she had that good-looking (yes, he was handsome), young (and young)—no, she wouldn't—

He walked to the liquor tray, poured a shot of scotch, and added a splash of water. He didn't gulp it down but raised the glass and sipped it slowly, steadily, until it was drained dry. Raffaello sighed; there, that was better; he could have a little pick-me-up to steady his nerves; anyone was entitled to that. He poured himself another drink and sat down. By the time he was halfway through it, he felt a numbing calm take hold. He lifted his hand, steady as a rock.

Still, the possibility that Maggie might have wiped the slate completely clean of him, might be embarking on another affair without so much as a backward glance at *their* relationship, nagged him, incubating such dark thoughts of revenge that he got up and poured a dividend to his second drink before he'd even finished it.

He was suddenly restless. He must find her; he must take steps; he couldn't just sit there fending off calls and questions; he could no longer bide his time waiting.

Her lawyer would know. He handled all her affairs. She was extremely close to him, the godmother of his child even. He had the operator look up the number.

"Hello, Arnold—Raffaello."

"Ah, Raf, how are you?"

"Fine," Raffaello said. Oh, how smooth and politic, a lawyer to his fingertips, not even a hint of the fracas.

"What can I do for you, Raf?" Not a trace of anything but friendship in the man's voice.

"I'd like to—" Raffaello started but broke off. "You know about last night?"

"Last night?" Arnold said; then, as Raffaello was thinking both in amazement and annoyance that the man could not possible play it so naively, the lawyer chuckled warmly and said, "Oh, yes, read all about it in the papers this morning." He laughed again. "You two, you're a prize pair," he sighed. Then: "Nothing serious, I hope."

"No, no," Raffaello replied, "just a spat."

There was silence for a long moment. As Raffaello took a breath to speak, Arnold repeated: "What can I do for you, Raf?"

"I wanted to speak to Maggie. Just talk to her on the phone. I wonder if you'd give me her number."

"Number?" Arnold repeated. "Why, golly, Raf, I haven't heard from Maggie today. I don't know where she is. I read where she'd checked out of the hotel. Didn't she leave a forwarding at the—"

Raffaello hung up on him. He knew from the studied innocence coming over the phone in thick waves of sugar-coated bullshit that he was acting on orders, that he knew damn well where she was. He would not be taken for a complete fool!

The phone rang while he was still cursing the man, his profession, and his ethnic background. He snatched it up. "Yes!"

"Mr. Tucci?"

"Yes!"

"Leo Goodman, Channel Seven News. I wonder if you could tell me something about your relationship with Maggie Banner?" Raffaello was about to slam the phone down again when the man asked: "Do you have any idea where Miss Banner might be?"

"Well, no . . ." Black thoughts swirled and tumbled in his head. If she wanted to play dirty, put him on the wrack, torture and humiliate him, he'd give it back to her. He'd drop a small cryptic message that would be certain to flush her out wherever she was. But it must be worded just right, nothing that would give away the secret they shared, just a calculated smidgeon. "Tell you what—could I have your number?" Raffaello asked. "I'll call you right back."

The voice on the other end was all appreciative eagerness. "Sure, sure, Mr. Tucci. Leo Goodman, Judson two, two thousand, extension four two one."

"Get right back to you," Raffaello said, putting the receiver down.

By the time he'd freshened his drink and sat back down at the phone, he coded a clever message that would insure a call from her. She'd had her fun; now it was his turn.

CHAPTER 16

For the rest of the afternoon, Suite 712 of the Southern Hotel was a staging center for their departure. Kelly was fascinated by their precautions. Maggie reasoned that since his picture had been featured so prominently on the front page, it would be wiser if he were to remain in the hotel. At the same time no bellboys or maids were allowed to enter the rooms.

Kelly wanted to go by his apartment to collect some clothing and personal items but Maggie was adamant about this; she would provide him with whatever he needed.

To secure maximum protection in leaving New York unnoticed, Flora and Stosh were taking a plane to Los Angeles, then catching a local flight to San Diego. Maggie and Kelly would take the only direct flight, a later one, to San Diego. Kelly was told of this, but San Diego was only to be a meeting place; he was not told their final destination. They were assigned fictitious names to travel by and given full instructions in conduct and procedure.

In the disguise of Miss Vaughn, Maggie made several trips out of the hotel. She returned from her last trip, clutching several packages, just as Flora and Stosh were ready to leave. Opening a bag, she took out a salt-and-pepper snap-brim hat. "Kelly, try it on."

"I never wear hats," he said.

"Put it on. You're still on the front pages and I don't want anyone recognizing you. These, too," she said, handing him a pair of dark horn-rimmed glasses. "They've just got regular glass in them, so don't worry."

They gathered around while Kelly put on his disguise. "Let's see," Maggie said. He turned to face them. "Marvelous, it makes quite a difference; you'd be surprised. Flora, Stosh?"

"Yeah," Stosh laughed, "Clark Kent."

Flora was all frowns. "It covers up his pretty hair and hides his beautiful eyes."

"Flora, honey, that's the point," Maggie sighed, taking Kelly by the hand and leading him to the mirror. "See?"

It was true. He looked completely strange and a bit silly to himself. Outside of the service, he'd never owned a hat and he'd never worn glasses.

"Hey," Stosh said, checking his watch, "we'd better cut out."

There was a flurry of excitement as they set the bags out in the hall and called down for a porter. Suddenly Flora said, "Maggie, I'd feel better if we all went together."

"Well, we're not. It's all planned. We've all been photographed together enough lately and you two aren't exactly inconspicuous, you especially," she added, pointing a finger at Flora.

"You don't think he'd have the airports watched?" Flora asked.

"I doubt it—how would he know I'd be leaving by plane? How would he know I wasn't staying in the city? Besides, look how many airlines there are. He'd need an army."

"I wouldn't put nothing past him," Stosh said.

Flora was still troubled. "But what if you should—"

Maggie cut her off. "No!"

Flora paused, glanced down at the floor, then up at Kelly. "Kelly, you take good care of her, and if—"

"Honey, I'm not going to fall out of the plane, I promise you," she said, herding them to the door.

Their repetitive good-byes, suddenly clumsy and shy, were evidence to Kelly of the true affection and concern they felt for one another, more than the mere fun and games they so often engaged in.

"Take care, the two of you'se." Stosh waved as they turned and walked toward the elevators.

"The two of you'se, too," Maggie said, quickly calling out: "Ey, give us an airplane joke!"

Stosh stopped, putting a finger to his lips! "Ah—the flight was so bumpy the stewardess poured the food directly into the airsick bags!"

"Two weeks at Loew's Dungeon!" Maggie said.

Stosh crossed his eyes, making a grotesque face at her. Then he took Flora's hand and they continued down the hall. Maggie put a hand around Kelly's waist. "Will you look at them?" she said softly. "Just look at them."

Kelly smiled at the lumbering giantess and the rugged Pole; they made a rare couple.

When they walked back into the sitting room, Maggie took off her wig. "Seven o'clock; couple more hours and we'll be off."

"Seven," Kelly said. "Could we turn on the news?"

"Sure."

When he'd switched on the television set, Maggie took off his hat and glasses. "That's better," she said. "Come sit."

They watched reports of the President's visit to Mexico and a warehouse fire in Chicago. Maggie took his hand and leaned up against him. "You won't believe what I'm pretending!"

"What?"

"That we're seventeen, having our first date at the—"

A large still photograph of Maggie Banner stepping off the plane flashed on the screen. "Maggie Banner, forty-eight-year-old two-time Academy Award–winning actress, arrived at Kennedy—"

Maggie's husky laughter filled the room. "That's right,

make a liar out of me!" The timing was perfect and the two of them laughed, missing the commentary accompanying an old photograph of Raffaello as Don Jose. When the current picture taken outside the Copacabana was flashed on, Maggie shushed for quiet.

". . . Kelly McDermott, young publisher—"

"Publisher!" Kelly said.

"Shh."

". . . gave Raffaello Tucci the count outside the Copacabana night club last night. Young McDermott—"

"Sure," Maggie sighed, "they give my age right off the bat and already he's called you 'young' twice."

". . . threw his punch after an incident involving a dance with Miss Banner inside the club earlier. Shortly after the fracas, Miss Banner disappeared. Mr. McDermott, too, is on the missing list. Tucci issued a terse statement in answer to questions about Miss Banner's probable whereabouts and plans: 'I believe,' said the former singer, 'she's made a commitment to do a film for an independent company—' "

"What?" Maggie said. Her face expressed total surprise as the commentator continued reading Raffaello's quote:

" '. . . something called *The Booking Agent*. She's tired of doing comedy and wants now to do a really serious film. That's all I know about her plans,' Tucci said."

Before the sentence was finished Maggie had gasped and was standing by the sofa. "Christ!" Her reaction was so violent—she had almost jumped to her feet—that Kelly found himself standing beside her. "Oh, Raf . . ." she muttered. The color was completely drained from her face. After a moment she moved to the television set as if she were in a trance, fumbling with the knobs distractedly until she'd managed to switch it off. She remained standing by the set in a daze, the fingers of one hand curled together and raised to her lips. After a while she moved her head back and forth slowly several times, as if she were denying something, or perhaps canceling out a thought.

She appeared so oblivious of Kelly's presence that he said her name tentatively, the way one would wake up a sleepwalker: "Maggie . . . ?" They stood where they were for a long time until he repeated in a louder voice: "Maggie, are you—"

She snapped her head around. "Hmn," she muttered. Her eyes were glazed, he could tell she wasn't really seeing him. "What?" she asked.

"Are you all right?"

"All right?" she repeated as if by rote. She shook her head briskly to clear her vision.

"Are you all right?" he repeated.

"Of course I'm all right," she said, almost sharply. She was seeing him now, and in a moment she was smiling. "Well, now . . ." She said, clasping her hands together. She started to walk toward Kelly, then abruptly stopped as she saw the confusion on his face and remembered her behavior was unaccounted for. "Oh, that," she said, waving a hand in the direction of the television set, "surprised me, that's all. I didn't really want—" She broke off, leaving the sentence unfinished.

Kelly wanted to ask what specifically surprised her, but her attitude discouraged questioning. Walking briskly toward the bedroom, she said, "I've just one more errand to attend to. You'll be all right for a while, won't you?"

He started to reply but realized, as she shut the door behind her, the question had been rhetorical. In less than five minutes she was on her way out as Miss Vaughn. Her leave-taking was distracted, her good-bye spoken more as a duty than anything else.

For the first time her disguise failed to strike Kelly as slightly frivolous; instead it seemed to be in deadly earnest. He also sensed somewhere not far beneath the surface of Maggie Banner a panic, kept tightly reined, but there nevertheless. Perhaps this was responsible for her kaleidoscopic behavior.

Raffaello had spent a blurred and not unpleasant afternoon awaiting her call. He continued drinking but he'd also eaten well: oysters, a minute steak, a green salad and coffee.

He'd sent for a masseur, too, and had a brisk shower followed by a soothing rubdown.

It was the same treatment he used to accord himself when preparing to sing at the opera. He was, in fact, preparing for Maggie. To guarantee his message reaching her he had phoned several other members of the press for wider circulation. He was positive he would hear from her. So certain was he, that he had finally left instructions with the operator not to put through anyone except Maggie Banner and Morty, his man in the field.

He didn't wait in vain; at twenty after seven the phone sounded. He let the operator ring several times, then waited through a short series of emergency bleats before picking it up. "Miss Banner on the line, Mr. Tucci!" The operator's voice was tinged with excitement, amounting to complicity.

Then a buzzing click and he heard the familiar husky voice: "Raf?"

One word and his scalp tightened and seemed to lift up off his head. "Maggie . . ." he said.

There was a pause and he heard her exhale a long breath. "Oh, Raf . . . how could you?" The words were spoken not with strength or anger but in a tone of sad resignation, not of reprimand as much as pity, and what was worse, pity for him.

He was stabbed, flattened, made ashamed in the pit of his stomach. He could only clear his throat and strike back at her with a forced brusqueness he was somehow able to summon up: "Come over and we'll talk about it."

"Oh, Raf," she said; again the same, sad, empty, almost detached sound.

"I said come over and—"

But he heard the phone click off and then a dial tone. He was left numbed by the brevity of their exchange. He stared at the receiver in his hand. The buzzing, like an angry fly, irritated him, but still he held it until he heard a click and a crackle, and knowing the operator would come back on, he quickly put the phone down.

Still he thought—*forced* himself to think—her hanging up

didn't necessarily mean she wouldn't appear. His ploy had got to her, of that he was sure; she wouldn't let it rest at that. He knew how quickly her mood could change. She'd have a drink or two, get her dander up, hop in a cab, and come tearing over to give him holy hell. They'd have a fine scrap, words flying, threats and counterthreats; then one or the other would say something ridiculous or non sequitur and in a second they'd be roaring with laughter and fall into each other's arms.

He poured himself a drink, only a small one. Just hearing her voice was plasma to him; the lifeline was still open; she'd arrive soon, he knew it.

CHAPTER 17

"Good Lord," Maggie said, taking in the enormous swirling concrete ramps as they stepped into the air terminal. "Why don't they make buildings that look like buildings anymore? Airports, banks, even churches—they're all getting to look like the inside of a whale's mouth."

When Maggie returned to the hotel from her last outing, her mood had changed entirely. She'd ordered a pitcher of daiquiris, and they'd each had three before leaving. Now Kelly was off the ground, high-spirited, feeling the adventure of setting off on a trip, albeit with a touch of the surreal, heightened by the unaccustomed sensation of a hat atop his head, glasses balanced on his nose, and, of course, there next to him, Maggie Banner, submerged in the looks, accent and clipped manner of Miss Vaughn as they crossed the floor, following the porter to the check-in counter.

She scanned to the left and right. "Wonder if he would have the airport watched?" she mused. "In Rome we had a battle and he actually had me tailed on a tour of the Vatican. Probably thought I was going to have a *really* private audience with the Pope." She chuckled. "Actually, I did, but that was later—Raf was there, too." She squeezed Kelly's hand. "That's one of the dear goddamn things about him. He was so nervous, so nervous! I thought he was going to *throw up* on the ring." She sighed: "Oh, well, they'd never spot me in this getup."

Outside of the cab ride, this was Kelly's first public appearance with her in disguise and he was highly aware of it. Entering the terminal, Kelly was struck by the sensation that they were stepping onto a brightly lighted sound stage: lights, camera, action. In the hotel during the day he'd come to think of these new friends as the Maggie Banner Players. He'd kept himself on the outside looking in, but here he was bobbing along now in costume, an active card-carrying member himself.

As Maggie tended to the porter and Kelly moved up to the ticket counter, he was extremely self-conscious. Feeling more like a disembodied hat and a pair of glasses than an entire person, he wondered if that's how he appeared to the young man who took his ticket. Maggie stepped up next to him as the man tagged his suitcase, stapled the check to the envelope, and handed it back to Kelly with a smile and: "Mr. Helm . . ."

"Hmn?" Kelly muttered, looking confused.

"That's fine, darling," Maggie cut in, giving him a little nudge to the side and handing her ticket to the man. Kelly suddenly remembered he was traveling under the name of George Helm and he was embarrassed that he'd forgotten. Again Maggie nudged him and he followed her glance as she nodded to a newspaper lying open on the lower inside counter next to the clerk's elbow. He could make out, between individual photographs of Maggie Banner and Raffaello Tucci, a picture of himself originally taken for an employee's booklet by Parade Paperbacks.

Maggie gave him a conspiratorial wink and he grinned in return. "Miss Vaughn," the clerk said, handing her ticket back, "your plane should be boarding now, Gate three. Have a good trip!"

Walking toward the ramp leading to the departure gate,

Maggie took his arm. "Little does he know," she said out of the side of her mouth, "that the innocent pair he so casually checked in are, in reality, Typhoid Mary and the Mad Bomber!" Five nuns scurried down the concrete ramp toward them; with their feet invisible beneath their long black habits, they appeared to be gliding on ball bearings. "Penguins—look at them," Maggie whispered. After they'd rolled past, she added: "Some of them are terrors, you know. Absolute terrors. Still, you have to love them—Brides of Christ. Friends of mine wouldn't fly on the same plane with one for a million dollars!"

After passing through security and checking in at the gate, they started walking down the forward gangway. Maggie squeezed his arm. "Catch the smile, twenty-nine percent less cavities in her group." A pretty blond stewardess stood in the entrance to the plane proper, the full beam of her dazzling professional smile lighting up the passageway. "Know why she's so happy?" Maggie whispered. "She's delighted to have a few suckers trapped on the plane with her. If *she's* going down, the more the merrier!"

They were welcomed aboard and shown to their seats three-quarters of the way back in the nearly empty first-class cabin. They'd no sooner taken off their coats and settled down when Maggie turned to him. "I didn't ask you—do you like to fly?"

"Well, I—no, not particularly," Kelly admitted.

"Great!" she cried out, leaning in and pecking him on the cheek. "Scares me to death every time we take off and land. In between, too. I just don't believe these huge monsters that weigh as much as an office building can get up in the air, let alone stay there—without divine intervention. If God had meant us to fly, he'd have given us tickets—right?"

"Right," he laughed.

They heard the muffled clamping sound of the plane door being closed. "Look, our umbilical's cut," she said. The accordion-pleated gangway retracted slowly, swinging horizontally toward the building. She patted Kelly's knee. "If you want to get out now, you'll have to parachute." Then she cocked her head to the side. "My God, do you realize I've practically *kidnapped* you?"

"Yes," he grinned.

"Well, why not?" she shrugged. "I've done everything else!" Every so often Maggie's voice dropped to her chest in a throwaway reading, reminding him of Tallulah Bankhead, whom he'd seen in *Lifeboat* and *A Royal Scandal.* As the plane moved out onto the broad expanse of field, she took his hand and squeezed it tightly. "Christ, it's good to be getting away. I'm excited!"

"I am, too." He wanted to add: about you. But he couldn't quite hear himself saying it. In an instant he recognized Maggie's most appealing quality: her complete and immediate reaction to each and every stimulus—the terminal, the ticket clerk, the nuns, the stewardess, flying. Wide open to the moment, she seized every second as if it were a strange and brightly colored piece of glass that had to be examined for its particular place in the mosaic of the day.

When the plane approached the runway, Maggie turned to him excitedly. "Let's knock ourselves out! We neither one of us are wild about flying. It's night, anyway, so we won't be seeing the wonders of the Grand Canyon or the Dallas A and P." She unsnapped a large leather tote bag and dug around in it. "We'll get us a little buzz on and sleep the trip away, be all fresh when we get there—if that is His will," she added.

"Where?" he asked.

"San Diego."

"I mean, where are we going after that?"

"Oh," she shrugged, sorting through a tortoiseshell pill-box, "you've gone along this far, let it be a surprise."

He sensed from the way she spoke this was her only reason for not telling him. "All right," he replied.

"Here." She handed him a round, white pill. "Doriden, not too strong, not too weak. But if we have a couple of drinks and keep talking, we can get a lovely jag on." She wagged a finger at him. "Must keep talking though, otherwise you just pass out—no jag." She took a silver flask from her purse and unscrewed the top. Popping the pill into her mouth, she washed it down with a quick gulp. "Kelly?" She handed him the flask and he followed suit. The whiskey fired his mouth and throat, scorching a path to his stomach and making him cough. He waved a hand in front of his mouth to cool the stinging membranes. "Good boy," Maggie said; "take another." He drank again and handed the flask back to Maggie, who tilted it up to her mouth.

The jet engines accelerated to fever pitch, the plane lifted up, came to attention and began its heavy, lumbering movement down the runway. "If you don't *mind!*" Maggie said, offering a hand, then clutching his when he reached over. "I also wouldn't mind if you'd lift up your feet—we need all the help we can get, you know." She slapped him on the knee with her free hand and although it was silly, of course, they both raised their feet as they felt the plane fight the pull of gravity and lift tentatively off the ground. "Umm," Maggie groaned, "higher, just a little more, come on, there's a good baby!" In a sudden spurt of freedom, no longer acknowledging its weight, the plane soared out and away, completely airborne. "We did it," Maggie said, shaking the hand she'd been holding. "Congratulations. I really feel I should get a discount for all the work I do on these damned things."

"That's another thing about Raf—" She stopped abruptly. "You don't mind me talking about him, do you?" Answering herself, she said: "Of course not, why should you—I'm with you, not him. It's Raf wouldn't care to hear about *you!* Anyhow, the first time we flew, from L.A. to New York, I was going through my usual panic during takeoff and there was Raf calmly reading this book. 'Well,' I said, 'you're not going to read during takeoff, are you?' 'Sure,' he said, about as cool as one can say sure. I grabbed a hand, he kept his eyes glued to the book, and after the plane was up there I glanced over to see what he was reading and the goddamn book was upside down! He was on hold, totally out of it. Just sitting there with an upside-down book! Mr. Tough Guy—you have to love it!"

They unsnapped their safety belts and made themselves

comfortable. "So," Maggie sighed, "here we are, phase one of kidnapping completed. Tell me, if someone had told you twenty-four hours ago you'd be on a plane to San Diego— what would you have said?"

"I wouldn't have believed it."

"And now?"

He shook his head. "I still don't believe it. It's not possible. I've probably been knocked down by a truck and I'm lying in a hospital with a ca-concussion. I'll wake up soon and there'll be a starched nurse standing over me saying—"

"Would you care for a drink?" It was the smiling stewardess. They laughed and ordered and when they'd been served and the stewardess went to get their trays of hors d'oeuvres, Maggie said: "Oh, how I'd like to wipe that smile off her face. There's about as much joy there as a garbage strike. Lord, I bet she makes whoever gets a little of that pay for it!" Maggie shuddered at the probable toll, clicked her glass against Kelly's and they sipped. "Here's to you," she said, once more squeezing his hand. "Good Lord, have you noticed how I can't keep my hands off you?" She pinched his forearm. "I insist upon grabbing you, pawing you. Could it be your charm, your brain or your cologne?" She took his chin in her hand and turned his face to her; she touched him so freely, she could have known him for years. "Or is it that one lone dimple that drives me wild?" She looked at him closely, then released him. "You're blushing."

"What do you expect?" he asked. "I can't ta-tell"—Maggie could not resist smiling—"when you're serious and when you're kidding."

And Maggie thought she could not remember when she'd met anyone so appealing. "When I'm kidding, as I was then," she said, "I'm usually serious, as I am now."

"I liked that . . . what you said." He ventured a further comment. "You say what you mean, don't you? Or did I mean—you mean what you say? Or both—yes, both." He raised a hand to his forehead. "I'm beginning to feel . . . funny."

"It's the pill," Maggie said, "and the drinks; they're getting together."

"Do you feel that way, too?"

"A little bit," she said. "We must keep talking."

"For how long?"

"Until we can't. Go ahead, I want to know all about you."

He cleared his throat. "How did you get the—how did you allow yourself to . . . *kidnap* someone you didn't know?"

She thought for a moment. "Same thing that allows me to say what I mean, or mean what I say."

"What's that?"

"Circumstances." She shrugged.

"But now," Kelly said, "you're not saying what you mean."

"Yes, I am."

"But you're being . . . vague—no, cryptic."

"Mmn, perhaps."

"Won't you tell me wha-what circumstances?"

"No." She sat looking straight ahead; after a moment she turned to him and smiled. "Everyone has special circumstances. For instance, how did you begin to stutter?"

He laughed. "Circumstances." In response to her wry glance, he added, "Which I'll tell you about."

"Funny circumstances?" she asked.

"Oh, no—no, no," he laughed again.

"But you're laughing."

"I know, but they're not. Are yours?"

"What?"

"Funny circumstances?"

And now Maggie laughed. "Oh, God, no!"

"If we both have unfunny circumstances, why are we laughing?" Kelly asked, feeling groggy and talkative at the same time. "And another question: if our circumstances aren't funny—what an odd word, *circumstances*—if they're not funny, how is it this all seems to be . . ." He rubbed a hand over his forehead.

"Seems to be what?" Maggie asked.

"A comedy," he grinned.

"Oh—oh," she said, "didn't you know?"

"What?"

"Life is a tragedy played out by comedians."

The stewardess returned with trays, a shrimp salad, cheeses, crudités, caviar and other appetizers. The smile never left her face no matter what she did, and she did everything with the utmost efficiency. As they ordered their main courses, the loudspeaker crackled and a good old boy's voice, dripping in homespun warmth and southern comfort greeted them: "Hello, there, this is your captain speaking. We sure do hope you all are gonna enjoy our flight this evening. We're mighty happy to have you on board. The weather out west is a darned sight better than what we're leavin' in the Big Apple—"

"Christ," Maggie said, "I hope we're not going to be exposed to a lot of cockpit charm. I wish they'd just fly the goddamn thing and leave the talking to us."

"What was that?" the stewardess asked.

"I said," Maggie looked her in the eye, "he sounds like a real pain in the ass!"

Without a fraction of her smile fading or the flicker of an eyelash, she replied: "He is!" and walked up the aisle.

"Oh, well, hell, she's won me over. She's absolutely heaven. What was I talking about? I was all ready to tangle with her. See how life constantly throws up little surprises."

Her switch on the stewardess endeared her even more to Kelly. She was not intractable.

"How do you feel?" Maggie asked.

Kelly took a deep breath. "I freel—"

"Perfect," she laughed. "Perfect—enough said."

"I feel," he enunciated carefully, "fuzzy and . . . *detached,* yes, detached from all frames of references I've ever known—unreal, I guess."

"Is that good or bad?"

"That's *good.*" He grinned. He looked around at the softly lit interior of the plane and out the small window at the cold billion-starred backdrop for the blackness of the night. He glanced at Maggie, who was observing him; it seemed to

Kelly she might be reading his thoughts and he didn't mind in the least. In case she wasn't he continued: "I'm having an experience. No, an event. I like it." A rush of optimism flooded over him; he felt incredibly safe and cloistered and he thought to himself: I can say anything; I don't have a si-lencer on me; besides, up this high, hurtling through space faster than the speed of a bicycle, it doesn't even count. And he gave voice to his thoughts: "I could say anything."

She smiled, then she leaned into him. "Tell me about your father. It's been killing me. Tell me some of your darkest secrets, go ahead. I mean, what else can we do up here? I suppose we could pray our way to San Diego but that would be so repetitive." She touched his arm. "Go ahead!"

Her enthusiasm was obvious. In the event she must find out about his inadequacy, despite the promising beginning in the hotel, he decided to tell her as much about himself as possible. "I'll tell you a secret."

CHAPTER 18

He sat there, thinking where to begin, how to begin. The stewardess brought their food; Maggie fell all over herself being nice to her. When she'd left, Maggie sensed his hesitancy. "All right, we'll start off with a few questions—where born?"

"Lemming, New Jersey."

"I don't know why, but that sounds tacky," she said, not cruelly, but with candor.

Kelly almost spit up his first forkful. "It was, it is!"

"And your father—doctor, lawyer, crook?"

"No, a minister."

"A minister?" She repeated it with enthusiasm. "A *minister*—of course that *could* fall into the latter category. Hmn, what must it be like to have a minister for a father?"

"I'll tell you!" he said with emphasis.

"Siblings?"

"One brother; I was four when he died. I remember him vaguely . . . but I heard of him endlessly. My father worshiped him. The only thing he would have accepted was an exact duplicate and I was far from that."

"How old was your brother when he died?"

"Sa-seventeen. See, I stutter when I talk about it. Freddie was away at his first year of college. He was a whiz, a fine student, but an extraordinary athlete, full scholarship in football. He came home for Christmas vacation. He and my father had built a tree house in this giant oak in our back-yard. I guess he just climbed up in the tree house to check it out. I'd been given a tricycle; I was riding it up the driveway. A dog, just a neighborhood dog, wandered back and sta-started to chew at my pants. I must have gotten frightened and I kicked at him. He growled, showed his teeth and snapped at me. I screamed and my brother started to climb down to get the dog away just as my father, who'd heard me yelling, came out on the back porch. My brother lost his footing right at the top. He fell and ha-hit his head on the edge of a flagstone patio. He never came to. He la-lived a few days in a coma, but—" He shook his head and left the sentence unfinished.

Maggie reached over and touched his arm. "And your father saw it happen?"

"Yes. That was our Pearl Harbor, my father's and mine. Only being a man of God, he couldn't declare outright war, it had to be under the surface. I don't think he hated me until I was older. He was disappointed in me, but he didn't hate me until later."

"Being a man of God, he shouldn't have hated."

"He did. Most of all, I remember my father would sit out on the back porch with a glass of wine—he liked his wine— and he'd look up at that tree sometimes for an hour until it was dark. I loved winter because it was too cold for him to sit back there. He'd sit in the parlor by the fire. I dreaded the coming of spring, knowing he'd be out on the porch soon, sitting in his white wicker chair, staring up at that tree house."

"But that's brutal—it should have been taken down," Maggie said.

Kelly nodded. "My mother tried, but he wouldn't hear of it. The tree house was a shrine to Freddie. But you see," he turned to Maggie, "when I was small, it never occurred to me my father was not a good man. He worked for God Himself, so he had to be kind and just and right in all things. I didn't catch on until much later. And he was a good minister. He—"

"He couldn't have been," Maggie said firmly.

"Yes, to his parishioners he was. He served them as a man would his family. And my mother and I, we were two people who tried to serve *him;* we were two people who disappointed him. We were two people he could ta-take out his—" He paused and a look of confusion clouded his face.

"Take out what?"

"I don't know. I—I think he came to regard us as his cross to bear. He could forgive many weaknesses, almost any failings among his flock, but when he got home he wanted perfection in his wife and son. There was only one thing he had no tolerance of—that was illness."

"Illness!" Maggie sat up straight. "But illness—"

"I know," he said, "is something one can't help. But imperfection in the physical body, not quite so much in an outsider, but in his family, amounted to—he took it as a personal affront. And I obliged him by catching almost every childhood sickness a boy could have: measles, chicken pox, mumps, whooping cough. And when I exhausted those, I came up with jaundice and had to be taken out of school for a year. That was when he began to ha-hate me, I believe. But all my illnesses were only a prelude to my stutter. That was the final outrage."

"Kelly," she said, reaching over and touching his arm, "what did he look like?"

Kelly glanced up at the ceiling, squinting his eyes as if he could bring the image of his father into focus there. "Tall, about six two; his body was lean but the frame of it was large. But his head didn't go with his body. It was too small; not the forehead or cheekbones, but his eyes were small and round and gray—turtle eyes—and the lower part of his face was out of proportion. His mouth was too small to contain his teeth; his lips were thin and his chin was short in the distance between the bottom of it and his mouth. The set of it was strong, but it was small and that made it . . . ma-mean looking. His neck was long and thin and held his head too far up from his body. Almost a cartoonist's head on Lincoln's body."

Kelly laughed. "His Adam's apple was enormous. We went to the county fair once and you know those—like huge thermometers? You strike a block at the bottom with a mallet and try to make the ball inside bounce up and ring the bell at the top?" She nodded. "Watching that, I thought: I'll bet if I hit my fa-father on the toe with a mallet, his Adam's apple would pop up and shatter his chin."

They both laughed. "Not at all how I pictured him, but what do I know? It's fascinating, it's all fascinating," Maggie said. "Do you mind, but I'm eating it up?"

"No," he smiled. He was experiencing a definite relish communicating his impressions to her—in a way, entertaining her. The pill and the alcohol were working now. His mouth was dry, his speech felt a bit thick, but he did indeed have a talking jag on. "This stuff—the combination is . . . heady! Can you get hooked on this?"

"No," she laughed, "this is only an in-flight situation." She touched his leg. "Go on."

"He wanted me to be an athlete, because that's what Freddie was. But I was a puny kid and—"

"Puny!" Maggie exclaimed. "You've got a good body; we checked you out last night; not a muscle builder's but such a lean, hard body."

"I've worked at it, but when I was a kid, I was skinny and weak and his hopes for me were so strong—they overpowered me, they attacked my nerves and my nerves wrecked what coordination I had. I tried to compensate by becoming an excellent student. I'd settle for nothing less than straight A's. When I'd bring my report card to my father, I was bringing him a gift."

"And it didn't please him?" Maggie asked.

"Yes, but not to the extent I wanted it to. But by that time my stutter had begun and that was the final straw." He turned to her quickly. "I didn't tell you he had a fine voice, deep and mellow like a lion; he could preach and talk extemporaneously for hours. I stacked myself up against him in so many ways: would I ever grow as tall, would my voice become as deep as his; not only tha-that but would I ever be able to summon up all those words and keep pouring them out?

"I first began to stutter in school when I was called on to recite. When I was in the eighth grade it ca-came upon me like an epidemic. By summer, the summer before high school, I was pretty much tongue-tied."

"Oh, Kelly . . . Kelly. But didn't they take you to specialists?"

"Yes, finally in Lemming and then Philadelphia. The stutter leveled off after a while so I could speak, but it was painful for me. It was also painful for those who had to listen to it. I learned to live with it and myself. I was always a heavy reader, but now I swallowed books one after the other.

"My stutter drove my father wild. When I'd get stuck on a word I could tell he had to refrain from slapping it out of me, so nothing could really help as long as I was living in that three-story Victorian battleground—with him."

"You've hardly spoken of your mother," Maggie said.

"She was almost in direct contrast to my father. She was short and pretty, in a way. She had a round face, large soft eyes, a very natural smile, beautiful skin. She was like a—I don't know, I always thought of her as a wren. I could never imagine the two of them meeting and courting. She must have loved him at first, but later on she was afraid of him.

"I think she was in awe of being married to a man of God. Almost like she fell in la-love with an *ordinary* man and after they were married—found out he was a minister. I think she was in awe of having children by a minister, shocked that one of them should be taken away from them, and saddened that the other should be constantly nagged by illness. And confused that she, too, was afflicted by a disease.

"When she first got 'flutters'—that's what she called

them—around her heart, she refused to believe it. This was several years after my brother died. 'Dizzy spells,' she used to say. 'I had one of my dizzy spells.' She blamed them on a bad sense of balance. 'I could never ride a bicycle, even as a young girl,' she'd say.

"She finally confessed to *me* that she did, in fact, have a bad heart, and we tried to keep it from him. I'm sure he sensed it, but he wouldn't permit himself to acknowledge it openly. Then one day, one Saturday afternoon, it fluttered right into an attack. I was upstairs. I heard a crash, followed by a thud.

"Then I heard footsteps and my father's voice. 'Loretta, get up! Get up, Loretta!' He was chiding her.

"I ran downstairs. She was lying in front of the stove ga-gasping for breath. There on the floor was a pot roast and a little pool of gravy and some carrots and potatoes scattered about. She was gasping for breath, her hand over her chest, and I started to go to her. 'Wait!' my father said, and he stepped closer to her, looking down at her, his face angry-red. 'Loretta,' he asked, 'are you sick? *Are you sick!*' " Kelly laughed nervously. "And—and I thought if she said yes, he'd actually kick her, lying there like that, panting, eyes flutter-ing, one leg in the gravy, like some poor bird that had crashed into the wall and dropped to the floor.

"I ran and called the doctor and after he came we finally got her to bed. I stayed with her while my father had a long talk with him and when the doctor came back into her room, you know what she asked him? Not—is it bad, will I be all right? She said: 'You didn't tell him, did you?' *You didn't tell him, did you,*" Kelly repeated, laughing nervously. "She'd been lying on the floor surrounded by the evening meal and: 'You didn't tell him, did you?'

"Even after that, I never saw her take one of those little pills in front of him. Never. If we were all out driving in the car and she got breathy, she'd say she had to go to the rest room and he'd stop at a gas station. It remained a fluttery heart to the end—until it fluttered out."

Kelly shrugged. "From then on my father was happier

away from home. When he was at church or out working with his parishioners or serving on committees. When he came home he was entering a disaster area, as if, with our afflictions, we'd actually conspired against him."

CHAPTER 19

Kelly turned, looking out the small window at the black night; there was no moon yet, but a billion stars were out; however, they burned with the white cold of diamonds beyond the blackness. Maggie thought he might be talked out for the present. He surprised her, turning with a grin: "The greatest thing about the past is that it's just that—past. I wouldn't want to la-live through it again for—" he hesitated "—all the chocolate malteds in the world!"

She grinned back at him. "What about friends?"

"Not many; I was a loner—it was the stutter mainly. One fellow, Kelly Munroe—I took my first name from him; it was David, David Greenall, but I changed it after what happened. Kelly was a great fellow, totally uncomplicated, moved to our block my sophomore year. He taught me how to play tennis. Another boy, Jason Kipps, a sensitive boy with a slightly gimpy leg and an alcoholic father. It was obvious my father didn't approve of him, so he didn't come over to my house much. Because Jason was ashamed of his father, I never went over there much. We mostly went to the movies together—we were movie friends."

"Was there never a girl?"

He turned to Maggie and his face lit up. "I was coming to her. Bethel, Bethel Anders. She was beautiful, in a special way, a calm beauty—chestnut hair, wide forehead, large blue-gray eyes. So poised it was almost unnatural for a teen-ager. She moved to town my senior year. I saw her walking down the hall the first day of school that September and I was in love. All day I kept hoping she'd turn up in one of my classes, but she didn't. I was miserable.

"Then the following Sa-Sunday she walked into our church, my father's church, with her parents. She looked at me and smiled—she recognized me and smiled. I got hot and cold running . . . everythings! I decided to play a game. I'd build up a romance with her in my mind, postpone for as long as possible letting her know I stuttered. After the service I saw my father welcoming her parents and I disap-peared. This went on for several weeks." Kelly laughed. "Oh, kids can be foxy. I'd see her in the halls or at lunch period and we'd smile and nod, but I'd keep my distance. She seemed to be a loner, too. She made one close friend, Mary Murphy, but that was all. After a while I could tell she was as much aware of me as I was of her. I didn't want to lead her on and disappoint her, so I decided to speak to her the following Sunday at church and la-let her in on my prob-lem."

Kelly's face clouded over; he took a deep breath and when he spoke again his voice was low and flat in tone. "That Tuesday noon we had an all-school assembly. A man and his wife and their trained dogs, little mixed breeds who opened gates, played house, pushed shopping carts, and a seal who played catch with the man and honked out a couple of tunes on a set of old-fashioned car horns. The star of their act, and the clown, was a girl chimpanzee named Alice. She wore a red skirt with suspenders, a white blouse, and underneath she had on blue panties, all very patriotic. When she wasn't actually doing her act, she sat in a little rocking chair to the side of the stage. If the dogs or the seal received applause for whatever tricks they did, Alice would jump up from her chair and lift her dress up, showing off her blue underpants.

"You can imagine how that went over with an auditorium full of high school kids. They clapped and howled and the woman would rush over and sit Alice down, scolding her like it hadn't been planned that way at all."

Kelly turned to Maggie and she thought she had never seen a face so darkly masked, his expression entirely out of keeping with this tale of a performing girl chimpanzee named Alice.

"The seniors sat in front of the auditorium; because Bethel's last name began with A, she sat in the front row. I sat about five rows behind her. The seal was winding up his act, slowly making it through 'America the Beautiful' on the horns. When he finished he smacked his flippers together, applauding himself. The kids clapped and Alice jumped up and lifted her red dress up, showing her blue panties for about the eighth time. The woman pushed her down in the chair and stood over her, wagging a finger in her face.

"There was a murmur to the left, down front in the audience. I heard someone shout, 'Hey!' Someone else giggled and the murmur grew. I looked over and Bethel was standing up—moving very slowly forward between the first row and the stage, which was raised about three or four feet. The spill from the stage lights struck her hair, highlighting it.

"I couldn't imagine what she was doing. I looked back up to the stage and the woman was no longer scolding Alice, she was standing there looking toward Bethel, a hand raised to shield her eyes from the lights. Because the show had been interrupted, someone called out, 'Sit down!' Then one section of kids in the rear began stomping their feet on the floor.

"The woman started walking toward where Bethel was standing. She took only a few steps when she stopped in her tracks. Bethel was standing there, arms rigidly outstretched now, clutching the hem of her skirt, raising it in the air." Kelly shook his head. "I don't tha-think—I don't ever remember being so shocked.

"The sound of seats clattered; kids in the back were stand-

ing up to see what was going on. Just then, those sort of
. . . harsh yellow auditorium lights went on. There she was
for all to see, standing there, holding up her skirt, showing
part of a slip and white underpants. Well, lots of kids
laughed, some even applauded and whistled. Alice, the
chimp, took this as another cue and jumped up and raised
her skirt. A roar went up from the auditorium as several
teachers rushed down the aisle from the back.

"The noise from the crowd surprised Bethel; she spun
around to face the auditorium and let go of her skirt. There
was a gasp as she stood there, her carriage perfectly erect,
head up, looking for all the world like a younger, prettier—it
sounds crazy—but Mona Lisa. A faint trace of a smile on her
face, a little smile of almost pleasant surprise as if she were
thinking: oh, you're here, I didn't know you were here.

"Then the teachers, two down the side aisle, one rushing
down the middle one, caught her attention and their running seemed to frighten her. Her eyes widened, her mouth
opened, and strange strangulated sounds came from her
throat. The first teacher that got to her shoved a slim book in
her mouth. I guess to keep her from swallowing her tongue.
By that time the others had grabbed her and she went completely out of control, twisting and wrenching, as they
started to drag her away. By that time the place was pande-
monium. I couldn't watch—couldn't stand seeing any more.
I ran up the aisle and home."

"Was it epilepsy?" Maggie asked.

Kelly nodded. "All that evening I planned what I'd say to
her. See, if I exposed my stutter now, if I handed it to her on
a platter, it would be too obvious, like saying: 'See, we both
have—' " Kelly shrugged in a gesture of helplessness. "Yet I
wanted to let her know. I had such an affinity for her. Now I
really loved her.

"She didn't show up at school for several days. In the
meantime—" he shook his head "—kids are so cruel—God,
the way they went on about that. You'd think that was the
only thing that happened all fall. Anyhow, about three days

later I turned the corner changing classes and practically bumped into her. There we were, face to face. She was immaculately dressed, as always; the only difference after that first attack was a heightened color in her cheeks, as if she'd merely decided to change the shade of her makeup, but that didn't alter her calm or poise.

"I realized I was the one who was blushing. Finally I summoned up courage to say something brilliant. I said, 'Hi.' She smiled and said, 'Hello.' About that time a covey of dizzy girls swirled by, giggling, hands to their stupid mouths. It was obvious what they were giggling about. We both looked down until they'd gone by. When she looked back at me she saw how ill at ease I was. I think she was about to move on, but I refused to let them sabotage our meeting. I blurted out, 'My name's—' But do you think I could say it?" He laughed. "I could not get the word out, all I could do was stand there and repeat, 'Da-da-da-da-da-da—' I'd wanted to stutter in front of her, to let her know, but I didn't want to sound like a complete basket case. I finally started over. 'David's my name!' I said."

Again Maggie saw his face settled over by a long-ago sadness. "She was confused. She didn't know I stuttered; I could tell by the expression in her eyes. It hit me as we stood there, if she'd only known before, it might have been a bond between us. The way it was now, it was simply wrong, we both felt it. I could tell."

"Didn't she say anything?"

"Yes. Even though I was tongue-tied, I was trying desperately to think of something to say, when the bell rang. 'I'll be late for class,' she said. 'Me, too,' I replied. And she left."

Maggie touched his hand. "But surely in time, you—"

"There wasn't much time left that fall. Oh, we still nodded to each other for the little time she remained in school, but then about five weeks later, in November, it happened again. Thank God, I'd had the flu and was still home recuperating. Because this time it happened in church, my father's church."

"Oh, Christ!" Maggie blurted out.

"Exactly," Kelly said. After they both laughed, he looked at her and said, "I don't believe I'm sitting here on a plane telling my life story to someone I've only known for twenty-four hours—not only that, I don't even know where I'm *going!* I don't believe it!"

"Ah-hah, but that's the sort of thing that keeps us young. Oh, for the life of a swinger—the same old differentness day after day."

The stewardess, beaming as usual, came to take their trays. "Thank you very much," Maggie said, adding: "You know, you have a fantastic smile."

"I'm sure," the stewardess laughed. "I just had four caps put on today; my mouth is riddled with Novocain; I can't do anything with my upper lip, it's frozen."

She walked away as Maggie looked at Kelly and shook her head, laughing at the same time. "See, the infinite surprises He has in store for us!" Then suddenly remembering, she grasped Kelly's arm. "In your father's church!"

"Yes," he said, shaking his head and blinking his eyes. "Anyhow—" He rubbed his forehead. "This combination is terrific; I feel like I'm on a submarine instead of a plane now. Everything's muffled. I think I'm beginning to wind down—like an old Victrola that's running out of . . . wind!"

"Try, force yourself," Maggie said, elbowing him gently.

"I wasn't there, so I didn't see it, but my mother did. Bethel had an attack while my father was announcing the week's upcoming activities. She got up and wandered in the aisle—before her parents could get to her. She'd been sitting with this friend, Mary Murphy. When they did try to get her out of church, she went all out of control. My father apparently didn't react too well."

He cleared his throat. "Anyhow, we usually had our Sunday dinner at four. I came down in my bathrobe and slippers; I was helping my mother set the table when she said, 'Your father's very upset; something happened in church. That pretty little Anders girl had a bad attack and—'

"I'd been upstairs in my bedroom all day; I hadn't known. 'Is she all right?' I asked.

" 'Is she all right!' It was my father's voice from the parlor. 'All right!' His voice dripped with contempt.

"And that was it, we were off and running. I suppose we'd been looking for an open escape valve for years and without even knowing it—we hit one.

"I thought maybe she'd been hurt. I walked past the parlor, mumbling something about, 'I'll call and find out,' and went toward the kitchen to use the phone.

" 'Where are you going?' he asked. He got up and followed me. I didn't answer him, but kept walking into the kitchen. I could feel him behind me as I picked up the phone. 'I forbid you to use it,' he said. I started to dial; I didn't even know her number and I knew I wouldn't get a chance to finish, but I had to display open defiance of him. He snatched it away from me and spun me around, shaking me by the shoulders. I heard my mother cry out, 'Frederick.'

" 'Stay away,' he called to her. Then to me: 'I might have known she'd be a friend of yours. You pick them, don't you?' I didn't answer him; he shook me violently. 'I suppose she's a *special* friend of yours. Is she a special friend of yours? Answer me!'

"I had only one answer for him: I hate you. But I could only say, 'I ha-ha-ha-ha . . .'

"He could tell from my expression what I wanted to say. He threw his head back and laughed. 'You can't even say it!' he roared at me. 'You can't even *say* it!'

"But I said it. 'Hate!' I screamed out. I didn't bother putting it in a sentence. 'Hate, hate, hate, hate, hate!' The more I said it, the louder he laughed. Soon he picked up the chantlike rhythm of it by clapping his hands together, applauding me. And there I was screaming 'Hate!' at him and my mother was hanging onto the kitchen doorway, ba-begging for us to stop.

"But I was determined to take the joke out of it for him. I stopped abruptly, just stopped and stared at him. He went on smacking his hands together, but after a while he must have felt ridiculous applauding all by himself and he stopped.

" 'Hate!' I screamed at him, wrenching it up from the pit of my stomach. I took a step toward him—he was across the room from me—I took a deep breath and there was no smile on his face when I delivered the word to him once more. Now he looked confused. 'David,' he said. And I thought: David will give you one more that will never stop echoing in this ha-house. I recoiled my entire body and screamed, 'HATE!' at him. I felt it tear from my throat.

"He leaned, almost fell back against a shelf and he looked frightened. And just as I was thinking I'd actually frightened him, I felt the warmth in my throat and saw the blood spurt out from my mouth onto the floor. And I thought, if it kills me it was worth it. My mother was screaming by this time—why she didn't have a heart attack I'll never know—and my father was dumbstruck.

"I thought: I'll get to the ha-hospital myself. I won't faint. I may drop *dead,* but I won't faint. I ran out of the house, still in my pajamas and bathrobe—St. Cecilia's Hospital was only four blocks away—and started to run down the sidewalk, blood still gushing out of me and down my front. After a block or so my fa-father came driving up alongside me, calling, 'David, David!' But I didn't look at him, I kept on running until I got to the side entrance and ducked in the hospital. A nurse grabbed me in the hallway and I passed out, but at least I did it without him. By the time he got there, I was in the emergency room. I'd ruptured a blood vessel."

"My God—" Maggie gasped. "Kelly, I—"

But he was too caught up in the reliving of it to stop. He was also working on his last stretch of energy; it was running out fast.

"I also heard later there was a nasty scene in the meeting room behind the church with Bethel's parents, after her attack had subsided. My father said or did something, I never found out exactly what. A Mr. and Mrs. Jackson, very nice, rich people, had become close friends of Bethel's parents. They were in church when it happened. Mr. Jackson had always been one of my father's prime fund raisers for the church. Whatever happened, my father so alienated the Jacksons they switched to another church. They never came back; of course, Bethel's parents didn't either.

"This was a blow to my father. He never got over it. And you know small towns? Lemming's not that small, about forty-five thousand, but the stain spread in little ways and na-nothing could wash it away. After that, my father liked his wine even more.

"When I got back to school after a week or so, I didn't see Bethel. I screwed up my courage that afternoon, looked up her parents' number in the phone book and called. Her mother said, 'Bethel's away at school. May I tell her who called?' I said, 'Yes, tell her David called.' Then I said, 'Tell her I'm sorry I didn't see her before she left.' I felt better, having done that."

"What about things with your father?" Maggie asked. "I mean after that happened?"

"From then on, I got a little more respect from him. We kept out of each other's way, gave each other more space."

"My God," Maggie said, "I wouldn't give that childhood to a nasty orphan."

Kelly grinned, then yawned. "Oh, I haven't even gotten to the grisly part yet!"

"You haven't? What about Bethel—is that the end of her?"

"No, well, it was for a while, until after graduation, but—no, she's part of it all." He covered his mouth and yawned again. "I feel like someone hit me over the head with a velvet mallet, a nice cushioned one, but I feel the hit even so."

"Haven't got to the *grisly* part," Maggie repeated, giving him a quick hug. "I can't wait, but I will. I will."

He was delighted with her curiosity, appreciative of her attention, and pleased that he could hold her as an audience of one. He was also feeling unburdened by several tons.

"Let's get comfy now." She snapped off the lights above

them, took blankets and pillows from the overhead rack, and tucked him in. She slipped off her shoes and curled her feet up under her, settling back in the seat up against him. The blackness outside the small window disturbed her, so she leaned forward and pulled the shade down. "Now," she said, leaning back into him again, "it's cozy."

She flexed her hand, spreading her fingers out over his leg, halfway between his knee and his groin. The response to her touch was immediate; even in his groggy, somnolent state he could feel the rush of blood, feel the pressure against his shorts and the pleasurable sleepy ache that followed. He reveled in the spontaneity of his reaction to her.

It was strange, this sensation, because this was the only part of him that was alive; the rest of him—brain, forehead, chin, neck, shoulders, arms, fingertips—was anesthetized and the total numbness of these parts seemed outside himself, looking in on the isolated arena of blood and muscle strength below.

When Maggie began to talk softly of the days they would spend together, he grinned and listened to her with forced concentration, but it was an uphill struggle against the drowsy contentment pressing down on him. Soon an entire sentence was too much to sort out and he could only reach out to grasp at phrases and then at individual words, which by this time seemed to have no relationship to one another.

When he was asleep, with the grin of an event still upon his face, she stopped speaking and gazed at him for a long time before leaning over and lightly brushing his cheek with her lips.

CHAPTER 20

By early evening Raffaello's nerves were badly frayed; no further word of Maggie. He'd tried phoning Arnold Lefkowitz again and was told he had left the office for the day. He'd found the lawyer's home number in Pound Ridge and called shortly after seven. A young boy answered the phone.

"Hello," Raf said, "is this the Viet Cong?" He remembered what a kick Maggie got out of the name.

"Yes," the boy giggled.

"May I speak with your daddy?"

"Sure, just a—" But the boy had been interrupted and a woman spoke next. "Hello . ... ?"

"May I speak to Arnold?"

"Who's calling?" she asked.

"Raffaello Tucci."

Not a moment's pause. "I'm sorry, Arnold's not home."

"Mrs. Lefkowitz?"

"Yes."

"We all had dinner together before Maggie and I left on our trip."

"Yes," was the answer, as chilly as it was noncommittal.

Raffaello guessed the word was out. "Your son led me to think Arnold was—"

"I'm sorry, he's not home."

The hostility in her voice prevented him from pressing the matter; he merely left word for Arnold to call when he came in. The moment he hung up he wished he'd opened up on her with the big guns. Now there was an organized conspiracy to keep him away from Maggie and strong feelings of persecution jabbed him.

Victor had called with tickets to the opera and he'd received other invitations from various friends, but he had courteously declined them all, claiming urgent business, long neglected while he was abroad, required his attention.

Raffaello possessed a formidable one-track mind which allowed him to think of nothing but his current obsession, and he was obsessed, as he never had been before, with Maggie Banner.

His obsessions, aided by small, ever-present voices whispering over and over again in his ear, worked for and against him. From the first day he began to study voice seriously he could hear them repeating: the Met, the Met, I'll get to the Met, I'll sing at the Met. And the rhythm of these inner voices, steady and reassuring in their persistence, propelled him toward his goal.

These same voices made it impossible for Raffaello to forget a slight, let alone a major wrong; they were responsible for the many acts of revenge he indulged in.

They also caused him to dwell unduly and miserably upon the misfortunes he'd suffered. For two years after his automobile accident, he was plagued by the perverse nagging of the voices reminding him he had caused his wife's death.

Only when he met Maggie and fell so completely under her spell did they begin to ease up on him.

Now the voices knew only her name: Maggie, Maggie, Maggie, Maggie . . .

At nine o'clock there was a knock on his door. "Yes?" There was no reply. "Who is it?" he asked. Still, no answer.

"Who's there?" he called. More gentle knocking. "Who is it!" He shot up out of his chair. "Maggie!" he shouted. "Maggie!" He rushed to the door and snatched it open.

An extremely pretty brunette, hatless and wearing a good mink coat, stood in the hall. She had a lovely complexion, a soft, dewy Irish look about her. "Nancy," she said, smiling and extending a gloved hand.

"Nancy?" he repeated.

"Yes, Nancy Donohue. May I come in?" She didn't wait for a reply but walked past him into the room. "Johnnie and Chuck sent me."

"Oh, Johnnie and Chuck," Raf said. "I talked to Johnnie earlier."

"I know, they wanted you to go out on the town. But since," she said, taking off her gloves, "you didn't seem interested, they thought you might like some company right here."

"Well . . ." he said, still not knowing how to react to her presence.

"May I?" she asked, getting out of her coat.

"Yes, of course," Raf replied, helping her, then putting the coat down across the back of a chair. When he turned around she was sitting on the sofa. She wore a simple, expensive gray wool dress. She didn't speak, only sat there smiling up at him. Large-eyed and lithe, she was a very pretty girl, indeed. He judged her to be no more than twenty-six or -seven. "Could I fix you a drink?" he asked.

"No, thanks. I don't drink, but you have one. Please," she added.

He picked up his glass and walked to the tray, wondering if she was really just a friend of Johnnie's and Chuck's or a high priced call girl. She didn't look like a call girl, no matter what the price, and she didn't drink. Perhaps she *was* simply a friend of theirs. The two men were in the construction business together on Long Island and he had never known them to go around with cheap women.

"This storm's quite something," Nancy finally said. "I've never seen New York like this, have you?"

"No, no, I haven't," he replied.

There was no other conversation until he'd seated himself opposite her, drink in hand. Then she smiled, a lovely easy smile. "I have several of your recordings. I especially like *Andrea Chénier*."

"Thank you," he said. She couldn't be a call girl. She was also not just talking off the top of her head; *Andrea Chénier* had been his finest recording; the part was best suited to his personality and his bravura style of acting.

"Could I get you anything?" he asked. "Cigarette?"

"No, I don't smoke. Perhaps later I'll have a ginger ale."

He looked to the bar; there were several bottles of ginger ale there. "I'll fix you one now, if you'd like."

"No, later will be fine," she said. "Did you take in any performances at La Scala or Vienna while you were abroad?"

"No," he replied.

"I hear that—" She broke off, raising a hand to her chin. "Oh, would you rather not talk about opera?"

"Oh, no," he shrugged. "No, I just didn't get around to it. I—"

The phone rang and he got up quickly. "Excuse me," he said, walking toward the door, "I'll take it in the bedroom."

It was Morty. "Listen, Raf, I got some news for you."

"Go ahead."

"I went up to this Parade Paperbacks around five. I just nosed around in general, you know; I asked if they actually read unsolicited manuscripts, like I was a would-be author. Well, I struck up an acquaintance with one of the secretaries and while we were talking I casually asked if she knew this Kelly McDermott that was all over the papers. When she said yes, I invited her out to dinner. Oh, incidentally, Hiram and a friend of his are still watching McDermott's building. I just checked with him and he still hasn't come home. Well, now it all figures—"

"What do you mean?" Raffaello asked.

"Well, I took this secretary, Barbara, to dinner. I just left her. Actually, she's quite a—"

"Get to the point!" Raf snapped.

"Okay. Anyhow, this Barbara said one of the other girls that works up there got a call from McDermott in the morning or afternoon, I don't know, and that he'd told her, some girl he used to go with, that he was with Maggie, that he was going away for a vacation with her." There was no answer from Raffaello's end. "Raf?" Morty asked. "Raf, you there?"

"No," Raffaello muttered.

"What do you mean?" Morty chuckled. "I can hear you."

"I don't believe it," Raf said.

"Maybe . . . but that's what she said this other girl—"

"Thanks, Morty. I've got to go now."

"Sure," Morty said.

Raffaello put the phone down and sat there on the edge of the bed. "No," he said out loud. "No, I don't believe it," he muttered, shaking his head. Then he got up, walked to the door, and opened it.

"Hi," the girl smiled.

Raffaello stepped back in surprise. She was sitting in the same position on the sofa but not as he had left her; now she wore only a black brassiere and black panties. The expression on his face triggered her next words. "What's the matter?" she asked. But he simply stood there, staring at her, taking the whole picture of her in. She sat completely at ease, one leg crossed gracefully over the other. He noticed a sizable black-and-blue mark on her right thigh. She followed his gaze and placed a delicate hand on the outside of her leg. "Oh, this," she said. Then she laughed, a light, little schoolgirl laugh. "Don't worry, I'm not into anything *that* kinky. I was painting my apartment and moving my furniture around, I—"

He winced. It was true, she was a call girl; an unusual one, at that, but a call girl nevertheless. They had sent a whore to take Maggie's place.

"What's the matter?" she repeated, uncrossing her legs and leaning forward.

"Please—" he said, not specifying the request.

"Please?" she asked. "What . . . ?"

"Please leave," he said.

"Oh . . . I'm sorry." She stood up and started toward him. "I'm sorry," she said again. "Did I rush things? I didn't mean—"

"Get out!" he said, backing away into the bedroom.

"Oh, Raffaello, don't be—"

"No, please—just leave. Please!"

He slammed the door shut and turned, leaning up against it with his back. "How much?" he asked.

"What?" She'd stepped up to the other side of the door.

"How much do you cost? I'll pay you," he said, both angry at his friends for this unsolicited expression of their sympathy and ashamed of himself for his reactions.

"Oh, no, that's all right. Johnnie and Chuck already took care of it." She spoke now in a matter-of-fact voice which irritated him all the more. He stood there, listening to the small sounds of her getting back into her clothes. After a while she called out: "Good-bye, Mr. Tucci. I'm sorry." Then he heard the front door to the suite open and close.

There was no replacement for Maggie; there could be no substitute for a woman like her. Jesus Christ, didn't they know that!

His mind was riveted to what Morty had told him. He had to know where she was, if he was with her, where they were going, if they were going. That's all that mattered—knowing about her.

He put in a call to his friend Ralph Bianco. After the amenities were over, Raffaello spoke what was on his mind. "Ralph, you said you could find out where she is."

"Sure, sure I can. Just give me a starter."

"Her lawyer-manager-friend is Arnold Lefkowitz. His office is at four forty-five Park." He gave him time to write the information down. "She might be going away somewhere; if she is, there'll be a record of it there in his office. Lefkowitz handles her finances, everything."

"Sure," Ralph said. "I'll get right on it. I'll get back to you, probably in the morning."

Raffaello thanked him and they said good-bye. He

wouldn't sleep until he knew where she was. Yes, he would. He opened the door to the sitting room and retrieved his glass. He took two sleeping pills with the rest of his drink and prepared for bed.

Lying there, letting the pills do their work, he attempted to send up a prayer or two but the effort was futile against the steady counterpoint of her name drumming against his ear. Instead of sheep, he counted Maggies until he could feel his blood thicken and eventually he slipped into unconsciousness.

CHAPTER 21

They were met at the airport in San Diego by Stosh and Flora. Their greetings overflowed with warmth and a joyful excitement more in keeping with a separation of months, Kelly thought, than a few hours. He sensed a bond between them stronger than friendship, as if they'd been through the wars together.

When Flora finally released Maggie, turning her over to Stosh, she embraced Kelly, pressing him tightly to her, and for a moment he was lost in the folds of her light topcoat. "Oh, Kelly, you took good care of my baby!" She squeezed the air out of him and he couldn't help grinning.

When she freed him, he straightened his glasses and hat, which had been knocked crooked. "Hi, guy!" Stosh said, taking him by the shoulders and planting a kiss squarely on his cheek. He was going for the other cheek when Maggie, imitating him, said: "Cool it, *guy*!"

"What—in Italy and Greece men do it all the time."

"You're in *California* now."

"Yeah," Stosh laughed, "the land of fruits!" He elbowed Kelly as Flora giggled. "Okay, guy, I'll give you a rain check on the other one."

Maggie held up a fist. "You *do* that!" she warned.

They laughed as Maggie took Kelly's arm, leading them into the terminal and then to the cocktail lounge. She walked to a booth in a far corner of the room and indicated for them to sit. "I'm going to freshen up." She put a hand on Kelly's shoulder. "Order me a scotch, will you, Tiger?"

As she walked away, Stosh said in his own heavy-handed brand of facetiousness: "So, *Tiger*—any excitement after we left?"

Flora leaned in toward him. "Yes, I was so worried, not that anyone would recognize Maggie, but I kept thinking— what if someone recognized *you*, Kelly. There was even a big picture in the San Diego papers, way out here."

Because Stosh had asked and also because Kelly thought they might give him a clue, he told them of seeing the news on television, adding: "Maggie was very upset when the newscaster read a statement from Raffaello."

"A statement from Raf!" Stosh exclaimed as Flora asked: "What statement?"

"Saying he had no idea where she was, but her next project was going to be a picture called *The Booking Agent*."

Flora snapped her head around to look at Stosh. "*The Booking—*" She stopped abruptly.

"Jesus!" Stosh muttered.

Flora made a little pounding gesture on the table with her fist. "He won't let her alone. I knew it, I *knew* it!"

"Flora . . ." Stosh said. She glanced at him; their eyes met and held for a moment until they both looked down at the tabletop.

"Why, what's wrong?" Kelly asked. Neither answered. "What's wrong, Stosh?" he repeated. "Was it supposed to be a secret?"

"Yeah . . . kinda." Stosh paused a second before asking, "What did Mags do? Did she say anything?"

"No, she reacted like the two of you did," Kelly replied candidly.

A waitress came and took their orders. When the woman had gone, Stosh attempted a smile; it was one smile that didn't require him to shield his teeth. "Well, at least we're all here," he said with forced enthusiasm. "Huh, Flora?"

But Flora was not up to the game. "Yes," she said in a voice that was barely audible.

It was obvious they were not about to share the true significance of the incident, whatever it might be. Kelly excused himself and went to the men's room to freshen up himself. By the time he rejoined the table, Maggie was there and their drinks and sandwiches had arrived. They were laughing. Either Stosh and Flora had not mentioned their previous conversation, or if they had, all of them were covering brilliantly.

Maggie was soon pressing the final leg of their trip against Flora's suggestion that they stay over in San Diego and continue in the morning. "I don't want you to get worn out. It's been a long day," Flora said. "It's so late now, by New York time it would be—"

"But I feel fine, haven't felt better in weeks." She looked out the window. "Look at this beautiful California night. Let's the four of us drive down tonight! Kelly, how about you?"

"Fine," he grinned, "whatever you say."

"Oh, let's," Maggie said, reaching over to take Flora's hand. "I'll have all the rest of the world once we're there. Wait till you see it, it's a dream. Not even a store for miles. You have to go all the way into Ensenada." She turned to Kelly. "We're going down to Mexico, Baja California, the peninsula below Tijuana. A friend of mine, Benny Sydow— directed me in two pictures—has loaned me his house. It has its own cove and beach and cliffs. It's so beautiful you could get a fracture. And isolated. Miranda's Cove, it's the most—"

"You're sure he won't spill where you are?" Stosh asked.

"Benny? Never! He's had his Mexican woman come in and give the place a thorough going over, but she's not to come around while we're there. There'll just be us. I can't wait; I haven't seen the place in five years. Oh, come on!

We're all here together, we pulled it off—let's go down tonight!"

Flora was helpless in the face of Maggie's enthusiasm.
Soon they collected their luggage and Maggie and Kelly sat
in the back of the car Stosh had rented as they drove the
length of the town with San Diego harbor directly to their
right, strung steadily with ships, the battleship gray glistening silver in the moonlight. Sailors in their whites dotted the
sidewalks on the way back to their ships after a night's lib-
erty. At a red light a flock of them crossed the street in front
of the car. Stosh leaned forward against the steering wheel.
"Look at all that good healthy American seafood. That's
enough to give you a reltney!"

"A reltney!" Kelly said. "What's a reltney?"

"A reltney's a hard-on so fierce the tips of your ears pull
down!"

Flora shrieked and swatted him on the shoulder; Maggie
and Kelly laughed as Stosh added: "Just look at them!
Wouldn't Hiram go outta his mind?"

Maggie nudged Kelly with her knee. "But you wouldn't
even notice?"

"No," Stosh sighed, "that stuff ain't for me. You know
me—I gotta fall in love first."

"But you fall in love like *that!*" Maggie said, snapping her
fingers.

"Okay, put me on," Stosh said, starting the car up, "but I
swear, trickin', one-night stands, only time I trick is when I
get lonely."

"That's like saying the only time you eat is when you get
hungry."

"Hey, Maggie," Stosh protested, "what do you make me
out in front of Kelly, some kind of tramp?" There was true
concern in his voice.

"Aw, baby, I'm only kidding you." She reached up and
squeezed his neck.

"Yeah, but—Kelly don't know me."

Kelly was touched by his anxiety; he was also made un-

comfortable by Maggie's open discussion of Stosh's proclivi-
ties. It made her too coolly wise, too knowing. It was slightly
off-putting.

They passed a sign: Tijuana—16 miles, and in a while
they were out of the city proper. The bay was no longer in
sight; instead flat marshlands stretched out to their right.
The car rounded a curve and the beam of the headlights
picked up a young Marine, clean-cut, no more than a kid,
standing by the side of the road hitchhiking. Maggie and
Stosh sang out together: "Oh-oh, fallin' in love again, Oh-oh,
Oh-oh!" They laughed along with Flora, who joined in on
the final two "Oh-oh's." The tune was vaguely familiar to
Kelly from a popular song belonging very much to the past.
Maggie took Kelly's hand. "We did that all over the world:
Tokyo, Calcutta, London, Paris, Berlin." She'd taken her
glasses off; her eyes caught a shaft of moonlight coming in
the window and reflected it back to him. Kelly thought he'd
never seen such large green eyes in his life.

After a few miles giant billboards appeared with increasing regularity on either side of the highway, advertising motels, restaurants, dog races, jai alai, and the bullfights. A
steady line of motels loomed into view, signs ablaze, vying
gaudily for the tourist trade, and Maggie read off the entice-
ments. "Heated Pool, Morning Coffee, Shuffleboard, Free
Breakfast, Piano Bar, Magic Fingers—"

"Magic Fingers?" Flora asked. "What's that?"

"Honestly, Flora, sometimes you worry me," Maggie said.
"It's that little . . . sort of slot machine thing by the bed.
You drop a quarter in and the mattress vibrates for fifteen
minutes."

"Yeah," Stosh added, "for horny people that check in
alone."

They came to a string of gas stations with signs: GAS UP
IN U.S.A. and a final one announcing: LAST GAS IN U.S.A.
and they were suddenly in a line, one of two lanes open for
cars entering Mexico. When they pulled up under the por-
tico extending from booth to booth, a middle-aged Mexican
in olive-green uniform stuck his head in the window. He

had a trim black moustache, a plump face, and the scent of roses entered the car with him. He looked straight past Stosh and smiled at Flora. "Visitors?" he asked.

"Yes," Maggie replied from the back seat.

"All American citizens?"

"Yes," Maggie said, "we're spending a few days in Ensenada."

Ignoring Maggie completely, he beamed several gold teeth at his target, Flora. "Yes, Ensenada. Tijuana not so good for nice people. You know," he shrugged, "border town, okay for sailors out for a good time, not so good for nice people," he repeated, staring at Flora. Flora blushed, smiled, and nodded in return. "Have a nice time." He tipped his cap to her and waved them on.

As Stosh pulled away he and Maggie broke into a chorus of "Oh-oh, fallin' in love again!" Flora giggled and Stosh said, "Why, Flora, I bet you worked up a little roynch there, didn't you?"

Flora clucked and Kelly asked: "A roynch—what's a roynch?"

"You don't know what a roynch is—that's like when a woman gets so hot in a movie theater looking at some sex symbol up there on the screen that all the air rushing into her pussy lifts the shoelaces up off her shoes!"

Flora let out a shriek, reaching over and giving Stosh a brisk swat. "Hey," he said, "one of those little love taps of yours could dislocate a shoulder!"

"Yes . . . but you're *terrible!*" Flora howled. "All of you!"

"*We're* terrible," Maggie laughed, "You're the one was flirting."

"Ahh!" Flora gasped, "I was not. Oh, I wasn't either. I never—ah!" But it was obvious from her clucking sounds she was pleased that the Mexican had paid attention to her.

The pitted road led them past a few small bars, an auto-insurance agency, the Tijuana Quick Marriage Bureau, and then approached a narrow bridge, spanning nothing more than a rock-strewn gully, with a footpath for pedestrians on either side. Stosh crossed it slowly. On the far side a huge boulder with red letters splotched on it proclaimed: "Christ is coming!"

"Hey, lookit," Stosh cried out, "they got a religious porno movie down here!"

Maggie reached ahead and swatted him. "Sometimes you go too far!"

Stosh ducked forward. "What is this—Beat Up a Polack Day?"

After a few blocks the road turned to the left and the main thoroughfare of Tijuana stretched out in front of them. Flora gasped and Stosh said, "Holy shit, Toto—I don't think we're in Kansas anymore."

The street, strung across with row upon row of colored lights for as far as the eye could see, was unusually wide, and although it was after two in the morning, the sidewalks were crowded with sailors, tourists, and natives: barkers, shoeshine boys, workers, Mexican women holding blanket-wrapped babies in one hand and selling chewing gum and cigarettes in the other, and an occasional lady of the evening; however, the whores, able to rely upon an army of pimps to guide their trade to them, stayed mostly close by their mattresses. Stores and arcades of all kinds—leather goods, perfumes, laces, watches, pottery and parrots—opened out onto the street. There was a bar or nightclub for approximately every three shops. A barker stood in front of each shop; the nightclubs and bars sported two and sometimes three, hawking the virtues of the emporiums they represented with manic enthusiasm, doing everything short of hauling customers in off the streets by their arms. The mixture of disco, country-western and Latin music ricocheted from these watering spots and collided in the streets.

"This is what you call Great Tacky," Stosh said.

Maggie spoke in her Bankhead voice: "Reminds me of Vienna—Christ, there's a nothing town!" Kelly laughed and she took his hand: "Down where we're going—it's not like this."

Stosh drove the length of the main street slowly. They stopped for a light and a Mexican couple in their late fifties, filthy, ugly, and blind drunk reeled out of a bar. As they stumbled past, the woman belched loudly. Kelly immediately sang: "Oh-oh fallin' in love again," and Maggie and Stosh joined in the final "Oh-oh, Oh-oh!" The ending was hideously off-key and they roared with laughter. Maggie flung her arms around Kelly. "That's our boy!"

On the last corner before the main street swung to the left Kelly saw a large shop advertising: NEWSPAPERS FROM ALL OVER THE U.S.A. "Could we stop and get a paper?" he asked.

"Sure." Stosh braked the car.

"No," Maggie said without looking at him. "Stosh, keep on."

Kelly was surprised by her abruptness. "Why not?" he asked.

"I'd rather not." There was a pause. "I'd rather not be bothered with all that trash."

Kelly had the temerity to add: "You don't have to read them." She snapped her head around to face him. "I mean," he said, "you don't mind if I do?"

"Yes, I do, I do mind. What do you think I'm talking about?"

Flora turned around. "Maggie . . ."

"Oh, use your head, Flora. God only knows what he'll—"

Stosh shook his head. "No, I don't think so," he muttered.

"You don't think so! How do you know? He already—" She cut the sentence off and left it hanging in the air. Nobody spoke for a few seconds until Maggie finally said, in a softer voice, "No papers, if you don't mind?" Kelly didn't answer, treating the question as a rhetorical one. His lack of reply galled her. "You don't mind all that much, *do* you?" He shook his head. "You're my guest, remember that. Think of the money as payment for not reading the papers, if you must. Ten thousand dollars for not reading the newspapers a few days! That's not half-bad, is it?" Her officious tone amazed him, preventing him from speaking.

"Well, is it?"

"No."

"Fine, then it's settled."

Their high spirits of a few seconds before vanished; a pall settled over the car and they rode in silence. Kelly squelched an impulse to say: What do you know, we've had our first fight; but he was annoyed by her tone and chose not to dismiss it that easily.

Stosh saw a sign pointing the way to Ensenada and turned to the right. A two-lane highway, bordered by dirt shoulders, led gradually up an incline beyond a group of motels and past a short stretch of sloping farmland, and then they were driving through gently rolling brown hills with shacks and small farms scattered along the sides, on ridges, in gullies, and in the open spaces to the left of the road. The countryside was asleep; rarely did they pass a shack or a small farm with a light. Mongrel dogs slept in the cluttered yards; a burro, a few goats, a cow and a horse now and then, stood frozen in the moonlight upon the lifeless hills. The only moving things were chickens, picking in the yards close by the roads; the only sound was the occasional complaint of a rooster, crowing in protest at the inertia surrounding him. To Kelly, the land had an almost Biblical tint of age about it.

They drove for fifteen minutes, still ascending, and then began a gradual descent. As the road curled to the left around the base of a hill, they could see, off to the right and below, the endless glistening plain of silvered darkness that was the sea. The road circled down, drawing close to it, and soon they were driving alongside deserted beaches. "If we're in the middle of a sulk," Maggie said, "I might as well have a snooze." It was spoken in a way that demanded no reply, and it received none. Stosh turned the radio on low. Maggie settled herself over against the luggage away from Kelly, who allowed the sea air, together with the implausible sum total of each part of this experience, to overcome him.

It was some time later that they changed positions almost unconsciously, as sleepers do, with Maggie mumbling, "Life's too short," and coming to rest up against him as he slipped an arm around her. He did not recall a further change until Stosh called her name and he awoke to find Maggie's head in his lap. Before he could awaken her, she opened her eyes, smiled up at him and winked: "Sometimes you find people who never lose their temper; they're kind, cheery, generous and—they usually run elevators. . . . Forgiven?" He grinned and nodded.

"Maggie?" Stosh repeated. "Which way now? We're coming into Ensenada."

"Already?" She sat up, rubbing her face and eyes. They were coming down a long easy slope into the sleeping Mexican town. "Stay on this," she said. "It leads right through town. It's the only road going south. Benny said the cove's almost exactly twelve miles beyond the heart of town. Check the mileage. I think I'll recognize it, but just in case."

They passed a church, then a square, empty except for two Mexican sailors asleep on twin benches, and followed the highway, which turned to the right and became, for eight or ten blocks, the main shopping street of Ensenada. A pack of stray dogs, big-eared, lean and hungry looking, trotted across the street in front of them. Two male cats faced one another head on in front of a Mexican bank, growling lowly, while a female cat rolled luxuriously in the gutter nearby, waiting to bestow her charms upon the victor. A goat wandered out of an alley next to a small theater and watched them drive by. Stosh sang out, "Oh-oh—" and they all finished together. Their laughter made a hollow sound in the empty town.

A large, old-fashioned bus, Mexican and American flags mounted side by side on the roof, sat parked by the side of the road. Painted in Day-Glo in a wraparound band at the top rear of the bus was this message: DO YOU FEEL FAR AWAY FROM GOD? Under it the sentence: GUESS WHO MOVED?

After Maggie read it aloud, Stosh shook his head: "What lives down here—a bunch of religious fanatics?"

"Oh, I hope not," Flora said. "They can be so pesky!"

For whatever reason, Flora's reaction together with her reading struck them funny. Kelly was grateful the mood had changed and their good spirits were restored.

Nearing the harbor, the street turned, leading them past several live-bait shacks and boat-for-hire stands and the main pier, stretching out in the water to their right. After this, only small native homes stood in irregular rows back away from the road; soon they disappeared and once more they were on the highway heading south. The road veered away from the ocean, running level for a few miles, then becoming hilly as it approached the coast again.

"Look," Maggie said, "the sun must be coming up beyond those mountains there." They looked to the east. The moon, now a pale lemon disc high in the sky, had lost its brilliance; the sky over the sea was still midnight-blue but extending in over the land it became a shade lighter above the jagged peaks of the mountains. "We'll be up for the sunrise," Maggie said.

Even as they looked toward the mountains the shade appeared to lighten another degree. The ocean to their right, now without the brightness of the moon to shimmer it, lay like dead lava, dark and motionless. Kelly shivered at the early morning chill. Maggie had finished touching herself up from her compact; her lips were freshly covered with pale orange lipstick. Leaning up against Kelly, she took his hand in hers. "Stosh, open her up, see if she's got any get-up-and-go. But keep an eye on the mileage."

Stosh pressed his foot down on the accelerator; the car, heavy in its hold on the road, lurched forward as the hum of the engine increased, moving higher in pitch. The scarf Flora wore streamed out behind her; Kelly reached up and touched the fluttering crepey ends of it with his fingers, and Maggie smiled at him. They flew along with a half-mile of low desertlike land between them and the sea and several miles of rugged sloping foothills leading up to the mountains on their left.

Gazing out the window at the spectacular spread of landscape before him, Kelly thought of his apartment on East

Sixty-third Street, so tidy and sheltered and citified. The difference between that scene, which he had simply walked away from, and this—speeding along the ocean with Maggie Banner and Company in the Mexican predawn—was staggering to him.

He blinked his eyes: *is it happening, am I here?* He glanced down at his hand; yes, he was holding her hand. But even his sense of touch didn't necessarily lend the scene truth. Testing reality, he squeezed her fingers. She squeezed his hand in return and looked over at him, smiling. This still did nothing to reassure him.

He looked up. Somehow, the hum of the motor and such a tiny detail as Flora's scarf snapping back in the wind made it all believable. If the sound and wind had been cut off, it could easily pass for a dream.

The road began to rise once more, turning and veering closer to the coast, forcing Stosh to cut down the speed. The beaches were no longer flat but took on the jagged look of the Maine coastline. "We must be near," Stosh said. "Almost twelve miles."

"I don't see any houses at all," Flora said.

"You wouldn't." Maggie leaned forward in her seat. "It's the only house for miles; you can't even see it from the road. It's built on a ledge below a bluff, hanging over the ocean."

The road descended, zigzagging in and out around cliffs, no more than a hundred yards above the sea until it dipped abruptly inland, snaking down into a rocky gorge along the side of a hill, climbing out on the far side, and making a wide, sweeping turn up and around to the left.

"Here, this must be it," Maggie said.

"Where?" Stosh asked, stopping the car. All that was visible was a flat, grassy, U-shaped bluff extending out ahead and to the right of the road, ending in a sheer drop to the beach, which could not be seen from the road.

"The bluff is right above the cove. The driveway must be back a ways."

Stosh backed up until he could see two dirt tire marks, weeds growing up between them, lead off the road and drop sharply down out of sight. He shook his head. "Hope my fuckin' insurance is paid up!"

"I didn't know you could get fucking insurance," Maggie said. "Is it expensive?"

"You ought to be in pictures," Stosh snorted. "We'll end up in the drink if we follow those tracks."

Maggie touched his shoulder. "No, I remember. But it's steep, put her in gear."

"Baby, you better come up with some brakes." He nosed the car down off the highway and followed the narrow dirt road. A clay bank, the northern end of the U-shaped bluff, shot up to their left; to their right, only a sharp drop-off into a rocky gorge. The road dived down to the left, straightened out, running parallel to and below the horseshoe prong, and suddenly they were in a wide, red-bricked parking patio with the long, low front of a Spanish house blocking the far side of it.

CHAPTER 22

Stosh eased the car to a stop by the front of the house, overgrown with magenta bougainvillaea except where it had been clipped away to free the door and several windows. Maggie grabbed her purse and leather tote bag. "I can't wait to show it to you. And wait until you see the view."

They got out of the car and Maggie fumbled behind one of two granite lions on either side of the door for the key. They stepped into a large tiled foyer, with a kitchen, utility rooms, and a maid's room leading off it, and followed Maggie down a long hall into the wide, comfortably furnished living room, its far wall of glass looking out over the ocean. Standing four abreast, they gazed out, beyond a brick terrace running the length of the living room, and down at the gently rolling sea.

"Oh," Flora whispered, "how did they ever *build* a house down here? It's breathtaking."

"The ledge we're on is midway between the top of the bluff and the beach," Maggie explained.

"It's the absolute fuckin' end of the world." Stosh pressed his nose up against the glass. "How do you get down to the beach?"

"Right out here." Maggie slid the glass door open and they stepped out onto the terrace, following her to a break in the sparse wood railing which guarded the far side of it. "See?"

Brick steps dropped steeply down the side of the cliff for a few yards. A wooden footbridge, lined with chain and rope handrails, led gradually from the steps down across an open space to the side of a large boulder rising up from the sand. Steps were chiseled around the side of the boulder and another wooden footbridge slanted steeply down to the left, anchored at the bottom to a low flat rock resting on the beach.

Stosh glanced down toward the beach, then around at the house. "Wild—like a house from one of those old Joan Crawford movies with some guy chasin' her around, trying to knock her off for the insurance!"

"Joan Crawford!" Maggie snapped. "I made a couple of those myself, you know!" She shattered the quiet with her husky bark. "You want to hear a terrible story?"

"Whaddaya think?" Stosh asked.

Maggie turned to Kelly. "When Joan died, I called up Bette Davis. I mean, they'd had their feuds and all, but they'd worked together and they were both pro's, legends in their time, so I phoned Bette and I said, 'Bette, I just heard about Joan; what a shame, you must feel awful!'

"There was a long pause and then Bette said, 'Sweetie, they don't change—just because they're dead, you know!'" Again her husky laugh could be heard along with Flora's censuring cluck. "I know, it's terrible, but it's Bette to the tits!"

Stosh peered down, taking in the precarious route to the beach. "I'd hate to try it down there with a load on."

"The bridges are solid," Maggie reassured him, "and there are handrailings all along."

"There's an island," Flora said.

Out in the ocean to the left, a large, jagged rock jutted up, sitting midway in the entrance to the cove. A narrow strip of sand hugged its base. They walked to the left side of the terrace where they could look down and see the cove and the half-moon stretch of beach curving out to the end of the rocky southern prong. Sheer cliffs dropped off from the flat bluff down to the beach.

"The master bedroom, to the left here, has the full view of the cove," Maggie said. "The other bedrooms, on the other side of the living room, face north and out to sea." She shivered; there was a snap in the morning breeze.

Flora reached out a hand. "Maggie, you'll catch cold, come inside."

"I'm not shivering from the cold—from excitement. I love this place." She took Kelly's arm. "I want to take Kelly down to the beach." Before Flora could protest, she added, "Just to show it to him. We'll come right back up."

"We'll bring the bags in. I'll lay out your things, but then it's time for bed. Please, Maggie."

"All right."

Maggie led the way down the steps. They picked their way along slowly to the footbridge and across to the boulder. The dramatic impact of the setting precluded speech. They gazed inland over the top of the bluff where streaks of lighter blue splintered out from behind the mountain peaks, shattering the illusion of a midnight-blue dome to the sky, fanning it out and presignifying the light-blue limitless sky of day.

"Come." She led the way slowly down to the second footbridge, which swayed gently in response to their shifting weight. When they stepped onto the flat rock, Kelly jumped down onto the sand, turned, and reached his hands up to her waist, swinging her down alongside him. They walked along the clean, packed sand where the tide had receded. Small waves lapped at the shore, retreated and lapped again. They continued on until the beach curved out to sea, narrowed, and became a jumbled strip of rocks toward the jagged end of the cliff. When they came to the rocky part, they stopped and turned around. The house looked tiny up on the ledge. The lights were on in the master bedroom; the drapes were open and they saw a figure move briefly past the glass window and disappear.

"Flora," Maggie said. "Dear Flora."

As if these words were a cue, they turned to one another, and she offered her face to him, now without disguise: the shock of tousled hair, the wide green eyes, the startling cheekbones, the nose with its slight upward tilt at the end, giving her face a fresh look of anticipation, the generous mouth and perfect chin. He kissed her, and he thought surely no mouth could be so lovely, so gentle yet responsive, so clean yet so full of passionate juices. The rest of him responded to their embrace, and she pressed her body up close to his. They stopped for a moment. She held his face against her cheek with the palm of her hand and whispered, "My Tiger." The words were not spoken lightly, nor sexually, but with simple endearment. They kissed again and Kelly began to tremble. He felt it between his shoulder blades and in the small of his back. She took her mouth away from him. "Chilly?"

He echoed her words. "Not from the cold—from excitement." His voice was low and husky and he cleared his throat.

They embraced without kissing. He held her body close to him, his chin pressed into her thick hair, and he thought: I wish it could happen right here on the beach, naturally and without any ceremonial preparations.

She took his hand and they walked back and climbed up to the terrace without speaking. Mixed planes of the palest red and orange overlapped one another, dispelling the blue sky above the mountaintops to the east. The dark slate-gray of the morning's predawn was losing its hold.

"Quick, inside," Maggie said. "We vampires melt in the sun!"

Kelly closed the glass door after them as Flora came out of the master bedroom. "I only unpacked one of your bags and your toilet case," Flora said. "We'll do the rest in the morning." A hand flew up to her face. "*Morning!* It's morning now." She gave Maggie a peck on the cheek. "Have a good sleep, dear."

"You found your rooms?"

"Yes, they're lovely. Kelly, sleep well." Flora kissed him lightly and walked to the far end of the living room. "Goodnight," she called back, and disappeared through the doorway.

"Kelly, wait here. I'll quick shower. Then you can, if you want."

"Yes, I'd like to."

She left him standing in the living room. The floor was covered by a thick mat of stitched-together wheat-colored squares. A large overstuffed sofa, mustard in color and nubby, dominated the room, flanked by five easy chairs, all angled to work from a massive irregular slab of California redwood, mounted on brass legs. A large leather-covered bar occupied the far end of the room, stretching from the plate-glass window overlooking the terrace to the hallway leading off to the guest bedrooms. On the wall behind it was a collection of rifles and pistols, several racks of glasses and pewter mugs, and a large wooden placard with the slogan: REMEMBER PEARL HARBOR! burned into it. Above this, there was a homemade placard strung across with a giant brassiere, which had been bronzed. The sign above it read: REMEMBER PEARL OLSEN!

He sat down on the sofa. He was full of anticipation; he sat suspended in anticipation. A small bird fluttered out on the terrace, disappeared, and dipped back into sight, settling on the guard rail.

"Hi . . ." It was Stosh, standing in a robe and slippers; he yawned and scratched his stomach. "Where's Mags?"

"Taking a shower."

"Oh." Stosh scratched his head. Kelly felt a mild resentment at this intrusion. "What do you think of the layout?"

"Couldn't be better." He realized it was not resentment he felt but a sudden shyness.

"It's the fuckin' nuts," Stosh said, yawning again. "Well," he rubbed his eyes, "I'm pullin' a quick fade. See you whenever we come to." He turned and shuffled toward the hall.

Kelly sat there sifting through his feelings but finding no real explanation for them; only an almost subconscious notion that they were no longer in transit, they'd reached their destination and that perhaps the Mad Tea Party was over, occurred to him. This, for some reason, augured a change, a settling in his relationship to them and, though he told himself to forget it, the idea nagged him.

"Kelly?" She stood in the doorway, recessed a few feet from the living room by a short hallway fitted with a stereo set and record cabinets.

"That was quick," he said.

"Why not?" she smiled at him. She wore a pale lavender robe tied around at the waist, and pulled a brush through her thick hair. "I'll give you equal time and not a second more." She stepped back, and he walked into the bedroom. "Looks more like Hollywood," Maggie said, strolling to the center of the room, "than Mexico. But Hollywoodians, most of them, are creatures of comfort. They drag their comfort with them whether it fits or not. Actually, who's to say—it *is* comfortable."

It was more than comfortable, it was plush. An oversized custom-made bed facing the glass window and looking out across the cove to the far arm of the bluff ruled the room. Its high, carved wooden headboard was fitted with twin reading lamps, a radio, an electric alarm clock, various shelves, and a small bookcase. There was also a panel of buttons built into it, regulating the electrically operated window draperies and every light in the house. A low oak chest footed the bed, and twin oak dressers sat against the far right wall. Built-in closets, fitted with louvered doors, lined the wall on either side of the dressers. Near the window twin love seats and an easy chair formed a seating arrangement, facing in to a low marble coffee table. The entire room was carpeted in rich beige with a heavy nap.

"I hung up your robe in the bathroom. Your comb and things are in there, too. Hurry up."

He showered, dried himself and brushed his teeth quickly, to keep active, to rush ahead of the feelings of tremulous alarm which threatened to seize him. When he stepped into the bedroom, the heavy draperies figured in black and tan had been drawn and the dawn filtered through them in diffused rays.

Maggie lay in bed; a soft headboard light shone down on her. She wore nothing, but the covers were pulled up to the top of her breasts. "Quick yourself," she smiled. Kelly stood where he was. He sensed immediate defeat. The scene was too much set. This elaborate room was overdesigned for the experience he had so long anticipated. Her beauty, lying there as she was, was far too much for him. "Come to bed," she said softly.

"Ya-yes." Walking slowly toward her, he was possessed by feelings of wonderment, not of passion or love. How could he love her? How could he break through such an impenetrable wall of awe and fall into love with this celebrated symbol of sex and humor and womanliness?

He sat on the far side of the bed and took his slippers off. She lifted back the covers for him, and he dropped out of his robe and slipped quickly into bed. The sheets were a cold compliment to the dead feeling within him. She moved toward him, turning to face him on her side. When she touched his cheek with her hand, he turned to her—because it was the thing to do. He kissed her gently, but his mind had killed the physical responses of his body. She moved closer to him and their bodies touched. The warmth of her skin glowed against him. If only he could absorb a fraction of her warmth.

"Cold?" she whispered.

"I—the shower." His voice broke on the last word.

She put her arms around him and rubbed his back with her slender, graceful hands; this brought them even closer together. They kissed again, and she drew her arms around his sides to the front of him. His body became rigid; he thought if she touched the inert part of him he was so aware of—he would die of shame.

But she did not. She lifted her hands up in front of him, grazing his chest, and eased her body so that he might place his arms around her. He did, and she shuddered slightly at the chill in his fingers. He removed them from her back and lay there, arms around her, hands resting awkwardly on top of one another out and away from her. He clenched his fingers, doubling them up into the palms of his hands to warm them.

He kissed her again, pressing his mouth against her lips in forced spasms of passion which only exaggerated his self-imposed impotency. Being experienced in love-making, she would not allow this for long and soon pulled away from him. He turned upon his back and she leaned up on her elbow, moving her head over and above him, touching his lips with her hand as if to quell any words he might utter and then kissing his forehead lightly.

"Tired . . ." She smiled at him. "Me, too—it's been a long day." She kissed him again on the mouth without parting her lips. "Sleep well." And she left him, turning to rest next to him on her back.

Her gentle, kind release did nothing to alleviate the disappointment he felt within himself. He heard the muted cries of a sea gull and hated it and all creatures without complicated brains to block their natural instincts.

So he was awake when her body jerked slightly and her foot touched his. He looked over at her; she had moved away from him somewhat. He saw her lips move, her mouth twitch as if in protest, her face contort, and before his eyes she bolted to a sitting position, swinging up from the waist and screaming out: "Oh, my God!" In an instant she had bounded out of the bed and was standing, arms tensely outstretched, fists clenched. She screamed out once more: "Oh, God! Oh, my *God!*" in such terror that it seemed to shake the house.

Kelly's blood ran cold. He sat up, hands braced back against the mattress. "Maggie . . . ?"

She spun around to face him. Her eyes, wildly dilated with fear, stared at him as if he were a total stranger. The veins in her throat pulsated from the sheer physical energy of her screams. Turning from him, she searched the room, her head moving in quick movements until her eyes focused upon her robe at the foot of the bed. She picked it up and put it around her.

"Maggie . . . Maggie, dear." It was Flora at the door.

"Yes," she replied in a choked voice.

The door opened and Flora entered. "I heard you." Although Flora was concerned, she didn't appear to be unduly surprised or alarmed; by her manner she could have appeared in answer to a request for some aspirin.

Kelly put on his robe and stood up from the bed.

Maggie raised a hand to her forehead. "That dream . . ." Flora went to her. "Don't leave me."

"No, no, never," Flora said, putting her arms around her.

Maggie turned to Kelly, her look now one of recognition. "Don't leave me," she said to him.

"No," he replied, and he was thankful to be included, although she only gave voice to the words—there was no emotion in them.

"We won't leave you," Flora added, guiding Maggie a few steps to Kelly. The three of them stood close together by the foot of the bed. After a while Flora said, "You go to sleep now."

"Yes," Maggie replied. "That stupid dream." She smiled and her mouth tugged over and down. "I must have frightened Kelly."

"Never mind, you sleep now. Kelly . . ." Flora patted him on the arm. She kissed Maggie and left the room, closing the door after her.

Maggie looked up at him. "Sorry. The witches fly low, the witches of the mind."

Slipping off her robe, she got into bed. Kelly followed her. She lay on her side, facing him. She looked at him with her warm green eyes, and he thought now they might talk, might exchange their fears, but after a while she said, "Hold me," and turned on her other side, facing away from him. He moved over, his front against her back, and put his arms around her. She held his hands in close to her below her breasts and sighed. He could feel the fatigue in her body from whatever it was, this fright she had undergone, and within minutes her breathing became regular, her hands relaxed upon his and she slept.

Her demonstration of panic diminished Kelly's feelings of insecurity; in questioning the reasons for her distress, his mind strayed from his own despair. That she could so easily find the comfort to fall asleep in his arms enabled him to relax, finally, and slip into unconsciousness himself.

CHAPTER 23

Kelly half-awakened, hearing the sound of running water. He lay now on his stomach, his head turned sideways, facing the unfamiliar oak dressers. Twisting his head around farther, he saw the trapped panel of muted light between the figured drapes and the windows. His next awareness was of the hardness pressing down against the mattress.

He turned his head around the other way to find that he was alone in bed. If only she were there at that moment, turned on her side, warm and outgoing and smiling at him. They would fall into an immediate embrace and—

Twisting over on his back, he sat up quickly, embittered by his convenient scenario. If consummation depended upon—what?—her sitting astride him as he awakened with what they called in the service a piss-hard-on (he winced at the memory of the phrase)—how misbegotten it would be.

He could hear Maggie brushing her teeth in the bathroom now, and he felt the need to use the room after her. On the other hand, as he sat up in bed and reached for his robe, he wished she would never come out. No sooner wished than the door opened and she stepped into the room, looking completely refreshed and so unlawfully beautiful his thoughts of failure were made all the more perverse.

"Good morning," he said, reaching for his robe.

She smiled at him. "It's almost two o'clock."

"Oh, that's right."

"Good sleep?" she asked.

"Yes." He excused himself and walked to the bathroom, closing the door after him. He undid his robe and, finding it difficult to urinate in an early-morning erect state, he turned on the water in the basin for help and soon began. As he passed his water, he also passed his state of excitement. He shook the last few drops from this traitor in his hand, flushed the toilet, and stepped to the washbowl where he faced the very real traitor in the mirror. For this, and he put a hand to his forehead, was where the signals came from, this brain of his, this treacherous, disobedient master control center. He quickly washed his hands and face, brushed his teeth, and combed his hair, not caring to be cooped up for long with his unhealthy thoughts.

He stepped into the bedroom to find her in bed, robeless, as she had been the night before. He wondered if she lay there in expectancy, if she imagined it was only fatigue that had voided his passion, that now, refreshed with sleep, washed and brushed and empty of bladder, another encounter might lead to fulfillment.

Walking to the side of the bed, he sat down facing away from her. He withdrew his arms from the robe, letting it fall down about his waist, and was about to slip under the covers when she reached over and touched him lightly on the back.

She spoke softly: "Do you want to get up?"

He thought if she had not touched him, if she had only voiced the question, he most likely would have replied yes. But her hand, her fingertips upon his back, imbued a gentle overture to the question and he said, "No, not just yet."

Immediately he regretted his words, for the combined pain of failure to himself and the inability to please this woman, somehow in distress, though he couldn't specify the distress he sensed, was sickening to face.

She withdrew her hand and he got into bed, where he lay next to her and stared up at the ceiling. And for a moment he *was* the ceiling, looking down upon this deficient scene, regarding himself, lying there upon his back in a pathetic delaying action.

He glanced over at her. She, too, was lying upon her back, her beauty mellow and primed to be shared. Again he could not help wishing she had been there beside him when he awakened.

She glanced over at him. "You don't look blowzy in the morning."

"Neither do you," he said.

"You want the truth?" He nodded. "I don't know how long *you've* been awake, but I was primping in there a good half-hour." She moved over toward him, now turning on her side.

Even words failed him now; he knew if he spoke he would stutter. He focused once more upon the ceiling, aware that she was looking at him. He wondered if Flora and Stosh were awake. If only they would burst into the room, engaged in one of their games, and the day could be got into and this purgatory between the sheets could be ended.

He was suddenly uncomfortably warm under the covers. He could feel his ankles becoming damp and the flush traveling up the insides of his legs to his thighs and stomach and the indentation of his chest and on up to his neck, until drops of moisture rested on his upper lip. Raising a finger, he blotted them. He heard her sigh and felt her foot touch his.

"Warm . . ." she said. She rubbed her foot along his shin. "Hot."

Yes, hot, he thought—hot with apprehension, if not outright terror. No longer able to sustain the suspense of this prickly limbo, in a spasm, more of anguish than ardor, he faced her, throwing his arms around her as she fell over on her back, enabling him to swing easily on top of her, his right leg pressed down between her legs, his other leg clamped against the outside of her thigh.

He thrust his opened mouth down upon her. Their teeth bumped, grazed, and bumped again, sounding a comic click-clack in the air, and he forced his mouth furiously against her lips to drown out this luckless beginning.

She murmured his name, but he would not ease up. He could feel her breasts pressed far up by her collarbone beneath the weight of his chest, and the coolness of her body, for a moment, seemed to draw the unhealthy heat from him. He could feel his limp parts pressed up against the gently curving mound of her soft pubic hair. It thrilled him, for no matter what, this was a closeness, a further kissing of their bodies. The smell of her, the texture of her skin, the entire aura of her, filled him with a desire which he ground down upon her.

"Easy . . ." she whispered, but he would not cease his frenetic approach, would not chance losing the desire he felt in his brain, as if he could fill his head to the bursting point with yearning until it exploded, blotting out his mind altogether, destroying it, and allowing his senses to take over.

She tried to move, to breathe free of him, but he raised his arms, grasping her head between his hands, turning her upright again and covering her mouth with his unsteady lips.

He was forcing the masculine role, taking it by the neck and shaking it for all its worth. There was even a satisfaction in the persevering gesture of it. And for a moment he experienced, or imagined he did, through sheer force of determination, a twinge of life, a pulsation where the center of their bodies touched. He pressed down harder upon her to test this life he sensed and she let out a small muffled sound of discomfort. He ignored it, redoubling his efforts, grinding their bodies together, thinking—I can, I can . . .

But his childhood leapt forward and dealt him a foul blow: his memory flashed storybook pictures of the little red engine chugging up the little blue hill, huffing and puffing: "I think I can, I think I can, I think I can . . ."

The analogy mocked him and he threw himself off her in a wrenching movement and lay upon his back. His breathing was irregular and heavy. He focused on the ceiling and again the ceiling ridiculed the athletic travesty played out under it. He closed his eyes, averting his face from her.

She moved quickly to him. "No, no . . ." she whispered. "No . . ." She kissed him gently on the forehead and down the side of his neck as he turned his head farther away from her and tears of anger and despair eked slowly out of his eyes and crawled down his cheeks. He constricted his stomach, holding back the sobs he felt within him. The effort made him cough and he froze on his side, fighting against a total rout of his emotions, refusing to show any further sign of his bankrupt manhood. Her fingers curled over his cheek and when they touched a wet spot, he cried out: "Sta-stop!"

She withdrew her hand immediately but continued to lie close to him. They remained there for what seemed to Kelly an eternity, until his tears were no longer drops of water but a mere dampness on his cheeks. After a while, a certain relief in the knowledge that this abortive attempt was at least over grazed him lightly. He raised his hand and blotted his face. In response to his movement she slid away from him, and he could hear her fumbling with a pack of cigarettes, hear the match being struck, and her first deep inhaling breath of smoke.

"I dreamt," she exhaled, without a trace of emotion, "after that screamer we started off with, that I was hanging in a museum. A rather good museum it was, too. Rouaults and Brueghels and Monets and Manets and some of the Dutch masters across and to the side of me. And there I was hanging without a frame." She chuckled. "I remember feeling pleased as punch with myself that everyone who turned the corner and walked into my . . . wing, I suppose it was, came directly over to stare at me. Then I remember thinking, on second thought, of course they're staring at you, here you are the only human being hanging in this entire museum, probably any museum in the whole world, so naturally they're *looking* at you, you fool! Oh, yes," she added, "and I was naked, to boot." There was a silence as she puffed on her cigarette, then she turned to Kelly. "What do you make of that?"

He cleared his throat. "I don't know." Yes, he thought, an ineffectual answer from him, the most ineffectual of humans.

"I don't either. I wish I had my dream book with me. I'm the foremost dreamer. I lost it in Japan, this tacky dream book I had. *The Queen of Sheba Dream Book, Policy Player, and Fortune Teller,* containing seven hundred and fifty dreams and their meanings. You simply looked up the dream under the heading; jail, kite, old lady, river or whatever you'd dreamed of and it told you, in absolutely contradictory terms, what it meant. I remember the dream for whale—did you know I have an almost photographic memory?"

"No."

"Well, I have. 'Whale: to dream of seeing one alive in the ocean is a sign of losing either life or property; to kill it, abundant good fortune.' Of course, I was *swallowed* by one in my dream, so it didn't help me a bit. I renamed it the *Queen of Sheba Infuriating Dream Book, Policy Player, and Fortune Teller.* It didn't make a bit of sense." She paused for a second, then shrugged her shoulders. "I suppose that's why I was so fond of it. I've always liked riddles."

Glancing briefly at Kelly, she sat up in bed, holding the sheets up to cover her breasts with one hand and taking the ashtray from her side and placing it on her lap with the other. "I suppose we'll *really* get to know one another today, won't we?"

There was no other answer. "Yes," he smiled at her. She had extricated him from his pit of self-conscious embarrassment; the day was being entered into, and he felt a burgeoning affection for her.

She tamped her cigarette out. "Yes," she repeated, as if she had finalized the decision, "we'll really get to know one another today." In a spurt of energy she added: "And you'll tell me what happened with your father—and Bethel!"

"Yes." He sat up in bed. "Oh, God—yes!"

She cocked her head and grinned. "Now that's the kind of reaction I like!"

He wanted to tell her, wanted to open himself up, turn himself inside out, unwind and unravel, stretch himself out in front of her, tell her everything, hoping the telling might be the easiest translation for the complexes he was stuck with.

CHAPTER 24

After breakfast with Flora and Stosh, Maggie rushed Kelly into preparations for the beach so they might catch the last hours of the afternoon sun. When he stepped into the living room in the bathing trunks Flora had found for him, Maggie looked up from the canvas beachbag she was stuffing with towels and smiled.

"They're a size too big." Kelly jiggled the waist of them with his hands. "But I suppose they'll stay on." The madras trunks hung low on his hips and the legs of them were loose.

"They're—I hate the word—but they're cute," Maggie said. "They are." She wore a terrycloth robe over her swimming suit. Holding out the beachbag, she said, "C'mon, you take this."

Stosh hurried into the room wearing a chartreuse and purple bikini. "Check the threads I dug up," he said, swiveling in imitation of a fashion model. His rugged, white-muscled body looked entirely incongruous in the suit.

"Wouldn't you know?" Maggie laughed. "Where do you think you're going?"

"Swimmin'."

"Who asked you?"

"Nobody. You gotta get asked?"

"How's about helping Flora get the rest of the things un-packed for a while? Then you'll come down and join us."

"We already got everything unpacked."

"Why don't you help her anyhow?"

"Oh." Stosh snapped his fingers. "You wanna be *alone*. Why didn't you say?"

"Just for a while."

"Sure," he said with good humor. "I'll come down later on. Flora!" he called out.

"Yes?" She came into the foyer from the kitchen and walked into the living room.

"I'll stick with you awhile," Stosh said.

They walked out onto the terrace and Flora and Stosh watched them descend the steps. "Have a good time," Flora called after them. "Maggie, if the water's at all cold, don't go in. If you do, don't do a lot of swimming. I don't want you to—"

"Flora!" Maggie swung around and looked up at her. "I graduated from kindergarten at *least* three years ago. I even go to potty myself now."

"Yes, but you really shouldn't—"

"Flora," she said curtly, "I even have my own checkbook. I know how to use it, I also know how *not* to use it!"

Maggie continued down the steps; she'd not gone more than five yards when she sighed and spoke to Kelly in a loud, strident voice guaranteed to be heard up on the ter-race. "Sometimes I hate myself for being so bitchy. Some-times I could just cut my tongue out. But they do drive me to it—however I put up with them because I absolutely adore them! I've even been thinking of threesies lately!"

Stosh could be heard giggling above them. When they stepped off onto the warm sand, they glanced back to see Flora and Stosh waving down to them. They waved back and turned, facing the cove and the rock jutting up in the entrance to it. The water was a calm blue-green. There was not a breeze to be felt; the sun held the cove in a silent mellow trance of warmth.

"So peaceful, I can't imagine any more peaceful place on earth," Maggie said, walking toward a gently rising slope in the beach. They unpacked the beach towels and stretched them out side by side on the sand. Maggie knelt and slipped her robe off. She started to lie down, then stopped, bracing herself with her hands. "Look at that, will you?" She bobbed her head in the direction of the master bedroom; Kelly looked in time to see two forms duck behind the draperies. "Checking on me," Maggie added. "Probably think I'm going to swim twelve laps out to the rock and back."

She lay down upon her back and Kelly settled next to her. "Where did you find them?" he asked.

"Stosh came with Raf. Incredible background. He was a hustler at the age of, I don't know, fourteen, I think." She shook her head. "No, he'll tell you. He loves to tell about his life and he does it much better than I. And much more colorfully. An extraordinary life. We took to each other right off. He'd been Raf's kind of, oh, court jester. There's something about him. All the right qualities are there. In spite of the life he's led, he's so untouched, in a way, so full of hope and kindness—I don't know how anyone can put in the years he did and come out of it naïve in many ways. I don't know how he could be as bright as he is and speak such brutal English, either. He doesn't seem to be touched by his environment on any level; he reached a certain stage of development and stayed there. Oh, his vocabulary has grown, but it certainly hasn't helped the double negatives or his accent or the malaprops. He comes up with some pips. When we were starting off on our trip, I took him on a shopping spree in New York. Going out to dinner that night—he was dressed in a gray flannel suit, oxford button-down shirt, striped tie, nice black loafers and cashmere socks—he turned to me and said, 'I feel like Little Lord Foy Da Roy.' I said, 'Little Lord Foy Da Roy?' 'Yeah,' " she mimicked Stosh to perfection, " " 'didncha ever hear of Little Lord Foy Da

Roy?' *'Little Lord Fauntleroy!'* I said. 'Yeah—that's the one!"

They laughed together and Maggie added: "Can't *drag* him to the dentist. It's a crime. Just the mention of it and he starts to tear up." Maggie drew her fingers down along a ridge in the beach towel and looked up toward the house. "But Flora, there's the dear. She's so good it's hard to put up with. She was a nurse, you know?"

"Isn't she still?"

"Yes, but she can't practice in California, not officially in a hospital. She went through a bad drinking problem, had a couple of little . . . accidents when she was practicing. Would you believe she was an alcoholic?"

"Never."

"She was, she was married once, too. After her husband died, she went on the bum for a couple of years, ending up on skid row, Main Street in Los Angeles, which there is no place more skiddier than in the land. Imagine Flora, God love her, crashing about the streets with a bottle of cheap wine in her paws. She'd been sober for years when I met her. She became a combination practical nurse and companion, good pay, mostly wealthy people. The producer of my last picture knew about her. I was working hard, overworking really, and she began massaging me, keeping me in shape, coming to the studio with me. We took to each other right off. Then she came up to the wilds of Utah for three weeks of location shooting. A good thing, too. I pulled a couple of surprise faints. And when we got back I found out," Maggie cleared her throat, "about this damn anemia business and it requires some—you know, taking care of, watching, so there was Flora and that's how it was. The timing was perfect, I don't know' what I'd have done without her." She smiled at Kelly. "Maybe the angels—" She broke off, as if the mention of them brought immediate doubt as to their existence, and added, "or *whoever*—sent her to me."

She flopped over on her back and lay for a long time looking up at the sky. The sun was moving farther out over the ocean, the deep yellow of it bleeding into orange. A warm afternoon trickle of a breeze filtered into the cove, not enough to stir the sand, only a faint brush to be felt upon the cheek or leg.

She sat up quickly and turned on her side to face Kelly. "That must be it," she said. "The angels or whoever must send us to one another." She grinned at him. "Maybe they sent you to me." She fingered the beach towel along the edge and found a loose strand of cotton hanging off it; she unraveled it down the side, wrapped it around her finger and snapped it off. She looked back up at him and smiled again. "Or maybe they sent *me* to *you*—who knows?"

They sat quietly for a few moments until she put a hand on his arm. "Can I ask you a direct question?"

"Yes . . . sure," he said.

"What happened—or what didn't happen . . ." she nodded her head in the direction of the house "—up there, does it have anything to do with Lemming, New Jersey?"

"Oh, Christ—yes!" he said, surprising himself.

She laughed. "Thank God. Then it doesn't have anything to do with—well, for one nasty instance, my age?"

"No, no."

"It's not a matter of personal daintiness? I shouldn't switch to Scope or something?"

"No."

"What about the movie star thing, that's been known to put people off?" She chuckled. "Even me, at times."

"It doesn't help, but . . . no, not really."

"Then," she reached over and gave him a loud, smacking kiss on the cheek, "tell me. You left off with Bethel away at school."

CHAPTER 25

Kelly was eager to fill her request; if he could not please her in the way he wanted to so badly, he could at least explain himself to her.

"It all happened so quickly. I hadn't seen Bethel since she'd left our school. My stutter had improved; my father and I avoided each other as much as possible. Kelly was my best friend, Jason my next best. But a few days after I graduated from high school my whole life seemed to change. I was in rare high spirits.

"I'd won a scholarship to the University of Pennsylvania. I'd got a summer job on the Lemming *Citizen News,* no more than a copy boy, but still a job. Most of all the idea of getting away from home in the fall was with me every minute; I couldn't wait. This was a Friday and Sunday my parents were leaving for a two-week trip to Maine. I couldn't wait for that either. I suppose everyone has a day after high school graduation when they feel they're really grown-up. This was mine.

"Even the weather that day was perfect, crackling clear and a light breeze. I came out of the bank, turned the corner and bumped smack into Bethel. She never looked more beautiful. We both laughed and I said, 'My name's David.'

" 'I know,' she said. We simply stood there. I knew at once we were intensely glad to see each other. After a moment, she said: 'You called, didn't you?'

" 'Called?' I asked.

" 'After I left.'

" 'Yes.'

" 'I'm glad,' she smiled at me.

"That did it. I just blurted out—'Would you like to have lunch?' She said she would and we walked down the street to the Lemming Inn." Kelly shook his head and laughed. "Lunch! I'd never taken a girl to the movies, to anything short of a church meeting, and suddenly I was taking Bethel to lunch at the Lemming Inn.

"Oh, I stuttered like crazy out of excitement, but even that didn't bother me. Bethel was doing most of the talking, about the school she'd been to in Virginia, and how well she'd been feeling lately—that was the only reference to her health—and a poem she'd had published in a small literary magazine. Toward the end of lunch, I was already antici-pating a summer romance. I asked her if she liked to play tennis and she said yes. I said we could get some games in now that the weather was good but then she told me she was leaving with her parents in a week to spend a month on some friends' ranch in Colorado. For a while I took a nose dive, but then I thought, what the heck, she'll be back in mid-July, we'll have the rest of the summer before college starts."

"You had it all sewn up, didn't you?" Maggie asked.

"Yep," he grinned, "and I'll never know why. After all, I wasn't exactly Don Juan. Still, with her going away, I thought I'd better make hay while the sun shines, so I sug-gested we play tennis that afternoon.

"We met later at the city courts. She looked beautiful in one of those classic tennis skirts and a blouse. She was a fairly good player, too. We played a couple of sets and I could have gone on forever, but she said it wasn't too good for her to get overheated, so we stopped and sat on the grass in the shade and talked, just small talk, but comfortable. We never spoke of my father or her attacks; it was too early in our relationship for any of that.

"I finally asked her to go to the movies that night, but she'd made a date to spend the evening with her friend, Mary Murphy, and didn't think it was right to break it. I quickly booked her up for the next day, Saturday—tennis in the afternoon and the movies at night."

"Good boy," Maggie said.

"I suppose," Kelly said, looking over Maggie's shoulder toward the side of the cliff, yet focusing on nothing but the gauzelike memory of a day years behind him, "I suppose that next day was perfect. Maybe I've romanticized it all out of proportion in the time since—" He shook his head. "No, it was perfect."

He spoke the words simply and without protestation. Maggie watched him closely and, for a moment, she thought he might never continue, that he had returned in full to that specific day and the perfection of it could not be expressed in mere words, let alone shared.

"I remember when I asked my father if I could have the car that evening. He'd had the basement of the house fixed up years before as a playroom for my brother. It was wood-paneled, fireplace, comfortable furniture, record player, Ping-Pong table. And there was a separate room down there with a desk and files, where my father spent more and more of his time working on his sermons. He could tipple at his wine down there without anyone knowing it.

"I knocked on the door. He asked who it was and it was a while before he opened it. I told him I'd like to borrow the car and he asked me what I wanted it for. I told him I had a date to take a girl to the movies. 'You have?' he asked. Only it came out like—YOU!

"He never failed to make me feel my lack of abundant friends. He'd talk about what a waste the playroom was, because I never asked anyone over to use it, meaning I didn't have anyone *to* ask."

Kelly moved his head around to face Maggie and smiled. "Mind if I don't tell you about the entire next day? The tennis, the long walk, the cleaning up before dinner—how many times can you comb your hair? The rotten-great chicken-in-the-basket at the rotten-great Red Horn Lodge on Route Twenty-two, or the warm, dark intimacy of the movie? It would only sound naïve and—why is it the good times are boring to talk about and the bad ones hold a kind of fascination?" Before she could answer he said: "I will tell you I chose a double bill in the worst of the three movie houses in Lemming. Two old revivals, *Spellbound* and *Rebecca*, picked because they were spooky and would help me in the hand-holding department. Worked, too. I sweated through *Spellbound* and finally made the big move in *Rebecca*.

"Then when I drove her home we parked out in front of their house, at her suggestion, instead of pulling up in the drive, in case her parents were asleep. We just sat there under a big tree and didn't say anything for quite a while. I finally mentioned that, because my job started Monday, it might be nice if we could spend Sunday afternoon together, after my parents left, which would be following the morning service. She said that would be fine. I wouldn't have the car while they were gone, but Bethel said her parents had two cars—she intimated she couldn't or didn't drive and I gathered that was because of her problem—and she was sure her mother would let us take her car. I suggested driving down to the shore in the afternoon for a swim.

"With our plans all staked out, we just sat there in silence. Finally, she took my hand, said she had a lovely time, and good-night. I said good-night, wishing I had the nerve to kiss her. Just then she leaned over and touched her lips to my cheek. As she began to withdraw, I shot a hand up to the side of her face, holding her head where it was. I think that surprised her; I know it did me. I could sense us both tensing, but I kept my hand there until I could feel us relax, first Bethel, oddly enough, then me. I turned my head slowly until our mouths met and there we were and we kissed."

Maggie sighed in relief. "Oh, thank you, all the saints in heaven—and Barbara Walters!"

Kelly grinned. "We kissed and kissed and kissed. I had my arms around her, finally, but there was nothing but kissing. We kissed until we were exhausted. Then a prowl car came along the opposite side of the street and crawled to a stop. We quickly said our good-nights; Bethel got out and trotted up to the house and I pulled away.

"I remember the drive home that night as the all-time high point of optimism. I just knew my life, my entire life, was in for a complete change, as amazing and sudden as turning the corner and bumping into Bethel on the street the day before."

He glanced at Maggie and she smiled at him. To her surprise her smile was not returned. Instead a wry, almost tough expression crossed his face. "I was in for a change, all right. Oh," he shook his head, "the angels or whoever had a change in store for me. They had a switch I'd never, in my wildest dreams, imagined.

"Right after breakfast the next morning, I called Bethel, who said her mother would let us take her car and she'd also invited me for supper that night.

"I could hardly wait for my folks to leave. My father preached the eleven o'clock service, we came home, and they changed into light traveling clothes. It was a scorcher of a day. I noticed my mother popped a pill into her mouth just before they got into the car. The heat, together with the excitement of the trip, must have got her.

"We said our good-byes and after they drove off—there was such an atmosphere of peace about the house. The enemy had left, for two weeks at least, and the battleground was silent. I walked from room to room, soaking up the feeling of being there alone. I even went down to the playroom. It was degrees cooler than upstairs; I tried the door to my father's room off in the corner, but it was locked. I remember I just had the idea I'd sit at his desk, see what it was like.

"I took a cab to Bethel's. Her folks were out playing golf, so I didn't see them. Then, for a brief moment as we got into her mother's car, I experienced a moment of panic. In hindsight—almost a pra-premonition. It was all—Bethel, my parents away, my job beginning the next day, going off to college in the fall, and Bethel again—the change in my life was too abrupt. It set off a warning: watch out, this is too good to last. I remember even thinking: drive carefully. It must have shown in my attitude or on my face—just sitting there behind the wheel—because Bethel said, 'David?' I looked at her, smiling at me, and shook the moment off.

"Traffic was heavy and the beach was crowded, but we walked down a ways and found a good place to stretch out. It was in the nineties so we went right in for a swim. Then we just lay on the beach side by side. We didn't talk much, it was almost too hot to talk. We went for another swim and rode the waves together and then lay back down again. I don't believe I ever experienced such a sense of well-being, lying next to her that second time. Already I felt we belonged together. She was my girl. Just the prospect of all the times we'd have together filled me so—I got to feeling so good I found it difficult to lie still, so I sat up to suggest we take a walk down the beach.

"Bethel was already sitting; she held a hand up to her forehead. She said she had a headache, only a slight one, probably from the heat. It was after four and what with the Sunday traffic, we decided to leave. The traffic was brutal and the car was hot. We talked awhile at first but then she leaned her head back against the seat and closed her eyes. I reached over and held her hand and we rode the rest of the way with only the radio going softly.

"The way the highway comes into Lemming from the shore was nearer to my house than hers. I wanted to change clothes and get all spruced up for her folks, so I suggested stopping at my house first. She asked if there was any aspirin and I said there was."

Kelly stood up quickly, almost jumped up. The movement was so abrupt Maggie stood up alongside him. He turned to face her. "If only I'd dropped her off at her house." He shook his head. "But you see, I was feeling—everything was so right. So right!"

Maggie noticed a small vein pulsating quickly, running from the base of his neck down across to his collarbone. When he spoke, his words came in short breaths.

"I drove up to the house. The driveway was on the far side and there were four or five little kids playing on the sidewalk in front of it, so I didn't turn in, just parked in front. I didn't sa-see the car parked in the drive by the backyard.

"It was much hotter in town than at the shore—not a breeze. Bethel was breathing heavily as we walked up onto the porch. Again she mentioned it was just the heat. It was cooler inside the house; I said it was really cool down in the playroom, that she could go down there. I got her aspirin and water and led the way to the basement. It was about six o'clock then, still light out, but down there it was dark. It was cold in comparison to the rest of the house. Bethel even shivered, but said it felt good. I turned on two lamps on either side of the sofa, put a record on the stereo, and told Bethel to lie down and relax, to let the aspirin go to work. I stood over her as she settled back on the sofa. I asked if there was anything else she wanted, but she shook her head and closed her eyes. She looked so lovely I wanted to bend down and kiss her, but I didn't.

"I walked across the room to the stairs. When I got to the foot of them I thought maybe I *would* go back and kiss her lightly on the forehead." He paused, closing his eyes briefly in remembrance. "Maybe I'll just kiss her ever so lightly and say some little thing—"

Kelly's eyes snapped open, his expression tightened. "I heard a noise; it wasn't quite a murmur, almost as if she had started to hum. I turned and Bethel was in a sitting position on the sofa, her feet still resting on the end of it. She seemed to be staring at her feet. I saw her mouth move, heard another humming sound, higher and tighter this time, through her teeth. I noticed her fists were clenched and resting on her knees.

"I said her name. I said, 'Bethel.'

"She didn't look over at me, but glanced up toward the ceiling. And I heard that humming sound again, almost as if she were trying to recall something." A shaky breath escaped Kelly. "I knew it was—I knew something was wrong. I said, 'Bethel, are you all right?' She didn't answer me; she clutched the hem of her dress with both hands and pulled it tightly down across her knees and I could see her arms trembling.

"I wasn't afraid. I didn't feel fear, only concern. I walked to within about two feet of the sofa and asked, 'Bethel, what can I do? Is there anything I can do?' She didn't answer, but her back hunched up—she was no longer sitting straight— and she began a sort of rocking movement, still clutching at the hem of her dress. She wasn't lifting it up, only pulling it down across the knees, so tight I thought it would rip. She was clinging to that skirt, as if by holding on to it she could hold on to her control.

"I sat down next to her. She jerked her head toward me for a moment, but her eyes were rolling up out of sight and I knew she didn't see me. I could feel her arm so tense up against mine. Rigid, like a cable. I said, 'Bethel, it's David.' She didn't react. I repeated in a loud voice, 'It's David.'

"She stopped rocking for an instant and said my name, 'David?' in a voice that broke my heart. It was halfway between a question and a cry for help. Then her body began a series of convulsions, centered inward, convulsing in toward the pit of her stomach. She lifted an arm and struck me in the jaw with her elbow. I could tell she'd get off the sofa if she could. I threw myself down on top of her, pinning her arms down on either side of her. It took all my strength. Trying to get up, she bumped our heads together, so I kept my head turned away from her, down between her face and the back of the sofa. She didn't scream; there were only those strange little strangulated noises coming from her throat. The convulsions were large at first. Gradually they decreased and I could feel her physical strength weakening.

"She began trembling; a steady vibrating took hold of her

body. I lifted my head and looked at her. Her eyes were no longer rolled up under the lids, but they were fluttering in quick little movements. Her lips were stretched tightly across her teeth; then she opened her mouth and began a series of gagging, choking sounds. Her mouth opened very wide and I could see her tongue curled back. I remembered something about pa-people swallowing their tongues, so I jammed the side of my hand in her mouth and she bit down as hard as she could. I yelled out as her teeth locked on my hand. I didn't try to pull away and after a while the pain stopped and my hand only felt numb.

"She seemed to use up the last bit of strength biting my hand. Then, very quickly, in little waves, her eyes stopped fluttering and focused on me and I could tell she was seeing me. After a moment, her eyes reflected confusion, then almost surprise, and the pressure of her teeth on my hand stopped altogether. I felt it was over and I was actually thinking it hadn't been half as bad as I would have imagined.

"Suddenly she took her mouth from my hand. I released one arm when I felt her wanting to raise it and eased my weight off her. She brought her hand up and brushed it across her mouth. There was a little blood on her lips from my hand. She wiped it off with her hand, looked at it, and shuddered. Then she looked at me, her brow wrinkled up, and she said, 'David?' In that instant her eyes filled with tears. She said, 'Oh, David . . .' and there was such remorse, such apology in it! She said my name once more, sobbed it, then she turned her head away from me and she was crying."

There were tears in Kelly's eyes now. He stood there, legs slightly apart, toes gripping the sand. "God, I was all over her, caressing her, telling her I loved her. It even made me love her more." He turned to Maggie. "It did, it made me feel strong. I felt I'd helped her. It even made me feel, well—passionate.

"I kept on talking and caressing her. I tried to kiss her but she kept turning away, sobbing into a cushion. I finally took her head in my hands and forced her to turn and I kissed her cheek, her forehead, but she struggled when I tried to kiss her lips. Suddenly I became very aggressive and forced her over on her back and once more lay on top of her with the weight of my entire body. Still, when I'd try to kiss her mouth, she'd turn her head.

"Eventually, I don't know what made me do it but—I bit her lips. She let out a little cry and we both froze, both became absolutely quiet. Then, after a while, I kissed her gently and now she opened her mouth and we kissed and I became terribly excited as our mouths moved together and now the sounds coming from her were sounds of pleasure. She felt me pressing down hard upon her and she pressed back and soon I was fumbling with her dress and then her breasts and she said, 'David. . . .' I thought she was protesting but then she murmured, 'David, I love you . . .' "

Tears rolled down Kelly's face and the muscles in his neck and shoulders stood out. His voice rose in volume until he was almost shouting, although he faced Maggie squarely.

"And whether this was the right time or not, I felt so strong, so full of la-love for her there was no stopping. She reached down to help me with the buttons on her dress and as she bobbed her head up—a small cry of surprise escaped her. She squinted, trying to see out of the light into the dark part of the room. Then a full-throated scream and she buried her head in my chest.

"I turned, looking across the room toward the dimness at the foot of the stairs. I didn't see anything, anyone. I turned back to her. 'Bethel,' I said. 'Bethel, there's nothing—'

"Then I heard his laugh. That deep, hearty laugh, a dirty laugh now. And before I actually saw him I already knew the position of his mouth, pursed together in that small, mean smile. And I turned my head around, looking past the stairway, and there he was standing in the doorway, now open, to his office. But the light was off in there; I couldn't see him too well in the dark. The rays from the lamps beside the sofa didn't quite reach that corner of the room.

"He kept laughing. Bethel cried out again, clinging to me.

I had to pry her off in order to get up. When I did, she fell away from me, turning toward the back of the sofa and burying herself from sight. My father tried to stem his laughter; it came in short gasps as he prepared to speak, to say something.

"My eyes were becoming accustomed to the darkness in the corner, and I could see he was only wearing his pants and an undershirt. He took a step forward, still laughing and hanging onto one of the two pipes that led from the basement ceiling down to the floor. A shaft of light hit his neck and face. I saw that grimace, that awful la-laughing mouth, and I wanted to kill him.

"He spoke her name on a gasp of laughter: 'Bethel!' And it made him laugh all the more. I realized he'd been at his wine. I didn't even wonder why he was there. I only knew he was trespassing on me, on us, and he shouldn't be there." Kelly turned to Maggie as if he had to drive this point home. "He sha-shouldn't have been there!"

He inhaled a long, shuddering intake of breath and continued. "Finally, clutching the pipe for support, he managed to control his laughter long enough to say: 'Don't let me stop you, don't mind me!' He laughed some more. I started across the room toward him and his face twisted up as he spat out his next sentence: 'The cohabitation of the cripples!' He threw back his head on top of that long, red neck of his, trying to repeat the phrase which caught his fancy so, but he was laughing too hard.

"I ran toward him. My eyes were glued to his neck; without a shirt and collar, it looked even longer, redder, more grotesque than ever. Before I even got hold of him, I could already feel the power in my hands—like an animal must feel in his teeth. His head was stretched back when I grabbed his throat and dug my fingers into him. I not only wanted to choke him, I wa-wanted to tear his throat apart, *rip* it apart. His head jerked forward and he lost his balance. Our bodies collided and I almost vomited with disgust as I felt his erection pressing against my hip—God only knows how long he'd been watching us!

"I think that was what made me hang onto his neck until his eyes bulged out and I could see the fright in them. In his terror he summoned up strength and began to resist me. He grabbed my hands and tried to tear them away, but I had my fingers imbedded in his flesh. That throat was such a target. And when I felt he might succeed and just as he went off balance and tipped to the side in front of one of the pipes—I smashed his head back against it.

"Bethel screamed; she must have been looking toward us now. He shook his head; he was dazed. Bethel screamed, 'David!' And I banged his head against the pipe again, harder this time. It made a weird hollow sound that echoed up the pipe and spread out across the ceiling. My father muttered: 'Jesus!' No, I thought, no Jesus, Jesus won't help you now. 'David!' Bethel screamed again and again and each time she screamed my name I smashed his head against the pipe until she ran screaming past me up the stairs.

"I could feel the dead weight of his body in my arms. I let go of him and he fell—such a long way it seemed—to the ground and lay on his side on the floor. His eyes were wide open and blood trickled out of his mouth."

Kelly held back his sobs, speaking with a trembling strength. "I kicked him in the stomach and spoke for the first time. 'There!' I said. And I kicked him maybe two or three times more. 'There! And there!'

"Immediately I was covered with horror at what I'd done. I called up the stairs: 'Bethel!' But I'd heard the front door slam when she ran out. There was only silence in the house. I knelt down by my father." A burst of laughter escaped Kelly. "And you know what I thought? I thought how ugly he looked, how *ugly* he was! And I got frightened, like I used to at horror movies, and ran up the stairs and out onto the street.

"Bethel was nowhere in sight; she'd run off. The car was there, her mother's car, and I got in it." He cocked his head and looked at Maggie. "Isn't it funny how I knew my mother wasn't in the house? I simply knew she wasn't there. I drove to the police station and parked right in front of it. A policeman was standing there and he said, 'You can't park there, son.' I paid no attention to him; I just walked up the steps into the station.

"A middle-aged sergeant sat at a high desk, like a judge's bench, writing something. I walked up to him and said, 'I killed my father.' I remember so well the way he looked up and then down at me with a tentative half-smile and said, 'What, son?' Both of them called me 'son.' I suppose I'd mumbled it; I was in shock. I repeated, 'I killed my father.' But the sergeant only looked at me and shook his head, as if to say: 'No, no, you didn't, now come on, son, what *did* you do?'

"Just then I heard the other policeman's voice—he'd followed me in—saying, 'This kid's parked in front of the green—' And I turned and yelled at him: '*I killed my father.*' That stopped him. The desk sergeant reached out and grabbed me by the shoulder and turned me around. 'What did you say, son?' There was concern on his face now. 'I killed my father,' I said for the last time. And they believed me."

CHAPTER 26

Kelly hunched his shoulders, holding his arms out in a gesture of helplessness. "And I did," he sighed. "I killed him."

Maggie put her arms around him and drew him to her. Having told her in so many words, Kelly felt immeasurably unburdened and this freedom opened him up and he could feel himself filling with love for her. To Maggie, the fact of his telling her was an act of love in itself. He held her in return and in their silent embrace, standing there on the warm sand, they exchanged unlimited messages of understanding, shaded with promises of help—more than any words could have accomplished.

After a long time, she released him, picked up her bathing cap, took his hand, and they walked across the sand. When they got to the water's edge, she turned to face him. "God, you talk a lot!" Her low, husky laughter echoed out over the water and Kelly laughed, too. She gave him a quick shove, catching him by surprise and sending him sprawling back into the water. She jumped in after him and, as he stood up waist high in it, she slipped her arms about his neck.

The sun had changed from late-afternoon orange to the color of a ripe persimmon, bathing the cove in warm tones of umber. Maggie's features, glistening wet and unencumbered by her thick hair now that she wore a bathing cap, reminded Kelly of a sculpted head: the wide eyes, the highlighted cheekbones, the smooth hollows of her cheeks sloping down to her chin.

And to Maggie, in light of this recent knowledge, he was an unbelievably tender and special person.

They stood there in the water gazing at one another. After a while she took one hand and traced her fingers from the cleft in his chin down his neck and between his pectorals to his flat stomach. She smiled as she drew her fingers around the waistband of his trunks to his back and then brought them up the hard valley of his spine and outlined his shoulders. "There," she sighed, "now that we've had Body Appreciation Class, let's have a go at the rock."

She released him and they started off, first doing the crawl, then switching to the sidestroke, and after a while, merely paddling in the water, getting their second wind. They looked at each other, expelling happy sounds on their breath. Maggie switched to the crawl again and Kelly kept even with her, marveling at her ability in the water. It was farther to the rock than it had seemed when they stood on the shore looking out at it. There was still a quarter of the way to go.

Once more they stopped and treaded water. "Feels good," Maggie panted.

"Yes."

"Invigorating," she added.

"Uh-huh."

"Invigorating—hell! I'm bushed."

Maggie lunged ahead, doing the sidestroke again, pushing forward in a final spurt of energy until she stopped long enough to put her toes down and touch bottom. She turned to him, smiling and breathing hard, and placed one hand on his shoulder; they walked ahead until the water was ankle-deep and then stepped up onto the narrow strip of clean sand at the base of the rock towering above them. The sun cut over a sloping shoulder of the rock, warming half of the beach, and after shaking the water from their bodies, they sat side by side in the weakening rays of it.

When they had returned to normal breathing, Maggie touched him on the knee. "Did you see Bethel after that?" She quickly added, "Matter-of-fact, what happened? You've left me on a cliff. And your mother? What about your mother?" She sounded indignant.

He smiled, but only for an instant. He looked down at the sand between his legs and made crisscross marks in it with his fingers. "My mother had had a heart attack after they'd been on the road only an hour or so. My father took her to the hospital, stayed awhile, and went home. I suppose later on he went down to his office and began drinking.

"She was in bed in the hospital when a nurse, coming on duty, told another nurse that Reverend Greenall had been killed by his son. They were standing out in the hall right by her door. She screamed, made a fuss, and started to get out of bed. While they were trying to restrain her—she died. I never saw her alive again."

Maggie inhaled a deep breath and controlled an impulse to embrace him again.

"They found," Kelly said with irony, "quite a collection of pornography on top of my father's desk and more in the drawers. A woman came forward the next day, the operator of a motel about thirty miles from Lemming, with stories about my father and a certain lady he'd been bringing there for the past three years. She didn't know he was a minister, or who he was, until she saw his picture in the paper. The lady was located in Lemming, a rather nondescript woman, a hostess at a Howard Johnson's restaurant outside of town. She liked to be beaten. My father used to whip her.

"Do you remember the couple I told you about that were friends of Bethel's parents, the people who left my father's church after Bethel had her attack?" Maggie nodded. "He brought a famous criminal psychiatrist from New York, Dr. Richard Vogel, in on my behalf and—it was strange, it was

all over the papers for about three days, headlines, everything. Then it was like everybody got together; there was a
speedy grand jury hearing, they listened to Dr. Vogel, and it
was all hushed up. Of course, with all the mess that came
out about my father, the Church—and I spell that with a
capital C—was anxious to have as little publicity as possible.
I was remanded to Dr. Vogel's custody. For a while I was at
a place in Long Island; later he turned me over to a psychiatrist in Cleveland when I moved there to live with my aunt.

"Because of the initial amount of publicity and then the
case dropping off to nothing, there were always people trying to trace it, follow it up. I got permission to change my
name. I picked Kelly because I liked it and Kelly was a
friend of mine. And I took McDermott from a character in a
book I'd read. The sound of them together, Kelly McDermott, sounded exactly unlike to me. I liked that. So here I
am, Kelly McDermott, né David Greenall."

"And Bethel?"

"I only saw her once, when she came to give testimony."

"Never after that?"

"No, it was too much of a shock for her. It was wrong. We
never, not the way the two of us were, we never could
have—what?—circumnavigated that afternoon in the basement. She's married now. We exchange Christmas and
birthday cards."

"But in all the years since then—how many?" Maggie
asked.

"Ten."

"What did you do all that time?"

"Oh . . ." Kelly sighed listlessly. "Four years at Western
Reserve in Cleveland, two in the Navy—I don't know why I
did that, enlisted, that is—and the last four in New York."

"That accounts for the time, but what sort of years?" Kelly
only shook his head; she sat watching him for a while.
"You're talked out, aren't you?"

He looked up at her. "Yes, I guess I am."

"I know." Maggie touched him lightly on the arm. She
stretched her neck around and looked at the sloping, jagged

edge of the rock. In the late rays of the sun their faces were the color of bronze. "This time of day, when you're with someone, when you have someone, can be the most quietly exciting. If you're alone, it can be the most frightening, can be panic-making."

Kelly nodded and they leaned together; as they sat in the ebbing warmth of the sun, he knew he had someone.

They heard a call and looked up to see Stosh waving to them from the beach opposite.

Maggie stood up. "Come on out," she called. Kelly stood next to her.

Stosh yelled something, but all they heard was the last word in a rising inflection: "—sharks?"

"No," Maggie yelled, turning to Kelly. "Tell him to meet us halfway. And tell him no sharks."

"No sharks," Kelly yelled, waving to him. "Meet us half-way." He glanced at Maggie. "There aren't, are there?"

"Let's hope not," she laughed.

The last sliver of sunlight was cut off from the sand by the rock as they walked into the water. They swam in toward the beach, doing the sidestroke and keeping even with one another. They didn't stop for a breather until they saw Stosh chopping water fifteen yards ahead of them.

"Swims with all the grace of a rock!" Maggie panted.

They waited until Stosh, breathy and grinning, splashed up even with them. "How'd you make it out there? Flora saw you." He ducked his head in the direction of the house. "She's sore as hell."

"Another demerit," Maggie sighed.

Stosh was dog-paddling. "The water's great. Hey, how come you're sure there ain't no sharks?"

"We didn't see any," Maggie said.

Stosh shouted: "You mean that's *all?*" Maggie nodded. "Jeez, I'll bet there's sharks." He looked down in the water.

"Look!" Maggie shouted, "there's one!"

Stosh screamed and thrashed in the water. "Where— where?" Maggie's laughter stopped him. "What a dirty— that's a dirty trick!"

She patted his shoulder "Stosh, baby, sharks—the kind that eat nice young Polish-American boys like you—don't come in this close to shore. And they don't usually attack unless they're frightened, or cornered, or there's blood in the water. So don't—"

"Wait a minute, wait a minute," Stosh said. "Answer me one question, will you? Who was it talked to a shark to find out they don't come in close to shore, or don't bite unless they're scared or there's blood in the water?" Maggie and Kelly laughed. "I mean it. What shark gave out this big interview and spilled the beans, huh?"

"There are no sharks," Maggie said. Without warning she ducked beneath the surface, grabbing Stosh's legs and pulling him under. He, in turn, reached out, clinging to Kelly and taking him down with him. The three of them ducked one another and when they emerged, laughing and spitting water, Stosh thrashed away in an effort to escape. "Easy," he sputtered, "I ain't no Superman."

"You ain't no Truman Capote, either!" Maggie cried. "To the shore!" and they began swimming in.

Kelly paced himself, first doing the crawl, then the sidestroke and back to the crawl until he felt he could touch bottom. He put his feet down, but he was not as close as he thought. Lunging ahead with a few more long strokes, he brought himself into water shallow enough to stand in.

He turned around. Stosh chopped water about twenty yards away, but Maggie moved slowly another ten yards behind him. The sun was sliced in half by the horizon. The sky above it was slashed with panels of red, orange and magenta. Stosh touched bottom, stumbled out of breathlessness and caught his balance. "This sure is different from when we used to swim in the Hudson River. You could hardly make your way for the scum-bags!" He turned around and faced out to sea. "Hey, Mags, c'mon."

She was doing the sidestroke, barely moving, holding her head up out of the water with effort, not at all the form she'd shown when they swam out to the rock.

"You all right?" Kelly called out.

She didn't answer, but kept treading slowly through the water. Kelly plunged out toward her; Stosh called out, "Hey!" and followed him. When Kelly neared her, he could see her mouth was open in a slack sort of way and her breaths were coming out short and sharp. "You all right?" he repeated.

She acknowledged his question by a small movement of her head and kept coming forward. Her eyes were heavy-lidded. She stopped for a moment; her mouth bobbed below the surface; she paddled her hands in front of her for buoyancy, and when her mouth hit the air again, she coughed faintly. Kelly quickly swam the last few strokes to her. "Here, hang on to my neck." He turned in the water and felt her hands upon his shoulder blades. They were icy cold. "My neck," he said, back-treading. Her long fingers slid up his shoulders until they clung weakly to his neck. He swam, lunging forward in long strides and pulling her weight behind him.

"Maggie?" Stosh called out, still coming toward them.

A few more strokes and Kelly let his feet down, touching the sand. She slid off him and he quickly turned to put an arm around her waist, as Stosh came to the other side of her. She smiled briefly and put a hand to her throat. "Whew, I—I suddenly gave out."

They walked slowly to the beach. Even in the fading light of the cove, Kelly could detect a milky blue-white pallor upon her face and a darker blue in her lips. She was so cold to the touch he wondered she wasn't trembling.

Coming out of the water, Kelly felt the dead weight of her body as she sank toward the ground. He bolstered her but she said, "Sit awhile." Stosh and Kelly lowered her onto the wet sand. "Ahhh!" She expelled a large breath. Her head tilted forward but she forced it upright, holding it back and stretching her neck.

Kelly saw the concern on Stosh's face. Maggie opened her mouth. "I—" Her head cocked to the right. "Stosh . . ." she said.

"Yes," he replied, as if she'd finished a complete sentence. He turned to Kelly. "Let's get her up to the house."

They knelt beside her while she stretched her arms out and placed her hands around their necks. Each one curling a hand under her leg they stood, raising her to a sitting position between them. They stepped off together and walked in silence across the sand. Maggie looked toward the west. "Colors . . ." she said, with an attempt at interest and vitality. Kelly glanced back, stumbled slightly and regained his balance. Maggie laughed, only it sounded more like a hiccup.

They stood her on the sand when they got to the rock. Hopping up on it, Kelly leaned down and slipped his hands under her arms. In a joint effort he lifted as Stosh swung her legs up onto the rock, jumping up himself while Kelly steadied her.

"For the climb up," Stosh said, "I think one at the feet, one at the head." As Kelly already had her under the arms, Stosh bent down and grasped her feet.

Maggie shook her head. "No . . . Stosh."

"What?" he asked, straightening up.

"You . . ."

"What? Me, back there?" He pointed to where Kelly held her, and she nodded. Stosh shrugged and relieved Kelly of his hold.

Kelly sensed she didn't want him to focus on her in this condition. She preferred having him by her legs, facing away from her. He bent down, taking an ankle in each hand and shifting his body between her legs. Together they lifted her and started slowly up the wooden gangplank.

"Maggie!" Flora's voice pierced the air. She had come out onto the terrace and stood looking down at them.

"Cheese-it, the cops," Stosh said.

"Oh-oh," Maggie gasped, not without a trace of humor.

"What is it?" Flora called out.

"Turned her ankle!" Stosh yelled.

They saw Flora place a hand to her chest in a gesture of relief.

"Stosh!" Maggie chided him.

"Shh," he whispered. "She won't heckle us all the way."

"Is it bad?" Flora called down.

"No," Stosh yelled, "just a twist."

"How did—"

Stosh interrupted her. "Stop making us talk—it's tough enough lugging her."

She made a little waving gesture at them and disappeared into the house. "Worked," Stosh said.

They reached the big rock, slowly navigated the chiseled part, and stepped off onto the second gangplank. "Good boys," Maggie said. She wiggled her toes in a show of appreciation at Kelly. He smiled without turning to look at her.

When they reached the steps leading up the side of the cliff to the terrace, Flora's face appeared over the railing. She watched closely while they carefully picked their way up them. She held a terrycloth robe open and her face sharpened with concern as she studied Maggie. She had barely opened her mouth to speak when Stosh interrupted her. "I lied, it's not her ankle, just one of her tired spells."

"Ahh!" Flora chuckled. "Maggie, you—"

Maggie spoke in weary resignation, "Flora . . ."

"All right," Flora snapped as they were about to set Maggie down, "keep on, right into the bedroom." She draped the robe over Maggie and led the way, turning to face them as they carried her through the doorway. "I should have known—"

"Flora!" Maggie summoned her remaining strength for this utterance.

Flora turned her head away and walked to the bed. They laid Maggie down; her eyes were half-closed; she was breathing faintly but more regularly.

"Stosh, get my bag," Flora said. "Kelly, you'd better wait out there." She didn't look at him, only waved her arm in the direction of the door. Her avoidance of him was a tacit accusation of complicity for Maggie's condition.

Kelly walked into the living room followed by Stosh, who

said out of the side of his mouth, "Don't screw around with Flora Nightingale!" and hurried to follow her instructions.

Kelly wandered out onto the terrace, where he stood looking out across the darkening waters of the cove at the spectacular remains of the sunset. Having shared his secret, it was as if Maggie had seen him through his crisis and now, when she needed help, all he could do was stay out of the way. He experienced a sense of helplessness and it demoralized him.

Remembering their beach things, he stepped to the edge of the terrace and looked down. In the deep twilight he could make out a dark clump on the sand and he set off down the steps.

When he'd folded the towels and packed the beach bag, he stared out over the water once more; the sky far out to the west was a solid swatch of magenta now, as if some great conflagration were raging beneath the horizon. He shuddered involuntarily, looking back toward the house and taking in the faint glow of light behind the draped bedroom windows. He turned his head around and glanced up at the edge of the cliff. In the murkiness, it was difficult to tell where the bluff ended and the sky began. Shuddering again, he experienced an inexplicable moment of uneasiness.

CHAPTER 27

For the first few seconds after he awakened in the morning, Raffaello lay very still, listening for the small sounds of Maggie moving about. Then, with a rude jolt, the realization that she was gone came to him.

He sat up in bed and rubbed a hand over his face. Feeling passionate in a heavy, drugged way, he turned on his side, facing where she usually lay when they awakened, to his left. How closely they fell asleep, legs and arms entwined, wrapped up in one another, more like young lovers than a couple in their middle years.

Their love-making was uninhibited and young, too; everything about their relationship was youthful; their appetites for one another, even their fights. They both enjoyed making love in the early hours of the morning; then they would go back to sleep for an hour or so, a complacent sleep of pure contentment.

He lay there drowsily rolling in sensual memories until he felt an ache in his groin; he censored himself for giving in to daydreams which could only add to the loneliness he was experiencing.

He showered and shaved quickly. Still, he felt stuffy and, in a way, unclean. He'd been in these same rooms for over twenty-four hours. He needed a change of scene, some fresh air. He decided to take a walk—"to wash the stink off," his father used to say.

The air was clear and brisk as he strode west on Fiftieth Street, but he was snug and warm in the cashmere overcoat Maggie had bought him in London; she'd given him the soft kid gloves and the cashmere scarf, too. He felt cleansed and mellow and—suddenly optimistic, too.

Catching sight of himself approaching in the angled mirror of an antique shop, he followed his image out of the corner of his eye. He still cut a striking figure. He possessed that intangible something, even if he wasn't actually recognized, the scent of a celebrity, someone to reckon with, that made heads turn and eyes follow him as he walked down the street, entered a restaurant, or crossed a hotel lobby. He could sense it and it gave him prideful pleasure.

There, those two girls walking together had both looked at him. He stopped at the corner of Fifth Avenue and turned to cross to the south side of Fiftieth Street. One of the girls glanced quickly behind her; no sooner had she turned back than the other, pretending to brush a strand of hair out of her eyes, sneaked a look. He smiled and crossed the street.

After coffee and juice at a stand near Times Square, he strolled south. In the back of his mind he had the notion to walk by the site of the old Metropolitan; even though an office building now stood there, he still felt an affinity for the neighborhood. But when he reached Forty-second Street the marquee of a movie house caught his attention. A Maggie Banner festival, a double feature, probably thrown on overnight to cash in on the publicity, was playing.

He found himself standing in front of the theater looking at the framed stills. One of the movies he remembered well; the other, one of her earliest and, he'd often heard her say, one of her best, he hadn't seen. He bought a ticket and walked down the mirrored foyer. The clock in the lobby read five minutes after ten as the doorman tore his ticket. He passed a woman reading a detective magazine behind the candy counter and entered the rear of the auditorium where the heavy odor of popcorn, smoke, garlic, urine and sleep hung in the air.

A shot of birds flocking across the night sky in silhouette against the moon filled the screen.

A black couple leaned together in sleep in the last row. Raffaello took off his coat and walked down the center aisle as a shot of horses grazing in a ravine replaced the birds. He could hear, along with the pastoral background music, the loud, rasping snore of a fat man slumped in a seat over to the right. There were no more than twenty people in the orchestra floor and the majority of them looked as if they'd spent the night there. Two skinny Puerto Rican boys, pompadours of dark hair glistening in the refraction of light off the screen, sat holding hands.

He took a seat as, up on the screen, the shadowy figure of a girl standing under a tree in an orchard appeared. The camera moved in closer and closer until a streak of moonlight caught the face of Maggie Banner.

Raffaello sat up straight in his seat. God, how beautiful she was—*is!* A smile showed itself in her eyes before her lips parted and she stepped away from the tree, one hand extended. A young man appeared out of the shadows and took her hand. "How long would you have waited?" he asked.

"All night," she replied in that familiar voice, husky even in her twenties, and with the same frankness that was her trademark.

Raffaello suddenly ducked his head around to see if anyone had caught him watching her. *Of course not, you fool!* His stomach constricted. What was he doing to himself— sitting in a Forty-second Street flea house watching her in a picture at least twenty years old at ten o'clock in the morning!

He walked quickly up the aisle. Her voice followed him out to the lobby: "Will we always feel like this, do you suppose? Even when we're old and wrinkled, like two prunes?" Then her husky laughter.

"Stop it, stop it!" Raffaello said. The candy lady looked up from her magazine as he hurried down the foyer and out onto the sidewalk. He crossed the street and walked into a cheap bar; the smell of the place almost rivaled the movie house. He ordered a scotch, neat, and when the man brought him the shot and a chaser, Raffaello noticed the scarlet remains of a woman's lip-print on the water glass.

"Dirty," he said, shoving the glass and two dollar bills toward the bartender, a greasy complexioned man with enlarged pores.

"Sure," the man said, but he was eyeing Raffaello closely. Before reaching for a clean glass he squinted and leaned forward. As Raffaello raised the shot to his lips the man said, "Say, aren't you that Raffaello—"

"No," Raf said. He downed the drink, coughed and wiped his mouth off.

As he walked to the door, the bartender snickered: "Sure, sure you are. Hey," he called out, "your lady friend's right across the street there!" The man's insinuating wheeze infuriated him, but he kept going.

Whereas the air was brisk and snappy in a friendly way when he left the hotel, now the cold was penetrating, damp and gritty and hostile. Still, he refrained from taking a cab. Instead, he stopped off in several bars on the way back to the hotel. By the time he left the third bar he felt a warm glow again. Passing a smart women's shop, Raffaello's eye was caught by a brocaded hostess gown of green and blue, a favorite color combination of Maggie's. Without thinking, he reached inside his breast pocket for his wallet.

Ah-ah, what are you doing? He removed his hand. The voices said: steady, steady. But he contradicted them. After all, why not buy it for her? Their separation was temporary; Ralph Bianco would find out where she was, and he'd have a present when he appeared to surprise her!

Stepping out of the store with the package under his arm, he turned and walked into the bar next door to celebrate his purchase. By the time he arrived back at his suite there was a slight weave to his walk and his breathing was interspersed with brief snorts and a gasp every now and then.

A long white florist's box rested on the floor inside the sitting room door. He lifted off the lid, folded back the white tissue, and found a large plastic Easter lily. A small card read: "Now you know how it feels. Sympathies! Jenny." She'd finally come out in the open and declared herself. He looked at the Easter lily; he was neither angered nor amused by the token. He only thought it foolish and somewhat psychotic of her.

It was a quarter past twelve. He put in a call to Ralph Bianco, but he was out. He called the desk to inquire for messages. A Hollywood gossip columnist had left her long-distance number; there were several calls from local newspapermen, and one from his widowed brother, Dominic.

He was knee-deep in guilt for not having contacted his family since his return. His father had suffered a stroke three years before and no matter what the doctors said about his mental alertness, Raffaello was certain that behind that sunken face and those blank eyes his brain was as numb as his power of speech. It pained him to see the man propped up in his favorite chair, his caved-in form bundled in a blanket, spittle on his chin, able only to fix a frozen stare at whatever came into his line of vision. As soon as he was reunited with Maggie he would pay them a visit, loaded down with presents for his spinster sister, Carla, his brother, and Poppa.

Raffaello was sitting on the sofa, not thinking of anything in particular, perhaps only listening to the voices say her name, when he felt something hot on his cheek. As he reached a hand up to see what it was, a gulping choke escaped him.

In an instant wracking sobs burst from his mouth and tears spilled down his face. A key clacked in the lock and the door opened. A maid stepped into the room, her arms filled with linen. "Away—get away!" he cried, half-sob, half-curse. She quickly backed into the hall and closed the door.

Taking a handkerchief from his pocket, he stood up and wiped off his face. He couldn't remember starting to cry.

Suddenly he was simply crying; now, just as suddenly, he had stopped. What was he crying about? He couldn't designate the emotion behind it. He'd been thinking of his father; was he crying over his *father?*

No, he knew why he was crying.

Was he drunk again? Yes, he'd been drinking and—he glanced around the room. How long had he been in this hotel, days or weeks? A quick, vicious wave of hatred for Maggie swept over him, that she could so reduce him to tears.

Oh, Lord, he never remembered feeling so blue. Flattened out, trampled upon, stomped down and drained. A funk, Maggie called it whenever—"Stop it with Maggie!" he groaned. "Stop it!"

He fixed himself a stiff drink. Until he knew where to find her, no use sitting around in misery. He took a sleeping pill and left word with the desk he was not to be disturbed unless Morty, Ralph Bianco or Maggie herself called. Although this last possibility had been whittled down to a splinter, it still pricked him.

When Kelly returned to the house with the beachbag, it was suggested he share Stosh's bedroom for the night so Maggie might have a complete rest. After cleaning up, he was plied with drinks by Stosh, who did his best to keep the stereo stacked with records and make small talk. During a brief lull in the music, while Stosh was getting some cheese and crackers from the kitchen, Kelly switched the radio on but found it wasn't working. Curiosity over his newfound notoriety was still with him; it also occurred to him there was a possibility his past might be exhumed. He would prefer to let it lie buried. He pulled the cabinet away from the wall and saw that the radio was not plugged in.

Stosh entered the room and made straight for the phonograph. "Radio's on the bum, no use pluggin' it in."

They ate dinner in the kitchen without Flora, who took her plate in with Maggie. They were drinking coffee when Flora called to Stosh. When he returned, after about five minutes, he said, "Maggie's resting," and sat for a moment without speaking. Then, taking a deep breath, he slapped his hand down on the tabletop. "Hey, let's go for a ride. Maybe on down below here, see what's down there." Kelly said he might read a little and go to bed early. "Aw, let's go for a ride. Huh, Kelly?" The addition of his name at the end of the suggestion implied a plea of sorts that Kelly found difficult to ignore; also, he gathered they were meant to leave the house for a while. Stosh's acting ability could not be classified as subtle.

The night was cool but not uncomfortable. Stosh turned onto the paved highway from the steep dirt drive and headed south. They drove in silence for a few minutes until Kelly reached ahead and switched on the car radio. This triggered a burst of energy from Stosh. "Hey, Maggie says you want to know about my life story."

"Well—" Kelly was taken by surprise. When had she told him that? It was true he'd inquired only that afternoon about how Maggie had met both Stosh and Flora, a far lesser request than asking for the story of Stosh's life.

He glanced at Stosh with a smile. "Don'tcha?" Stosh asked.

"Sure," Kelly replied, feeling he would be remiss if he said anything else; then hoping to lighten the atmosphere slightly, he added, "—but you're not going to do it in *Polish,* are you?"

"Some wise guy." Stosh reached over, snapping off the radio.

It was obvious that Maggie, for whatever reasons, had given orders for him not to listen to the radio. He was equally certain Stosh had been drafted to keep him occupied and entertained.

Stosh plunged into the story of his life with enthusiasm, telling of his upbringing on the Lower East Side, of his large Polish family, of the early death of his father, and his job as delivery boy at the age of fourteen for an exclusive market in the East Fifties. He told of the chance delivery to the man who first propositioned him, offering him money, of later becoming houseboy for an interior decorator and his "friend," and of his eventual employment as call boy for Maureen, a select madam who catered to the various requests of men and women in need of companionship and more.

"Oh, by the way," Stosh said, "I forgot to tell you, you won a scholarship in case you're ever interested. You get three trial lessons," Stosh sounded his Clem Kaddidlehopper laugh. "Ever fool around in a car goin' around cliffs at sixty miles per hour? Can getcha real hot!"

"For the time being," Kelly said, "I'll take the Arthur Murray lessons."

"I'm gonna take about one more rejection from you and then knock you on your ass!" Stosh giggled before going on with his story. Although the life he described was alien to Kelly and the details often raw, Stosh spoke with candor, a certain naïve wisdom and humor. He told of the treatment he received from his family when they first learned of the life he was leading and of his estrangement from them. He spoke with sadness of his mother, who refused to see him, then suddenly added: "If only *I* was elected first Polish Pope—that'ud get the old lady, she'd have to make it up to me, then. But they passed me by. I think it was my teeth."

When Kelly reacted with surprise to the story of Stosh's long affair with Hiram, the man who had been a part-time bodyguard for Raffaello, Stosh said: "What—you didn't think there was gay hoods? Think again. Hoods are into everything—the gay scene, the dope scene, everything—just the way normal people are."

When Stosh delved into his own working relationship with Tucci, Kelly used this as a wedge to question him about Maggie's alliance with the man, but outside of relating several anecdotes of their trip abroad, Stosh was careful to skirt the main issue, always managing to lead the conversation back to himself.

They drove for miles, passing scattered native shacks, a

small farm here and there, and an infrequent settlement. The countryside was rugged in its beauty, dominated always by the jagged range of mountains slashing down the middle of the peninsula to the east and by the ocean to the west.

"They sure don't go in for towns, do they?" Stosh asked. "I guess if anyone wants to fool around, they gotta go all the way to Ensenada." He glanced at his watch. "We been gone way over an hour, might as well go back," he said casually.

He turned the car around at the next flat stretch of road they came to and drove north. If Kelly imagined Stosh might be talked out, he was mistaken. When the road curved out toward the sea, turning at a sharp bend and descending down into a valley, Stosh said: "Must be right before our place." He was suddenly quiet and Kelly sensed an air of apprehension as they curled down to the floor of the valley and climbed the far side, finally swinging out in an arc with the bluff overlooking the cove to their left. Stosh slowed the car to a crawl, searching for the dirt tracks leading off the highway to the driveway.

The beam of headlights loomed up from the left, crossing theirs and highlighting the clay tones of the cliff bordering the far side of the road. A dark blue Pontiac nosed up from the driveway and stopped at the edge of the road. Stosh braked to a stop and waved for the driver, a well-dressed middle-aged man wearing a dark suit and a hat, to go on. The man nodded and smiled briefly before pulling out into the road and driving off in the direction of Ensenada.

Kelly glanced at Stosh; his face masked out all expression except for a look of rather overintensified concentration as he turned the car off the highway and maneuvered it down into the worn wheel tracks of the dirt road.

"Visitor," Kelly said.

"Yeah," Stosh mumbled. "Boy, I'd hate to come home boiled and try this." He pulled the car up in front of the door and they got out. As they entered the living room, Flora slipped out of Maggie's bedroom and closed the door after her.

"Did you boys have a nice drive?" she asked in a soft voice.

Before Kelly could reply, Stosh said, "There was a car leaving."

"Oh," Flora said. "Yes, I ordered some things from the drugstore and they delivered. Imagine, twelve miles. I suppose distance doesn't mean a thing down here. What did you do?" She quickly thought to add: "Of course, if I'd thought of it, I'd have asked you to pick the things up for me. That is, if you went to Ensenada."

"No," Stosh said, "we drove down the other way—forgetsville!"

"Well, then," Flora said, clasping her hands together, "it worked out just as well."

Kelly was quiet, allowing them to finish whatever scene they felt obliged to play out, acknowledging with an inner smile that neither one was in danger of winning an Academy Award.

"How's Mags?" Stosh asked.

"Feeling much better," Flora said. "A good rest tonight is what she needs."

Stosh stretched and yawned. "Can we say good-night?"

"She's been dozing off and on. You'll see her in the morning." Flora turned to Kelly. "Would you like a drink or a bite to eat, Kelly?"

"No, thanks. I'm ready for bed."

"Me, too," Stosh added.

"Well, it's been a long day." Flora patted his arm.

And the three of them, standing there, agreed to end it.

A phone call awakened Raffaello in the late afternoon. He was groggy, sticky with sleep, but Ralph Bianco's news brought him quickly to his senses.

"Sorry it took so long, but there was no getting in the building last night, no porter or anything. The office was open until noon today, so my man had to wait until the afternoon. Only took a hundred bucks to the janitor—before you say anything, Raf, it's on me. Fred Bellow should be over there soon." Ralph Bianco chuckled. "Even used Lefkowitz's own Thermofax to have it copied."

"Have what copied?" Raf asked.

"The stuff, a page or two from his file on her. She's gone to some place in Mexico."

"Mexico?"

"Yes, Ensenada." The man paused before continuing, then: "Raf, there's a notation or two might interest you. Fred'll be there any minute. Listen, I've got to run, Brooklyn's got my ass in a sling. Check you tomorrow."

Raffaello thanked him and they hung up. Anticipation teased him; he could hardly wait. He'd gone to sleep in his clothes and he felt rumpled and sweaty; he wanted to be alert when he received the information on her. He had just stepped out of the shower when he heard knocking. Without drying himself, he threw on a terrycloth robe and hurried to open the door.

"Ralph Bianco sent this over." The man handed Raffaello a manila envelope.

"Yes, he just phoned." Raffaello wanted the man to vanish, wanted to rip into it.

"I put the original back where I found it. Nobody'll know it was—you know—fucked with." The man must have read his mind, because he tipped his hat and started to leave.

"Wait a minute," Raf said. "I'd like to—"

The man held up his hand. "No, it's taken care of, Ralph's orders." He stepped outside the door. "Hope it's the right stuff," he said, and he was off down the hall.

Raffaello called out his thanks and quickly shut the door. Hurrying to the small hotel writing desk, he ripped open the envelope to find copies of three memorandum sheets with the name Arnold Lefkowitz printed at the top. All of the sheets were dated and written in a longhand he guessed belonged to Lefkowitz.

The first one read: "Codicil to M.B. will being typed, filed on Monday. Check, make sure delete section 3, para 1 & 2. Call Miss Anderson, Underwriter's Trust Co. on Monday, regards deposit box and transfer of funds to Bank of America, Calif."

On the second sheet were the words, "M.B. care Miranda's Cove, Box 24, Ensenada. Contact Benny Sydow, 1700 Roxbury Drive, Bev. Hills."

Raffaello vaguely remembered Maggie's talking about Benny Sydow, a favorite director of hers, and his house in Mexico. So that was where she was off to; there was even a certain logic to it; Mexico was one of the countries they hadn't visited. He would as soon confront her in Mexico as anywhere else.

It was the third memorandum that riveted his attention. "Check #1264, $500—payable Flora Bostwick. Check #1265, $500—payable Stosh Sadowski. Check #1266, $750—payable to sister, Mrs. Beatrice Keathley, 82 Elm Court, Little Rock, Ark. $2,000 cash to Kelly McDermott, services companion. $8,000 balance payable on arrival or termination of services? Check with M.B. on this. Plane ticket for K.M. name of George Helm, San Diego, check #1267, payable Koerner Travel Agency."

A safety catch deep within him suspended his total gut reaction and allowed time for a brief phone call to a woman who had once been his secretary. She was an adoring fan and he kept the conversation to a minimum, only asking her to get information on flights to San Diego or Ensenada, if possible, and call him back.

When he hung up he picked up the piece of paper again. No telling how long he would have remained glued to that third memo, his brain stalled in a traffic jam of emotions, none of them healthy, if the phone hadn't rung. He answered it in reflex, without really thinking what he was doing.

"Hello, Raffaello . . . ?" It was a woman's voice.

"Yes."

"Radie Hughes." It was the Hollywood columnist. "I phoned you earlier, person to person; didn't you get the message?"

"Yes," he muttered.

She allowed time for an explanation of his lack of reply, but when none was forthcoming, she pressed on. "Raf, I was so sorry to hear about you and Maggie. I'm sure . . ." She went on consoling him, saying she knew they'd patch things up, Maggie this and that . . . "dear but impulsive . . . of course, one had to realize . . ." She went on in a jumble of words.

But Raffaello's mind was listening to its own jumble . . . services companion . . . *companion!* . . . together with him in Mexico, sharing with *him* . . . dragging him off, a pickup, that young-wet-behind-the-ears-skitterish—

Morty had told him but he wouldn't let himself believe it; now he'd seen the proof written down in black and white. "Christ!" he said out loud.

That stopped her. "Raf?" she asked.

"Yes."

"Anyhow, Raf, I'd love to know how you feel, for the record. Your own personal reactions to the breakup. Mind you, I know things will work out."

All reason defected; his emotions made up his mind for him. If Maggie could do this to him, she was acting without regard; yes, without any regard whatsoever. She'd left him in a dishonorable way, sneaked off. He'd given her a warning, but she paid no attention. In that case, no matter what covenant they shared, she deserved to be treated without regard. She was playing mean and dirty games and he would play mean and dirty back at her.

"As I said, Raf, I know things will work out between you, but in the meantime—"

"No, Radie, I don't think they will."

"Why do you say that, Raf?"

He could almost hear her ears growing to a point. "I'm afraid I have some news about Maggie . . ."

Still, he had to close his eyes and take a deep breath before he could continue.

CHAPTER 28

"Sleepyhead." Fingers lightly traced across Kelly's forehead. "Sleepyhead." He opened his eyes; Maggie's wide green eyes were looking down at him; her generous mouth was tugged over in a half-smile, backed up by cheekbones and swirls of smoky-blond hair. "It's me."

He smiled, too, thinking: how amazing to wake up and have Maggie Banner right there, bending over you in close-up and Technicolor. She wore an emerald-green blouse.

"I've been up for two hours. I couldn't stand waiting any longer. You might have slept all day. It's almost eleven; we didn't give you another mickey, did we?"

He shook his head, licked his dry lips, and cleared his throat. He'd read until the early morning hours; even then he'd had a hard time going to sleep, what with Stosh snoring and occasionally talking in his sleep in the bed next to him.

"Are you still tired? I'll leave if you want. And creep quietly out into the living room where," she added, "I'll play the stereo at fever pitch and do my world-famous military tap on the coffee table."

He laughed, then quickly remembered. "How do you feel?"

"How do I look?"

"Fine, you look fine."

"That's how I feel."

"Where's the gang?" Kelly asked.

"I sent them off to Ensenada. They love movies. I told them to have lunch, to *go* to one, shop, stay away as long as possible. Know why?"

"No."

"Because," she said, getting up from the bed and crossing to the window, "it's the most incredible day. Look!" She pulled the drapes open. "Isn't it fantastic?"

There was only gray to be seen. A dark, gray-flannel cloud bank hung low over the sea; trapped beneath it, a lighter gray fog moved slowly inland in wisps and patches and ripples. The ocean was gray, too, a leaden gray. "Look at the sea, like mushroom soup, only cleaner," Maggie said. "Do you like it?" And not waiting for an answer, she continued: "I love a good, honest, rainy, foggy, gray day. Of course, it's not raining yet, but there's still hope. A secret day." She turned to him. "Get up, sleepy creature! Do you like days like this?"

"Yes," he grinned at her.

"Good." She was already on her way out of the room. Below the green blouse she wore beige slacks and flat beige slippers, which shortened her and gave her a girlish walk. "I'm fixing your breakfast." She disappeared, only to pop her head back around the corner of the door a second later. "When I make a recovery, do I make a recovery, or don't I?"

"You make a recovery," he said, adding: "You have about the greenest eyes."

She tugged at the center of her emerald blouse, pulling it out from her chest and dipping her head down alongside it. "What do you think *this* is supposed to match—my teeth? Come on," she growled in a tough voice, "quit stalling, I wanna hear those feet hit the goddamn deck and *shake* it!" And she was gone.

During breakfast Maggie pumped him for an account of the time after his parents' death. Telling of those years, he let her know he'd never been able to consummate a love affair.

When she brought their coffee into the living room, she announced: "Now I'll tell *you* a few things. You've had your share of bad years, more than your share. But look how things have picked up! In what—only a few days. My God, you've got movie stars kidnapping you, pawing you, fawning all over you, they're even fixing breakfast for you! Right?" He nodded and smiled at her. "So they're getting better all the time. Oh, you've had a problem, but—" He snorted, surprising himself. "Yes," she said, "a problem, but we'll end all that. We will!" Raising a hand to her chin, she threw her head back. "Good Christ, I sound like Mistress of the Games." She thought that one over. "Well, hell, I guess I am." She took a sip of coffee and interrupted herself with a thought; putting the cup down abruptly, she spoke with a burst of energy. "May I tell you what the right experience, the first one, did for me? Of course I can, it's my house, my experience!"

"Yes," he said, thinking how the little girl in her kept making surprise appearances.

She paced back and forth in front of him. "You've probably read all the trash about my tacky background and family. It's true, most of it. I was actually brought up as one of a litter of pigs. A piglet, residing outside of Fayetteville, North Carolina.

"My father was a farmer, my mother a brood mare. Fourteen kids. I was third from the oldest. When I say farmer, I don't mean a pretty, manicured, nice little green farm. I mean a muddy, rutty, stump-filled, ugly, brown, scrubby farm that would have made Jeeter Lester crow with delight.

"I didn't hate my folks. You couldn't hate them. All they did was work, eat and sleep. Obviously they didn't sleep *all* the time—the sneaks. I can't remember when my mother wasn't pregnant. And as I grew up that was strange, because they hardly paid attention to one another otherwise.

"There was only one struggle I was aware of, but it was a lulu—survival. Then, later on, escape entered into the picture. But I'm not going to drag you through my entire child-hood. I will tell you this: I was an unattractive little girl. I was fat—all we had to eat were starches. Oh," she placed the backs of her hands up to her cheeks, vamplike, and winked, "I suppose all this fantastic bone structure was be-hind the blubber someplace, but it would have been a pure case of dynamiting to get at it." She tugged at her hair. "And this hair, it was thick all right, but a nasty shade of tan. Tan hair. It was," she shuddered, "terribly undistinguished.

"To be frank, I got the idea early on that sex was dirty. If it made people live like we lived, if what it did was bring you into the world I knew, then it was a dirty word and I wanted no part of it.

"I also remember my thoughts of marriage—later on, I did think of marriage as a means of escaping the farm—con-tained involved plots for never allowing my husband to touch me. Mainly because I didn't want to start all over again like my parents. On our wedding night I was going to spring heart disease on him, along with a note from my doc-tor saying if he ever so much as touched me 'that way,' it would mean certain death. Then I would tell hubby, with great largesse, that I understood this was a bit of a surprise and that yes, I *was* naughty waiting to let him in on my little secret until our *wedding* night, but I thoroughly understood and expected he should take a mistress.

"When I reached high school and began to read books, I thought of love in that pure, sickening, platonic way that some young girls do. I was a romanticist, but only for the setting—skip the romance. My dreams were based on living in a nice clean house with a bed to myself. There could be a husband under the roof, but not in my bed.

"I looked at boys in school if they were clean, not if they were good-looking. If they were rich, all the better. I was in awe of clean rich people. You see, our home was filthy. It was one huge diaper repository. The ones not in diapers were in various stages of self-training. The folks were too busy trying to keep the kids fed and alive, without worrying about whether they were washed or not. I can close my eyes and smell our house now. In Paris, in the hot weather, strolling by a pissoir always gives me a little twinge of homesickness. So you see," she winked at him, "life was basic, life was real where I came from."

Kelly shook his head. "I can't believe you were unattractive."

"Truth!" She held up her hand in swearing fashion. "Know what did the trick? A case of whooping cough, the likes of which you haven't heard of. No whooping, though, not a cough in a carload. It went on for over six months and I about wasted away to nothing. They didn't know what was the matter with me. I eventually went to the clinic in Fayetteville after six months of swilling down all the medicines in the world, and some young doctor, an intern, finally diagnosed—whooping cough! Did you ever hear of a case of whooping cough where you don't whoop?"

"No, I had the regular kind. I whooped like a crane."

Maggie brushed her hair back from her forehead and laughed. "What does a crane whoop like, anyway?"

"Like me when I had the whooping cough."

She laughed again. "But here's the lovely part. By the time I found out I had whooping cough, I also found out I had a face. Let's see, what was I then, about sixteen? Yes. When all the weight melted away, these," she placed her hands lightly under her breasts, "suddenly appeared. They'd probably been there all along, lost in the baby fat. I've always been rather *for* whooping cough ever since. So there I was, shaping up. I mean my legs now looked like legs, instead of pudgy stumps dissected by great dimpled knees. I not only lost weight, I seemed to have stretched up and down. Oh, there was about as much character in my face as a baked potato, but the raw materials were there to work with. All it took was a little living.

"Boys began noticing me and rather regularly. I do believe my sainted father—rest in peace—even gave me a glance or two. Mother was a bit frayed at the edges then."

"Is your mother still alive?" Kelly asked.

She cast her eyes down. "No. And the frightening thing—

after thirteen children, she died bearing her fourteenth. That doesn't seem right. Poor dear, didn't have a chance in this world." She glanced at Kelly and smiled. "And don't you know my father remarried a year or so later and sired three more! I believe his prostate finally blew up like a poisoned dog, exploded and killed him." She shook her head. "Not really. He hurt his foot on the farm and died of blood poisoning.

"So—to get back. All the malarky about working in a dime store's been overplayed. I did clerk at Neisner's in Fayetteville for a week or two. Then I got a job at a cigar store, friend of my brother, Ned. I'd dropped out of school when I had the whooping cough and never went back.

"I have to tell you that simply because men were noticing me didn't mean I was having any of them. Not at all. In fact, now that they were paying attention to me, I was even more hostile. I'm not going the way of my mother, I thought. Now that I've lost this weight and found out I'm here, you want to domesticate me, impregnate me, fatten me up, and cover me with children and I'll be lost for all time. Because of my mother's record, the idea of one or two children never occurred to me. I thought of having children as a sort of chain reaction. Once you started—there was no stopping."

Maggie dropped to her knees on a stack of cushions in front of the sofa. "Anyhow, my older sister, Franny, worked as a part-time cleaning girl for three families, all wealthy. She worked for one lady, a widow, a Mrs. Barnard, and her son. Mrs. Barnard died and about a month after her death Franny called in sick one afternoon. Mrs. Barnard's son, Peter, was leaving for England in two days and was in need of help. He asked if she could send someone in her place, and she sent me.

"It was early spring, April, a nippy evening. I took a bus right after work at six. It was a lovely old colonial house, all white and columned. I rang the bell; when the door opened the most beautiful young man I'd ever seen was standing there."

"And clean?" Kelly asked.

"Scrubbed and shining," she nodded at him. "He said hello and I said hello, and we just stood there looking at one another. Kelly, I'd never even had a crush on a boy. Oh, there'd been some I liked as pals, or admired—but never a crush. And standing there, I fell in love."

She got up from the cushions and walked to the window. "I honestly believe if he'd taken my hand and led me straight upstairs and to bed, I'd have gone." She turned and smiled at him. "I think he said hello again before asking me to come in. Once inside, we stood again and looked at each other.

"Finally, he spoke. 'Did Franny send you?' I told him yes, I was Franny's sister. 'Oh,' he seemed surprised. 'You don't look like Franny.'

" 'I know,' I heard myself saying, completely at a loss for words, 'I've been sick.'

"And he laughed, a sweet, gentle, lovely laugh, and I laughed. You see, Franny was out-and-out fat; in my own way I was explaining to him why I didn't look like her.

"He asked me if I'd had supper; I told him I'd just got off work and I'd eat later on when I got home. 'Please have a bite now,' he said. 'Especially if you've already put in a day's work.' I said I'd fix myself a sandwich, but he took me into the drawing room—the most beautiful house I'd ever been in—asked me to sit down, and excused himself.

"When he came back he said dinner would be ready soon and handed me a glass of something. I told him I didn't drink. He said, 'It's only sherry.' I declined, but he said, 'Oh, please do,' like I would be doing him a favor. So I sipped it. I expected to be given a bite in the kitchen, but when the cook, a lovely old black woman, announced dinner, he took me into the dining room and sat me down across from him. I'd never in my life ever—" After all these years, delving back to that day she was still speechless.

"Cinderella?" Kelly smiled.

"Yes, Cinderella. I was so out of my element I could barely

eat, but that wasn't the only reason. The slipper might not fit me, but he was certainly the Prince. And I was in love. Who could eat?

"He spoke to me not as a cleaning girl, but as an equal, spoke openly and warmly. I missed a lot of what he said because I was completely stunned. And he asked me about myself. I told him about having the whooping cough without ever whooping, by far the most exotic fact I could dredge up about myself. He inquired about Franny and my family. When he found out about all my brothers and sisters—of course, we were only twelve then, my mother was carrying number thirteen—he was fascinated.

"After dinner he took me upstairs. It was his mother's bedroom and dressing room and sitting room that needed cleaning. Her two sisters had been over, and they'd been sorting through her things. Still, there was a pile of perfectly good clothes they hadn't wanted. Peter said to please take anything that anybody I might know could use. Mind you, not a word about my family. He wouldn't embarrass me.

"I worked, cleaning up her rooms for a couple of hours. I helped him take some things to the attic. Then he took me to his bedroom and study. He'd been packing, and I straightened up his rooms while he carried some things down to the basement.

"I remember just standing in his room after he left, seeping up the feeling of him, soaking up the essence of him through his things. I went on a touching spree. I knew I would never touch him. I pressed my hand down on his bed: this is where he sleeps; I placed my hand on the top of his desk: this is where he writes; I put my hands in his slippers, like hand puppets: these are his slippers.

"And I had a cry for myself. Not a big cry and not a cry of sadness because I couldn't have this beautiful, clean, lovely Prince; but a small cry of happiness at experiencing the *emotion* of love I felt for him.

"When I finished working he asked if he could drive me home. I'd made up quite a bundle out of the clothes and although it meant a bus ride downtown and another bus out to the farm, about nine miles, I said no. I didn't want him to see where I lived."

"Didn't you want to be with him?" Kelly asked.

"Yes, of course." Then, just as quickly and with vehemence: "No!" In reply to Kelly's questioning glance, she shrugged: "I mean, what was the point? It was hopeless, out of the question. I'd met my Prince, I'd fallen in love, and I had that. He was off to London. I could love him no matter where he was. Meeting him, that one night, couldn't change me that much. I was still an incurable romanticist.

"He insisted, even when I suggested he must have friends he wanted to see before he went to London. He said he'd been away most of the last four years at college and he'd recently broken off his engagement and—he drove me home.

"I didn't enjoy the ride. I wanted to, I tried to, but I had the memory of him all tucked away, and I'd just as soon his memory of me, if indeed he'd have one, end at his house. I could only anticipate his reaction when we arrived at 'home.' Driving into our yard, you'd have sworn you were entering a combination swamp and city dump."

"I'll bet he didn't bat an eye," Kelly said.

"Why—why do you say that?"

"A real Prince wouldn't."

"He didn't. He might as well have been dropping me off at Tara. Tara!" she snorted. "With three mongrel dogs barking; our sow, Henrietta, caught nursing her newest litter, lurching up out of a giant mud hole; assorted chickens sending up a flurry; my fifteen-year-old brother, Elson, and a kid from the next farm scooting out from the tool shed—Lord knows what they'd been up to; and to top it off, my father opening the door to see what the commotion was, squinting out at us in his long underwear and joined by Jeremy, age nine, without *any* underwear.

"I was on the floorboards from embarrassment, but Peter didn't flick an eyelash. 'It's only *me*, Dad,' I shouted, with murder in my voice. You know what he called out? 'Which one?' 'Maggie,' I yelled. 'Oh,' he mumbled, as if saying: 'Oh yes, I remember that one.' He scratched himself, shoving Jeremy out of the way, and closed the door.

"I said a quick good-bye, thanked him for the ride and the things. I was reaching for the door when Peter suddenly said in a firm voice: 'No, no!'

"He startled me. I hadn't done anything for him to say, 'No, no!' to.

" 'What?' I asked.

" 'No,' he repeated. He reached over and took my hand. 'Have dinner with me tomorrow.' I couldn't answer. 'Will you have dinner with me?' I was speechless. I couldn't look at him, let alone speak. 'Please.' Then he said my name: 'Maggie.' There was an entire book in the way he spoke it, a book I'd never read, never even opened, but nevertheless understood.

"Some wisdom beyond my years, way beyond, told me the Prince wanted to be with me, with *me*, Maggie Herget, now, at this minute, and the prospect of me even meeting another Prince was slim. Still, I was unable to answer. Then he said something else in a low soft voice.

" 'What?' I asked.

" 'Stay with me tonight.'

"I said—yes. I heard the very short echo of my saying yes.

"He pulled around out of the yard, and we drove back to town without speaking, Peter holding my hand all the way. When we walked into the house, he turned to me and said, 'I'm leaving the day after tomorrow.'

" 'I know . . .'

" 'I don't think it's right,' he said.

" 'Yes,' I replied, 'it is.'

"He asked me if this was my first time. I told him it was. He took me upstairs to his room, gave me a robe and slippers, told me to shower or bathe if I wanted, to make myself comfortable and call him when I was ready.

"I went through the motions of undressing and bathing in a trance. When I did call down to him, he came up and sat on the bed and we lay there kissing and making love, he with his clothes on. After a while I wanted his clothes off so

badly, wanted the feel of his body, his skin, next to mine."
She smiled. "He knew what he was doing. So that by the
time he undressed, desire had completely dissolved my
virgin fears."

She held her hands, fingers entwined, up to her chin.
"His love-making was—here's that word again—clean, ex-
quisitely gentle, yet passionate, so timed and executed to
please and excite me, and wildly successful. If every
woman's first experience equaled mine, frigidity would be
obsolete." A smile of remembered delight stretched her
mouth, then she snapped her fingers. "How's that for winning the race the first time out?"

She stood up from the sofa, once more examining the endless gray vista outside the glass doors. After a moment she
turned to him. "I didn't go to work the next day. I stayed
with him that night and until he left the following day. He
said he'd write, but I didn't pin my hopes on it. He'd made a
woman out of me and I loved him. That's all that mattered."

"Did he tell you he loved you?"

"No, he was too kind to leave me behind like a stuck but-
terfly. After he'd gone I lived off him, I actually fed off my
memories of him. I looked at men differently, too. Maybe
this man or that one had a part of Peter hidden in him, had a
secret gentleness, a kindness.

"I didn't hear from him for over three weeks. Then I got a
letter. When I opened it there was a plane ticket from New
York to London and a check for five hundred dollars. He
wrote that he loved me and would I join him?" She snapped
her fingers together again. "Made Cinderella look like Apple
Annie."

"And you went?"

"Almost without the plane," she laughed. "No, practically
immediately. I gave my father and mother two hundred dollars—they'd have seen me off to the jungles of New Guinea
for that, poor dears—and away I went."

Maggie knelt in front of him, taking his hands in hers.
"Kelly, the whole thing was miraculous, but that first experience was the most miraculous of all, miraculous by means of

being right." She kissed his hands and pressed her cheeks down upon them. After a moment, she spoke in a level voice, looking him straight in the eye. "I wish I could do that for you. I would rather be able to do that . . . than almost anything I can think of. And I'll bet I can." She smiled. "But we won't push it, we'll just see." A small shake of her head. "Life's a son of a bitch, isn't it?" Again she lowered her head, pressing her cheek against his hands.

He looked down at the top of her head; he felt as much love in his heart as it could possibly contain, but the fear that his body was as dead as the farthest burned-out planet smothered any physical response he might have. Wishing for no more scar tissue, he asked what happened to the Prince.

She waved a hand in the air. "Not the point, that's the past. You're the present."

"But I want to know, I'm curious—like you."

"And stubborn," she added, standing up and walking away from him. "I lived with him in London. He'd been left a great deal of money; he didn't have to work, but he went into the printing business with an uncle."

"But you didn't get married?"

"I wanted to in the worst way. He spoke of eventual marriage and of having children—he wanted a family. But he was well aware of our ages. We were both so young. He was only twenty-two and I was seventeen. He wore his youth as he did his wealth, graciously and wisely.

"After a year or so I even tried to trap him. I began, now and then, not taking precautions. I knew if I became pregnant he'd marry me. But nothing happened. After a while I never took precautions. Finally, there was much more specific talk of marriage and having children and a cottage outside London. One night, at our neighborhood pub, he popped the question. Of course I said yes. But the next day I did a strange thing, for all my plotting: I went to a doctor and had tests to see if I could have a baby.

"I learned I couldn't. One of fourteen children, and barren

myself. Oh," she thrust a hand up in the air, following it with a wry look, "the Old Boy has infinite surprises in store for us. Another strange thing I did: I told him."

"But if he loved you—"

"He did, but I could tell it was a great disappointment. So much so he wouldn't believe me, not until several doctors later. By that time he could no longer deny the disillusion he felt with words. It was in his face, in his eyes. Our relationship was altered, in a subtle way, but it was altered. As much as I'd never wanted children, now it was coming back at me. I thought I was too young to have my sins thrown back in my face. But there it was. There was mild talk of adoption at first. We went on for almost another year. We were together for a total of almost three years. He met an English girl. What could I do?" Maggie shrugged and smiled at him, adding: "She said, smiling what in a script would be described as a 'brave little smile.'

"I loved England by then. I began going around with a wild crowd, lugging a torch just a size or two larger than Big Ben. Then, as a joke, I took a small role in a play, through friends, playing an American girl, a tart. I found I had a flair for acting and away I went."

"I remember," Kelly said, "that famous interview you gave about what would have happened to you if you hadn't become an actress."

Maggie laughed. "You mean if I hadn't become an actress, what would I have been—a whore? True, what was I trained to do? Nothing. I'd have become a whore. Same qualifications. Acting, if you have the flair for it, is a snap. I'm not talking about actors who *aren't* born with the gift, or the looks, or the chemical scent an audience sniffs right off the bat. When *they* become what we call 'stars,' that's no snap. That's hard work, grinding hard work. So is the life of a journeyman actor.

"My kind of actor, pictures mostly, if you have it, it's a breeze. And the work, outside of long hours and a lot of boring sitting around—what is it? What do you do but pump up

your ego day after day? You have the greatest writers, direc-
tors and technicians behind you, plus an ulcerated producer
or two. They're doing all the real work. You don't even comb
your own hair, simply get out there and have yourself. Oh, of
course, dedication creeps into it. Dedication to yourself, to
your image, your looks, your voice, your body, your sex appeal, your—"

"Talent," Kelly interjected.

"Talent!" she cried. "The talent I started out with con-
sisted of a pair of legs, a pair of tits, a mouth, nose, eyes, hair
and a good set of teeth. That's not talent, that's an accident.
Try to play the piano or dance or write a book with *that* talent and see how far you get."

"But you became a fine actress."

"I became a good one and why not? *You* work at something continuously for twenty years, vastly overpaid, with
the best possible people guiding you, whole legions of them
pushing you—you'd become pretty damn *fine,* too. Unless
you're a vegetable. No, of all the arts, acting's the—writing,
now there's work. Composing, painting. Ballet dancers! I
shudder to think of their lives. Acting—my kind, I'm not
talking about Olivier or—*my* kind requires about as much
discipline as attending a party. In style, mind you. Matter of
fact, my early years in pictures, walking on the set each day
was like going to a party. And the party was always for me.
And there were always the most beautiful people to play
games with, even to make love to."

"That's all there was to it?" Kelly asked. "You were never
proud of a particularly fine job you did?"

"Are you mad!" She threw back her head. "Of course I
was proud. Proud!" she laughed. "Proud's an under-
statement, I have been absolutely trans-fucking-ported by a
good job I've done—what do you think?" She stood there,
feet apart, hands planted firmly on her hips. "What in God's
holy name are we standing here in a living room in Baja California talking about *acting* for?"

Kelly could only grin at her kaleidoscopic change of
moods.

"Then let's take a walk, let's get out there in all that good fog!"

To insure his privacy, Raffaello had bought two first-class tickets on the plane. He was suspended in anticipation of seeing her; he wished for no word or event to come between. He merely sat staring out the window. When the hostess offered him a drink he avoided an exchange with her by briefly shaking his head.

He had sneaked out of New York and he was feeling slyly content with himself. His brother Dominic had finally reached him Saturday night and reminded him that Sunday was his father's birthday and Raffaello, though he knew he would be leaving in the morning, promised to appear.

But here he sat, staring out and down at the billowed layer of clouds below the plane. He had committed one disgraceful act by his disclosure to Radie Hughes (and therefore the entire Free World) and now he was unconsciously reverting to childhood behavior he had never quite left behind.

As a boy, when he had been bad and knew he would be whipped, he invariably committed a series of punishable acts one after the other in quick succession, so that retribution, when it eventually caught up with him, was well deserved. This pattern afforded him a certain perverse pleasure which he accepted without probing the reasons.

Having learned her whereabouts, the scent of her stung his nostrils and he was blinded to everything but seeing her. He was magnetized to a straight line, the shortest distance in time and space between them. His brain was too impacted by a confusing mixture of desire and anger to rehearse what kind of confrontation it might be. He would see her that evening, that's all he knew. In the meantime, he was merely allowing himself to be transported from one place to another.

CHAPTER 29

They stood on the bluff overlooking the cove. "You know what I think sometimes? Look—" She guided him gradually around in a slow circle, holding her left arm out in front of her and describing the expanse of their view while they turned. "Think of the earth, the bare earth, as it was in the beginning. Think of what it was: the sea, mountains, forests, plains, deserts. That's all there was, all we were given, the raw materials. Here—" She let go of him and bent down, scooping up a fistful of dirt in her fingers. "Dirt—not much different from any other dirt the world over.

"Now think of the World Trade Towers, submarines, airplanes, electric lights, radio, television, brain surgery, marching around out in space, taking a potshot at the moon and *hitting* it! My God, and we, people just like you and me, dredged everything we have out of this!" She crumbled the dirt in her fist, allowing it to sift through her fingers and fall to the ground. "Now that's a miracle and you can't say it isn't."

"I didn't." He grinned at her.

"But I mean . . . it's no accident. There has to be a plan for all this. It couldn't happen by people simply bumbling about. It must be part of a larger plan we have no concept of, don't you think?"

"I would think so."

"And if there's an enormous plan to it all, there must be a planner. And that's where God comes in. There must be a God. Or some higher power we can't comprehend." Once more she swung her arm out in front of her. "This simply couldn't happen by itself. It's too miraculous; miracles don't happen without somebody *making* them happen. They don't know enough; miracles don't have minds or brains. They must be the result of forces that are all-knowing, all-seeing, and whatever they/it/he/she/them is adds up to God—at least as far as I'm concerned." She glanced down at the ground, then looked up and asked the question hesitantly: "You believe in God, don't you?"

"Yes, I do."

She leaned into him, kissing him hard on the cheek, a firm kiss of gratitude one might receive for having bestowed a special gift. She spoke to the clouds: "Can't fool us, we know you're up there!" She shook her fist in the air. "But you can be a perverse bastard when you want to—you little devil, you!" She aimed a cadenza of laughter at the edge of the cliff, sliced her laughter in two, and snapped her head back to Kelly. Her face was tight with concern.

"Why does he make one woman a Farrah Fawcett Whatever and another a hopeless mental case? How did the Old Boy ever come up with war and poverty and crime and toothaches, termites, Hitler, Anita Bryant, and the delicious aging process? And when he does give the nod, hand out a goody—watch out! That's just to give you the taste of it, so you'll goddamn well know what it's like when it's snatched away. Why can't even a love affair last? Why do the scales almost always tip after the first royal flush, so that one's hanging by his fingernails for a smile or a kind word and the other's breaking his jaw stifling a yawn?"

Another burst of laughter, more a cough, brittle and derisive. "And what's the one certain thing we have dangling in front of us all our lives—death! That's a beaut, there's a *charmer* to look forward to. Must have really taken some doing on the Old Boy's part to figure *that* one out. 'Let's see,' he must have said, 'what can we give them at the end as a little present for crawling through all the muck? Ah, yes— *death!* And we'll give them a good healthy fear of it just in case they might be tempted to get a decent night's sleep along the way.' " Maggie snorted. "Why—why all that? Hmn? Or are you thinking—what incredibly naïve questions, *incredibly* naïve and simple!" She looked him straight in the eye. "Can you answer them?"

He shook his head. "No."

"But if they're so terribly childlike, so simple, why can't they be answered?" She placed her hands on his shoulders. "Why is that?"

"I don't know," he said quietly.

"Damned right you don't know. That's a whopping part of it, too—not knowing. Millions of people suffering continuously—for what? Original sin! Certainly not because that silly cunt took a bite out of an apple. Or was it Adam bit it? No matter, there's no answer."

She released him, turning and once more gazing out over the edge of the bluff to the ocean. As if by signal, the fog and mist were dispelling before their eyes, eradicated by a solid curtain of dappled gray rain moving inland from the sea. A ruffle of steam curled ahead at the base as it struck the surface of the ocean and crawled steadily forward.

"Look," Maggie said.

They were hypnotized as the fine line of steam edged forward, was broken by the rock jutting up in the ocean, mended itself inside the cove, and crept on, roiling the surface of the water as if a million tiny pebbles had been hurled down upon it. And finally the rain, cool and fresh, overtook the two figures standing on the bluff, striking them with the solid force of its easterly movement.

They looked at one another through the heavy drops that slashed between them and joined hands.

"The old son of a bitch must have heard me," she laughed. They hurried across the grass-stubbled bluff and by the time they reached the road they were drenched. "Easy," she panted, "we can't get any wetter." They walked leisurely now by the side of the road, hands interlocked, arms swinging, exchanging smiles in acknowledgment of slippery faces and matted hair.

The rain appeared to have drenched Maggie's outburst, too, to have dissolved her thoughts and fears. But Kelly recognized this query regarding God to be no curious, periodic reflection, but a deadly earnest quest. It made her eminently vulnerable and all the more lovable. He stopped short, wrapping his arms about her and swinging her up to him. He kissed her, then set her back down in front of him.

"Oh, yes," she said, "I liked that." As she stepped off alongside him: "What brought that on?"

"I felt like it."

"Oh, well, that explains it!"

It didn't, but Kelly again experienced stirrings deep inside him, tinglings and a sexual adrenaline released not only by his feelings for her, but also triggered by sky, sea, rain and earth. There was an undeniable connection between nature's wildness and whatever wildness lay buried in him.

"If we stand here much longer we'll drown—c'mon." She took his hand and broke into a run. They laughed together as they picked their way down the steep, rutted driveway, alive with rivulets of water, slipping now and then and balancing off one another until they rounded the corner and stepped onto the asphalt. They ran across the parking area and into the house where they quickly removed their jackets and kicked off their shoes.

Maggie shivered. "Didn't feel cold out there, but now it does." Running her hands down her dripping face, she said, "Look at us! Good thing Flora isn't here. C'mon." When they reached the living room, she winked at him and jerked a thumb toward the master bedroom.

He gathered his toilet articles together along with his robe and slippers from Stosh's room and when he walked through the doorway to her bedroom she was tying her terrycloth robe around her waist. Her wet clothes lay in a pile by the bathroom door. She quickly toweled her face and hair dry while he put his things in the bathroom and took a large towel off the rack for himself.

"Here, let me," she said when he stepped back into the bedroom. Dropping her towel on the bed she walked to him and touched his cheek lightly. "You remind me of the Prince. I did tell you that, didn't I? Not your looks exactly, more your quality, a chemistry."

The mention of a former lover, at this moment, even a favorable comparison, was disquieting to Kelly, especially one who represented the epitome of love-making to her.

"Listen to it come down." Maggie looked up at the ceiling. "Mm . . . nice." She took his arm and turned him so the two of them faced the large glass window. The downpour was torrential now. The beach and the water were barely visible through the gauzy sheets of rain. The steady pelting upon the roof was mesmerizing.

She stepped in front of him and unbuttoned his shirt, unfolding the two sides of the clinging wet material and peeling them back off his chest. She helped him out of his shirt and dropped it to the floor.

She traced her fingers down his chest between his pectorals. "Duck bumps." She kissed him lightly in the center of his chest. Drawing her head back, she smiled up at him. Looking down at her, then where she had kissed him, he noticed the nipples of his chest were hard and saw the "duck bumps" surrounding them.

She took his towel and blotted his neck and shoulders and chest. *No, he was the man, he should do the ministering.* He saw a wet spot upon her temple and reached out, tamping it with two fingers of his right hand. The motion was abrupt; it surprised her and she looked up at him.

"Water," he said. *How to explain? Don't explain, don't think!* He closed his eyes, as if by doing this he could shut off his treacherous brain. She was drying his waist when, suddenly thinking he was about to suffocate, he snapped his eyes open. The room was close and stuffy. Looking to the window, now misting up on the inside, and hearing the drone upon the roof, he felt trapped—entombed almost. The room thickened with the musty atmosphere of a sealed chamber. He cocked his head around. The king-sized bed dominated the room. Yes, it was a chamber, made for the bed, for the pleasures of the bed, a bedchamber. Bed-chamber—torture chamber. *Stop playing word games!*

"Here . . ." She was unfastening his belt. His stomach constricted violently, and she looked up at him. "What?" she asked in a gentle voice.

"Tickled," he lied. A sad little lie, he thought, a pathetic lie.

She loosened his belt and released the top snap of his pants, undoing the zipper and slipping them down along his hips until they dropped to his ankles of their own weight. "Here . . ." She guided him to step out of them.

He held his breath, waiting for her to unsnap the top of his shorts, but to his relief she continued guiding him back-wards and sat him down on the edge of the bed. She started to kneel in front of him, glanced beyond his shoulders, and walked to the bedroom door. The sound of the door shutting did nothing to ease the flow of anxiety within him.

She returned to him and, kneeling on the soft carpet at his feet, tugged off his wet socks and began drying his feet.

He looked down at her: *such beauty, how gentle she is, what man wouldn't—*

"Tickle?" she smiled up at him.

He shook his head. She went on to dry his legs, beginning with the calves and working up to the solid part of his upper leg by the edge of his shorts, as his irrational fear worked up inside him until it lodged in his throat and threatened to strangle him.

It happened so quickly. When she had finished drying him, she dropped the towel next to his feet. Still on her knees, she gazed straight ahead at a point slightly above his navel and on impulse thrust forward between his legs, pressing her cheek up against his stomach, at the same time slipping her arms around the small of his back.

"Sta-stop!" It tripped out of him like two bursts from a machine gun, brittle, tense, several decibels above his usual voice. *She was only caressing you.* Then, in a lower and calmer voice: "I didn't mean . . ."

But already she was pulling away and looking up at him: confused, hurt, the green of her eyes flecked with—what? Annoyance? She stood up, backing away from him at the same time. His words caught her in a half-turn: "Maggie, I—"

She wheeled on him, striking him speechless. "Yes?"

He shook his head, looking down, loathing his legs, his feet—his flesh.

"What did you think I was going to do?" she asked.

"Nothing," he mumbled.

"Quite a reaction to nothing. Was I that frightening?"

"No." He focused upon the carpet with such intensity his vision became blurred.

"Do I repel you?"

"No!" He jerked his head up.

"Methinks thou dost—" She turned away from him, disgusted at her resort to triteness. She stood with her back to him and stared out the window. The gap between them widened in the silence until he thought the house would crack in two. He saw her back stiffen. She fought the rising metabolism of her temperament, but panic, too, her own unshared panic, stabbed her and sabotaged her control. "Perhaps," she said coolly, turning once more to face him, "you'd be happier in there with Stosh."

He shook his head and looked down again.

"Who knows? Maybe you should investigate it?" She sighed, sickened at her cruel innuendo. His concave posture indicated such a measure of damage that she stifled an impulse to go to him and take him in her arms. She cleared her throat. "That was tacky," she said in a low voice. "You know I didn't mean it."

He nodded his head.

"Still," she added, pacing the floor, "you might as well sleep in there. No use making one another uncomfortable. These little forays take their toll." She snorted, "I hate days like this." Then: "Of course, I'll have a drink. Care to join me?" Although it was a question, it required no answer; she crossed the room and opened the door, leaving him alone.

It was over now. They had not been in the house ten minutes, but the "foray," as she labeled it, had exhausted him. His mind, which had plagued him into crisis, now slid without protest into a stunned dormancy.

He heard a crackling sound from the speakers in the bedroom, heard a record plop down, the arm move over and settle upon it with a tiny grating sound. The music began softly. It was Ravel's *Bolero.* As Maggie recognized the low-keyed beginning of the piece, she laughed huskily and called out: "A little late for that, huh?"

In spite of his misery, he smiled.

He heard the record being rejected and another one fall into place, heard Maggie walk down the hall to the kitchen. Standing up from the bed, he gathered up his pants and shirt from the floor and walked silently across the living room to the other bedroom.

So she wouldn't think he had used her absence to sneak across the living room without having to face her again, which he *had* done, of course, he swung the door to Stosh's bedroom shut with a slam. This small, ineffectual gesture salvaged nothing, only causing a wry smile of self-denigration to curl his lips as he flopped down on the bed.

He lay there searching for some degree of consolation, no matter how small. And there was a consolation of sorts, a loser's consolation: it was over, she could no longer set the scene, and he could no longer offer up hopeful preambles to the fulfillment of love-making. No more forays, no more gymkhanas.

But he did feel love for her and he did, at least in his mind and heart, too, feel desire. Then *why–!* How many times had he trod this familiar ground, how many times had he asked himself if the outlet for his emotions would be blocked for all time?

Inundated by questions, he lay there becoming numbed by the endless whys of them. He could hear the restless sounds of Maggie moving about in the living room, a minor counterpoint to the heavy drumming of rain, which he allowed to deaden his senses until he tumbled into a sleep of depression.

Kelly was awakened from a damp, inverted nap by Flora and Stosh. Maggie was not in her room, nor was she elsewhere in the house. Without the full details, Kelly explained they'd taken a walk, returned to the house and talked for a while, after which he'd come to the bedroom for a nap.

After a further check of the house, Stosh and Kelly stood in the living room as Flora walked out from Maggie's bedroom. "Her wig's not there and the tweed suit is gone. Kelly, was she feeling well?"

"Yes." Better to indicate the truth; he added: "A little restless, perhaps."

Inspecting the bar, Flora picked up a used glass. "Was she—had she been drinking?"

"Not while I was with her. She was fixing one when I went to lie down."

"How come you didn't bunk back in there?" Stosh indicated Maggie's bedroom.

"Like I said, she was restless. I didn't want to be in the way if she felt like using her room."

"Oh." Stosh was not completely sold. "I'll get on the horn. She hadda take a cab, she couldn't walk. How many cab companies in Ensenada? I'll check where they took her, we'll go find her."

"I'll go with you. I'll just shower and clean up; won't take me ten minutes." Kelly walked toward the bathroom.

While Kelly was shaving, Stosh knocked at the door and pushed it open a crack. "I found her. She took a cab, all right. Some restaurant down near the water, El Diabolo."

The ride into town was spent mostly in silence. They

found the place easily, on a wharf jutting out between the boats for hire and the commercial fishing fleet. The restaurant was a large, rustic, weather-beaten wood structure, resembling a converted shed or warehouse.

Walking across the broad planks of the wharf leading to the door, Flora asked, "What will we say?"

Stosh shrugged. "Depends on what *she* says. Play it by ear."

An attractive Mexican woman greeted them and led the way through a small anteroom, beyond a partition decorated with fishing nets and glass floats, and into the large beamed dining room. Soft music came from speakers at either end of a bar extending half the length of the room. Handsome roughhewn wood tables, most of them occupied by Americans or well-to-do Mexicans, filled the rest of the room, with a large wall of plate-glass windows facing the breakwater and the ocean beyond it and individual windows set in the north wall looking across the bay to the fishing fleet bobbing at anchor.

"Three for dinner?" the hostess asked.

"We're looking for someone first," Stosh said.

The woman stood by while the three of them searched the room. Kelly spotted Maggie first. "There she is, over to the right, fourth window from the end."

When the hostess approached the side of her table, Maggie glanced up, saw the woman, then the three of them, and feigned a complete lack of surprise. She wore her wig and tweed traveling suit with the high-necked blouse, but she hadn't bothered with the bandage on her nose and she'd replaced the bifocals with a pair of black, horn-rimmed reading glasses.

"Sorry we're late," Stosh said casually.

Maggie smiled, playing along with him. "I thought you'd never get here, so I ordered a drink for myself. Well, don't stand there like the Three Stooges—sit down." After they ordered, Maggie leaned back in her chair and grinned at them. "Well, fancy bumping into you in Ensenada of all places."

"Yeah," Stosh replied. "Flora here just found out she was

knocked up—we think it was that Mexican border guard—
so we decided to celebrate."

"Good, I couldn't be happier. May I have pick of the litter?" Flora giggled; Maggie glanced at Kelly, sitting next to
her and took his hand. "Sweet dreams?"

"Not particularly . . ."

She lifted his hand and kissed it lightly.

"That's nice," Stosh said. "Don't fight."

Flora grinned ferociously and asked how Maggie was feeling.

"How do I look? Fine."

When their drinks were delivered, Stosh raised his glass
in a toast. "Hail Mary, full of grapes—" he began, but Flora
swatted him before he could finish. After ducking, he raised
his glass again. "Okay, what did Abe Lincoln say after he
woke up from a three-week binge?"

"What?" Maggie asked.

Stosh shook his head groggily, then blinked his eyes: "I
freed the—*whaaaat?*"

Now it was Maggie who raised her glass. "Here's to a real
little trooper—Ginger Rogers. And let's all remember, it's
love that makes the world go round." She started to sip,
then added: "—that and hate!"

They all drank; Maggie turned to Stosh. "Give us one
about the neighborhood."

"Uh—my neighborhood was so tough, there was graffiti
on the walls of the confessional. We even had an express
line for six sins or less!"

They laughed. The Maggie Banner Players were back in
full swing. Maggie held her glass out again: "What the
hell—let's have a night out on the town!" She immediately
glanced at Flora, who did her best to camouflage her disap-
proval. "Flora . . ." Maggie smiled, but there was an im-
plicit warning in her voice.

The music stopped and the early evening news came on
in English from an FM station in San Diego. The steady
hum in the dining room decreased only slightly as the first
items dealt with the President's latest message to Congress,

a border incident involving China and India, and the bombing of a home belonging to a union labor leader outside San Diego. He had gone to the corner cigar store; his wife and mother-in-law were killed while watching television in the living room.

News of this tragedy brought the room to a near hush, followed by a brief murmured undertone. The next sentence cut the room like a knife:

"Motion picture fans the world over were saddened today over the report that one of its brightest stars, Maggie Banner, is fatally ill with Hodgkin's disease."

Several short gasps were heard, a few people shushed for quiet, and the woman seated directly behind Maggie sighed a deep, heartfelt "Ohh . . ." across the table to her husband. Then virtual silence enveloped the room.

Kelly did not look at Maggie, but glanced up at Flora and Stosh to see their eyes flick from Maggie's face to his own. No one moved at the table as the announcement continued: "So Raffaello Tucci, Miss Banner's constant companion of the last ten months, disclosed in New York last night. Tucci gave that as the reason for her abrupt retirement from films, her loss of weight, sudden fainting spells while on a round-the-world trip, and her recent disappearance after a fracas at the Copacabana nightclub in New York City.

"Miss Banner's Los Angeles physician, Dr. Ludwig Pahlmann, refused comment, but a London physician's office, a specialist in leukemia, Hodgkin's disease and other forms of cancer, confirmed the report that Miss Banner was afflicted with the incurable disease and was not expected to live for more than six months.

"To show the extent of the grief of her many fans, one woman who preferred to remain anonymous, called the *Los Angeles Times*, requesting them to print the following message: 'Maggie, wherever you are, we love you.' This would seem to be a majority opinion."

As the announcer went on to other news, low whispers of concern filled the room.

At their table Maggie was the first to speak. "Too bad I

wore my wig. We could hold a memorial service right here."

"I didn't think he'd do it," Stosh mumbled.

"Neither did I," Maggie said. She took a large gulp from her drink, brushed her fingers across her lips and stood up. Flora stood, too. "I'm just going to freshen up, Flora."

"I'll come with you."

"For God's sake," Maggie snapped, "I'm not going to drop dead in the john!" She walked quickly from the table.

CHAPTER 30

Flora sat down. The room was stunned by the news; the very air seemed to have been deadened by the newscaster's voice. Kelly sat there dazed, still sustaining shock waves, numbed beyond thinking, much less speaking.

"I didn't think he'd do it," Stosh repeated.

After a while Flora turned to Kelly. "You see . . . ?" But she needed to go no further for an explanation of the various small mysteries inflicted upon him since their meeting.

The news ended and music began once more. Gradually the level of noise increased but not to what it had been before; the pall cast over the room would not be dispelled so soon. Their waiter returned, hovered near them in the event his services might be required, and was engaged by another table. A woman across from them began a series of fond reminiscences of Maggie Banner pictures. To drown her out both Flora and Stosh spoke at once.

"Maybe I—"

"They said—"

After a moment, Flora asked: "What will we do now?"

Turning to Kelly, Stosh shook his head slowly. "Raf must

be flippin' out to do that, he really must. He knows how much Maggie—Jesus!"

In the distance cacophonous music—trumpets, coronets, a drum, the sounds of a small parade—could be heard coming from the direction of the highway. The discordant strains, coupled with shouting singsong voices, grew louder, clashing inharmoniously with the soft music coming from the speakers inside the restaurant and then gradually fading away.

The voice from the next table reached their ears once more. "So many of the great ones end tragically: Jean Harlow, Marilyn Monroe—"

It was that more than anything which caused Flora to stand, say, "I'll just check on her," and leave.

Kelly and Stosh sat there, not drinking, but each grasping his glass and staring down at the table until, as if by prearrangement, they raised their heads to eye level.

"Why does it gotta be her?" Stosh asked.

They gazed back down at their drinks until they heard Flora's breathless voice. "Stosh, she's gone!" Flora lumbered up to the table, a hand pressed to her bosom. She began to speak, gulped, swallowed and found her voice. "She—she wasn't in the ladies' room. The hostess said she left, walked out the door."

"Here we go again," Stosh said in a tight voice. He stood up and left a ten-dollar bill on the table.

When the Mexican parking-lot boy saw them crossing the highway, he broke away from the girl he was talking to and walked to get their car.

"Hey!" Stosh shouted. The boy stopped and turned around. "Did you see a lady with a wi—" He caught himself about to say "wig," shot an embarrassed glance at Flora and Kelly, and corrected himself. "A lady with bangs over her forehead," he pantomimed. "And glasses and a tweed suit?"

"Ah!" the boy grinned, looking to his girl friend. "She went with wedding parade." His girl giggled, nodding in verification.

"Wedding parade?" Stosh asked. "Where to?"

The boy shrugged. "Some party, I guess." He pointed back down the highway. "Couldn't be far." He waved in the same direction. "Few blocks down, then in that way." He pointed inland. "Lots of clubs."

"Clubs?" Stosh asked.

"You know, clubs. Nightclubs for Mexicans. Not so much for tourists."

He left them with a shrug and returned with their car. With Flora in the back seat they drove slowly down the highway. "That's what all that noise was," Stosh said. "I guess we gotta cruise around till we find 'em." Turning left onto a dirt street, he scattered a flock of chickens and slammed on the brakes. "Don't they got pens in this country? Everything runs around loose!"

Raffaello checked into the El Convento Hotel in Ensenada shortly after eight in the evening. After signing the register he asked the desk clerk if he knew of a place nearby named Miranda's Cove. The young man said no, but he had only recently arrived from Nogales. Raffaello waited impatiently while the clerk went to find the assistant manager. The same question to the middle-aged Mexican brought a smile and a nod.

"Oh, yes, it's—oh, somewhere between twelve and fourteen miles south on the main road. It's private," he added. "No fishing or swimming. It belongs to a Hollywood director."

"Yes," Raffaello said, "that would be it."

He inquired about renting a car and was told nothing could be done until Monday morning. A fifty-dollar bill to the assistant manager wiped Sunday off the calendar and a car was promised by nine thirty. A ten-dollar bill to the young Mexican bellboy produced a bottle of scotch soon after he was shown to his room.

He needed a good scrubbing up after his trip and the bathroom was inviting, immaculately clean and large. Stretched out in the oversized tub, he felt like the old Raffaello. There were no direct Sunday flights to San Diego so he'd gone to Los Angeles and hired a private plane for the trip down to Ensenada. Something like that, hiring a plane or a boat, even a limousine, still gave him a buoyant hey-look-at-me-I-did-it feeling, adding a touch of luxury he never ceased to relish.

Now, too, the knowledge that he was close to Maggie excited him. He could feel vibrations, good ones, in his stomach, small tremors like he used to feel at five o'clock on the afternoon of an evening he was to sing. Not stage fright, but the healthy tension of preperformance adrenaline.

He was in good shape, he'd only had two drinks between planes in Los Angeles. He told himself he could drink in moderation. Perhaps all it took was the mellowness that came with age. Yes, he was feeling mellow. He would have one more after his tub and soon the car would be there and he would surprise her.

Now he allowed himself to dwell upon the possibilities of their meeting. In a way, he was choosing scripts. It was so easy to be seduced by past memories; he had total recall of the days of her infatuation for him, of the days when not a second could go wrong between them. These flashbacks were so pungent they completely anesthetized him from reality. Lulled into daydreaming by the warmth of the bath, he sat there editing their meeting.

He could hear a burst of her husky laughter now. She'd get a kick—give the devil his due—that he'd tracked her down so soon. She'd turn to Flora and Stosh (who would be shaking in his shoes) and say, "What am I going to do? Can't do with him, can't do without him! Certainly can't *shake* him, that's for sure. One more for dinner, Flora!" And they'd be together again.

He'd treat her gently now, no outbursts, no scenes. He'd cherish her, protect her, please her. Did she feel like going to Mexico City for dinner or the bullfights? Or Acapulco? Or up to Los Angeles? Whatever she wanted.

As for the extra character in the libretto, there was sound reason to suppose she'd actually hired this Kelly McDermott as a companion. Attractive he might be, but hardly what she would look for in a man, *as* a man, young, skittish, shy and frightened. During their trip abroad, how many orphans had they dissuaded her from adopting, how many oddballs had she picked up along the way? Her curiosity about people was all-encompassing, irrepressible. She needed a coterie about her—he was merely the newest member, an acquisition. They were usually people she felt she could do something for, too, and this McDermott fellow looked like he could use help. Raffaello promised himself he would accept the young man's presence graciously and without malice. He was determined to be well mannered.

An intruding thought jolted him from his reverie. He sat up straight, sending a splash of water over the side of the tub. How could he forget he must reckon with what he'd done to her! He'd betrayed her and he could see the scalding look of reproach in those wide green eyes. He suddenly felt chilled sitting in the tub.

He got out and dried himself vigorously, at the same time rubbing away the fears he had of facing her by telling himself the news was bound to come out sooner or later. How often had she acknowledged the remarkability that there hadn't been a leak so far.

Still, no matter what he told himself, he could not rationalize away his guilt or the consequences of it. She was adamant, and rightly so, regarding her privacy. She refused to dwindle away in public view, her every move examined under the microscopic beam of notoriety.

No, he could not easily avoid her scorn. On the other hand, she was not one to waste energy clinging to emotions once they'd been given full expression. She would soon— she would what?

By now he had conjectured himself into a sort of stage fright at the prospect of confronting her. With only a towel wrapped around him, he quickly went for the scotch bottle.

Stosh drove slowly up the dusty street, passing rows of sagging patched cottages, two small groceries, several run-down bars and a pool hall. He looked down the next street they crossed but outside of a beer bar on the corner there were only dilapidated shacks and an open-air fruit stand. Coming to another cross street, they could hear the jangled sounds of several jukeboxes. They sighted three bars on the opposite side of the street; turning the corner they saw several more bars on the near side and a nightclub, La Paleta, advertising entertainment. Toward the end of the block, steps led up to a building which resembled a meeting hall or small church except for its neon sign: La Fiesta.

The sound alone indicated a street of well-populated honky-tonk bars, but as they drove slowly past them, all open to the street except for the nightclub, they found them to be virtually empty. In one nobody was to be seen, not even a bartender. In the saloon next to it a small Mexican boy sat cross-legged atop the bar, playing checkers with a waitress.

"The place is fuckin' spooked," Stosh said, stopping in front of La Paleta. "Check in there, Kel."

When Kelly opened the front door he found the room large and dark. The small bandstand was empty. Several couples danced to canned music, four tables were occupied, and two middle-aged men and a woman sat at the bar.

He returned to the car. They started up and the strains of live music reached their ears from La Fiesta toward the end of the block. The building sat on a mound and although its windows were too high for a proper view of the inside, they could see colored lights revolving and make out strings of paper decorations crisscrossing the ceiling. Stosh pulled the car up by the dirt walk leading to the steps. The music stopped and a burst of applause echoed from the building followed by laughter and the high chatter of Mexican voices. "Some live ones in there," Stosh said.

"I'll take a look." Kelly mounted the steps as the music began again. One side of the front door was half-opened; he opened the other half and stood in the doorway. A revolving many-sided contraption hung suspended from the center of the ceiling, bathing the room in rainbow hues which glanced off the walls and ceiling at uneven angles. A six-man band occupied the raised platform to the left of the room. Plastic-tableclothed card tables, three deep, bordered the spacious dance floor, and one large table, the wedding dais, stood opposite the door. Beyond this long table an archway led to a back room where five or six women were busy arranging bowls and platters of food.

The dance floor was crowded with couples of every age, size and shape; gleaming black hair was the one common denominator. Several small boys, eyes glued to their feet, dragged little girl partners around the floor, and three pairs of women danced together in one corner. The male members of the immediate wedding party wore wide-lapelled tuxedoes and the women were got up mostly in three-quarter–length dresses of lace or satin. A flash bulb went off to the far corner of the bandstand and Kelly saw the bridal couple, she in a long white satin gown and veil, he in a tuxedo. A baby, tended by her grandmother, lay in a wicker basket on top of a card table. Several ancient couples sat at other tables, staring vacantly at the dance floor, and a few young men in dark suits slouched around in a loose group to the left of the band.

Kelly was about to leave when a gap opened up between couples at the far right hand corner of the dance floor and he caught sight of Maggie's profile. He lifted a hand to attract her attention at the same time the young man she was dancing with slowly turned her so that her back was to him.

Kelly waved down the stairs, gesturing to Stosh and Flora. When they reached the top of the steps, Stosh took one look in the door and said, "Just like a Polish wedding. Where is she?"

Kelly pointed her out as the music stopped to healthy applause. Several couples left the dance floor to investigate the food in the back room and Maggie's escort led her to a table to the right of the floor, opposite the bandstand.

"Might as well," Stosh said, leading the way.

She caught sight of them before they reached the table. Quickly covering up the brief jolt of surprise she was unable for a second to hide, she lowered her eyelids to half and displayed a weary smile of resignation. The young man looked confused as Maggie waved an open hand at them. "My *amigos*," she said. "What do you use—radar? Or have I got on strong perfume?" she inquired of Stosh. Before he could reply she snapped her fingers. "I *did* tell you I had this wedding to attend, didn't I?"

"Yeah," Stosh said. "Only we forgot to tell *you* we was invited, too. May we?" he asked, indicating a chair.

"By all means," Maggie said. "This is Angel, my intended, pronounced Ahn-hel!" At the sound of his name the Mexican rose from his chair and executed a small bow. "And this is Agnes, a de-frocked priest. And my son, the pest, El Pesto, a raging homosexual—watch out for him! And this," she indicated Kelly, "is Georgie Jessel. Would you believe he's ninety-six? Yogurt did it all. But he can't pee anymore. When he went to the doctor and complained of this the doctor said, 'How old are you?' 'Ninety-six,' said Georgie. 'Oh,' said the doctor, 'in that case it's all right because—' "

" '—you peed enough already!' " Maggie and Stosh spoke in unison.

"Give us another age joke!" Maggie asked.

"He's so old, when he played the slot machine in Vegas—it came out three prunes!"

"*Gracias*," Maggie said, adding: "Well, here we are, together again. Odd the way we keep crashing into each other, *nicht*?"

Silence fell over the group. The young man, Angel, perhaps twenty-five or -six, was extremely good-looking. His black hair was thick and wavy, his skin was smooth and mocha-colored, and his nose was aquiline. His eyes were the only obvious imperfection; although they were a rich, dark brown, they were too small and round for his face and set in too close to his nose. This, together with his slight nervousness, gave him a shifty look. He wore a dark suit and, underneath it, a purple shirt of satin and a black string tie.

Glancing from Stosh to Kelly, he attempted to solve their probable relationship to Maggie. When his looks were returned without innuendo or apparent animosity, he made a gesture of prior claim by raising a hand from under the table and placing it over Maggie's hand. Having done this, he once more checked for any possible adverse reaction and relaxed a bit.

Kelly felt a twinge of jealousy and chided himself for it; a dirty feeling also grazed him.

Maggie sighed, looking from one to the other of her friends. "Oh, incidentally, my fiancé here is about as unilingual as they come, so feel free to talk dirty." She patted Angel's hand and smiled. He nodded and smiled in return. Maggie looked at the map of distress outlined upon Flora's face and stuck her tongue out at her. "Flora, sometimes your reactions can be boring in their predictability."

Angel glanced nervously around the table, sensing that perhaps it might be his turn to carry the burden and break the silence. He cleared his throat, smiled self-consciously, and then, neck muscles straining tautly, uttered a few words as if communicating in English not only required a foreign language but a completely different set of vocal cords. Each word appeared at a regular interval, individually strangled from his throat.

"Me . . . Murican . . . fran . . . Mee-sus Schultz." He heaved a sigh of relief and flashed a smile at his accomplishment.

Maggie put a hand on his arm and cried out, "Oh, Mrs. *Schultz!*"

His face could barely contain the excitement. He bounced on his chair and prodded Maggie's shoulder with a finger. "Mee-sus Schultz?" he nodded, grinning widely. "*Conoce* Mee-sus Schultz?"

"Of course," Maggie said, "*Mr.* Schultz, too."

"Nu Jork?" he asked.

"Of course," Maggie smiled.

"He talks like that comic on television," Stosh said.

Angel fumbled with his tie, loosening it and undoing the top two buttons of his collar.

"What's he gonna do?" Stosh frowned, "take it *out?*"

Maggie and Flora chorused: "Stosh!"

"You said to talk dirty."

Maggie shot him a withering look as Angel reached inside his shirt and took out a thin gold cross suspended on a delicate chain. "Mee-sus Schultz," he grinned.

"I'll bet she did," Maggie cracked.

Stosh added, "That don't look like Mrs. Schultz."

Their attitude had reached the limits of patronization and Maggie turned on him. "All right, that's enough. I know, *me*, too, but enough's enough!"

"Okay," Stosh shrugged.

Angel did not miss the rebuke in Maggie's voice. He carefully tucked his cross back inside his shirt, buttoned his collar, and tightened his tie. When he was finished he turned to address Stosh. "No Catholic?"

Maggie touched his cheek. "Oddly enough—yes, and he only speaks English a teensy-weensy better than you."

"Thanks for nothin'," Stosh said.

Maggie poured straight shots of tequila for herself and Angel. After they drank them down, she said, "Now if you'll excuse us," and led him off to the dance floor.

Before Flora could get the words out, Stosh faced her and said: "I know—what will we *do?*"

"What *will* we do?" Flora asked.

Stosh shrugged. "What do I know, a poor Polack from the Lower East Side?"

"Kelly . . ." Flora turned her pleading face to him, "we should get her home."

"We'll get her home," Stosh said. "Leave me think." He touched Kelly's arm and spoke in a low voice. "Did you and Mags have a fight?"

"Not really . . ."

"But something must have happened. Else—why's she with *him?*"

The music stopped abruptly. A burst of applause greeted the musicians and they left the stand for a break as a mountainous woman appeared in the archway to the back room, an apron over her electric-blue dress and artificial fuchsia flowers entwined in her wiry black hair. She shouted in a booming voice, *"Alimento! Alimento! Alimento!"* Those nearest her picked up the cry and soon the entire crowd was moving toward the archway.

Maggie and Angel were not far from her. Angel grabbed Maggie's hand and, as they escaped through the arch before the stampede, she waved and called out: "We'll bring food!"

In no time at all there was a bottleneck which lasted a full ten minutes before the tail end of the jostling crowd was able to squeeze through the archway. "I'm hungry," Stosh said, standing up. "I oughta go help them, but I'd get murdered." He sat back down and poured shots of tequila for himself and Kelly.

Two small boys appeared at the table and stared solemnly at Kelly, Flora and Stosh as if the three of them had dropped down from the moon. Four large brown eyes followed each sip of tequila, each movement either of them made, no matter how small. Stosh finally winked lasciviously. "Hey, the two of you'se meet me out in the car and I'll give you some candy. Want some candy?" Flora clucked and slapped his hand. The boys giggled when she did this and ran away. "They couldn't understand me," Stosh said. "They was givin' me the willies!"

A steady line of people straggled back juggling plates of food through a single service door in the corner of the room near the bandstand. After a few minutes the crush was over and others were able to return single file through the main archway.

Kelly and Stosh looked at one another at the same moment and with the same thought.

"You don't think—"

"What?" Flora asked.

Stosh ignored her, muttering, "Christ!" and hurrying to the back room, followed by Kelly. There were still a goodly number of people in line for food but no sign of Maggie or Angel.

After Flora's first flurry of panic, it was Stosh who insisted upon driving to a coffee shop and eating before returning home. Flora fought him all the way, but he was adamant; their argument continued over dinner.

"Supposing he does something, hurts her?"

"Why should he do that?"

"I didn't like the looks of him," Flora said. "He touched her ring."

"He held her hand," Stosh said.

"He touched her ring with his finger and looked at it. I saw him." As Stosh was about to speak, she snapped, "Besides, he shouldn't be holding her hand."

"So," Stosh sighed, "what are we gonna do? You know Maggie. We tagged her enough tonight. How far can we push our luck?"

"All I wanted to do was go home," Flora said. "She's got her own room, she has her privacy. Just so we'd be in the house."

"Flora, we don't even know if she went home. They skipped out on the food; maybe they're at a restaurant—or at his place, or a motel!"

"Then we should start looking for them," Flora insisted.

"Where?" Stosh asked. "What do we do, go around knockin' on every shack in town, yellin', 'Here, Maggie, Maggie, Maggie!' Or supposin' we found them at a motel, what do we do—haul her out of the sack?" Stosh was suddenly aware of Kelly's silence. "Sorry, Kelly, but—" He turned back to Flora. "She's over twenty-one!"

Frustrated by Stosh's logic, Flora burst into tears. "But why," she sobbed, "did she . . . have to . . . she's . . . she's got Kelly!"

Yes, Kelly thought, she's got me. As if she hadn't enough problems—she's got me.

Kelly and Stosh did their best to soothe her. She stopped sobbing, but her bout with tears had destroyed her appetite and she sat the rest of the time, red-faced and distracted, picking at her food.

Leaving the restaurant, they passed a newspaper rack by the cash register. *The San Diego Union* featured a picture of

Maggie on the front page. The heavy black type above it read: MAGGIE BANNER FATALLY ILL.

Stosh mumbled, "Bastard!" On their way to the car, Stosh glanced up at the sky. "Freaky weather." The mist and the fog had been replaced by a soft breeze with a touch of tropical warmth to it. Several luminous billows in the clouds gave evidence of a moon somewhere up above.

With the news out, it was permissible to play the radio and they listened to music on a Mexican station while they drove along the ocean, now roughing up with a heavy surf. No one spoke during the trip back.

They could hear the stereo blasting away as they rounded the corner and drove onto the parking area in front of the house. The front lights were on; two kitchen windows were open and a strong breeze blew the ends of the curtains out of them; the front door was half-open and from what they could see, all the lights were on inside the house.

Flora gasped and Stosh muttered, "Jesus!"

Kelly sensed the moment with them. The violent sound— it was *La Valse*—and the blazing lights, without human movement in sight, combined to signal distress.

CHAPTER 31

Stosh slammed the car to a stop. He called out, "Maggie!" as he and Kelly ran into the house, down the hall, and stepped into the living room with Flora lumbering after them.

"Jesus!" Stosh stopped short, bumping shoulders with Kelly.

There she sat in her terrycloth robe, wig off, drink in hand, an amused look upon her face. Leaning back in a fan-shaped wicker chair near the bar, she raised her free hand in a gesture of pretended surprise at their sudden entrance. "*Hola*—the troops have arrived!"

"Jeez." Stosh reached for the sound on the hi-fi and turned it down.

Maggie raised an eyebrow and stretched her arms out. "Mad about your entrance!"

"You had us scared," Stosh said.

"Why, Flora," Maggie gasped, "you're ashen-faced."

"We didn't know . . . we thought—"

She sprang up from her chair. "You thought what?"

Flora took a step backwards. "We didn't—we were frightened—"

"Frightened of *what?*" Maggie demanded. "Will you tell me, for God's sake, what you're saving me for? You want to wrap me in cotton bunting and keep me all pretty and nice—for what?" She tilted her head back and laughed. "You were frightened—of *Angel!* I scared the hell out of him. Stosh, it was a camp!" She turned to Kelly. "You see, Kelly, even with my fright wig and glasses it seems I have this fatal magnetic charm." She prowled the room, speaking to no one in particular. "When we left—nothing against you all, I simply feel five's a crowd—we repaired *a mi casa.* I speak a little the language."

She scuffed a slipper along the matting. "Now this Angel, shy as he might seem, is not one for lengthy overtures. His approach is basic as all get out, he believes in a strong attack. Well, one embrace led to another, led to my wig being knocked askew—swiveled smack around on my head, in fact. The gimmick was up. He was a bit disconcerted when he found he had control of my hair. So I figured, what the heck, Maggie, give the guy a break, maybe he'd even get an extra kick out of it."

She laughed again. "So, off with the wig—the glasses were already removed, it was dark in the playroom." She waved an arm in the direction of her bedroom. "On with a light and you should have seen his eyes. They crossed, did a pinwheel, and registered—TILT!

"The first thing he said was, 'Maggie Banner!' which I felt was appropriate. I mean this kid has been to the movies, no dolt he. Then as he got to his feet, rather quickly I might add, he crossed himself, which I felt was *in*appropriate. I mean considering—but it was his second gesture that gave me a bit of pause. He wiped off his mouth, all the while staring at me as if I were the White Witch Goddess.

"I made entreaties for him to rejoin me in the continuation of our former game, but thereupon ensued a lot of jabber about what, I couldn't quite make out at first. Finally, it dawned on me. Can you imagine what the gist of it was? Apparently the Mexican papers have the news, too, and dear old Angel couldn't get it out of his head that Hodgkin's disease might be *contagious*.

"He was terrified. I tried to assure him it was a disease of the lymph glands you either have or do not have, but there was a great deal of nervous mouthwashing and when I swore, cross my heart and hope to die, that it wasn't catching, the lad, being resourceful and not easily conned, made it clear he'd like to use the phone. When I gathered he was calling the family doctor I'm afraid I got testy and slapped him.

"He was only too relieved to use that as an excuse for a display of outraged Latin manhood. We had a dual temper tantrum, followed by a stormy exit, each screaming one another down in our own language, each completely unintelligible to the other. The humor of it struck me when he tripped running across to his car and took a header—it was a beaut—into a puddle of water.

"So," she sighed, "there you have it. But here we are, the original group, together again!" She walked out onto the terrace, finished her drink and flung the glass off the far side down into the rocks at the mouth of the gorge. Returning to the doorway, she said, "What good is an empty glass? *Nicht?* Might as well put it out of its misery."

She stepped back into the living room. "You have no idea, Kelly, the references we make to dying until you stop and think: 'Put it out of its misery; cross my heart and hope to die; I'm dying for a drink; laughed so hard I thought I'd kill myself; surprised—I almost dropped dead; stop, you're killing me!' "

She walked to Kelly and grazed his cheek with her fingers. "So, Kelly, pet, you haven't been heard from since you learned of my . . . problem. No reaction at all? Come, come!"

"Maggie . . ." There was quiet entreaty in Flora's voice.

Kelly averted his eyes, looking down, and shook his head slightly.

"Mmm, you should have seen *me* when *I* found out. Right, Flora?" In the time Maggie allowed for a reply, Flora, too, sighted the carpet and remained speechless. "No answer!" Maggie snorted. "I, for one, was actually plussed! I'd been fainting. It was hard work on location. I'd also developed a rash on my hands and on my upper chest, around my neck; I went in for a complete checkup. I was in the hospital and—"

"Stop!" Flora cried out. "Maggie, don't—"

"Why not?" she asked. "It's quite an item. Kelly must be at the very least *curious*. So, I was in the hospital, actually with what I thought was exhaustion, having ground out four pictures in a row with no time off. When my doctor finally came in with the results of my various tests—looking rather like your friendly neighborhood undertaker—I mean he knew me, knew I liked things straight from the shoulder, that type, me, I mean, not him. Anyway, after a rather metaphysical conversation, which had me properly confused, he asked if I'd ever heard of Hodgkin's disease? So happens I had, but only vaguely, just the name. Never knew anyone that had it, knew nothing about it. And here's the laugh on me—oh, brilliant one! From the sound of it, I presumed he meant it was the rash. I held up my hands and said, 'Isn't there some kind of treatment, shots or medication?'

"He said the rash was an allergy, they'd have to do some scratch tests.

" 'What on earth is Hodgkin's disease?' I asked.

"And damned if he didn't tell me!" She spat the words out contemptuously: "Hodgkin's disease. Good Christ, it has a piddling sound to it. *Like* a rash, or a bad case of pimples. 'What's that all over your hip and around the small of your back?' 'Oh, I've got Hodgkin's disease.' 'Poor puss!' " She clucked in mock sympathy, then she snorted: "H-o-d-g-k-i-n-apostrophe-s. Tacky, tacky, tacky! It even has to carry the word 'disease' with it. Why must it lean on that? Now—cancer! There's a single frightening word, a sign of the zodiac, a word to be reckoned with, strong enough to stand by itself. *Cancer!* Don't fool around with Big C. And leukemia—

rather exotic-sounding, I always thought. Reminds me of a luxury liner. 'We're sailing for Bangkok on the *Leukemia,* April twenty-ninth.' " Her face contorted with disgust. "But Hodgkin's disease—good grief, it's as regal as oatmeal. Do you suppose I could bribe the obits to say I died of—"

"Maggie, don't—"

She ignored Flora. "Oh, let's see . . ." Putting hand up to her mouth, she wrinkled her brow in thought. "Why not say I died of nymphomania? Fun way to go—huh?"

"Mags, don't," Stosh pleaded. "You never talk like this."

"Of course not. But we've got to get it out in the open with our friend, Kelly, thrash it to death—there, you see, Kelly, how it creeps into the conversation, ever-present—then we'll drop it. You can't just say, 'I've got this incurable disease, have a grape.' " She walked to the bar and busied herself making another drink.

Flora uttered a half-sounding, "Mag—"

"What, dear?" Maggie spun around, holding up a glass. "You want one? No, of course not, you don't drink, do you? Oh, just have *one*. One can't hurt."

Kelly was shocked by the perversity of her suggestion and surprised at Flora's genuine smile in response to it.

"No, you see," Maggie explained, "I've always teased her that way." She quickly stepped to Flora, kissed her on the cheek and returned to the bar. "She knows I'd never give her a drink. Still," she said, holding the glass up again and wagging it back and forth in her fingers, "just a little taste of mine won't hurt, will it? Just a sip, Flora?"

Flora giggled. Outside and down below, the breaking waves formed a steady, rhythmic background; out on the terrace a strong breeze whipped the air with a sound of its own. The room itself was silent. When Maggie finished making her drink, she turned around, toasted them and sipped it. "If anyone wants one . . ." She waved a hand to the bar and walked out onto the terrace.

Stosh turned to Kelly. "Scotch?"

"Sure."

"Strange weather," Maggie called in, reaching up and

feeling the air with her hand. "So warm, yet there's a heavy surf." As Stosh handed Kelly a scotch on the rocks, she said, "I'm going down for a walk." Flora and Stosh were exchanging looks when Maggie spun around. "Don't worry, pets," she smiled. "Relax." These words did nothing to lessen their concern. "You do understand I'm just a tiny bit depressed, upset, whatever—you understand that?"

"Yes," Flora mumbled.

"So you won't begrudge me a few minutes alone to try to get *un*depressed, will you?"

"No," Stosh said.

"Then will you please try to scrape the cement from your tight little faces, for Christ's sake! Or I'll get some new people around who won't look at me like I'm constantly about to drop dead. Let's just go on pure faith that since I didn't drop dead yesterday—I'm not about to drop dead today!" She turned, started to walk toward the steps, then suddenly wheeled around. She'd worked herself up too much to cut the scene off just yet. "By the by, if I do decide to pick my time and place for dropping dead *myself,* as long as it is my life, you will honor that, won't you? I really do think one ought to have autonomy over one's own death. I mean—if we can't have that, what can we have!"

"Maggie!" A little plea from Flora, in tears again.

"Oh, Flora, grow up for Christ's sake!" A full burst of laughter. "Have a drink!" She picked up her long robe in one hand and disappeared down the steps. Flora moved instantly for the terrace.

"Let her alone," Stosh said.

"Yes," Flora replied, raising a hand to her forehead. After a moment she excused herself. "I've got such a headache, I'll just lie down for a while. Stosh, call me if . . ." she trailed off.

"If what?"

"I don't know." She left the room.

Kelly and Stosh stood in the living room; neither of them moved or spoke for a long time. Stosh finally cleared his throat. "That's why she split with Raffaello. He was so hung on her he wouldn't believe it. At first on the trip it was great. We went every place, seen everything, had a ball. Then he started draggin' in these specialists wherever we were. This doctor, that doctor. Drove her crazy. She didn't want a leak. The money he spent, like for hush money, thousands and thousands! When none of the doctors said there was any hope, he started lookin' for miracles. Then it got spooky. There's a place in Japan where they got miraculous cures. He hauled her up this sacred mountain to some temple. At first she went along with it, like for a gag. In India he came up with some pips. We was tearing all over the country from this quack to the other quack. Then she started to get bugged, and he was getting frantic." Stosh thought for a moment. "Did you ever hear of this place, ah—" He snapped his fingers. "Ah, Lloyd's? Yeah, Lloyd's."

"Lloyd's of London?"

"No, in France. Crippled people go there, take one look at the place and eighty-six the crutches. Wham-bam-ala-kazam!"

"Oh, Lourdes."

"Yeah, *Lourdes,* that's it. We was there. That was sad, though. Something about that place even took Maggie in. That's the only time I seen her really want to believe something could help. That got me. Something about the place makes you think maybe a miracle could happen."

Stosh took a long sip of his drink. "Then in Arabia—Mags was nuts to see Arabia and Egypt—in Arabia Raffaello springs on her they're going on a tour of the Holy Land. How come, she wants to know, it wasn't on the itinerary. He tried to play it cool. Because it's right next door, he says. By this time he was really buggin' her. He keeps tellin' her that's where God was born. But she wouldn't go. She says if he's only there, in that one place—good luck!

"In Rome's where we had the big blowup. Raffaello arranges through the Italian Mafia for a private meeting with the *Pope!* Ain't that a camp? Mags had a fit. She says to him: 'What are you going to say to the Pope? You really going to put him on the spot, tell him he'll go for a ride if he doesn't do something? Or just have him roughed up a bit?'

"Then's when she got hysterical. She tells him he's driving her crazy, that he's killing her more than the disease. She says: 'I'm dying and you're rubbing my nose in it!' He screams at her she's *not* dying. She screams she *is*. She yells at him one day soon she'll prove it."

Stosh shook his head. "It was a wild scene, freeze your blood. She called him a sadist, every name in the book. He keeps yelling he won't let her die and she screams back: 'Just try and stop me!' Then's when he hit her, a real sock on the jaw, knocked her out. I tell you, he's so fuckin' crazy about her. I never saw one man so crazy about one woman—ever! Anyhow, get this—Flora tried to strangle him right out there on the terrace overlooking these seven hills they got in Rome. We all had to pull her off him.

"Boy, she's got class, Mags has. 'Course he could of killed himself for hitting her. But when she comes to, when we got her inside on the sofa, she opens her eyes and when she sees him—you know what she does?" Kelly shook his head. "She kinda purrs up at him: 'Morning, dear, what's for breakfast?' Then she reaches up and feels her jaw. 'You know, sweetheart,' she says, 'I had the damnedest dream about you.' "

Stosh's voice broke, his eyes welled up with tears. "How—how about a broad—like that?" he sobbed. "I—I—love her. She's—" He choked on his words and stood up. "Shit!" he said, and walked quickly to his bedroom.

Kelly went out to the terrace, stepping to the far left end and gazing down at the beach, searching for her. When his eyes became accustomed to the stretch of darkness beyond the direct reach of the terrace and stairway lights, he could make out a dark form, so tiny she seemed, leaning back against a rock formation and facing out to sea. Gradually he could see the general blurred outline of her profile and her movements as she sipped her drink, lowered her glass, sipped it again, and held it in both hands pressed close in against her chest. He stood watching her for a long time, filled with a compassion that threatened to overwhelm him. Was it his misty vision that tricked him into imagining he saw her glance up briefly in the direction of the terrace? Perhaps. For now there she stood, facing the irregular margin of white foam lining the cove, kept constantly roiled by the monotonous breaking of the waves.

He rubbed his eyes to clear his sight, saw her finish her drink, throw her glass over her shoulder, and step forward from the rock. She drew her hands up through her hair, shook her head, and—what was she doing now?

Slipping out of the terrycloth robe and dropping it on the sand, she stepped off quickly in the direction of the waves.

Kelly lunged forward, grasping the handrailing in front of him. "Maggie! Maggie!"

The moment she heard him, she stopped and swung around, facing up toward the terrace. She clasped her hands in front of her, tossing her head back and executing a virtual backbend, and he could hear the husky bark of her laughter as she rocked back and forth in delight that he had been caught up by her trick. His heart was still pounding when she walked back to the rock and put on her robe.

"Was that you?" Stosh ducked out onto the terrace.

"Oh . . . yes."

"What was you yellin' for?"

"Nothing," Kelly said, looking down at the beach without exposing his face to Stosh. "I was just calling to Maggie. I thought I might go down."

"Oh." Stosh stepped up behind him and placed a hand on his shoulder. "Yeah, why don't you?"

"Yes, I will." He felt Stosh's hand leave him and heard him walk back into the house.

Raffaello's car was an hour late arriving. It was all he could do to hold back his temper. But he did, he reined himself in. He had very little patience for people who provided services. Often he secretly wished for a depression so that working people in the United States would starch up, step to, pay attention, and perform their work with pride and dignity, on time, and without a lot of bullshit excuses. But he was in Mexico now, only miles from Maggie, and he accepted the fact that it was, like his own Italy, a Catholic country and it was, after all, Sunday. Also, he wanted to impress Maggie with his calm demeanor, so there was no use heating up. His boiling point was low to begin with. He wanted to impress her so badly, wanted to make this seem like the end of a sophisticated little game of hide-and-seek, the kind perhaps Cary Grant and Irene Dunne would play in a Lubitsch film. So, immaculately dressed in sport clothes, he sat in the El Convento Hotel, his hands folded in his lap, looking across the lobby but restraining himself from crossing those immaculately scrubbed tiles leading to the bar some thirty yards away. For the ninth or tenth time he opened the piece of paper containing a crude drawing of the highway and the approximate X along its curves indicating the location of Miranda's Cove. The head bellman crossed the lobby carrying some luggage. Raffaello wanted to strangle him for the delay. The man glanced at Raffaello and said, "Emilio is on his way with the car now."

CHAPTER

32

Maggie stood facing him and when he was within a few feet of her, she said, "You don't think I'd do anything that . . . quaint?" He was appreciative of the darkness for hiding his blush. He turned, leaning back up against the rock next to her, and they faced the foamy lip of waves snapping up not fifteen yards from where they stood. "The tide must be coming in," she said.

"Yes." His voice sounded hollow to him, hollow and ineffectual. He closed his eyes, overcome by a desire to be of comfort to her, by phrase, by gesture, or by simply—*being*. He wished for this more than he'd wished for anything in his entire life.

She said something, but his wishing had shut out her words.

"What?" he asked, opening his eyes.

"I'm sorry for this evening . . ."

He made a little sound, shrugging it off. They stood for a long time gazing at the steady roll of the waves, inhaling the pungent sea smells being carried in on the warm breeze.

He heard her take a deep breath. "I have a dream," she said. "I'm *stuck* with a dream, rather. Recurrent. It comes in

that . . . delicate, never-never margin between consciousness and sleep. I'm aware and yet I'm not. Now, after a year,
I suppose I anticipate it. I'm at the center, I *am* the center of
it, in the blackness of space. The earth is next to me, very
large and yellow and warm. I'm aware so much of its
warmth and of the cold and the dark where I am. I want to
get on the earth, climb on it and be *with* it. But as I reach
out, it begins spinning, slowly at first, and then faster,
quickly gaining momentum, spinning faster and faster and
moving swiftly in a wide arc out and away from me. It
becomes smaller and smaller and fainter in color and—"
Maggie's hand shot out in front of her, fingers curled, grasping the air; her voice was breathy. "And I realize I'm being
left alone in a cold, black spacelessness for eternity and I
can't—" She lunged forward a full step, caught herself, and
quickly brought her arm down to her side.

Stepping back against the rock, she turned to Kelly.
"That's what it was the other night. I usually come to standing on my feet and screaming bloody murder. A switch," she
shrugged. "Stop the world—I want to get *on*. My doctor suggested I consult a psychiatrist." She laughed. "We're a little
late, folks."

Reaching into the pocket of her robe, she withdrew a
package of cigarettes and a book of matches; Kelly took the
matches from her and lit her cigarette. Her green eyes
regarded him in the flicker of light. "When I was young,"
she said, "I thought I'd never die."

"I did, too," Kelly replied.

She smiled at him. "Was it a secret you were keeping—
that you were the only one who wasn't going to?"

"Not exactly," he said. "I was sure I wasn't going to die
because I was a minister's son—that was when I was very
little—but I think I included my mother and father. I don't
remember believing I was the only one."

"Oh, I did. I was the only person in the world who wasn't
going to leave, and I was keeping it an immense secret so's
not to upset everyone else. I think that was considerate of
me, don't you?"

"Yes," he laughed.

"I didn't dummy up until I was—oh, I don't know how old. I remember when they carried my grandmother in, my father's mother—she lived with us—all rigid and stony-cold and glassy-eyed. Oh, I thought, I'll never be like *that*." She reached out abruptly and touched his arm. "I didn't tell you where she died?"

"No."

"In the outhouse, sitting in the outhouse. She got up in the middle of the night and they didn't find her until the next morning. She was a mean old crone; nobody liked her. It was more like spring housecleaning when she went." She took a little catch-breath. "That's terrible to say. What do I know about what went on inside her? She lived sixty years of God only knows what before I was even born." She paused and spat out her next word: "Eternity! I don't know what it means. I can't conceive of it. I don't believe anything can go on and on and never end." Her voice was edged by a contained staccato of panic. "I try to imagine an afterlife stretching into eternity and I can't envision it. I can't! Or heaven or hell or their equivalents stretching into—where? *Eternity!* No, I can't conceive of it. There's got to be an end to everything!" She searched through the planes of darkness for the reaction upon his face.

"You know what I used to worry about?" he asked. She shook her head; an urgency in the movement said: quick, tell me. "—that is, outside of the whole idea of the sun burning itself out."

"Oh, yes," she said, "I had that one, too. After all, it's only a fire, a big one, but even the biggest fire has to burn itself out."

"Exactly. I always thought it would be my luck to have it fizzle out during my stay on earth, that it would simply go down one night and not come back up in the morning."

"What else?" she asked.

"It was a whole thing about balance. We were always told the earth was spinning away on its axis. If it *was* spinning, I could never understand how you could balance—like my uncle used to—a cigarette on a tabletop or build a house of cards without them falling down. I always thought one day something's going to go just a little off, a mere fraction of a—whatever the measure of the universe is—and things would start falling, oceans sloshing over, houses coming apart at the seams, mountains crumbling—and the more things got off balance from the original imbalance, well, it would be self-perpetuating until we'd all start spinning off into space and finally the entire earth would come apart and disintegrate—and that would be that."

She squeezed his hand. "Oh, I'm so glad you were tortured, too."

"I didn't want you to be the only one," he replied.

She laughed, then stopped walking. "If I could believe in Heaven or Hell or Purgatory or that we'd all be floating around playing games together in the cemetery, all cozy and Our Townish—I wouldn't be so—" She lowered her head, glancing down at the sand and speaking softly. "You see, underneath everything, all my—I am absolutely terrified." She gave a slight shrug of her shoulders. "I am." Lifting her head, she turned to face him. "There," she sighed, "I've said it. Funny thing, I'd have never thought I would be. I thought I was up to anything, any announcements they had for us. Not true. I am just plain undone scared."

For a moment she was the most vulnerable human being he had ever encountered. He, oddly enough, felt incredibly strong. Not only strong, but tall, big, muscular, in control. He felt himself filling up with strength as he stood there. Perhaps, having contemplated his own death for so long, having even willed it, he had defused the idea. He really had no fear of it. But she did. The sensation of physical growth was so eerie, so strong with the background of waves pounding close to them, it derailed his concentration until she spoke again: "Oh, and angry, too. Furious and bitter that I won this particular lottery. It's a jolt when you think you've got the world by the tail, then one day you wake up and find out the Booking Agent has canceled your entire act—show closed!"

"The Booking Agent!" Kelly said, going back to Raffaello's statement.

"Oh yes—his little clue. Cute, isn't he? We used to kid about the Big Booking Agent in the Sky—booking us into adolescence, marriage, the hospital, an early grave—whatever! So, yes, I was handing out demerits to the Booking Agent, but first and foremost—I was just plain undiluted scared. And you see," her voice was picking up momentum, "not of the *moment* of death, of dying *itself*—I can play that scene—but at the thought that after, there might be—nothingness." The word shuddered and stuck in her throat.

"Oh, God! If I thought it were all to end, all of us, you and me and Flora and Stosh, all mankind." She stretched her arm out to the sea. "All this, all creation. If I thought it was a dead end to *nothingness,* I couldn't—sometimes I think the sooner I die the better, get this suspense over. But if it *is* nothingness—" she laughed bitterly "—I won't even know that, will I?"

Brushing a hand across her forehead, she said, "Colossal nerve, yes, but I can't imagine the end of me for all time to come. I can't! There's something so strong in me wants to go on, in *some* form. Maybe if I had children . . ." She shook her head. "No, it's even more—more personal, more egotistic. I can't imagine *me* being finished and done with forever and the world twirling on with no more recognition than if another leaf had dropped. And me—where? All traces gone, no soul, no consciousness. Cold and black and—" She grabbed Kelly by the arms; her fingernails dug into him through his clothing. "I don't want to be in the ground." A quick little shudder shook her. "I don't want to be in the ground!" she repeated.

Her speech was stabbed with small sobs. "Even if there were a Hell, we'd be together—people—but locked in the ground—rotting away to nothing!" She clung to him fiercely. "It's in my will, cremated—but I won't be put in the ground, don't let them put me in the ground!"

Her body shook convulsively; she jammed her head

against his chest and he held her tightly. "No Maggie—I won't. I won't let—"

"But you can't stop—stop the *nothingness*—nobody—can stop that!"

"Maggie, listen. Listen—"

"Yes," she sobbed, "yes?"

"You said there must be a plan, that God—"

She tried to pull away from him. "*I* said, but I—" He clutched her to him, but she pulled to get away. "What do *I* know!" She wrenched her body away from him. "Bull-shit!" she cried out. The bitterness in her voice vitiated any sense of the comical.

He reached out for her. As he grabbed her shoulders, she twisted to the side, losing her balance and falling backward. In a lunge to break her fall, he threw himself off balance and was taken down with her. His left leg and thigh half-covered her, but the full weight of him rested on the damp sand.

"Maggie, I—"

"Don't con me! What do you know!" she shouted, struggling to get out from under him.

"As much as you do!" He gave it back to her with equal intensity. The disdain with which she addressed him was debasing; he refused to let her strip him further of what little pride and manhood was left to him. Sliding on top of her, he covered her with the full weight of his body.

Her eyes flashed through the accustomed darkness, no longer black but a slate gray. "You're all con artists!" Unable to move, she spat in his face. He checked an impulse to slap her cheek as her physical energy, trapped and backed up within her, escaped in choking hysterics.

Although he could not, even if he had found the words, have reasoned this deluge of panic until it was purged from her, he felt a strange and undeniable power over the terror she was experiencing.

Her words were no longer strung into sentences but emerged in bursts of gibberish: "Can't—I *can't*—can't forget—*nothingness*—if only something—*someone* could—make me forget—"

"I will." He pressed his body down upon her. "I will, I will," he repeated, because he wanted to, not because he knew how.

"Nobody—*nobody!*" She shouted up at him. Her voice was high and shrill, unlike any sound he'd heard from her. "*Oh, Christ!*" she screamed out. The sound wracked his eardrums. She sobbed uncontrollably, writhing and twisting to be free of him.

"Stop it! Maggie, stop it!" He moved his hands up toward her face, meaning to shake her, but his elbow slipped in the sand and a lack of leverage caused him to press down on her neck, choking her.

I must. I must do something for her. I must not fail her eternally. No—interminably! He jabbed his head down to correct the word slip in his thoughts, and the pressure of the movement exerted itself in the strength of his hands.

"Ah—Kel—" she choked, fingers still pressing her neck. A trickle of fear, of incomprehension at his action, invaded her brain and, seeing it reflected in her eyes, he eased the pressure long enough for her to speak his name, frightened and confused—"Kelly?"

His eyes locked in his head. Familiarity or déjà vu? Another time, his name uttered the same, tentatively—"Kelly . . . ?" Another panic quelled. Even as he pressed down with his body as if his force upon her could summon the answer, the years rushed forward and told him. But Maggie's eyes had already signaled danger and, seeing danger's alarm reflected from her, destructive and intriguing, sweet and vulnerable, unleashed a sensuous wave which swept over him, washing into his brain and drowning out all thoughts as a quick brush with death leaves only a shudder of life in its wake and a moment of breathless excitement.

He was excited, he felt it pressing down against her hip. The pressure made her cry out, still sobbing, his name again: "Kelly?"

And her sobbing made him feel strong and the physical

power he was exerting upon her added to his feeling of strength. He took his hands from her neck; she gasped and adjusted her breathing. "Yes, *Kelly*," he said, reaching down and pulling one side of her robe up and away from her body.

"What . . . ?" she asked.

He pressed down once again to test the hardness without the thickness of the robe between them.

Now she was aware of his excitement, aware and confused, too, that it should be happening now. "What?" she repeated, bringing her sobbing under control. "Kelly . . . ?" Her voice was the voice of a little girl.

"Yes," he replied, sliding his hand down between their bodies and touching her, the skin so warm and soft. She inhaled in three short gasps and he stared down at her, suspended as she was in a moment of realization and looking very small underneath him. Their eyes held one another as he arched his body up, relieving her of his full weight. Her sobbing had stopped, but she still breathed heavily. He glanced down between them to where his hand rested; she followed his gaze and pulled her robe open all the way. Taking his hand away, he gave her back the easy weight of his body, adjusting his position so that even with his clothes on he found a concave resting place between her legs.

She sighed, trembling and pushing up against him.

Her hands met his at his waist as he once more arched his body up. "I'll do it," he said, wanting and needing to be the aggressor. She stiffened, holding her position motionless while he undid the snap at his waist and started the zipper sliding down. Her hands, trembling now, joined his, guiding his pants down over his hips to his knees. He kicked his shoes off and used his feet to rid himself of his pants, then slipped his fingers under the waistband of his shorts, expanding them and tugging them down until the warm, erect part of him was released and struck down against her.

"Oh . . ." she said on a catch-breath, trembling and tentative. His entire body quivered as she reached down, taking him in her hand and guiding the head of his cock to touch her lips. He met resistance at first, persisted—she helping by adjusting her body to receive him—and soon he felt the firm heat of her as he entered. She arched her body up to meet him as he pressed down, sliding slowly and with great pressure inside her. Both gasped, then held their breaths as he forced his way farther into her and when, finally, he was fully encased she cried out a pleasurable sound of pain. At first he was afraid to acknowledge his ecstasy by word or sound, afraid he might shatter the reality of this sensation so long hoped for. He could only shut his eyes in silent joy.

She constricted, clutching the center of him and locking him inside her. Her warmth was unbelievable to him, more than warmth—it was an exquisite burning. After she once again exhaled a shuddering breath that translated her passion to him, he cried out "Oh, God . . . Oh, God!" both in rapture and thanksgiving, feeling every inch of skin on his body tighten, closing off his pores and restraining his own heat to the point of combustion.

He remained inside her without moving until her natural lubrication worked up, easing the pressure and turning the sensation from delicious pain into liquid ecstasy. Then she moved away under him, half-unsheathing him, and he felt the coolness of the air strike him and plunged back into the warmth of her.

They repeated this undulation only three times when he felt the stinging birth of orgasm. It seemed to begin in his feet, curling his toes and sweeping up his limbs, threatening to peel the skin back off his legs as it swirled in circular speed toward his groin. With one great freeing motion he drove back down into her and the force burst from him.

He cried out a wild, animal sound he would have denied ever came from him, had he heard it. Then, as the sensation of orgasm overwhelmed him and gave promise of blacking him out, he held his head up, straining his neck, contorting his face, and attempting to focus his eyes.

She cried out, too, feeling his ejaculations and accompanying each one with a jabbing upward motion into him. And he moaned as the spurts became shorter and weaker and finally stopped until she slid her arms down his back and placed one hand on each of his buttocks, pressing him down farther into her and releasing the last of his fluid.

In a spasm of affection for him, she leaned up, kissing his arched neck and working up to his jaw until he lowered his head and found her mouth for kisses as passionate as if their love-making were only beginning. If he could have spoken, he would have uttered one long, thunderous yes.

While they kissed, he remained warm and hard inside her, burying himself in her, and after a time and in a certain rhythm with the regular pounding of the waves, she began a slow, rotating movement under him. He caught the pattern of it, joining perfectly in the thrust, the circular grinding, the partial withdrawal and the forward upward plunge; gradually their movements became larger, with a wide, swinging pendulum stroke which separated them as he withdrew until they were no longer able to kiss and she moaned in prelude to her slow-mounting climax.

Once more she grabbed his backside, clutching her fingers into him and driving him into her. And when they met together, the rhythmic slapping of their bodies seemed to initiate the swirling fluids within him as the faint tingle of fulfillment trickled along the delicate fuse connecting the base of his spine to the front of him, and the soft skin of his balls tightened up and up, preparatory to the final act of expulsion. By the growing vibrations engulfing her body and the never-before-heard sound of woman's release from gravity, he knew they would meet together.

The roar of the surf sounded close to him and, although it could have been the pounding of blood in his ears as consummation's adrenaline throbbed in his veins, the breaking of the waves urged him to match the ocean itself in the driving power of his thrusts until he marveled that her body could withstand this assault.

She was equal to the challenge, rising up off the sand and lunging up to him, and it was her force and cries of love and pleasure and exhortation that triggered the sweet, aching explosion from him as they met together in climax with all the gentleness of a head-on collision.

Falling, falling, falling—until their bodies, coupled ferociously, were struck by a solid lip of the incoming tide.

They shouted and clung to each other as the water struck
them, skidding them up several feet on the sand, swiveling
them around, and sucking them back a ways.

"Oh—oh, a wave!" Maggie shouted. "A wave—how
great!"

"I'm still, *still*—" Kelly cried out, wincing.

"Yes, yes—me, too!" she gasped and was then dissolved
into sobbing postcoital laughter.

And he was trapped into laughter with her as the entire
world went liquid and their exclamations of delight shot the
air. They had no sooner focused upon each other when a
smaller wave sloshed over Maggie's head and splashed up
into Kelly's face, too. They sputtered and coughed and
laughed even more, now that the full release of their passion
was behind them.

Kelly felt the violent pounding of his heart, not only from
the physical energy expended but from the wildest joy he
had ever experienced, and then the realization struck him
full force. He covered her breasts and neck and lips with
kisses as his hands flew over her in trembling caresses and
then he laid his cheek against her cheek and pressed the
tears of joy into her face.

And he whispered: "Oh Maggie—it happened, it *happened!*" He kissed her again. "Maggie," he sighed, "we made
it, we did."

"You made it," she said, taking his face in her hands.

They were exchanging salty kisses when a wave, larger
than the first, smacked them, dislodging Kelly and sending
them sprawling.

He quickly stumbled up from the receding water and
rushed to Maggie, hopelessly entangled in the mass of her
water-soaked robe. He hauled her, swaying under a sodden
heap of terrycloth, to her feet.

"Here—help me out of this cement robe before it takes me
down with it!" she cried. He held the robe up as she peeled
it off, extricating herself from the heavy folds. "Saved from

the Iron Maiden!" she gasped. Each taking hold of an end, they wrung it out between them as best they could, although their efforts were weakened by bursts of laughter.

After he helped her back into the robe, pounds lighter now, she said, "Oh, that's better, nice and clammy, like a skinned goat getting back into its hide!"

Kelly suddenly glanced down at himself. "My God—my pants! And my shoes!"

"Where are they?" she asked.

"I don't know," he said, scanning the wet sand around them. "Where did we start?"

His question set off another bout of laughter as she pointed to him, dressed in jacket, shirt and tie, and nothing below except for a pair of socks; and he pointed to her, sagging under wet terrycloth, hair plastered to her head.

They were ridiculously lovely in each other's eyes.

"They're gone," he shrugged.

They fell in toward one another, clinging together as another wave foamed past their feet, splashing their legs. "What is this—the end of the world?" Maggie laughed. "Let's head for the high ground." When they stumbled up where the sand was dry, she turned to him and took his face in her hands. "Will you stay with me?"

"Forever!" he said, filled so with happiness—until he realized the choice of his word and it was immediately reflected in his face.

"Ah!" she shrugged, "there'll be lots of those."

And to blot out the moment, he put his arms around her and kissed her with all the passion he felt and with all the fervor to which performance entitled him.

CHAPTER 33

When they climbed up to the house, Kelly with his jacket tied around his waist, they dispelled Flora's fears at the sight of them by the sheer exuberance of their spirits. While Flora toweled her hair dry and Stosh stood by, looking wisely from Maggie to Kelly, Maggie outlined her new plan.

"Much as I love this place, we'd better start thinking about moving on. Our friend Angel's bound to spread the good word and—"

Flora gasped and Stosh slapped his forehead. "What a dummy. I didn't even think of that."

"Indeed," Maggie said. "We're safe for the time being, for a day or so, but not much longer, especially with the other news out. They'll be looking for me in packs. I want someplace I can't be got at. So what I thought is this, Stosh. You and Flora go to Ensenada tonight, stop at a motel, then first thing in the morning scour around, see what kind of a yacht we can hire for a couple of weeks. And, Stosh, I mean a yacht, something we can walk around on, price no object. We'll go up the coast to Coronada, Catalina, San Francisco— wherever we want."

"Great," Stosh said, "but how come we gotta stay in a motel? Why don't we just get up early here?"

"For the very simple reason," Maggie winked at him, "that my friend and I would like to spend our last night here alone."

Stosh looked quickly from Maggie to Kelly. "I knew when you came up from the beach you didn't get that way from makin' muddy pies," he grinned. "I think somebody's been foolin' around!"

After Stosh and Flora had gone, high with plans for this newest excursion, Maggie and Kelly stood out on the terrace looking down at the cove. He put his arm around her, feeling the full measure of himself. After a while he squeezed her. He opened his mouth to speak. Maggie looked at him, waiting, but nothing came out.

"What?" she asked.

"I—I'm full of so many words, I feel so—full, I ca-can't get any of them out."

"Try."

"I—" A sudden gulp escaped him. "Oh God—I think I'm going to cry. Of all times to—" And he did; small, soft sobs of relief, thanks, joy and other crosscurrents of emotions poured from him. Maggie put her arms around him, holding him close. When he was finally purged, he pulled away from her, grinned and said: "I guess you know what *that* was about?"

She leaned in and kissed him; he returned her kiss and they stood close together, their mouths feeding gently and sweetly off each other, until she could feel him once again excited and pressing up against her.

She broke the embrace. "And you were *worried?*" she laughed. "Maybe it's cumulative. Maybe your celibacy is paying off in endless residuals." She touched his mouth with her finger. "You blush the best of anyone. Your mouth turns down at the corners and gets all frownlike. You blushed when I first looked at you."

"I love you."

"How much?" she demanded. He opened his mouth to

speak, but when the amount was not immediately forthcoming she said, "Oh, I don't know, if you have to think . . ."

"Enough to black out all of Rhode Island and—start World War Five!"

"Come now," she said, "let's keep a tight bead on reality here!"

"I swear it, may Mickey Mouse drop dead on his fifty-first birthday."

"Then, for God's sake, take a shower with me!"

Raffaello drove through town in his rented Buick Regal, in immaculate condition, and soon the road turned left and he was moving along the harbor heading south. The breeze was gusty but warm and he reached up, cranking back the sun roof to let the scented ocean air in. He found an FM station beaming from San Diego playing Leontyne Price's recording of *Tosca,* conducted by von Karajan with Di Stefano and Taddei. He hummed along with the music; his mood was high and optimistic. He would be seeing her within a half-hour.

Balance was the operative word. Above all he would maintain his balance. He promised himself he would withstand any onslaught she might hurl at him with gentlemanly poise. If he could not win certain battles regarding his previous conduct, he could at least come through now with honor and bravery. He knew how she awarded points.

If she happened to be so unforgiving as to order him away, he would even cope with that. For that very reason he'd kept his hotel room. He would tell her he understood her anger and he would be at the El Convento; he loved her and she loved him and he would be there waiting for her call. She could not afford to waste time, nor was she the kind of person to spend it on foolish delaying actions.

So armed with preconceived images, he drove to see her. Once he passed the last of the motels and houses on the outskirts of the town he was struck by the beauty of the rugged coastline. The solid gray sky was breaking up, as evidenced by choppy glimpses now and then of the moon high above.

The crude drawing lay on the seat next to him, but he thought there would undoubtedly be a sign, either the name of the cove or the owner of the house—Sydow. He was surprised when the dashboard showed he had traveled eight miles, that there were no houses, no buildings of any kind to be seen on either side of the road, which now sloped irregularly in and out of small canyons, always winding within sight or sound of the ocean. He glanced at the drawing; it could have fit almost any part of the coastline he drove along now.

When he'd gone twelve miles he began to be concerned. He looked at the drawing again; the X marked on it meant nothing, not with all the curves and windings this road took. Crumpling it in his fist, he tossed it up and let the wind whip it back out of the sun roof, muttering: "Fucking Mexicans!"

There were no lights to be seen, no signs of any kind except warnings for curves and inclines. He continued, driving slowly now, on the lookout for what might be even a darkened house. After another mile or so the road circled out, rounding a jagged point; Raffaello stopped the car, glancing back up the coast from where he'd come, and there, perhaps a mile back, he could see lights glowing faintly halfway between what looked like a large bluff and the ocean below it.

He turned around and drove back, slightly annoyed that he could have missed it. The road soon ducked inland a ways and then down along the floor of a small valley and the lights were no longer visible to him. After a while the car snaked up the side of a gorge and swung around the bend of a cliff and there to the left was a large grassy bluff jutting out over the water.

He pulled off the side of the road and stopped the car. He could see up the coast but there were no lights showing. Perhaps this was the bluff he had spotted from the distance. Still, he could see neither a road nor steps leading off it, nor did there seem to be any driveway at the far end where the road turned right, heading inland again.

He got out of the car and closed the door. The bluff was

covered with thick wet grass that gave a springy bounce to his step as he walked toward the edge. The moon disappeared behind a thick puff of clouds and in the darkness he thought he could detect a faint ray of light out in the black drop-off at the end of the bluff. He walked carefully now, testing the earth, aware that the soil might be eaten away by erosion underneath the cliff.

There were several scrubby, brushlike trees out by the edge; he moved toward the one on his right. There *was* a light of sorts streaking out down there. Reaching the tree, ten or twelve yards from the end of the bluff, he took hold of a branch with one hand and leaned forward, straining for a view below.

He caught a glimpse of the end of a terrace, outside lights aglow. He was at once amazed that there could be anything down there. He smiled: if there was a crazy house jutting out from nowhere, Maggie could be counted on to find it.

He judged he was too directly above the rest of the structure to see it without moving forward to the edge of the cliff and lying stomach down, head hanging off into space. For a better vantage point he moved farther away from the house to his left, at the same time stepping closer to the edge by following the natural configuration of the bluff which jutted out to form a prong.

Soon he was in position to look over and down into the master bedroom, open to view through the plate-glass window running the length of it. He could see the entire room, the seating arrangement, chaise, the low marble table by the window, and beyond it, the luxurious king-sized bed. Two reading lamps, one on either end of the headboard, were lit and a stand-up lamp glowed by the chaise.

Raffaello looked around him, taking in the surrounding terrain. To the north, the gorge running inland cut off the house; to the south, also a canyon, and beyond it, not a building or light to be seen. The house, not visible from the highway, was totally isolated.

When he looked back down at the bedroom he coughed

up a small involuntary sound of surprise. Maggie was just stepping into view from the right.

She was wrapped in a mustard-colored beach towel; there was a frosted window next to the large plate-glass onc and Raffaello guessed it to be the bathroom. As she moved across the room she dried her neck with a smaller towel. Stopping by the bed, she dropped the smaller towel on it, then walked to the dresser. Her back was to him and for a moment he couldn't tell what she was doing. She picked something up and, yes, she was patting something, cologne perhaps, on her neck and shoulder. Finished, she picked up her ring and slipped it on her finger, walking to stand in front of the large window just as the moon bobbed out from the swiftly moving clouds.

Raffaello quickly stepped in close to a scrubby half-tree/half-bush for protection. She only glanced up at the moon briefly and then stood there framed in the center of the window looking out and down at the beach below. He held his breath. Her beauty, even at a distance, was unmistakable and awesome. The rays from the stand-up lamp highlighted the planes of her face, the cheekbones, the sculpted hollows below, and the generous mouth. Although she was not looking up in his direction, he remained standing very still and close by the gnarled, leafless branches next to him.

She brushed a hand across her forehead.

He felt such love for her he could imagine, could almost will, his arms to stretch down across the space between them until he could trace his fingers lightly across the glass and then she would tilt her head, looking up and smiling at him, one corner of her mouth tugged down, as it always did.

Lifting her hands, she ran her fingers through her hair. He smiled at the familiar gesture, then laughed as her stretching caused the towel to come undone and drop down, exposing her breasts for a second before she clutched it, raised it again, and reached behind, tucking a fold to hold it in place.

Watching her, Raffaello was becoming excited. He silently

cursed, and not without humor, his immediate response at the very sight of her.

The moon slid behind a cloud and the resulting darkness outside seemed to magnify her image in the light down there behind the window.

As he was thinking she might have put on some weight, a few pounds, so beautiful was she, she turned and smiled in the direction from which she had appeared. She said something, then she was laughing and—

A young man, towel around his waist, stepped into sight. Raffaello ducked his head forward, recognizing him at once. His dark hair was wet and part of it was matted down across his forehead. The shock of seeing him didn't manifest itself in a specific emotional reaction at first. Raffaello was more hypnotized by his mere appearance than anything else. He was riveted to him, to the difference between the brief memory he held of him and the reality of the way he looked down there in the lighted distance with Maggie.

They stood talking for a moment; now it was as if Raffaello were watching a film with the sound track turned off. He even leaned out, ducking his head forward for a second as if he might hear them, before he caught himself. The only sound to be heard was the breaking of the waves. She threw her head back in laughter once more, then reached out, putting her hands on his bare shoulders and bobbing her head forward for a brief kiss, no more than a brush of the lips, upon his forehead.

"No . . ." Raffaello muttered.

As if obeying him, Maggie took her hands from his shoulders and Kelly walked to the bed and sat on the edge of it.

His build was more substantial without clothes. Why had he thought of him as skinny, almost puny? Though not overly developed, he appeared to have good muscle tone, definition in his chest leading to a small waist, and his legs were sturdy and well shaped.

Raffaello found himself wondering a more intimate question. He shuddered, a shiver of disgust at himself. Still, he had time to brush this off as no more than the average locker-room curiosity men have about one another, before Maggie walked to the bed, climbed up on it and knelt behind Kelly.

She took the towel from his hand and began drying his hair. At one point she leaned forward and kissed the crown of his head. As she did this he reached up to her and she kissed the palm of his hand, also. When she straightened up from this kiss, the towel she was wearing came undone again and dropped away from her. She paid it no attention and remained kneeling behind him, drying his hair, her breasts visible above his shoulders.

It was an unmistakable scene of two lovers; their intimacy and ease with each other were so painful to observe that Raffaello was locked in a masochistic trance. Like a man with his finger caught in an electric socket, he could do nothing but keep the beam of his stunned gaze focused upon them.

After drying his hair, she massaged his scalp with her fingertips. The pain increased, for this was something she had done each day for Raffaello.

The full and brutal news was in. She was not simply playing games, this was no frolic, no come-on, no bit of hide-and-seek. He had been replaced. He was a casualty, forgotten, dropped behind and left for dead on the battlefield of their affair.

Having carefully smoothed Kelly's hair back during her massage, Maggie surprised him by lunging forward with both hands and roughing it up. Laughing, he looked up at her and she threw her arms around his chest, pulling him backward on the bed.

The towel came undone from around his waist as he turned on his side to face her. They fell into an embrace and while they kissed they slowly rolled, she on her back, he covering her. Her hands moved caressingly up his back to his neck.

It was a youthful body, trim and firm, stretched out now for Raffaello to see.

An instant of rage struck him and in the darkness of his mind—a brief and violent desire to douse them with kerosene and ignite them while they were lying there together.

It was a small but meaningful byplay that ended Raffaello's capacity to watch. She drew a hand around Kelly's neck and poked a finger in his ear, wiggling it playfully. In response, Kelly shook his head and lifted his face up and away from her. They froze like this for a long moment, gazing at each other with smiling eyes, lips parted.

Raffaello was caught in this tableau, a discarded third party in exile. The pain was unbearable. He jerked his head away, facing out to sea and the rock sitting in the entrance to the cove.

The incoming sea breeze, touched by the mild gulf current, carried a tropical warmth, but Raffaello stood on the cliff numbed and cold. He was not conscious of time; he didn't know whether he'd been staring out at nothing, held in a stunned limbo, for seconds or minutes when he heard a vague whirring sound followed by the cough and sputter of a motor as an ancient pickup truck rounded the curve and for an instant skimmed the top of the bluff with its headlights.

This attracted his attention and he turned to see the truck disappear around the side of the cliff heading south. Moving his head slowly around, he once more stared down toward the warmly lighted scene in the distance. But he wasn't seeing clearly; the numbness that threatened to start his teeth to chatter also blurred his vision.

He was aware of the progression of their love-making, aware of the two figures undulating almost as one down in the bedroom, but he allowed his focus to remain fuzzy.

The voyeur in him was not anxious for further details.

Again he lost track of time. It was a large movement that made him clear his vision. Shaking his head, he rubbed a hand across his eye.

They had changed positions. He was lying on his back (and now whatever curiosity Raffaello had about him was satisfied and not happily so; he was a man, there was no mistaking that) and Maggie was standing on the bed over and astride him.

Now, while Raffaello watched, she sank down, straddling him, knees bending, closer and closer until she had closed the distance between them and he saw her spine arch as she experienced the delicious sensation of enveloping him in a different way and, from the position of her body, head thrown up and back, neck straining, arms outstretched, her ecstasy was all too apparent.

Suddenly, to Raffaello the scene was unspeakably filthy. An inhuman sound, a mixture of anguish and disgust, escaped his throat. At the same time, feeling dizzy, he reached out with his right hand and made a clutching grab at the bush for support.

Screaming in pain, he ripped his hand away and looked to see the source of his agony. The palm of his hand bore several deep gashes from the thorny branch he had so firmly grasped.

He cried out, cursing, and then moaned, cradling his injured hand in his good one and rocking back and forth on his heels. As he held it up closer to his face, the clouds obliged by once more parting and he was able to see the sight of his blood, shiny black in the moonlight.

A sticky hot lump bolted up from his stomach and burst out of his mouth and he was violently ill. When he finished, he fumbled for his handkerchief and, without looking back down at them, picked his way across the bluff to the car.

Driving toward Ensenada, he could feel the blood, warm and sticky, seep up his sleeve and dry along his wrist. He was forced to stop the car twice and twice he got out and leaned up against the fender while he retched, convulsed with dry heaving long after his stomach was empty.

CHAPTER 34

Maggie and Kelly, their breathing still heavy, lay next to one another. "Did I say exorcised or—exhausted," she panted, squeezing his hand.

Kelly leaned up on his elbow and looked down at her. Her beauty struck him far differently than before; she was pale and her skin seemed to be drawn tightly over her face. "Maybe we shouldn't have . . ."

"I wouldn't have missed the Late Show for the world!" She grinned at him.

He leaned over and kissed her, then put his face down beside her cheek. "You know what I like? What started out to be a Mad Tea Party turned into a love affair." He kissed her again. "I love you." He leaned back down, but in a moment he was up on his elbows again. "I'm practically unconscious but my motor won't stop." After a moment he asked: "Do I have a lot to learn?"

"How?"

"You know . . ."

She reached over and patted him on the hip. "I'd say you're what we call—a natural."

"How can you tell?"

"I've been around."

"You're not just saying things to make me feel good?" he asked.

"Couldn't you tell?"

"I don't have anything to compare us with—*me* with."

"Take my word."

"I will, if you mean it."

She smiled. "I'll get a notary public." She glanced at the firm round shoulder next to her, at his lips partly open in thought, and her mouth tugged over and down in a small smile, unseen by him, for she knew he was about to speak; she was almost certain of his thoughts and it warmed and tickled her.

He coughed a little cough, which had no physiological basis, and spoke without looking at her. "Do I please you as much . . ." His words trailed off.

"As much as . . . ?"

He shrugged, attempting a casualness. "Oh, say—Raffaello, for instance?"

"I'm with *you*, aren't I?"

"Yes, but—"

"If you didn't 'please me'—such a *mild* phrase!—I'd be with him. Not him," she corrected herself, "but someone else."

"I suppose. Except . . . here we are in the middle of nowhere. There's not much choice."

"But I chose you to *take* to the middle of nowhere."

"Yes, but you didn't know anything about me. You had no other choice than to—just make do."

"If you call the last couple of hours 'just making do'!" She slapped his leg. "What do you bloody well want from me?" she laughed.

He laughed, too. "I told you, I'm punchy." They lay in silence for a moment and then he said: "A day or so before I met you, I prayed for a miracle—and, by God, I got it! Isn't that incredible?"

"Mmnnn . . ." she said on the long end of a purr.

Looking over at her, lying there in muzzy fatigue, he propped himself up on his elbow. "I might just stay up all night and watch you."

"Watch me what?"

"Just watch you." He yawned.

"Oh, no, you don't. If you're going to watch me—no yawning."

He covered his mouth and yawned again. "Sorry."

"Deal's off. No watching."

"God, I'm happy," he exhaled, lying back down. "Remember the first time, when you said: 'Great—a wave!' I'll always remember that."

"Will you always remember me?"

The question stabbed him, but he quickly said: "I doubt it."

She poked him with her elbow and they laughed easily. "Will we try all sorts of other ways?" he asked.

"What? Oh, why—" She made a little clucking sound. "You're getting to be a fanatic."

"Will we?"

"I suppose," she laughed.

"When?"

She chuckled. "I'll consult my *engagement* book." Then: "May I at least have a cigarette break?"

"Uh-huh," he laughed.

"You're terrible." She slapped him on the leg.

"Don't touch me!" he warned. "The sleeping giant has been awakened."

"Lock up your daughters," Maggie said. "And while you're at it—hide the canary." Now it was Maggie who yawned. "I just realized—I'm starved, I haven't had dinner. I've performed several 'live, exotic shows' and I haven't been fed. I ought to quit this house!"

He was off the bed in an instant. "Let me fix you something. Please!"

She laughed softly. "You don't have to plead—get in the kitchen, put your money where your mouth is!" Slipping on his robe, he was about to leave the room when she added: "Nothing monumental, no duck or poached salmon—a sandwich, a snack."

"All right."

"Kelly . . . ?"

Her tone made him turn around. "Yes?"

She beamed an unmistakable smile of love at him. "What am I going to say?"

"Isn't it all—just terrific?"

"Exactly."

In the kitchen he found the makings for an omelette. He was chopping up green peppers and onions when he heard the soft padding of slippered feet. "Just lonesome," she said, crossing to a stool at the end of a long free-standing butcher-block counter. She sat, resting her chin in the cup of her hand while she watched him.

As he went about the preparations, it seemed to Kelly he had acquired an unusual dexterity. There was an economy and certainty of movement he had never experienced before. Not particularly adept with his hands, he was used to the maximum fuss and tension when working with them. Now tension appeared to be eliminated and he worked with an easy grace. He wondered about this as he broke the eggs into a bowl, beat them, and added a tablespoon of cold water. Then it came to him—he was enveloped by a natural high. He also realized this was the first time he was engaged in an everyday activity under the influence of love. He smiled and looked at her; she smiled back at him. The need for words was no longer present. The subtext provided by their feeling for each other wiped out the need for all but the most basic speech.

"May I have a glass of milk?"

"Coming up."

When he handed her the glass, she kissed his hand before he could take it away. He went back to the stove and as she watched him, she marveled at the strength of her emotions. She thought she might have worn down her capacity to love that fully, that perhaps it had been diminished by overuse. Not at all. Watching him pour the ingredients into a frying pan, she could barely resist embracing him.

He flipped the omelette onto a plate and brought it to her with a piece of toast. "You don't use catsup, do you?"

"Of course, I do."

He got it for her and, while she watched, poured some on the plate next to the eggs. "And a big glob on top, please." She took a forkful. "Ummm—good."

"Thank you."

"But *you* haven't eaten—don't you want—"

"No, not hungry. Happy, satisfied, content."

Before going back to the bedroom they stood outside on the terrace for ten minutes or so, he with his arms around her. The surf was heavy; the sounds it gave off, the heavy pounding, the hiss of foam sucking back down the sands, the silence between waves, was mesmerizing. The longer they refrained from talking, the more they said. Both felt it. After a while Maggie chuckled lightly, "I hope you're getting all this."

"I am," he replied.

"Good. Remember it."

"I will. And vice versa, I presume," he added.

"Definitely."

When they were finally back in bed, resting next to each other, she yawned and after a moment spoke his name softly.

"Yes?"

"Go to sleep inside me."

"Can I?" He leaned up on his elbow. "How?"

With one hand she drew his head down and kissed him; with the other she touched him where he was limp. Sighing, he said: "Your touch." She kissed him again, fondling him gently until he came to half-life and then more. He slid on top of her, keeping his weight light, and she guided him inside her.

They both sighed, putting their arms around each other, and she turned them slowly, at the same time drawing her

legs up around his thighs to his waist, until they rested easily on their sides. "There . . ." she said.

"Oh, yes," he replied, adjusting his weight. "I'm not too
heavy on your leg?"

"No." She yawned again. "We won't be able to stay this
way all night, but for a while . . ."

"I love you," he whispered.

She whispered back: "Considering the position we're in—I
should hope to Christ!"

She fell asleep very soon. Her breath, faint and fresh,
grazed his cheek and for a while, lying so entwined and
growing completely firm inside her, he was concerned that
he would be unable to sleep. But when he had reached his
maximum erection, there was a cutoff in his sensations; he
felt a numbness; a creeping paralysis of happy exhaustion
began in the calves of his legs and before it reached his
brain he was asleep with a smile of pure delight upon his
face.

When Raffaello returned to the hotel, he called for a doctor who cleaned and bandaged his hand, gave him a shot to
ward off infection and a small white envelope containing
pain pills.

His injury was only a coda to his true misery, but it provided an added excuse to begin some serious drinking. With
a pain pill, a sleeping pill, and his bottle of scotch, he soon
managed to anesthetize himself, to reduce the nasty mixture
of emotions boiling within him to a mean squint-eyed simmer.

There were no prayers tonight when he finally stripped
himself of his clothes, leaving them on the floor where they
dropped, and tumbled onto the bed. Instead there were
drugged exhortations to God for this latest twist of the finger
of fate, not so fickle as it was determined to prod and poke
and natter at him until his last hour on earth.

Even in his groggy condition he could still tote up the misfortunes visited upon him. Then a quick maudlin reflection
back to the days of glory: nights, standing there on that

stage, the waves sweeping over him, bathed in adoration, dripping with the wild joy of it all. He had the world so by the tail he could have swung it around his head.

God, the swift descent from glory, down, down, where in Christ's name is the bottom?

"No," he muttered. He wouldn't hit the bottom. And he wouldn't lose her. *I'll kill her first, I swear to Christ—*

The voices picked up the refrain and he laughed as they added: she's a dead duck anyway!

Then he passed out. Though his sleep was drugged and heavy, Raffaello fought his way to the surface of consciousness several times, wondering vaguely where he was and if what he'd witnessed the night before had been real. In his soporific state he rejected the reality of the view from the cliff as only one episode in the sick nightmare of the last few days and fell back into a self-induced sleep.

The throbbing in his hand, now puffy and tender, awakened him as the orange Mexican sun crawled over the rim of a bare brown hill in the distance. For a while he lay there beaming waves of anger at it, loathing it as a symbol of God. God, who was in the doghouse.

He stared at his hand, proof that what he'd seen was not part of any festival of dreams. His eye ached and his stomach was as hot and jumpy as his nerves were chilly. He glanced around the room; now, even Mexico came in for a share of his scorn. Mexico, what a ridiculous, make-believe country!

His stomach demanded liquids. He wanted a cold glass of tomato juice. Abruptly reaching for the house phone, he slammed his hand against the edge of the night table. He cursed and groaned in pain, clutching his hand to his chest.

Such a small mishap firmed the tone for the day. The desire for tomato juice was canceled and he poured himself a neat scotch and downed it.

By nine o'clock he'd finished off, along with juice and coffee, what remained of the bottle. He'd showered and dressed but his hand annoyed him too much to bother with shaving.

His nerves were still not back in place but they were no

longer chilly; they were heating up, percolating, and in answer to the litany of persecution the voices had drummed
into his subconscious, he was feeling a certain fighting-back
recklessness—as much toward the world in general as
Maggie in particular.

The tilt he so often struggled to avoid had taken over. He
felt tipped, cocked at an angle, and his mind, now jarring
along the singular rut of his obsession, told him only to end
the status quo of his misery, not how.

A final cup of black coffee to reduce the fuzzy and not unpleasant edge he felt, to clear his vision, then he would get
in his car and drive down there. But there would be no game
of hide-and-seek, no playing peekaboo this time.

CHAPTER 35

When Kelly opened his eyes, he was immediately and joyously wide awake and in a state of excitement. He didn't remember when during the night he'd become disengaged from Maggie, but he recalled staggering up to close the draperies at the first pastel hint of dawn creeping over the mountaintops, remembered falling back into bed and clutching her in his arms, the two of them on their sides, his front to her back.

Leaning up on an elbow, he gazed down at her, sleeping so peacefully. He wanted to kiss her cheek, but he refrained for fear of disturbing her. He felt he could no longer contain his excitement in the same bed without awakening her, so he eased his body over to the side and stood up.

Picking up his robe from the floor, he slipped his arms into it. He looked back down at Maggie and was seized by a desire to dive upon the bed and nuzzle up next to her. The world was so much with him he had to stifle an impulse to shout. Grinning, he quickly and quietly left the room.

He crossed the living room and stepped out onto the terrace. The brilliance of the morning and the utter silence of it stunned him completely. The day was crystal; the water in the cove was mirror-calm and a transparent light turquoise in color. He could see a rock, a swirl in the beige sand, and in close by the shore, a school of silver fish, suspended, motionless in V formation. The water out beyond the cove was level and tiny-rippled—miles of finely ridged dark green corduroy. The horizon was sharp in delineation; the royal blue of the sky planed down to meet the deep green of the water, neither sacrificing any of its individual color to the other, but, somehow, striking up a black line between them where they met.

But it was the very air, tangible and grainy-blue and so sharp in its freshness that it stung his nostrils, which hypnotized Kelly. Never had a day struck him with such impact. The breath was knocked out of him and, for a second, he felt compelled to grab the wooden handrailing for support. When his senses had recovered from the pure shock of the setting, he slipped out of his robe and let it fall to his feet. Standing there naked, he flung his arms up and out as far as they would stretch. He threw back his head and laughed and his laughter echoed down into the cove and bounced back up at him, causing him to laugh again. He walked to the far end of the terrace, overlooking the gorge and bottomed by nothing but rocks and a growth of wild underbrush, and relieved himself, seeing how far he could make his stream travel. Again he laughed, reveling in a new and total freedom.

He decided to fix a breakfast tray and bring it to Maggie. Putting on his robe, he stepped into the living room, and at that moment he was so filled to the brim with happiness he thought it impossible to contain such an overload. For a brief second, he hadn't any doubt that he would simply—disintegrate.

But the second was short-lived. Stepping into the dark hallway leading to the kitchen, he stopped short. The change from the bright sunlight was too abrupt for his eyes. He felt dizzy and put a hand out against the wall to steady himself.

It was then, an eerie moment grazed him. It—the scene, the day, his absolute contentment—was too much what it was, the essence was too pure, too perfect to continue, if not to be true. He remembered what Maggie had said—nothing lasts forever—and panic struck in the form of a very real doubt at the existence of the day he had just viewed.

He turned, rushing from the hallway across the living room and out onto the terrace. It was all there: the sky, the sea, the rock in the center of the cove, the sandy strip of beach bordering it, the air as clear as before. He feasted upon the lush display spread out before him. Of course, the day was there.

Still, there was something else. He shook his head, looking down at his forearms, stretched out as they were, bracing him as he leaned into the railing. They were covered with gooseflesh.

Instantly the true cause of his alarm came to him when his memory dredged up the one other time he had experienced such total happiness. Then, too, it had been followed by an inexplicable moment of apprehension: getting into the car with Bethel, that last Sunday on their way to the beach. Yes, that moment too was—

"Hey you!" a voice called out loud and clear from behind him.

The shock of it would have sent him off the terrace had it not been for the handrailing.

He spun around. Maggie stood barefoot inside the open glass door, her mouth still twisted down and to the side from the mock toughness with which she had called out to him. She caught the expression on his face immediately. "Why, I—I frightened you," she laughed.

"Yes," he smiled. "And I'll make you pay for it. I don't know how or when but I'll manage to extract some small perverse toll."

"Oh . . ." she said, in a mock combative tone, "like—what?"

The sight of her there in front of him, early-morning fresh and glowing, was enough to send his spirits into a triple somersault. "I'll probably get you very close to climax—then just leave and go to the movies."

"I hope you'll remember to zip up your fly." He laughed and she added, "Just remember, that kind of threat can work two ways."

"As long as we're having our first sexual war—come here and kiss me good morning."

"Hmn . . . I like the orders." She walked to him; he took her in his arms and kissed her.

After a lazy breakfast, they got into their bathing suits, found an inflatable rubber float in a closet, and set off down the steps to the cove. Stepping off the wooden planking onto the first large boulder, Maggie stopped and looked around her. "Now this is a day." She stretched an arm out. "This is a day and a half." When they stood on the beach, Maggie looked out to the rock and he followed her gaze. "The sand out there, so powder-white and—let's go out to our rock." He remembered how the swim had exhausted her and started to protest. "Couldn't you tow me out on the float?" she asked.

"My pleasure."

Kelly put the float in the water and when Maggie was balanced upon her back with the towels and cigarettes on top of her midsection, he pushed it into deeper water and began swimming behind it, kicking his feet easily out behind him, propelling them forward in gentle spurts.

Raffaello was on the lookout for a driveway and, as the car rounded the bend with the bluff widening out toward the sea and blocking the view of the cove, he caught sight of the weed-lined tire tracks sloping sharply down off the road. They looked precarious at best and, deciding to walk down to the house, he pulled the car onto the dirt shoulder of the road and parked.

Coming within sight of the paved parking area, he was surprised to find it empty. As he approached the house, he could see in through the kitchen windows and also into another room; there was no sign of activity. He stepped up to the front door and listened but he could hear nothing.

When he turned the handle it swung open easily. Glancing down the dark hallway, he could almost sense the house was empty; the echo of his footsteps on the tiles as he walked the length of the hall toward the sunlit living room at the end corroborated this feeling.

Stepping into the large room, he immediately looked to his left, where he imagined the bedroom he had viewed from the bluff above would be. He was correct; he saw an open door beyond the small recessed hall and walked toward it. When he entered the bedroom, his nostrils dilated. He could detect the slight and not unpleasant musk of sleep and, of course, her perfume. The bed was unmade and the covers were comfortably rumpled. He avoided looking for more than a second.

The idea that she might be down below at the beach occurred to him and he walked to the large picture window. He gazed down at the half-moon stretch of sand curving out toward the prong of the cliff but the beach and area of water he was able to see were empty. He glanced up to his left where he had stood the night before.

He quickly returned to the living room. The glass doors leading onto the terrace and facing out to the full view of the cove were closed; he walked to them and was about to slide them open but the glare outside annoyed him. From the moment he had left the hotel there was something about the beauty of the day, the clear purity of it, that jarred him, in a way, mocked him by reflecting the complete antithesis of his mood. Even his sunglasses could not dim the crackling brilliance of the day.

Walking past the bar, he inspected the other two bedrooms. He recognized the huge flowered housecoat over the back of a chair as Flora's; in the far bedroom he saw a loud plaid jacket of Stosh's hanging on the closet door.

He grinned; he hadn't thought much about them lately and what thoughts he had were far from pleasant but now, suddenly and oddly, he missed them. He strolled back into the living room and found himself liking the house; there was a good feeling about it. It was the perfect house for Maggie and him.

He looked over the well-stocked bookcases, the bar, the guns and mementos hanging behind it, then moved over to the wooden cabinets and traced a finger across one section of the large record collection. On the narrow ends of the albums his eye caught the names: Tebaldi, Milanov, Merrill, Björling, Warren, Callas—yes, and Tucci, there he was, several times. He slid out the albums featuring his name: *Bohème, Andrea Chénier,* and *Carmen.*

He glanced at his watch: ten thirty. No car, no one down on the beach below the house; he guessed she must be off on one of her excursions. In spite of her illness, her natural curiosity provided a false boost to her energy. He remembered the many side trips she'd organized on their tour.

He sat down in an easy chair and suddenly, without a thought to her companion of the night before, he was simply waiting for her, for his Maggie. As it should be. He leaned back, wrapping himself in warm memories. When he'd skimmed the cream of them, a certain restlessness came over him—what would she say, what would her expression be when she found him there?

He stood up and walked to the bar. Her tortoise-shell compact rested on the end of it next to a pewter mug and a pair of binoculars. He picked the compact up and fingered it, squeezing it in the palm of his hand. Then, after making himself a drink, he sat on a barstool to continue his vigil.

When they reached the strip of sand out by the rock, Kelly put the float and towels up on the beach and joined Maggie back in the water. They stood together waist deep, looking in across the brilliant turquoise, so liquid light and silky, to the beach opposite. The sand shimmered under the dominating sun until heat waves, a field of steamy fingers, curled up from the beach and became invisible at a height of three or four feet. The sheared-off side of the cliff facing them was three-quarters exposed to the sun, yellow clay, baked bright.

The lower quarter, in shadow still, lay a deep uncooked mass of terra-cotta.

The house perched up on the ledge to the left looked amazingly flat and miniature; it was difficult to imagine anything but a windup doll walking out the doors onto the terrace. The mountains looming up in the background, their surfaces flattened out by the invading rays of the sun, took on the unreal appearance of an enormous painted cyclorama.

Maggie put her hands on his shoulders, then slid them down his sides until her fingers curled inside the waist of his trunks. "Take them off." Kelly inhaled to make his midsection smaller as she slid them over his hips. He joined his hands with hers and slipped them down past his thighs and below his knees, experiencing a delightful freedom as the water rushed in and caressed his genitals. Stepping out of his trunks, he wadded them up and tossed them over to the dry sand.

When she was out of her suit and Kelly had thrown it up on the sand alongside his own, she turned to face him and they stood grinning at each other. Maggie lunged forward, throwing her arms around his neck and knocking him back into the water. Her body floated on top of his for a brief time until they sank beneath the surface and emerged coughing and sputtering.

They stood now in deeper water. Maggie's breasts, buoyant and even with the surface, appeared to be floating. Kelly cupped one breast in his hands and, leaning down, kissed the nipple of it, moving his tongue back and forth and around it in tiny circles. Arching her head back and closing her eyes, she exhaled murmuring breaths that sounded her pleasure. Filled with gratitude that he could be the source of her enjoyment, Kelly took her other breast and repeated his actions.

Soon he reached his hands up, drawing her head to him, and they kissed passionately. After a time they separated and, as if by prearrangement, ducked down beneath the surface where their mouths met underwater. They kissed furiously, working against time, and their kissing, silent and blurred, was unbelievably surrealistic until a rush of bubbles burst from their mouths as they exhausted the last gasp of air between them.

When they broke the surface they stood clinging to each other, and Kelly felt the weight of sensual gravity increasing in his groin. He pressed up against her and she shivered and stood still for a moment. Then she reached down and took the semierect part of him in her hand.

Before he realized what had happened, she had dropped down to her knees. The shock from the coolness of the water to the warm membranes of her mouth caused him to wince and cry out in delicious sensation. His voice echoed across the water, shattering the stillness of the cove.

He looked down, but he could only see her thick hair swirling in the water up against his stomach. And while she was still holding him this way, he was so filled with love of her that he reached down and pulled her up from the water and thrust his mouth against hers.

"I love you, I love you," he murmured while kissing her. He broke the kiss and dropped to his knees in the water, placing his mouth full up against her, though he didn't know quite what to do, and Maggie smiled at the unselfish eagerness of her young lover.

He broke the surface of the water coughing violently. "I forgot to take a breath," he sputtered.

She took him in her arms and whispered: "Here, in the water."

"Can we?"

"Yes—here." She put her arms around his neck, at the same time swinging her legs in around his thighs and drawing them up around his waist, straddling him and holding him in a scissor-grip. She released one hand from his neck, taking hold of him beneath the water and guiding him until he touched her. Leaning in to him, she rested her face up against his cheek. "Now," she whispered, adjusting her position for his entry. "Now," she repeated.

He thrust forward and up from his hips and the tip of him

pried her lips open and entered up to the ridge of his circumcision. There he met resistance and she leaned back away from him and cried out his name.

"Am I hurting?"

"Yes . . ."

He began to withdraw gently, but she quickly contracted, holding him inside her. "No," she said, "stay!"

She closed her eyes, bending forward to kiss him and as they kissed it was as if they willed a transfer of the warmth and lubrication worked up in their mouths to where their bodies met beneath the surface of the water. And while their mouths worked together, it was the desire to contain all of him which caused her to begin rocking delicately back and forth from side to side, the center of her body poised as it was, balanced upon his sex. And, in turn, he moved his body in easy counterpoint to hers, careful to maintain the balance and not dislodge himself.

They continued pressing together and then, as she swung sideways, there was a joyous slip, and he edged inside her a fraction deeper until the head of his erection was completely encased and her lips closed in over the narrower length of him.

"Now . . ."

"Yes," he answered.

They arched away from each other and, feeling the danger of movement which would uncouple them, pressed forward with all their combined might and slowly and with incredible pressure he bore down inside her. They uttered sounds of sensuous pain, two pairs of eyes closed, two necks arched back, veins standing out, throbbing, two heads bent back addressing the sky, mouths distorted in ecstasy, until he could go no farther and their bodies collided, her legs tightly wrapped around his waist, not a particle of space between them.

They cried out again as she contracted upon him and he, in turn, toes clenching the sand, squeezed from his buttocks, one throb, two, three and four, each throb ending in a pulsation where he rested swollen inside her. And she tightened upon him, contracting in return for each one. Their faces acknowledged this underwater communication with grins as exhaustion forced them to pause, the muscles of their bodies gone limp, and they rested, together as they were, with the climax of their passion still ahead of them.

"Am I too heavy?" she asked, for her legs were still entwined around him.

"No, the water makes you light. You're light, you're lovely."

She moved, sliding away a bit, and he felt the cool liquid of the water surround the base of him and then experienced the onrushing warmth as she moved in on him, encasing him completely once more.

This gesture touched off desire in him again. He moved slowly, slowly, pulling himself out and away from her. A look of surprise came into her eyes, a momentary squint of questioning, which he dispelled by thrusting forward again.

She gasped, her body jerking toward him in response to his vigorous movement. She leaned in to kiss him; their lips met and their mouths worked together with such deliciousness they could do nothing but prolong their kissing until it seemed endless. After a while they began moving their bodies in easy unison. They moved as one, neither pulling away from the other; soon the undulation grew in intensity until it became a grinding motion and they rotated in and against one another with a mounting pressure until she could no longer contain herself and, pulling her mouth away from him, she cried out phrases of love.

She braced her hands against his shoulders for leverage, drawing her body back away, taking the long, delicate slide the length of him, and Kelly, within a fraction of an inch of withdrawal, again feeling the titillating sensation as the cool water replaced the heat of her body, closed the liquid distance between them with a plunge and their stomachs met with a resounding slap, sending a spray of water flying up between them, splashing their faces and trickling down their cheeks in heavy, glistening drops. As she dug her fingers into his shoulders and they separated for another assault, they laughed, exchanging tight grins, teeth bared, chins dripping and glancing down into the water between them, they tacitly agreed to make such waves as they could stir up.

So locked with her in the water, surrounded by sand, cliffs and mountains, with the sun blasting down upon them, Kelly felt a raw abandon that was more animal than human.

They embarked upon a series of near withdrawals, quivering at the delicate balance remaining between them, the tip of him resting in the saddle of her, then rushing together to meet head-on. She winced and cried out as he became more expert at adding an upward motion to the thrust until he could feel himself striking the core of her; he knew there was a special place and angle which touched off fire in her and he knew he had discovered it.

When they reached the apex of this delightful round and their rhythm suffered from a certain exhaustion, they came to rest once more, she sinking down upon him, and they heaved sighs of love at one another. But Kelly was too aroused to rest long and soon he took her face in his hands and leaned forward to kiss her with trembling tenderness and now their kisses were pure heaven.

Slowly, while kissing, their bodies engaged in the most graceful ritual yet, sliding in and away from each other while gradually increasing the movement and lengthening the distance traveled. Their love-making was liquid, each dedicated to the gratification of the other and as each felt the fulfillment of his partner, this joy, this sight of sensual pleasure mirrored in the eyes opposite, acted as an aphrodisiac and turned delight inward as well, until they were transported, no longer anchored in the waters of the cove, but riding a tidal wave of orgasm.

Experiencing the warning tingle that precedes eruption, they increased the motion of their bodies, strengthening the attack without sacrificing any of the gracefulness which distinguished this final round of love-making from the sheer physicality of their earlier efforts, until they were no longer able to keep their mouths together.

They separated and, for the solid leverage needed to withstand the final impact of their passion, Maggie leaned back
away from him, hands braced, palms flattened against his
shoulders. Their eyes remained locked in hypnotic embrace,
and he surpassed himself with the long, expert withdrawal,
the head of him now entirely emerging into the water every
second or third time and immediately reentering before her
lips were completely closed and driving full up into her.

Soon, a high shuddering cry, completely foreign in tone
from her husky speaking voice, escaped her at the finish of
each thrust and as these cries increased he saw the veins in
her neck stand out and the muscles in her chiseled face,
especially around the mouth and jaw, tighten. Her nostrils
dilated and her eyes became glazed as he added a rotating
motion now each time he entered her, rocking from side to
side as he drove up, burying himself in her.

He felt the palms of her hands disappear and her fingernails dig into his shoulders. A ripple began at her glistening
solar plexus, traveling up across the rib cage to her breasts
and extending to her neck and face. She called out, "Kelly!
Kelly! Kelly!" in urgency and mounting intensity, at the
same time ceasing her part of the long, sliding, rocking
thrust and parry as her body grew rigid and she was seized
by a series of tremors. Her eyes opened wide, so wide Kelly
felt they could swallow him with their mixture of shocked
surprise and ecstasy.

Quickening his assault to attain the maximum pleasure
for her, he heard a shrill, piercing whistle followed by a dis-
tant roar, and for a second, he imagined the entire earth was
joining them in shattering climax. Maggie was oblivious to
this sound and, about to fall into the consummation of her
desire, she cried out his name in invitation to accompany
her.

As the echo of her voice reverberated over the water, the
sound was joined by an ungodly shriek slashing the sky at
the very moment he felt the burning fluid surging forward to
escape him.

In midclimax, their heads were drawn upward as a glistening trio of silver Air Force jets, barreling south from San Diego, creased the blue low over the ocean out beyond the rock and were gone, soundless now, from sight.

"Oh, God!" he cried out.

Their eyes met in orgiastic delight.

He cried out again and she felt his fluid gushing in to join hers, already released, and shouted: "My darling, my darling!"

They jammed together, locked firmly, as a shattering explosion rocked the air, ricocheting madly in the cove, and the sound barrier was broken.

Kelly flung his head back and it was he who cried out this time: "Jets! Oh, great—*jets!*" He thrust once, twice, and three times into her, giving her the last of him, before bursting into laughter as the backwash of passion tickled and drained him, leaving him exhausted.

He was suddenly and dazzlingly aware of sun and water and rock and sky surrounding him, zoning in on him. Struck blind for a moment and, in the blackness, with shooting stars skyrocketing in front of him, he shook his head, staggered two steps forward and one back, losing his balance and tipping precariously to the side. He heard her cry out in laughter and surprise and felt her weight fall away from him as he tumbled over into the water, becoming completely disengaged from her.

He was aware of opening his eyes underwater and of laughing and of the bubbles bursting from his mouth while he groped for a foothold in the sand. Breaking the surface with his head and shoulders, he saw Maggie's head emerging a short distance away and heard her husky laughter mixed with coughing.

They careened toward each other, sloshing in the water, arms outstretched and flailing in the air, until they clung together in a wet embrace.

"Oh—how wonderful—it is for us!" she gasped. "Waves yesterday—jets today! Twice blessed!"

"Yes . . . yes," he laughed. "Oh, Maggie, I can't imagine it ever being better. Ever, ever, ever!"

"No argument!" she gasped.

"On a scale of one to ten I'd give it—at least a twelve."

"You sold out cheap," she said. "Fourteen—take it from one who knows."

"Oh, God," he suddenly shouted, "I feel like screaming!"

"Go ahead!" she urged.

"I can't, I'm afraid my heart will attack me!"

"Try."

"Ahhh . . . that's terrible!"

They laughed softly and held each other while their breathing returned to normal.

From the tedium of waiting and a second drink, Raffaello was about to fall asleep in an easy chair when the explosion sent him jumping to his feet. With the plate-glass windows still vibrating, he stood there for a second, frightened and groggy, thinking first of an earthquake.

He stumbled to the glass doors, sliding them open and stepping out onto the brick terrace to discover the source of the noise. Looking around, he scanned the sky, then stood there in the brilliant sunshine shaking his head and rubbing a hand across his forehead to clear his thoughts. He glanced out across the water to the rock sitting in the entrance to the cove, then down to the strip of sand at its base and—jerked his head back abruptly.

He saw the two figures standing in the water. He quickly removed his dark glasses, pressed a hand against his eyes to clear his vision, and replaced the glasses as he stepped forward and grasped the railing.

Though he wasn't able to see their expressions, there was no doubt about their identity. They stood close together, she with her hands on his shoulders and—were they naked?

Remembering the binoculars, he walked with quick steps into the house. Unaware of being discovered himself, he hurried back to the terrace and took his position by the railing, raising the binoculars and slowly bringing them into focus. Their positioning enabled him to see Maggie's face and shoulders and—yes, they were naked—her breasts and only the profile and side of him. Raffaello steadied his arm against the railing as he brought her face into sharper focus.

In an instant, the essence of the scene pulled together and transmitted itself in close-up. She standing, leaning against him almost, her hands upon his shoulders, their faces dripping with water, hair matted, her breathing heavy—he could tell even at this distance from the rise and fall of her breasts—and as he watched, she took one hand from his shoulder and placed it against his cheek in a gentle caress. The intimacy of this gesture, together with her smile, made the journey all too well through the lens of the binoculars. No further translation necessary.

Stunned, Raffaello slowly withdrew the binoculars. All the time he was waiting and planning—she was mocking him! She was rubbing his nose in the cold remains of their affair.

Now, seeing them so intimately together for the second time, Raffaello was suddenly faced with shocked disbelief that he could have so easily passed over what he'd seen the night before and just as suddenly he was enraged with himself. What was he doing—blacking out when it was convenient! He could tell himself no more stories, no more fantasies.

The only catharsis for the emotional overload of lopsided love, hurt, pride, and jealousy he carried was hate and the juices were released. He began to tremble. She might not be playing games, but he would play a few.

He sensed movement down there and once more turned his attention to them. They were walking out of the water, their backs to him. He had his arm around her, supporting her.

Watch out, my young cocksman, she can leave any time now. That would be a case of coitus interruptus if ever there was one.

As they stepped up on the beach and Kelly began laying down their towels, Raffaello became concerned that he might be seen. Quickly he ducked inside the living room, stepping to the left of the sliding glass doors where he stood protected by the thick folds of draperies pulled to the side.

So camouflaged, he raised the binoculars and continued watching them. Perhaps it was his position, half-concealed as he was, but soon he became possessed of a sly cat-and-mouse madness. Now that he had unequivocally branded them the enemy, he relished observing them, so obviously unaware of being seen! She stretched out on her back; he lowered himself onto the towel next to her, stomach down, head turned facing her. They lay quietly, not even speaking, until she inhaled a deep breath of smoke, turned her head sideways and blew it in his face. Now they were both laughing.

Awful cute for you, Maggie, old girl—remember, you're no ingenue!

They were talking; soon he inched over closer to her. The movement was jerky, puppetlike. Yes, they looked like two naked puppets, dirty little puppets, stretched out down there in the sand.

If they were puppets, he would pull the strings. He would make them hop to his tune.

Lowering the binoculars, he glanced around the room until he sighted the pistols and rifles on the wall over the bar. He recognized a high-powered .22 rifle and laughed as he walked to get it. A search in a cabinet at one end of the bar yielded more than enough ammunition for a good shoot.

With the gun and shells lying on the counter in front of him, he poured himself a quarter-glass of neat scotch. He raised it to his lips and as he sipped it his eye caught sight of the stereo set across the room.

The idea so struck his fancy he uttered a small sound of delight and some of his drink spilled out of his mouth and dripped down his chin.

Fetching the binoculars, he quickly returned to his position by the drapes. Perspiration broke out on his forehead and his hand trembled in anticipation of his plan as he worked them into focus.

They were lying next to one another, eyes closed, holding hands; yes, they were going to nap. Perfect—he would provide them with a surprise awakening.

CHAPTER 36

Though Kelly had only been asleep a few minutes, it was a heavy, damp sleep and he awakened slowly. He was on his side and facing her. Maggie lay on her back, one hand raised, the back of it covering her eyes and part of her forehead. Her breathing was deep and regular.

There was something, yes, he could hear music from somewhere. A bit louder now and he recognized the end of the overture to *Carmen*. Then he could hear the soldiers' chorus and Moralès and the light music before Micaëla's opening bars.

Maggie's hand moved slightly. "Hmn . . . ?" she mumbled and her eyelids fluttered. She turned slowly on her side, facing Kelly. "Hmn . . . ?" she mumbled again.

"Music," he said.

"Music . . . ?"

"Flora and Stosh must be back."

"Oh . . ." She smiled at him and closed her eyes, ready to go back to sleep. Kelly leaned up on his elbow, shielding his eyes against the sun and looking toward the house. The doors to the terrace were open but there was no one in sight. He rested back down on his side facing her, ready to go back to sleep himself.

The music stopped abruptly. He knew *Carmen* well, knew the record didn't end there. After a while he heard Carmen's voice; he didn't recognize the singer, but he knew it was early in the second act. He lay there listening to the duologue after her song, thinking Stosh or Flora must have rejected a record or two. Now the volume seemed to increase once more and there was a scratching sound as the needle was being moved over the record. Again Kelly sat up and looked toward the house.

"What?" Maggie mumbled, rolling over on her back.

"I don't know," Kelly said.

Again the sound jumped up as Don José's Flower Song began, until the quality was rasping and unpleasant to the ear.

Maggie raised herself to her elbow. "Loud . . ."

"Yes," he agreed. They remained leaning on their elbows, gazing up toward the house. Just as Kelly turned to look at her, a frown wrinkled her forehead. "What?" he asked.

Reaching out a hand, she grasped his wrist and spoke in a voice tinged with disbelief: "Raf . . . it sounds like Raf!" She listened closely. "Yes, it is. I have that recording, I know it. Why would they . . . ?" She broke off and, shielding her eyes, looked up toward the house. "If we can hear it all the way out here, it must be . . . *deafening* up there. Why would Stosh . . . ?" Again she interrupted herself. There was something eerie, a total discrepancy between the jarring sound of the music and the otherwise absolute stillness of the day, not even a breeze. "Oh, well," she shrugged, "Stosh is crazy anyhow." She laughed. "If they've seen us, I'm surprised Flora isn't having a fit out on the terrace. C'mon." She took his hand and they settled themselves down on the towels. "I'm having my snooze, *Carmen* or no."

"Me, too." He lay back down and rolled over on his stomach. He was accustomed to the music now and, after a while, seeing that Maggie was breathing regularly and feel-

ing close to sleep himself, he braced himself with his hands
and leaned over to kiss her lightly on the cheek.

A sharp crack, followed by a whistling zing of a sound
echoed in the cove. Something struck the rock several yards
above and in front of him and he jerked his head up in time
to see a drift of powdery dirt sliding down the veined side of
it.

In late response to the sound, Maggie flung her hand from
where it rested on her forehead, striking Kelly on the shoulder. He spun around and sat up; at the same time Maggie
rose up on her elbows beside him. "What's going on?" she
mumbled.

"I don't know." His eyes fought the glare of the sun upon
the water as he scanned the cove. "I thought it was—"

Another shot cracked the air. A blip of water splashed up
at the sand's edge, not ten feet in front of them. The echo of
the shot reverberated wildly in the cove as Maggie cried out
and Kelly jumped to his feet, shielding his eyes and looking
up toward the house.

"God!" Maggie gasped. He turned to see her clutching the
beach towel he had lain on and covering herself with it.
"What . . . ?" she asked again, shaking her head and struggling to clarify the meaning of this second awakening. Her
gesture reminded Kelly of his own nudity and he reached
down, snatching up another towel and wrapping it around
his waist.

A volley of coarse laughter barked out across the water,
echoing as the shots had.

"Raf . . . ?" Maggie mumbled; it was a question.

Tracing the sound, they quickly looked from the house in
the far left of the cove to the top of the bluff directly across
from them. When Maggie saw him, a hand shot up to her
mouth. Raffaello laughed again. He tossed back his head;
his dark glasses caught the sun and blazed golden for a second.

"Raf!" she said again, staggering to her feet. "Raffaello!"
she said firmly, the very real fact of his presence up there on
the cliff striking her full force. "But—" She turned to Kelly,

an expression of panic and confusion upon her face, then looked back across the cove. "My God, how did he—"

Raffaello took several steps closer to the edge of the cliff. The way he walked, together with his stance once he stopped, feet apart, one leg cocked at an angle, caused her to say, "Drunk—he must be drunk!" She took Kelly's hand.

Raffaello lifted the rifle to shoulder position and Kelly leaped in front of Maggie to shield her.

"No!" she screamed. "No!" With all her strength she wrenched him away from her and he fell sideways on the sand.

Raffaello laughed again and lowered the rifle.

"Listen to him," she gasped. *"Listen to him!* He's mad."

No one moved for a few seconds, then as Kelly got to his feet and Maggie instinctively went to him, Raffaello shouldered the rifle once more. Wincing, they both held their breath, waiting for the next shot, but a flock of gulls flew in low across the cove, drawing Raffaello's attention. With a reckless arcing swing of the rifle he fired several shots in quick succession into the center of them. Kelly felt Maggie shudder against him as the gulls separated, flying off in all directions, and the stricken bird, one wing outstretched, the other hanging at an unhealthy angle, wobbled down in the air and hit the water, flopping grotesquely several times before floating still on the surface.

"Monster!" she whispered. Turning to Kelly she said, "He's *playing* with us!" She quickly looked around her. They were trapped on the strip of sand. On both sides the rock sloped jaggedly down to the water and it was apparent there was no beach on the other side, only a sheer drop-off into the open sea. "We're sitting ducks against this rock," she said, looking up to the figure on the bluff.

"If we could get around in the water to the other side of it," Kelly said, "he couldn't hit us." His suggestion didn't register with her; she simply stood staring out over the water, her face glazed by an unaccustomed expression of vagueness. "Maggie?"

"Yes . . . ?"

"If we could make it around outside the rock in the water, he couldn't hit us."

She ignored his words, throwing her arms around him and pressing her face up against his cheek. "How did he *find* us!" Immediately annoyed with herself, she banged her head against him. "What difference does it make—he did! Oh, Kelly!"

A shot rang out and she jumped away from him as the bullet sang past them and struck the rock yards to their left.

"Leave me alone!" Maggie screamed across the cove. They heard the words echo back: "Eave-ee-own . . ."

The question came back. "—ut?"

"Leave me alone!" she shouted, giving each word its beat.

In reply, Raffaello raised the rifle and shot aimlessly up into the air.

"Ask a silly question," she said, shaking her head and facing Kelly.

"Look!" Kelly said.

She followed his gaze to see Raffaello holding the rifle idly pointing toward the ground with one hand and with the other hand, the palm of it bandaged, waving her on, indicating for her to swim across the cove to the beach below him.

"He's got something on his hand," Maggie said. When he kept waving, she pointed to herself. "Me?" she called out.

"Yes!" came the reply.

"Go to hell!" she said, not bothering to project and turning to Kelly again.

"What?" Raffaello called out.

She spun around and shouted up to him: *"Go to hell!"*

In an instant he had raised the rifle and fired a shot. It winged past her ankle and a puff of sand popped up not five feet from where she stood.

"All right," she muttered, *"don't* go to hell." She stepped back and jabbed her toe into the pock mark left by the bullet. "That was pure luck; he didn't even take time to aim."

Kelly was amazed by her apparent nonchalance. "Maggie, do we have to stand here and *talk* about it?"

"I suppose not, but—"

Feeling it no longer possible to remain motionless, Kelly snatched up the rubber float. "Quick, get in the water." He grabbed her by the arm and dragged her to the edge of the beach, throwing the float down into the water in front of them. They pulled their towels off, dropped them on the sand, and waded out until they stood beside it.

"Look at him waving us on," Maggie said. "Coming, darling!" she snarled in a sarcastic whisper.

"We'll have to swim in a ways to get past the edge of the rock," Kelly said. "Tag on the end of the float. I'll tow."

"The tide, damn the tide," Maggie said, seeing the steady flow of water coursing in the cove through the channel between the edge of the rock and the jagged southern end of the U-shaped prong curving out from the bluff. "I can swim," she added.

"Wait till we get to the channel."

Kelly swam ahead doing the sidestroke, holding the cord attached to the float and pulling it after him. Maggie clung to the rear, kicking her legs out, helping to propel it forward. There was no sound except for the splash of water and the continuing harsh strains of *Carmen*. When they were fifteen yards out from shore, Kelly changed course and swam to the right in the direction of the channel.

A shot rang out. Neither one saw where it hit, but they stopped, treading water and looking to the top of the cliff in time to see Raffaello reloading the rifle.

"I wonder if he can hit us?" Kelly asked.

"I don't think he's really aiming," Maggie said. "I shouldn't think he could, one eye, drunk, and bright light of any kind bothers his good eye."

"I mean—I wonder if he's a good shot if he really tries?" Kelly asked.

"I don't know," she replied, "he's never shot at me before." A burst of husky laughter escaped her. "I mean—I don't know. God, I'm cracking up!"

They froze as Raffaello raised the rifle to his shoulder, quickly ducking their heads beneath the water when the sound of the shot cracked in the cove. Emerging, they heard the soft hiss of air escaping the float and looked to see a smooth hole angled in along the side of it.

"Yes, he's a good shot," Maggie said, running her hand along the top of it. Already the rubber ridges were flattening out and the raft was going limp. "We've lost our ship," she said.

Without replying, Kelly shoved the raft away from them. He could not equate the ordinary pitch of her conversation with what was actually taking place. He was momentarily stunned.

"By the time we hear the shot, does it do any good to duck?" she asked.

"I don't think so," he replied.

She grinned at him. "Still, it feels better, doesn't it?"

"Yes." He caught himself smiling at her in return, until the reality of their predicament returned to him: *here we are, floating around in the water, shot at by a maniac, with real bullets, and here we are trading smiles with each other!*

He looked at her incredulously as she glanced down into the depths and chattered on: "I suppose if you were hit below the water, it would slow the bullet down, the water would, wouldn't it?"

"Maggie, this is crazy!"

She glanced up at him. "You're telling me!"

"No, *this*—treading water, talking it all over! Can you make it out beyond the rock?"

"I suppose." She looked toward the channel where small waves rippled in on the advancing tide, and a frown creased her forehead. "I'm frightened," she said, turning and clutching his shoulder.

Another shot exploded from the cliff; their heads disappeared beneath the surface and bobbed up again.

"I'm beginning to get the idea," she said. "If we really want to get shot at, all we have to do is go into a clinch. It's forced rape in reverse."

"Maggie, come on—"

"What do we do?" she asked. "Just paddle around out there in the ocean? For how long?" She gasped. "Stosh and

Flora—what if they come back! I can't let them walk into this, I couldn't!"

"Maggie, we can't stay out here either."

"No . . . but—"

"If we get out of the cove, we'll find a place you can hang onto on the other side of the rock. I'll swim up that way or down below us and into shore. I'll get help."

"Down here, in the middle of nowhere? How?"

"I don't know, but I will!" He was becoming angry. "Come on." He lunged ahead in the water and she followed him. He glanced back after several strokes to see that Maggie was keeping the pace, but as she swam she turned her head, keeping a check on the figure at the top of the bluff. "Don't look at him!" he called back. "Keep going!"

They'd only taken several more strokes when it was obvious to Raffaello they had no intention of swimming across the cove but were heading, instead, for the channel and a means of escape out beyond the rock. A shot pierced the air and Kelly called out without stopping: "You all right?"

"Yes!" she shouted.

Another crackling shot sounded and his silent prayer that it, too, would go wild was shattered by a bleating cry from Maggie. He stopped, turning back to face her as she cried out his name in a small, choked-off breath.

He saw her flailing her left arm in the air, saw it flop down into the water; but mostly it was the expression of surprise upon her face that told him she'd been hit. The expression changed as she lifted her hand up for a second, gazing at it, seeming almost to question it. She let it fall back into the water again. A look of revulsion crossed her face.

"Wait!" he called out, swimming to her as fast as he could. Kelly didn't interrupt his stroke even when he heard another and fuller scream choke itself off in her throat. Nearing Maggie, he could make out the pastel stain floating next to her, suspended in the water. She lifted her arm up and they both saw the wound. Maggie uttered a little sound and turned her head away. Treading water with the other arm, she moved her legs to keep herself buoyant.

"Float on your back," Kelly said.

"Yes." She rolled over, kicking her feet up in front of her and floating as best she could.

She kept her head turned away from her injured hand while Kelly took hold of her forearm. He felt the warm blood, slippery from having mixed with the water, and inspected the wound. The bullet had entered the heel of her hand below the thumb and in toward the palm and torn its way out back, shattering a few small bones in her hand. It was a messy sight.

"Is the bullet still in me?" she asked.

"No."

"That's good." She turned her head to him for a moment. "It *is* good, isn't it?"

"Yes."

"It stings. In the water—it stings." She turned away again. "I don't want to—see it."

"Let's get in to where you can stand."

"Yes."

"I'll get a towel, wrap it up. Here, put your other hand around my neck."

Kelly maneuvered in the water, positioning himself so that he could tow her in to where it was shallow. She clung to him with her good hand and repeated, "It stings."

CHAPTER 37

"I hit her!" Raffaello spoke excitedly at first, like a schoolboy. "I hit her," he repeated, lowering the rifle and regarding it almost as if the rifle had committed the act without his assistance. Then, shaking his head and wiping his hand across his chin, he spoke in a daze. "I didn't mean . . ."

He stood there bewildered. He wasn't sure if he was trying to hit them or not. He was trying to *separate* them, he knew that, but she kept clinging to him. She was making him pull the trigger; she was bringing it upon herself.

Every time he pulled the trigger his hand ached. His eye was aching, too. He threw a mean glance up at the sun. He disliked direct sunlight when he was drinking; it made him woozy and sickish. He wanted another drink and he wanted the sun to go away.

Suddenly curious about where exactly he had hit her, he put the gun down and picked up the binoculars. He worked them into focus as they reached shallow water and Maggie stood, holding her left arm up, crooked at the elbow.

He studied her closely and Kelly aided him by holding her

wrist steady as he, too, examined her hand. Raffaello saw the blood spreading down from the palm and trickling along her arm to her elbow. He steadied the glasses, staring at the large splotch of red on her hand.

Yes, it was her hand that had been hit. Immediately he connected their injuries, his hand and hers. He could hardly believe his eyes. In his drunken, manic state, he interpreted it as fate giving them a sign, divining the bond between them. What further proof did she need!

"Does it hurt terribly?" Kelly asked.

She shook her head in a series of quick little jerks, keeping it averted from her wound. "It hurts," she added with a shrug. He took her elbow in his hand. "Mind if I don't look?" she asked. "Am I still bleeding like a stuck pig? I can feel my heart beating in my hand."

"You're bleeding," he said. "I'm going to squeeze hard." He placed both hands around her wrist and pressed firmly. She made a little sound. "Sorry, I just want to see . . ." At first blood spurted from the torn spot in her hand, but as he continued squeezing harder, the flow gradually ebbed and then almost stopped completely.

"Maggie—Maggie!" There was pure excitement in Raffaello's voice as he shouted across the cove and they both turned to look up at him. "Maggie—look!"

"What's he doing?" she asked.

"Pointing to his hand," Kelly said, shielding his eyes. "I don't know, I think that's a bandage on his hand."

"So?" she shrugged. Raffaello called out her name twice again. "What do you want—a medal!" she shouted, transmitting her pain to anger. She turned her back on him and when Kelly took hold of her hand again, two shots walloped in the air and they ducked. "Get a *cannon*—bastard!" Maggie hissed between clenched teeth.

Kelly laughed nervously. "I love you." Leaning forward, he kissed her on the cheek. This gesture earned another shot. A small geyser popped up only a few feet to the side of them.

"Don't love me anymore," she said. "Not for a while."

"I can't help it."

"All right, but no visible demonstrations." She nodded her head in the direction of the cliff. "Don José's touchy this morning." She started to turn to Kelly, then suddenly wheeled around and shouted up to Raffaello: *"Laisse-moi passer."*

"What?" he called down.

"Laisse-moi passer!"

Raffaello laughed, then spread his arms out wide and sang in a hoarse but strong voice: *"Pour la dernière fois, démon, veux-tu me suivre?"*

And in her husky voice, Maggie croaked back at him: *"Non! Non! Cette bague autrefois, tu me l'avais donnée— tiens!"* She spat into the water and then, to Kelly's complete amazement, she laughed.

Raffaello shouted, "Bravo! Bravo!"

As Maggie bowed, Kelly said, "You're both crazy! I'll wrap it up, make a tourniquet with the towels," he added, wading in toward the beach.

"Wait for me," she called out.

He turned to see her following him. "No, stay there. You're safer in the water."

She shrugged and stood her ground.

Stepping onto the dry sand, he heard Maggie call out something. "What?" he asked.

"I said, you've got a cute pair of buns there."

He could feel himself blush as he bent down and picked up the beach towel and a smaller bath towel. Trotting quickly back into the water, he glanced up at the cliff and saw that Raffaello had the binoculars trained on them. Aware of his nudity, he held a towel in front of him until he was waist deep. Grinning at his own modesty under fire, he looked up to meet Maggie's eyes, now blazing green and brimming with tears. Though she had every reason to cry, the change was so abrupt he was stopped. "What . . . ?" he asked.

"Oh, Kelly!" she sobbed. "Not now—not with us so—" She fought back the tears and blurted out: "And wouldn't it be my—my luck to get shot in the *hand*. I mean it's all so—so tacky! Hodgkin's disease and now I'll probably die of a bullet wound in the *hand,* wailing and—and weeping because it *stings!* It's so minor—" she choked "—minor league! Couldn't I—" she broke off.

"Couldn't you what?" he asked.

"—I don't know—go out *big!*" she sobbed.

"You're not going out at all."

"How do you know?" she snapped at him, back in control.

"I just do," he grinned at her. "Same way you know about sharks."

"Don't con me with that boyish grin." She put her good hand up to her forehead. "I'm afraid, too," she said, sniffing and clearing her nose, "and that's the tackiest part."

"Whoever died of a bullet wound in the hand?" he asked, walking to her.

"Nobody—till *me,*" she answered. "Goddamn it!"

He had torn a part of the towel into narrow strips. Lifting her arm, he wrapped a piece of it tightly around her wrist. She sucked in a breath and, exhaling, spoke on a sigh. "Oh, well—I don't care . . ."

Even now, he found himself loving the many unexpected moods of her. He bent forward and kissed a spot on her forearm below the tourniquet he was applying, but she was not aware of it. Keeping her eyes always turned away from her left hand, she gazed down at her right shoulder. "I'm getting sunburned."

He tied two strips into a knot. "There." She made a little grunting sound. "Too tight?"

"It's tight, but if it stops the bleeding . . . is it stopping?"

"Yes."

"Good." She looked around at her hand and quickly darted her head the other way. "Put something on it, so I don't have to see it, will you?"

"Yes." He wrapped the rest of the towel gently around the injured hand and used the last two strips to secure it at her wrist.

Raffaello had watched the proceedings carefully. He had seen her crying and it sickened him. He'd seen her cry only once during the time they were together but it had destroyed him. His vision blurred as he watched them down where the sun shimmered on the water.

He was suddenly disgusted by what he had done. But again, she had forced him. He called out in anger: "Have you had enough—have you had enough!"

Maggie spun around in the water, facing up to the cliff. "Yes!" she screamed back. "You can fuck off now!"

He jerked the gun up to his shoulder. They cringed for a duck beneath the water when Raffaello abruptly lowered the rifle and sneezed. He sneezed three times in a row, sneezed hard; his entire body doubled up and kicked back from the impact.

"Hay fever," Maggie muttered. He sneezed again and the echo sounded unbelievably comic ringing out across the cove with the "fate" theme from *Carmen* for a background. *"Gesundheit!"* Maggie called out.

"What?" Raffaello asked, a hand to his nose.

She shouted up at him: *"Gesundheit—you bastard!"*

"Maggie!" Kelly whispered, in warning.

There was a moment of silence, during which the sun, now high in the sky, seemed to beat down upon them ferociously. There was almost a sound to its intensity. Then Raffaello threw his head back and a sharp burst of laughter exploded from him. Maggie laughed in return and when he heard the sounds of her husky laughter, he laughed even harder. Kelly looked incredulously from Maggie to the dark figure up on the cliff. He thought perhaps they were suddenly sunstruck until he realized that he, too, was laughing, silently at first on short gasps of breath and then uproariously when he heard the first choking sounds escape his throat.

Maggie glanced from Kelly to Raffaello and back to Kelly again as the three of them laughed hysterically until the cove rattled with the hollow echoes—sounding like a recorded come-on to some amusement park fun house.

At the height of their laughter, Raffaello sneezed twice again and Maggie, weakened from this nervous release, withdrew her good hand from her stomach, clinging to Kelly and leaning her head against his shoulder.

Suddenly there was no more laughter from the top of the bluff and what laughter remained down in the water was cut off when they saw the rifle go to his shoulder.

Maggie pulled away from Kelly. "Stop it!" she shouted. "Stop it!"

"You give up?" Raffaello called out. "Do you give up?"

"No!" she shouted back.

He fired at them and the bullet struck the water several yards to their right. He fired quickly again and Maggie screamed as a blip of water shot up inches from Kelly's hip. He pulled the trigger again but there was only a click in return.

Raffaello quickly bent down and loaded the gun. Raising it to his shoulder, he was taking aim when the record stuck and the music began repeating itself, the end of a phrase of Don José's: *"Elle se trompe, hélas!"*

"Hélas! Hélas! Hélas!" repeated over and over.

Raffaello lowered the gun and gazed down at the house. From their position in the water they, too, looked to where it came from. *"Hélas! Hélas! Hélas!"*

Now, even the record mocked him. Raffaello shook his head as if that would dislodge the needle and get the record going again. Raising the rifle, he aimed it once more down at the cove, then suddenly swung around and fired five shots in rapid succession in the direction of the bedroom and terrace.

They heard the splinter of glass as the bedroom window was shattered and a dull thwumping sound when the brick was struck.

The record continued: *"Hélas! Hélas! Hélas!"*

Maggie clutched Kelly's hand as Raffaello knelt down to reload the gun again. She tilted her head as the hum of an approaching motor worked into the sound of the stuck record. Raffaello heard it too and looked toward the road. The sound of the engine grew louder and soon a car eased into sight coming around the bend. Raffaello remained crouched down, hidden by one of the low scrublike bushes as it slowed and then nosed off the road and disappeared down the driveway.

Though they were unable to see the car from their position down in the water, Maggie sensed from the sound that it wasn't continuing on around the bluff. "Flora," she gasped, "and Stosh!" She turned quickly to Kelly. "I'll go in, I'll talk to him. You stay here."

"No, Maggie—he's crazy!"

"We can't both stay here indefinitely, like this, here in the water. For God's sake, use your head! And if Flora—"

Her tone infuriated him. "I'm using my head. How can you get in without me—walk on the water? You can't swim, look at you!" He pointed to her hand, which she held up, arm bent at the elbow, completely useless.

She said, "I can get in if I want to, don't worry." She stepped off into deeper water, but Kelly grabbed her good arm and swung her around. They were arguing like children when a shot exploded and the bullet whistled between their faces. They felt the air rush past their cheeks, felt the coolness of the breeze graze their lips. The sensation it produced was almost heady.

Maggie gasped; Kelly whistled lowly.

The record stopped.

The abrupt silence was jarring. All three of them, Raffaello, Maggie and Kelly, looked to the house as Stosh stepped out on the terrace.

"Stosh, get back!" Maggie cried out.

Stosh stopped, but Flora lumbered out past him.

"Flora!" Maggie cried out.

Another shot exploded, missing Kelly and Maggie by several feet. Flora hurried to the end of the terrace. They saw a hand go up to her mouth when she sighted Raffaello. He, in turn, saw her and raised the rifle to his shoulder as Maggie once more called out: "Flora—Flora, get back!"

But Flora stood her ground. She held up her hand, palm flat, rather like a stern policeman stopping traffic. "Stop it!" she shouted. Raffaello laughed and fired a shot in her direction without really aiming. Flora merely raised an arm up in front of her face, as one would ward off a stone. Shaking her fist at him, she called out sharply: "You stop that!" He lifted the rifle again, but she went right on shouting at him. "Haven't you done enough! *Shame* on you!"

Maggie couldn't help a nervous giggle. "Listen to her," she said to Kelly, and there was a poignant, almost pitying quality in her voice that Flora should attempt to stop him with such scolding words.

"Shame on you!" Flora repeated.

"Oh, Flora," Maggie gasped, full of affection.

But Raffaello suddenly lowered the rifle and turned to face them down in the water. Again silence filled the cove. Flora, too, was quiet as Stosh stepped up alongside her and they waited for his next move.

Raffaello half-turned, facing away from the edge of the cliff; abruptly he whirled around and cried out: "Maggie, I love you!" He held his arms, one hand still grasping the gun, outstretched in front of him and shouted again, fiercely this time: "I love you!" He took a deep, gasping breath and cried out her name once more: "Maggie!" His voice cracked as the word tore itself from his throat.

Kelly's scalp prickled with embarrassment; he turned his head away. Maggie, too, averted her eyes, staring down into the water. On the terrace, Flora reached out and grasped Stosh's arm.

The sudden quiet was heavy; it hung in the air; the silence took on a humming sound of its own.

There was no answer to this bald declaration from the top of the cliff.

Raffaello cried out for the last time: "Maggie—why!"

Again there was no answer.

Raffaello had capitulated in front of them, to Maggie and the young man down there in the water with her and, most of all, to his pride. He blinked his eyes, turning his head and looking up to the mountains in the east. What was he doing, standing on a cliff along this Godforsaken peninsula jutting down into the middle of nowhere?

Nothing really mattered as he stood there numbly, coated with the shame and hopelessness of a loser. The unsavory events of his past joined the debacle, too, caving in on him like an avalanche. He looked down at his feet and shoes, streaked with mud, and his hand, the bandage dirty and loose and about to fall off. Don José? It was never a good part but he'd ended up stuck with it, a sad-assed, rag-tailed Don José if ever there was one.

A hornet buzzed his head in furious circles before shooting wildly off over the cove, but he paid it no attention. The perspiration stood out in heavy drops upon his forehead. Three beads of water ran together on his brow and trickled down the side of his nose. Even when the salty liquid dripped into his parted lips, he made no move to clear it away either with his hand or with his tongue.

Raffaello suddenly swung the rifle back with his left arm and sent it hurtling off the cliff with all his might. It spun end over end like a dry stick, down and down until it smacked against the water.

They saw a hand go up to his head. Then slowly he turned and stumbled away from the edge of the cliff. Soon they could see him only from the waist up, then his head, and in another moment he had disappeared altogether.

They heard the motor start up and then the abrupt jarring sound of tires spinning off on the macadam as the car, out of sight to them, lurched away. Maggie squeezed Kelly's hand as they heard the angled whining sounds of the tires when the car rounded the bend and sped down into the gorge.

And now Stosh and Flora were hurrying along the wooden footbridge and over to the rock, quickly picking their way down the steps.

They heard further unhealthy complaints from the tires as the sound of the careening car diminished in the distance. Maggie shuddered and turned to Kelly, embracing him and pressing her face close up against his cheek.

After a while he whispered: "I thought our time would be cut short." She trembled and pulled away from him. She looked incredibly small and tender standing there in front of him, her arm bent at the elbow, hand held up in the air like some animal's bandaged paw. If there was any awe left in his emotions for her, it was only awe at the overwhelming amount of love and admiration he felt for her. She looked from her hand to Kelly. "I suppose I'll have to cancel my harp recital tonight."

"Oh, Maggie," he said, squeezing her to him, "I love you."

"You have to," she replied, "I'm your first."

"Yes," he smiled, "my first. And you were worth waiting for."

She stepped back away from him, caressing him with a look; her mouth tugged down and over to the side in that crooked half-smile he had come to love so. "Your first and my—" She stopped abruptly.

Her words chilled him; he was unable to speak and he looked away from her. His reaction made her doubly aware of her rashness in speaking. Annoyed at herself, she tried for a recovery. "See," she shrugged, "I told you the Old Boy's always got something up his sleeve. There's always a catch."

"I di-didn't say there wasn't," he answered, still looking down.

His stammer and the sight of his eyes blinking back the beginning of tears was too much for her. "Oh, my Kelly!" She embraced him and he clung to her. "No more, I promise, I do! Forgive me!"

"Yes," he said, still fighting his tears.

"Why, the days we have ahead of us, crammed full of— nobody will have racked up such a score as us!"

But she, too, could not help thinking of the uncertainty of time. Her body jerked toward him and she cried out: "Stay with me!"

Her sudden jolt of panic filled him with strength again. "They'd have to drag me away," he said. "And even then—I wouldn't go."

On the beach opposite them, Flora cried out her name and Stosh, stripped to his shorts, shouted: "Are you okay?" and belly-smacked into the water for the swim out to them.

Maggie pressed her head against Kelly. "Keep me busy, keep filling me up with love."

He opened his mouth to answer, but she silenced any reply by kissing him full on the lips.

CHAPTER

38

or Epilogue

They had not been able to find a ship in Ensenada, but Maggie's hand needed serious attention so they'd gone on to San Diego, where they found a yacht belonging to a Greek shipping magnate. Two hundred and ten feet long, it was a joy, a luxurious toy, a beauty. The Greek crew, warm and outgoing, even provided a divertisement for Stosh, a second mate named Panos. Stosh called it "an affair-ette on whole wheat with sliced tomatoes, hold the olive oil and ouzo!"

When Maggie was well enough, they sailed up the California coast to San Pedro, Catalina, Santa Barbara, Monterey and San Francisco, where, throwing disguise to the winds, they registered at the Mark Hopkins Hotel for several days of San Francisco–seeing-eating-being.

Kelly was bursting with love for Maggie; he had never experienced such emotion in his life and this emotion spilled out of him, washing away assorted rigid patterns of behavior and releasing a clown nature he was not aware he owned. Keeping her interested, occupied and entertained every waking moment—this was his goal. It was not a difficult chore; she was profoundly curious about every single person, object and idea with which she came in contact.

Stosh and Flora were the perfect companions, there when it was time for a group, in the background when it was time for Maggie and Kelly to be alone.

If their love-making changed in any way, it only mellowed with time. He was amazed at his newfound potency; Maggie called him "My Priapic Prince." Deep within him he harbored a secret hope that by constantly making love to her, he could keep her filled up with life. Their time together was golden and richly textured, the quality of time one relishes moment to moment exactly as it is taking place and then again a few minutes or an hour later in instant replay—it was that pungent.

While they made love in their suite the last night in San Francisco, a minor earthquake, no more than 3.6 on the Richter scale, struck. The building swayed slightly, a ceiling light fixture swung lazily to and fro, dishes on a service cart rattled. They froze for a moment, eyes locked, wondering if it might grow in intensity. When it seemed to level off, Kelly glanced down at her: "Do we make the earth move or do we not?"

She smiled back at him. "At least!"

The phone rang. Kelly reached to the night table, snatching up the receiver and speaking without even listening to the other end. "Yes, Flora, we're all right, but we can't talk right now—"

Taking the phone from him, Maggie added: "—Because, darling, we're phuquing. For the record—that's spelled with a 'p,' an 'h' and a 'q.' "

She hung up and they continued.

On their way to Hawaii, they ran into a storm, a major disturbance just short of a hurricane. Pitching and tossing like a piece of balsa wood, the ship nevertheless became a fun house for them. The steward attempted to serve dinner in the dining room but even with skidproof surfaces, edged tables, and other maritime aids, it was a disaster. They fell into fits of laughter as one dish, then another, then a glass of wine went scooting off the table until eventually, assisted by Flora and Stosh, they staggered to their cabin exhausted and virtually unfed.

In their master stateroom they helped each other undress and remain upright until they managed to crawl into bed. Still laughing, Maggie said, "I feel like all three Marx Brothers in *A Night at the Opera*!" They lay next to each other, nuzzling and kissing and enjoying the storm.

"Are you frightened?" Kelly asked.

"No, are you?"

He smiled at her. "No."

"Why not?"

He kissed her. "Love wipes out fear. Besides, I'm into risk taking."

"Hmmn," she mumbled. "Still, I don't think we'll create the world tonight, do you?"

"Probably not," he agreed.

"I was never good at trapeze work."

After a while they fell asleep. In the middle of the night the violence of the storm awakened them. The stress upon the ship, the various creakings, groanings, and other sounds it gave up, created a sensual background for their kisses. Soon they were making love, although the ship still bucked and tossed fiercely. As they neared mutual climax, she murmured: "Oh, Kelly . . . wild, it's wild!"

"*Gracias,*" he said, not without humor.

Reaching up, she cuffed him on the shoulder. "The *ship*—you fool!"

When he felt the beginning of the most incredible sensation ever devised for man, he called out in warning: "Oh, Maggie, I—"

At that instant the ship gave a giant wrenching twist that sent Kelly flying off the bed onto the floor as the yacht shuddered in the trough of whatever wave had struck them.

"Oh, my God," Maggie shrieked, "has anyone seen my lover? He was right here!" Then: "Are you all right?"

But Kelly was laughing too hard to reply.

When she'd made sure he wasn't hurt, Maggie, too, was convulsed in laughter. Winding down, she gasped, clutching him to her as he careened back onto the bed with the ship lurching from side to side. "Oh, Kelly, my dear, as they say on the stage—I think the phuque is off!"

They spoke together: "That's spelled with a 'p,' an 'h' and a 'q.' "

She held him close to her. "Did any two kangaroo rats ever have it so good? Oh, I thank God for you, I do. I love you, my darling Kelly." And she whispered such words of love and true endearment as he thought he would never hear.

By late afternoon the next day the storm had diminished, although the seas were still rough and foamy and the sky was brushed by fast-moving billows of dark gray that allowed the deepest colors of red and burnt orange to be reflected far out to the west where a spectacle called sunset was taking place. The ship still rolled, but more gently now, and walking was possible with care.

Several whales had been sighted earlier by the crew. Flora, Stosh and Kelly, all wrapped in foul-weather gear, stood on the starboard side holding on to the railing, watching the sunset and keeping a lookout for the mammals.

They heard the heavy click of a hatch door opening and turned to see Maggie, in a yellow rain slicker and hat, step out onto the deck. There was a glow, at least an inch thick, on her face, a secret smile, a look of expectancy in her eyes that riveted their attention. They were so struck by the vibrations emanating from her that she was the one who finally said: "What?"

"I'd bet my entire gerbil farm—there's an announcement," Kelly said.

Her smile broadened as she stepped up alongside them at the railing and glanced out across the sea. "Good Lord, it's a sight, isn't it? Don't you wonder who put it all there? And how it was accomplished? There's an act I'd have liked to have caught!"

"Honey," Flora said, "you look—you just look so beautiful!"

Maggie stepped back away from them, holding on to a metal stanchion for support. "I've been doing some serious thinking and I don't care what any doctor or anyone says. I know I've had a lot in my life, more than my share, but I'm having a spectacular love affair—" She looked directly at Kelly. "—Look at him, he doesn't even blush anymore! Oh, how they change!" A heavy gust of wind slapped them and Maggie raised her voice to be heard. "I woke up this morning and I thought—what do I want? What do I really want? And I honestly had to answer—*more!* I want just a little more. I'll settle for a year. I know everyone told me not to think of remissions and I'm not. I'm thinking of miracles. Miracles—goddamn it!" She quickly glanced up at the storm clouds whipping past. "Sorry—delete that. Well, there *are* miracles and I don't see any reason why I shouldn't get in on one. I've gotten in on almost everything else they have to offer—why should I stop at miracles? So I'm going on record right here and now as expecting a miracle. That's all."

Her radiance was stunning to witness; they could only stand there looking at her. "Do you think I'm crazy?" No one replied. "Do you?"

Kelly smiled and said, "No."

"Flora?"

Quickly the ferocious grin appeared. "Oh, no—no, honey, I don't."

"Stoshalito?"

"Do I think you're cracked? Yeah—but what else is news?" Maggie raised an arm and he ducked back, grinning, then shielding his teeth. "But that's why I was in love with you from the start."

Maggie looked back up at the sky. "And what does the Booking Agent think?"

As the words left her mouth a Greek sailor up forward shouted: "Whale off the starboard bow!"

They turned, looking out over the churning water to see, not a hundred yards away, a blue whale roll majestically out of the waves and send a geyser of water and steamy air spurting up out of its blow hole. Stosh was immediately in hysterics. Flora looked confused but Maggie joined in the laughter as a second whale, its mate, hove into sight, breaking the surface and blowing out another geyser. Maggie took Kelly's arm and clung to him. "They think I'm full of hot air—but I'll show them!"

Three days later Maggie awakened pale and weak. She remained in bed for two days, militantly attended to by Flora. The evening of the second day Kelly moved back into the master suite. As he lay in bed next to her, she smiled and said: "I didn't say I wouldn't have to struggle a bit, did I? I only said I was expecting a miracle and I still am." She reached over, caressing his cheek with her good hand. After a moment, she took her hand away and leaned up on her elbow. "But you know something—I wouldn't be surprised if a few weeks or months of exquisite happiness weren't equal to years and years of just plain living. Would you?"

Looking her straight in the eye, he said, "I'm positive of it." He suddenly got to his feet and stood there on the bed over her. "And do *you* know something else?"

"What?" she asked, surprised and delighted at the strength of his attack and his position looking down on her.

"You're not the only one that gets to talk about miracles. I looked it up in the dictionary: 'a person, thing, or event that excites admiring awe.' You are two out of the three."

"Which two?" she asked.

"A person and an event."

"I'm an event?"

"Yes, you are."

"No one ever called me that before—and I've gotten a lot of reviews!"

"You are. You are my event—my wonder. I wonder at meeting you, I wonder at your loving me, I wonder at the epidemic of 'p,' 'h' and 'q'ing that's been taking place." Kelly changed his stance on the bed, planting his feet far apart. "But there's something you don't realize. We—you and I—we've already had one whopper of a miracle. Meeting.

Us. Because, you see, the second greatest item on the list is falling in love."

"The second?" Maggie asked. "What's the first?"

"The first is falling in love and having it returned. Consider that for a miracle!" He dropped back down on the bed to a prone position next to her. "Now—please roll over on your side and let me put my arms around you."

Smiling, she turned on her side, drew her knees up slightly into the spoon position and felt him slide down in the bed behind her, his front to her back. She eased her body so he could slip his right arm under her shoulder, then she took both his hands and held them together beneath her breasts. Feeling comfortable, loved and secure, she could not imagine ever wanting to leave this position. Exhaling a long breath, she pressed back against him. "When I think about it—I have been one lucky broad." A small chuckle. "I could not only have missed out on *you*—I could easily have been a pizza waitress." She turned her head around slightly toward him. "You're right, my Kelly—we've had the miracle! Of course, we have. My God, anything else is pure . . . rainbows and hot fudge sundaes."

She turned her head back and he held her close to him until he could feel her relaxing, about to fall into sleep. Just before she drifted off she spoke on the drowsy end of a sigh: "Nevertheless, Lord—hit me with a rainbow."